ACCLAIM FOR
KATE Q. JOHNSON

Daughter of Carthage, Son of Rome

Kate Q. Johnson has woven a compelling tale that brings to life the high stakes of political rivalries, a daring heroine and an honorable but torn military leader. Daughter of Carthage, Son of Rome is a vivid recreation of the ancient world and a sensitive portrayal of the demands of the human heart.

—**Linda Cardillo**, award winning author of historical novels such as *Love That Moves the Sun*, *Dancing on Sunday Afternoons*, and the *First Light trilogy*.

Kate Q. Johnson's sure-handed debut novel tells the story of a wartime Romeo and Juliet, two star-crossed lovers whose lives collide at a moment when history might have swung off in a different direction

—**Sherry Christie,** author of the *Roma Amor saga*.

ABOUT THE BOOK

Elissa Mago, a Carthaginian heiress, recklessly flees the prospect of a despised arranged marriage and arrives in Italy vulnerable yet defiant on the cusp of Hannibal's audacious crossing of the Alps and invasion of Roman territory.

Marcus Gracchus, a brilliant and celebrated Roman Centurion, questions his own loyalty to Rome after his brother is murdered and he is ordered to serve under the leadership of the vindictive man who orchestrated his brother's death.

A chance encounter thrusts the two together, first as captive and captor. But violence both on the battlefield and within the Roman legion eventually leads them into an alliance that is tested repeatedly by their ties to home. Ultimately, they must choose—their love for one another or their loyalty to their people.

DAUGHTER OF
CARTHAGE,
SON OF ROME

A NOVEL

KATE Q. JOHNSON

Bellastoria Press

Cover design by Wicked Smart Design.com
Interior design by Author E.M.S.

Bellastoria Press
P.O. Box 60341
Longmeadow, MA 01116
info@bellastoriapress.com
www.bellastoriapress.com

ISBN Ebook: 978-1-942209-86-7
Paperback: 978-1-942209-88-1

To Alex,
You're the reason I write love stories.

WESTERN MEDITERRANEAN
THIRD CENTURY BC

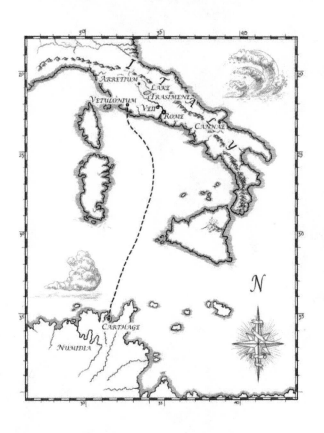

INTRODUCTION

At the turn of the third century BC, Rome and Carthage were the two greatest civilizations in the western Mediterranean region. The mere proximity of their massive empires might have made collision inevitable, but they were also cities founded on fundamentally opposing principles. Rome was a militant, aggressively expanding city whose citizens had recently subdued the entire Italian peninsula after centuries of war. Carthage was a prosperous city of merchants who had acquired large swaths of land in North Africa and Iberia (modern Spain) through trade and skillful negotiation with allies. Rome and Carthage first clashed from 264-241 BC in a war that involved the greatest naval battles of antiquity and left hundreds of thousands dead on both sides. After fighting to a bitter loss, the Carthaginians were desperate to retain their dominance over the seas and chafing under humiliating reparations to Rome. The rise of the Barca family, led by the brilliant young general, Hannibal, who had a blood debt from his father to pay against Rome, was the ember that set the fires of war raging once again.

CHAPTER 1

When Elissa Mago had first reached her hiding spot, she'd feared her heart was beating so loudly someone would find her. A sentry on the watch-tower could probably hear its thudding. But no one had appeared, and she had to go. She couldn't let all her hopes and dreams die today with her marriage to Merbal. It was too soon to give them all up.

Although it was still early, the night sky had brightened enough for Elissa to make out her surroundings. She'd been crouched behind this wooden crate for nearly an hour, and her knees were growing stiff. The straps of her leather sandals dug into her ankles and calves. Elissa picked nervously at a loose strand of wool on her dress. She had taken it from a slave girl; the only daughter of Hanno the Great shouldn't be seen in such unstylish garb. The dress suited her well enough, just an inch too short for her long frame. Her seamstress would have wanted to take it in around her chest.

Elissa noticed some straw sticking out from the corner of the crate. It most likely held something fragile, perhaps pottery that had arrived yesterday after the long voyage from Tyre.

1

Elissa hugged the cloth satchel in her arms tighter and the handful of coins she had stuffed inside pressed into her skin.

She would never see her people's ancestral homeland now.

Her father had said he might take her there one day, but now...well, now she was quite sure her father would never speak to her again, much less take her to Tyre. He'd probably never intended to take her in the first place. Men rarely took women on voyages merely for pleasure, especially men like her father. Her brother, Barro, might have taken her, but he was gone now, too.

Remembering her brother's absence was painful, and it brought Elissa back to the present. The water lapped gently against the dock in front of her. The air was hot and sticky; it filled her nostrils and throat as she breathed. A stench hung all around. Yesterday's catch soon to be mixed with today's; it was so unlike the fresh countryside where Elissa had grown up. The walls of Carthage loomed over her back. They were originally built to be taller than any building in the city, but its citizenry had grown tenfold since then. Cramped, multifamily dwellings now reached above their rim and jutted into the sandstone. From her vantage at the merchant port outside the city, Carthage appeared to be bursting at its seams.

Just like Merbal. Elissa shuddered involuntarily at the thought of her husband-to-be.

Merbal's tunics often appeared to be at risk of splitting under the strain of his gut. As his wife, it would have been her responsibility to see to their mending. She would have been no more than a warm body to bear an old man pleasure, a prize piece of jewelry to be paraded at society events. And for what? Some silver for her father and a few votes in the Council of Elders for Merbal? Surely she was worth more than that.

Her father's ship was moored ahead of her, gently bumping

against the wooden dock. Its lower bay was open and ready to receive its cargo. There was no cover between her crate and the hull of the ship at the end of the dock, but she might be able to run fast enough. She'd only need a minute, and she'd be hard to spot in the dim light of dawn. Sweat beaded underneath her hair. *Was this her moment?*

Hoof beats could be heard in the distance along with a high-pitched neighing.

They're here!

She would stick to the original plan. A herd of her father's horses, some of the finest in Africa, would round the corner at any moment. The poor beasts would be driven onto the ship and sold across the Mediterranean to the highest bidder. Taanit, a Numidian, and Hanno's freed slave turned merchant, would do the selling. With war declared and the lucrative silver mines in Iberia shut down, her father needed the money. What her father didn't need was Taanit helping his daughter escape a carefully arranged marriage. What he didn't know was that Taanit had been as dear to her as a brother during her childhood exile outside the city. Elissa tightened her jaw. She regretted what her actions would cost her father; truly, she did. But there was no other choice.

Elissa couldn't see the horses from behind the city walls, though the planks of the dock were already shaking beneath her. She imagined their churning hooves throwing up dust as they trotted briskly down the road outside Carthage and toward the gate in the wall that opened to the docks. Elissa peered around the crate and saw the gate was still closed. No sentry appeared to be manning it. That wasn't good. Any horseman knew better than to try and stop a herd of thundering horses; if they were forced into a closed wall they'd flow like water to the openings on both sides. It would be chaos, and her chance of escape would be gone.

Thud.

The gate swung open, hitting the sandstone wall behind it. Elissa exhaled shakily. A familiar figure came out from behind the gate.

Elissa moved lithely to the other side of her crate. It was Taanit. He was still far away, but Elissa couldn't risk letting him see her. Not yet anyway. He might be a dear friend, but there was no chance he'd help her onto the ship, and only a slim chance he wouldn't turn it around once he discovered her at sea.

One hundred glimmering warhorses trotted toward Elissa's dock. They were tied together in tightly packed rows of five, with no more than a few men from the neighboring territory of Numidia at the back and sides of the herd to guide them. The horses sped to a gallop as the Numidians tried to pre-empt their fear of the water around them by driving them harder. The first row of horses approached, a tangle of sinew and bones speeding toward her. They were packed so closely together, you could hardly see where one horse ended and the next one began.

Elissa sent up a prayer to Astarte—whose symbol was the horse, after all—and crouched low, the bag slung tightly over her shoulder. The horses were so close now she could touch the legs of the one nearest her. The air was thick with their panic. Their hooves whipped up a frenzied wind as they collided with the planks and darted back up again. Elissa's mind raced with fear; surely she'd be trampled in there! The center of the herd reached her. It was time to choose between probably being trampled and certainly being married.

She leaped.

The resolution in her legs surprised her, and she handily caught the mane of the small bay nearest to her. It skittered to the side, pressing hard against a larger gray next to it. Elissa hung tightly to the horse's mane, half-running, half being carried toward the ship. But this wasn't good enough!

She was on the outside of the herd and clearly visible to the Numidians if they bothered to look. She had to move to the center.

Elissa gulped in a final breath of air and jumped. Still holding her bay's mane with one hand, she swung under the horse's neck, grinding against its chest as the rump of the horse in front shoved against her. Elissa couldn't see anything other than the sweat-darkened hair on her horse's neck. She blindly thrust out her hand, searching for the mane of the gray beside her. Got it! She swung free of the bay and onto the other horse, her satchel still bouncing on her shoulder.

A sudden jolt of pain shot through her left foot and up her leg.

"Shit!" she swore. The thundering horses easily drowned her out.

The horses were so close to each other, there was hardly any ground not covered by a hammering hoof. Elissa tried placing just the toe of her left foot on the ground and cried out in pain. She bit down on her lip. Hard. A broken foot was the least of her concerns at the moment. Not when a broken body could soon follow.

Fear coursing through her veins, Elissa swung her injured foot onto the back of the gray so its withers were under the crook of her knee. She flattened her torso against the horse's neck to keep from sliding down and let her other leg dangle helplessly. The gray dashed forward to escape the added weight on its neck but had nowhere to go. The pressure on her back from the horse beside her was increasing. She could taste the sweat on her horse's neck. Salt wet her tongue; grainy hair filled her mouth.

Panic rose from Elissa's stomach and into her throat. She couldn't see. She couldn't breathe. The air in her lungs was being squeezed out by the horse at her back. The strap of her bag fell to her elbow, then her wrist. She tightened her left

5

leg, trying to bring her body higher, toward the light, but she was falling away instead. She was slipping down!

The churning hooves thundered in her ears. Her body reverberated with noise, motion, fear. She was squeezing the gray as hard as she could, but its hooves only got closer. She would be trampled, her escape for naught. Her desperate stab at freedom, crushed under their uncaring feet. Her sandal remained hooked over her horse's back; if it came free she would tumble to the ground headfirst. Taanit would find her body after it had been obliterated by a thousand hooves. Would he even recognize her? Her father would never know what had happened.

The sound grew to a deafening roar. A horse's knee clipped her chin, snapping her head against her back. This was it then, her story over before it had really begun.

Her foot slipped.

She managed to hold on to the gray's mane to keep her head above the hooves. But something was different. The horses' feet were on soft straw instead of wooden planks, and they were motionless. The roaring in her ears had receded to only the stomping and rubbing of restless horses. She'd made it onto the ship!

Elissa let go of her gray, slid down and blinked. The light was dim, but she could make out the curving black wood of the ship's hull. A horse neighed shrilly nearby and her gray stomped its feet in answer. Footsteps echoed on the gangway.

Elissa forced herself to take a deep breath and still her trembling body. She wasn't safe yet, and it was too soon to be seen. She had to hide. She pulled the satchel onto her shoulder and willed her legs back into motion. She weaved between rumps and under necks until she reached a corner of the hull. There was a pile of straw here, deep enough to cover a body. If the Numidians were coming to check on the horses, she'd be hidden from their view. Elissa looked toward the open door in the hull. Bright light was streaming in. The sun had risen over Carthage, and a tiny rectangle of blue sky was illuminating the darkness. All she'd ever known was through that door. Elissa turned away slowly. If only it was all she'd ever wanted.

She stepped into the piled hay, crouched down and rearranged the stalks until everything but her face was covered. She would wait until nightfall to find Taanit. Then she'd beg him to take her with him to wherever this ship was headed. Elissa didn't know what he'd do when he saw her. He might turn around immediately and return her to her father, or send her back to Merbal. Perhaps her oldest, and only, real friend might help her. He might choose to share the freedom he'd bought since his childhood as her father's slave. Either way, her fate was still in the hands of a man. She would have paid anything for a different life, but no one had told her the cost.

CHAPTER 2

Taanit leaned over the side of the ship, gazing at the inky water below. He gripped the rail with brown-skinned, work-hardened hands. Water wasn't natural to him. Numidians were horse people, bred in the plains and rolling hills of Northern Africa. The smell of salt, the thick moisture hanging in the air—it all felt foreign to him. He knew the dryness of a desert wind whipping across his face, the pounding of a horse between his legs, the ache in his back after a long day of harvest.

Unfortunately for him, none of those skills was useful to a merchant in the Mediterranean. He would have been better off with a knack for lying and a love of swimming. At the very least, he mused, if the horses could get used to the water, then so could he.

Taanit ran a hand through the short spirals in his hair. It was the same color as the water, and cropped too close to be fashionable. He didn't care; there was nothing fashionable about being a poor freedman. Still, he was proud of what he had accomplished in his twenty years. He'd been born a slave on the country estate of a wealthy Carthaginian man, and though he had always been treated well, he'd never been able to forget that his life was not his own. He carefully saved every coin he'd ever been given until he was able to buy his freedom from Hanno four years ago. He would have left immediately, but he had been waiting for the opportunity to buy his mother as well. Sadly she'd died and he was alone for the first time, but he had enough money to purchase a horse. It fetched a nice profit at the city market, and his career as a merchant had begun.

Taanit glanced up at the sky, lost in memories. It was brilliant black tonight, lit by the glow of a thousand tiny pinpricks and the sliver of a new moon. Not even a puff of wind to disturb the air.

An oar clattered to the deck behind him.

"Gods take it!" someone swore harshly. It sounded like a woman.

Taanit strode quickly to where the noise had come from. A figure was crouching behind the mast, trying to prevent a second oar from following the first. He reached out and grabbed a fistful of dark hair.

"Ow! For the love of Melqart, let me go, Taanit!"

He recoiled in shock at the familiar voice.

"E...Elissa?" he stuttered in disbelief.

"Yes, Taanit! Let me go!"

Taanit released his grip and stumbled backward. He blinked rapidly, trying to clear the apparition in front of his eyes. The woman's dark hair hung in heavy waves around her pale face, interwoven with occasional stalks of straw. She had the same high cheekbones, arching delicately down to a pair of full lips that he remembered. Her nose was curved upward at the tip, and held high in typical stubbornness. Yes, it could only be Elissa. When he had last seen her, she'd been a tall and gangly fourteen-year-old, but now, four years later, she'd grown into a woman of remarkable beauty.

Taanit was incredulous. "What...what are you doing here, Elissa?"

Even in the dim light of the stars he could see her pale-green eyes flare with emotion. He knew from memory that

9

they were flecked with amber, giving them an almost feline quality.

"Taanit, I'm sorry. I had to come," she said quickly. There was a touch of desperation in her voice.

"What have you done, Elissa?" Taanit said, more loudly this time. His mind had almost caught up to the reality of the situation. "You *can't* be here! Your father will be livid, and your brother, he might just kill me!"

Heat rose in Elissa's cheeks. They looked vivid against the night sky.

"What have *I* done?" she protested. "Only taken what little freedom I have to escape a lifetime of misery shackled to an uncaring, greedy husband!"

Taanit took a step backward at that. She was right. When he'd met with Elissa's father a few weeks before to discuss the Numidian horses he was going to sell, he had also endeavored to determine Elissa's whereabouts. It had been nearly four years since her father had moved her from his property in Zama where they'd both grown up. Hanno had informed him that she was in Carthage and engaged to be married. "A very prosperous match," he had explained smugly, looking uncharacteristically pleased with his daughter. Taanit had wanted to know more but didn't push his luck, since his fledgling career as a merchant depended on Hanno being happy with him.

"Elissa." He made his voice softer. "If you've run away from your husband…"

"Husband-to-be," she corrected.

"Nevertheless, you can't do this. Your father would never allow it. We'll have to turn around."

"Don't you dare, Taanit," Elissa said sharply. "I'm not going anywhere. I didn't almost get run over by a hundred horses to turn around now."

"Run over by *what*?" Taanit inhaled sharply as he

understood her meaning. "That's how you snuck on? With the horses?"

"Yes. I hid on the dock and jumped into the herd. They carried me onto the ship."

She said it so matter-of-factly that Taanit nearly missed the audacity of what she'd done. They'd always tried to surpass each other with their exploits when they'd played together as children, but her daring today certainly exceeded anything they'd accomplished then.

Taanit didn't congratulate her. He turned away instead.

"We have to go back," he said, facing the water. "I'm turning the ship around and we're going back. Where we're headed is no place for a Carthaginian. No place for a woman."

Elissa paused. "There's no wind. Taanit We can't go anywhere right now."

"In the morning then. I'll tell the crew to return to Carthage."

"Please, Taanit. I have a plan. Just hear me out."

Taanit shook his head but turned back to face her. Her shoulders had sagged but she still looked nowhere near giving up.

He sighed. "What's this plan, Elissa? Although I'm sure whatever it is won't end well for me."

"It will. It won't even affect your business with my father."

Taanit scoffed. "Not likely."

"Please, just listen," Elissa pleaded. "I'll stay hidden on the ship until we dock, wherever that is. When your men see me, they'll be shocked, of course. They might even insist that we return to Carthage. But at that point, the quickest thing to do will be to sell the horses and then sail home. You can send word to my father that I'm with you and that you'll escort me back to Carthage as soon as possible. Whatever he might think of me, my father wouldn't want to risk having me sail back alone. In the meantime, I'll help you or hide. I'll do whatever you wish while you're selling the horses. Then we'll go home. I'll return to my cage and you to your business. As simple as that."

"As simple as that?" Taanit repeated wryly.

"Yes, Taanit! There will be no harm to my father's opinion of you or his precious trade, and you'll have helped me out of an awful situation. If you can try and remember, we used to be great friends."

He softened. "Elissa, I want to help you, truly I do, and I have not forgotten what we were to each other. But what will this plan accomplish? You'll be going home to the same situation, only with your father furious and a thousand times less likely to be sympathetic to you."

"No," Elissa said with utter conviction. "Everything will not be the same when I return. I didn't just run away before getting married, I ran away on my *wedding* day. While I hid in the straw on my father's ship, the elite of Carthage gathered to watch the daughter of Hanno the Great marry a man even older and richer than he. Silver for my father and a fledgling political career for my husband-to-be—it was the perfect arrangement. Except there was no bride to meet him there, and the nobility of Carthage is shaking tonight as a result, half of them with fury at my presumption, and half with excitement at scandal besetting the Magos yet again." Elissa paused at this, her voice tight. "My reputation will be utterly ruined. Merbal will never want me after this humiliation. No man in Carthage will."

"But what if he does still want you?" Taanit asked gently. "What if he convinces your father to increase your dowry exorbitantly to compensate him for the humiliation and then marries you anyway?"

Elissa looked past him at the dark water below. "I've thought of that, too," she muttered.

"And?" Taanit prompted, trying to catch her eye.

She turned to look at him directly, and her face hardened with resolve.

"I'll say I was raped on the journey. No amount my father can give will be enough to induce a man to take a ruined bride."

Taanit stepped back, staring at her.

"And if you're going to point out that my father will have a doctor verify my story, I already know that," She bit out. "I know how to bleed myself like a man would," she said more quietly, but her eyes danced with fury.

The moonlight cast Elissa in sharp relief; dark hair framed ghostly white skin, a sphere inset with glowing green eyes. She looked every bit the fallen goddess.

Taanit wanted to protest more, and he had the right to worry. If it came to the worst, Elissa couldn't guarantee that her father wouldn't have him exiled or worse for allowing her to be raped in his care. And this plan of hers...well, she might avoid a marriage because of it, but most women would choose an unhappy marriage over the fate of a ruined woman. In this world, there was no real life for a woman without a man. She would be an outcast, forever dependent on the generosity of her father or brother for protection and care. But Taanit held his tongue. She knew the consequences, and besides, Elissa was not most women. He couldn't stop her, not really; she would always find another way. And she'd already come so far.

"All right," Taanit said. "You can stay."

CHAPTER 3

Moonlight streamed in through the open window; pale curtains danced on a gentle ocean breeze. An infant slept on a small couch raised above the cold floor, safely swaddled in silks and illuminated by a pale beam of light. The moonlight was mottled with dark spots, Luna's tears staining her celestial cloak. A shadow passed through the light, temporarily obscuring the infant, and a dark figure approached, drawing an aimless circle through the room. The figure cast the soft notes of a song around itself: a thin tether of chord clinging to the moving air. But the air cast off its binding and swirled about the figure with indifference. The song grew more melancholy, the notes stretched longer and longer, reaching into the space of another time. The figure leaned over the infant, and Elissa felt the soft brush of lips on her forehead. Then the figure was gone, the thin spectre cast out of the light. Only her song remained, and the faint imprint of warmth on Elissa's forehead.

Elissa involuntarily brought a hand to her forehead. She felt cool skin under her fingertips. A familiar surge of disappointment swelled in her chest.

What did you expect? She thought bitterly. She'd had this dream many times since she was a child. Elissa used to think it was her mother trying to bring her some message from the other side. But she was too old to believe that now. Her mother was dead and not coming back in any form. Besides, she'd taken herself to the other side, so what possible reason could she have for trying to get back?

Hazy memories flooded her mind—servants whispering in hushed tones behind doorways, her father white-faced and numb, refusing to even look at her. Elissa was far too young to understand at the time, of course, but later, Barro had gently explained it to her.

"Mother was very sad after you were born, Elissa. She grew quieter and quieter until eventually she refused to leave her room or speak to anyone. Father said he tried everything—presents, promises. I used to listen outside their door at night and hear him whispering to her like one of our nurses. But it was no use and finally she ended her sickness with a knife. It was very hard for Father. He didn't leave the house for weeks afterward. And when he did, the shame of it nearly killed him. People are not kind to the family of a woman who kills herself after giving birth to a healthy baby girl."

Elissa read between the lines on that one. He meant that people wondered what was so wrong with her that her mother had killed herself. Her father sent her out of the city, to Zama, shortly afterward. Barro said it was to protect her from the malicious whispers of society, but Elissa knew it was more than that. There was a reason she'd hardly seen her father twice a year until she was fourteen. He had only brought her back to Carthage because her absence from society at such a marriageable age had become more conspicuous than her presence. He blamed her for his beloved Jezebel's death. And truth be told, she understood why.

Even now, nearly eighteen years after her mother had died, Elissa still felt the lingering stares of councillors' wives—their eyes watching her, dissecting her, wondering what was wrong with her. They looked the other way when her father approached, of course; Hanno the Great had made it clear that any child of his was beyond reproach. Occasionally, Elissa would catch her father staring at her with pain in his eyes, and Elissa knew his true thoughts.

Elissa turned on the straw mattress and tried to shake that old feeling of guilt. Besides, there had been distinct advantages to growing up in the country, away from the watchful eyes of a father or mother. The best tutors in Latin, Greek and history had attended her, but after her morning lessons, she'd been left to roam the estate freely. She'd made the most of her liberty, running wild with Taanit and the other children in nothing but a dirty frock—climbing trees, stealing horses, forever on the hunt for the next adventure. Barro had continued to visit her several times a year even after he reached manhood, and had belatedly tried to enforce some discipline, but he left for the army before his rules could stick.

Elissa was half-awake now, and the pain from her bruised foot brought her back to the present. The dark wood of the ship's walls seemed to close in around her narrow cot. Taanit had brought her to his cabin after he agreed to let her stay. She had objected to taking his bed, but his quarters were the only private ones on the ship, and there was no other way to hide from the rest of the crew. Dim light filtered into the room from the gap under the door. What time was it? The crack suddenly widened and the spartan cabin was cast in gray light. Taanit slipped inside.

Elissa propped herself against the back wall and rubbed the remaining sleep from her eyes. Taanit set a plate of dark bread and figs at the foot of her bed and turned to leave.

"Wait, Taanit." Elissa swung her legs out from under the scratchy blanket and nearly upended the tray.

He put his finger to his lips and shook his head. Elissa paused, and then nodded. No talking. Taanit left the room quickly.

Elissa felt a bump and she lurched forward, absently pulling straw through the porous blanket on her mattress. She put out a leg to steady herself. Taanit had been very generous to offer her his cabin for the weeklong journey, but the small wooden box had quickly come to feel like a prison.

She sighed. Cell or cabin, she had to remember she was lucky to have it. She'd tried leaving the cabin one night after the ship's crew was long asleep, and had nearly stumbled over Taanit's sleeping body outside her door. Her protests had died in her throat with one look at his angry face. She'd retreated to her room with promises to remain there. One of Taanit's conditions for letting her stay was that she not be seen by any of the crew until after they docked. It was simpler not to have to provide any explanations until it was too late to turn back, and besides, there were superstitions about women suddenly appearing at sea. Taanit did not want to risk a mutiny. After they docked, he was planning to tell the other Numidians that Elissa was a distant relative who'd unexpectedly become stranded in Italy and required his assistance in returning to Greece. The lie wasn't outrageous; Elissa had inherited her pale skin from her Athenian mother. But beyond that, her Greek resemblance abruptly ended, and her dark hair and angular features were distinctly Carthaginian. Elissa could only pray that the Numidians hadn't seen too many Greeks.

A week had passed in the dim silence of the cabin. Elissa tried to stay occupied by playing dice with herself, and recalling distant facts her tutors had told her about Greece, but the passage of days was painfully slow. It had given her trampled foot a chance to heal, though. The bruises above her toes had faded to dull splotches of yellow and green, and she could walk normally now. Taanit came twice a day to check on her and deliver her meals, but he never stayed long. He claimed to be too busy caring for the horses and making sure the men were working. Elissa knew she'd put him in a difficult position, and she regretted it, but she didn't understand his aloofness. Growing up, he'd been as close to her as a brother; she wondered what had been lost between them.

A second bump brought the ship to a sudden stop. A horse whinnied below deck. Apparently the horses were as anxious to get off the ship as she was. The door to the cabin opened and Taanit briskly walked in. He shut the door quickly behind him.

"We've docked," he said, turning to face Elissa.

He must have seen the excitement rising in her face because he quelled it immediately.

"Elissa," he continued gruffly, "no one can see you yet. I'll escort you from the cabin once we have the horses unloaded and on their way to Vetulonium. We'll ride together after them. If we're fast, we should be there by nightfall."

She bobbed her head in understanding.

"Thank you, Taanit!" she said eagerly.

Taanit sighed and gave her a slight smile. "I'm sorry to have kept you here this past week."

He turned to leave but took a step toward Elissa instead, watching her intently. "Elissa, I need you to understand the seriousness of the situation. We're in Etruria now—an ally of Rome who's at war with your city. I know the fighting will happen far away in Iberia, but it's imperative no one find out where you're from," Taanit finished uneasily. He seemed hesitant to even say "Carthage" out loud.

Elissa's temper flared. Did he think she was still a child, incapable of taking the world seriously? At eighteen years she might be young, but she'd never been a child. Her mother's actions after her birth, and her father's reactions, had ensured that.

"I understand perfectly, Taanit."

Taanit dropped his eyes and nodded curtly. The door closed behind him.

"We're ready for you now." Taanit ducked his head into the cabin several hours later, looking a little less grave.

Elissa grabbed her bag from the chair and followed him out of the cabin. After a week spent in the dim light of the ship, the bright light on deck was blinding. She squinted as she climbed out of the hull, and craned her neck to get her bearings. The deck seemed deserted, and the horses no longer stomped down below. Perhaps they'd already left for the village Taanit had mentioned.

Her eyes widened as she looked past the deck to the surrounding vista. Turquoise water met jagged gray cliffs at the shoreline, which faded into rounded green hills stretching far into the distance. The slopes of the hills were verdant with leafy trees and grass that was still thick from summer. Carthage was a place of brown and blue, sand and sea, with the occasional oasis of color. But this land was vibrant green; lushness and fertility seeped from the very ground. Even the sky appeared bluer, as if the sun knew that such a land would need special attention.

"It's magnificent," Elissa whispered.

"I thought you'd like it." Taanit placed a hand on her shoulder. "Come. We should be on our way."

Elissa noticed the cautious warmth in his eyes and smiled up at him gratefully. She followed him down the gangway and along the dock toward a narrow strip of brown sand that comprised the beach. There were two horses waiting there. They'd been tied to a stake in the ground and tacked in the Numidian fashion—that is, with no tack at all. Riders had a loop of rope around the horses' necks to give them direction; their backs were otherwise bare. One of the horses, a large roan, pawed the ground eagerly. The smaller black mare beside him dipped her head in response. Taanit walked up to the roan and twined a hand in his mane. He swung himself up on the horse's back before Elissa had even reached her steed.

Elissa ignored his impatience and ran her hand across the mare's forehead. A triangular white star peeked out from between her fingers. Her hand shook slightly as she moved it to the mare's mane and wound her fingers through the coarse hair. She had abandoned her father and fled to a foreign country full of enemies and only one friend—a reluctant friend at that. She had come so far already; where would this horse take her now? Elissa pulled down on the mare's mane and swung onto her back almost as smoothly as Taanit. She squeezed her legs and quickly pushed the mare into a trot to hide the nervousness on her face. It was too late for second thoughts.

They rode away from the sea on a worn dirt road. The land quickly grew hilly, and they wound along the bottoms of the slopes in silence. The rhythm of the mare's gently moving withers gradually soothed Elissa's worries. As they rounded a bend in the road, she even started to feel some excitement about seeing what was next. Elissa had always felt confined within the sand walls of Carthage, and she longed to see more of the world. Barro said their mother named her Elissa after the great queen and founder of Carthage. Queen Elissa had run away from the ancient city of Tyre to escape her brother's cruelty. With a small band of loyal followers, she had sailed to Africa and negotiated to rent a narrow finger of land from the local Libyan king. Her city had prospered on the lucrative Mediterranean trade routes and the Libyan king had grown jealous. He demanded Elissa's hand in marriage as compensation for his loss. But Elissa was in love with another—Aeneas, the great hero of the Trojan War. She couldn't follow her love and still protect her city from war, so she built a great pyre and flung herself into the flames. The Libyans called her Dido, the wanderer, the woman who could never find peace.

Elissa glanced at Taanit absently. Would her story end as tragically as Queen Elissa's? Was it possible to have both peace and love?

Taanit looked back at Elissa. His eyes were bright, and his shoulders were no longer drawn up near his ears. He was clearly enjoying the ride.

"I think we should catch up to the rest of the horses in case the men are having trouble."

Elissa felt a familiar surge of guilt at his anxiety, but stopped herself. Perhaps there was a better way to make him forget his concerns.

"Shall we see who can get there first?"

"Elissa…" Taanit's voice was low in warning, but without the hard edge that would make her change her mind.

Elissa laughed lightly and gave her horse a mighty squeeze. The mare launched into a gallop that sent them flying down the road. The wind tore across her face and whipped her hair from its plait. It streamed behind her over the mare's back.

"Elissa!" she heard Taanit shout from behind.

Elissa looked over her shoulder, but Taanit had already kicked his horse into a gallop and was following her down the road.

Taanit closed in quickly, and soon Elissa's horse was only a neck ahead of Taanit's. A wide smile had cracked through Taanit's dour expression. Elissa grinned and bent lower over the mare's neck. The mare strained forward and lowered her back, allowing her legs to extend farther over the ground. Her breath came in even puffs that matched her pounding hooves. She was relishing the freedom as much as Elissa.

All too soon, they rounded a corner and the Numidians and their horses came into view. There was still a large meadow between them and the Numidians, but Taanit would want to stop before they got too close and scared the horses. Elissa sighed and eased her weight back to tell the mare to slow.

But Taanit didn't slow. He was directly across from her now, and their legs jostled together as they ran. Taanit curled his legs up his horse's sides and pulled his feet underneath him until he was half-crouching on its back.

His grin turned fiendish as Elissa protested. "Oh, no, Taanit! Don't you dare!"

It was too late. Taanit sprang from his horse and let out a ferocious shriek as he jumped—a cry that would be instantly recognizable to any Numidian.

Elissa ducked low on the mare's neck to avoid his hurtling body. But there was no need. Taanit landed behind her with practiced precision. His legs straddled the mare tightly, and he moved his hands to the loop of rope around her neck. Elissa grimaced and shifted forward to add some space between them. Taanit pulled on the mare's lead and they began to slow. His roan trailed closely behind despite now being riderless. It was for good reason that people halfway across the world wanted Numidian horses.

Taanit grinned. "I couldn't be outdone by your clever escape, now could I?"

"That was not necessary!" Elissa said severely. But soon she was laughing. It was just as it had been when they were children.

They continued at an easy canter astride her willing mare until they reached the Numidians. The horses were tied together in the same rows of five as when they'd boarded the ship. The Numidians were directing them down the road from the back and sides at a brisk trot.

The man at the rear of the herd looked at Elissa with mild surprise as they approached. Elissa felt her cheeks color when she remembered Taanit's nearness, his arm wrapped tightly around her to hold the horse's lead. Elissa squirmed uncomfortably; she didn't want these men to get the wrong impression. Taanit took certain liberties only because they were accustomed to a time when there was little distinction between girl and boy.

"Ababaal," Taanit nodded briskly at the nearest Numidian.

The man returned his nod, staring straight ahead.

Elissa frowned. Acceptance wouldn't come easily with these Numidians.

Taanit chuckled, reading her mind. "Don't worry; you won't see much of them."

He might have meant to sound reassuring, but his words had the opposite effect. Elissa wondered where he planned to stow her away this time.

They reached Vetulonium at dusk. Elissa stayed well back as Taanit and the Numidians drove the horses toward the city gates. She didn't want to be a burden to them, and she didn't mind the solitude. Elissa had never been to another city apart from Carthage, and even that city, her birthplace, made her uncomfortable. She felt uneasy within its high walls and its labyrinth of narrow streets. Carthage was a city teeming with bodies, faceless people going about similar lives. They rushed to the market to sell their wares, then to the temple to pray for good fortune, then home, to children they hoped would have better lives than theirs. Elissa would spend hours watching them from her father's home, and wonder if you needed a master to be a slave.

As the dark stone walls of Vetulonium drew nearer, she considered whether it would be the same in this city. It had once been one of the great Etruscan cities that had ruled western Italy. But the ancient civilization of Etruria had been brought to its knees by Rome nearly a century ago. The Etruscans were probably Roman in all but name now, another formidable people lost to the tide of Roman civilization.

The gate into the city was still open when they reached it, and the horses passed into Vetulonium without incident. The men drove them hard along a narrow road beside the wall. It was just wide enough for five horses abreast. Red thatched roofs circled upwards from the wall, and the tip of a white temple peeked over the summit of the city. The tidy rows of stone houses were so different from the tangled yellow bricks of Carthage.

They turned a corner in the road and the familiar shape of a stable appeared ahead. A corral had been left open in front of the stables. The Numidians directed the horses toward the entrance, and the sound of cracking whips cut through the still night air. Once they'd driven all the horses inside, the men convened outside the closed gate of the corral. They spoke quickly in Numidian, but from what Elissa could gather based on the few words she'd learned from Taanit, they intended to move the stallions to the stables to prevent fights from breaking out.

Elissa nudged her horse closer to get Taanit's attention.

"Wait there, Elissa," Taanit called without looking back.

She sighed. She could have helped.

Dusk had darkened to night by the time they were finished with the horses. Elissa had grown cold waiting. She shivered without a cloak. Her trepidation had returned with the darkness, and her body felt heavy as she stared up at the blank sky. She truly was far from home.

Finally Taanit approached. He nodded at her in silent acknowledgement and took off at a fast walk in the direction of the city. Elissa lowered her head and followed behind. They walked up the narrow streets of Vetulonium, Elissa taking two steps for every one of Taanit's. The dirt road had become stone, and the houses were clumped less closely together. The temple loomed large at the top of the hill when Taanit stopped.

"I sent one of the ship's crew ahead to secure us lodging. He mentioned an elderly couple who live alone in a comfortable house and occasionally accept boarders."

"So you'll be staying with me then?" Elissa asked hopefully. She did not relish the thought of being left alone in a room for another week.

Taanit led her down a smaller street on their right.

"No. I'll be staying with the men outside the stables. We need to keep an eye on the horses."

Elissa stared at her feet through the darkness. "But you'll come get me when you're showing the horses." She tried to make her voice sound firm.

They stopped in front of a doorway and Taanit put his hand on Elissa's shoulders. She shifted to face him.

"Elissa, I would love for you to come. I know you'd be helpful, and I…I know you'd be helpful," he finished lamely.

"It's settled then," Elissa said quickly.

"But I can't. My duty is to keep you safe, and that's what I'm going to do."

Elissa sighed and gave him a weak smile. She shouldn't ask more of him. Taanit had helped her so much; she couldn't make his task any harder than she already had. Elissa took a deep breath and tried to let the cool air rinse away her nagging loneliness. She squared her shoulders and knocked solidly on the door.

CHAPTER 4

E lissa leaned against the feather cushion at her back and forced herself to stop fidgeting. She was in the *triclinium*, waiting to dine with Messia and Laris, her hosts of the past three days. She was already growing restless. Elissa made herself study the mosaic on the wall across from her. It was difficult to distinguish a pattern among the worn colors, but it appeared to have something to do with gods and men. She looked down at her feet, resting flat on the simple stone tiles. Elissa was still staring at them when the sounds of movement came through the open door.

Messia walked toward a table at the center of the dining couches and set a plate of roast goose in front of Elissa. Laris trailed closely behind Messia. He sat rigidly on the couch opposite Elissa.

"This looks delicious, thank you." Elissa tried to catch Messia's attention with a smile.

Messia nodded curtly without even glancing at her.

Elissa's mouth went slack and she resisted the urge to sigh. It would have been easier to believe that her hosts didn't understand her, but she'd had enough tutors as a child to know that she spoke Latin flawlessly. It wasn't that Laris and Messia had done anything worthy of reproach. They'd provided Elissa with everything she needed to be comfortable, often before she asked. Nor were they overly controlling; on the contrary, they seemed to avoid her whenever possible. It was only when she tried to leave their simple home that Laris started shadowing her. She had ventured into the streets of Vetulonium on the first and second days of her stay, but his hawkish presence had made her so uncomfortable, Elissa hadn't even bothered today. That at least seemed to make her hosts happy.

Taanit must be paying them well to keep her hidden away. Elissa curled her lips in distaste. Her grand escape, passed in the company of hired childminders.

"Is the bird not to your liking?" Laris interrupted her thoughts.

"No, no, it's excellent," Elissa replied quickly. She tried to smile pleasantly. "Did you buy it at the market today?"

Laris nodded and looked back at his own plate.

Elissa followed suit. She had yet to find a conversational topic that was acceptable to them. Thankfully, the need for conversation died away when a sandy-topped ball of energy bounded into the room. Arnza, Messia and Laris's young grandson, saw Elissa sitting alone and scampered onto the cushion next to her. He curled his legs underneath him and turned to Elissa with his arms outstretched.

"Hello, little Arnza," Elissa cooed as she pulled him onto her lap.

Arnza wriggled around so he was facing her. He fell still as he peered at her with wide-eyed curiosity.

"Arnza, don't bother our guest while she's eating," Messia scolded.

"She doesn't mind," Arnza replied confidently in his high-pitched voice. He twisted around to reassure her. "She told me today I'm the handsomest man she's ever seen."

"Now, Arnza," Elissa scolded with mock seriousness, "It's unbecoming to brag." She tugged at his snub nose with her fingers. Unlike the adults, Arnza had taken to her immediately. He'd followed her around the house all day, trailing in her wake and peppering her with questions. Elissa had indulged him gladly, happy to have his company.

"What's this?" Elissa asked as she pulled a small wooden sword out from the back of Arnza's breeches.

"My new sword. Papa got it for me at the market."

Not one to sit still for long, Arnza jumped off the couch and lurched across the room, waving his sword and vanquishing invisible enemies with each strike.

Elissa laughed and clapped her hands. She glanced quickly over at Messia and Laris, and noticed they were smiling indulgently at Arnza. The elderly couple's love for their grandson was obvious.

"Oh, look, it's a Roman legionary!" Elissa exclaimed. She pointed at a new enemy in the corner of the room.

Arnza approached the new foe in a cautious crouch. When he was a sword's length away, he jumped forward and thrust his weapon in a vicious undercut. His opponent, the unfortunate footstool, clattered to the floor.

"Aha! No Roman can stand against Arnza, the fearless Etruscan warrior." Elissa proclaimed triumphantly.

Arnza dropped his sword and beamed at her in response.

"The Roman legionaries will be quaking in their perfumed armor before you're fully grown," she continued.

Arnza puffed out his chest with pride. "I'll be the most fearsome warrior of them all!"

Elissa laughed and ruffled the top of Arnza's sandy hair. He was such a happy boy. She lifted her head to smile at Messia and Laris. Her hand dropped away from Arnza.

Messia looked on the verge of tears, and Laris's face was tight with tension. "That's enough, Arnza. Put the sword away and return to your room," Laris said roughly.

"But Papa..." Arnza whined.

Laris jerked his head in the direction of the atrium with an expression that brooked no argument.

Arnza's sword fell to the ground and he stared at his feet.

"Yes, Papa." He dragged his feet across the stones as he left the *triclinium.*

Messia stood and hurriedly cleared the dishes from the table. Elissa watched her expectantly for some clue as to what she'd done wrong, but Messia's face was unreadable as she left the room. Laris studiously avoided Elissa's gaze as he followed.

The sun set and the *triclinium* grew dark. Elissa remained on the couch. She listened to the sounds of Vetulonium, muffled and indistinct through the thick stone walls around her. Night air filtered into the room through the open roof in the atrium. It wrapped Elissa in its cool embrace and filled her with longing. Her shoulders sagged with an invisible weight.

"Shall we put this here?"

Elissa carefully placed her wooden block atop the growing stack they were constructing on the floor of the atrium. She sat on the low step surrounding the small pool of water in the center of the room. Arnza was cross-legged on the floor in front of her. Morning sunlight streamed in through the open ceiling, and a breeze ran through the room, smelling of the potted roses in the corner. The rainwater collected in the pool behind her rippled. Arnza placed his block to the left of Elissa's and watched her expectantly.

"Very good, Arnza." Elissa pointed to the block she'd just placed. "See, if you'd put it on top of mine, the whole structure would've toppled."

Arnza nodded seriously, clearly pleased by her attention.

At least one person's opinion of her was unshaken after last night. If only the same could be said for his grandparents. Messia had dropped off Elissa's breakfast, leaving it outside her room this morning, and Laris hadn't said anything when she wished him good day on his way to the market. Elissa shook her head in frustration. How could she make amends if she didn't know what she'd done wrong?

Arnza set another block on top of his last piece.

"Uh, oh!" he squealed.

Elissa looked up and saw the whole structure swaying precariously. The block on the top fell loose and hit the ground. A second block on the side followed. Arnza jumped up and scurried to the back of the tower to stop it from falling. But it was too late. The wooden blocks tumbled to the floor around his outstretched hands. Arnza lunged for an errant cube as it fell toward the pool of water behind him. As he stepped forward, his foot caught on the step Elissa sat on and threw him off balance. Arnza waved his arms desperately to right himself. It was no use; his body tumbled into the pool and he hit the water with a splash.

Elissa jolted to her feet in time to see him strike the bottom of the pool. The water was only chest-deep, but that was enough to drown a little boy who couldn't swim. She lurched up the step and jumped into the pool feet first. Arnza had risen back to the surface, squirming frantically to turn his body. Elissa slipped her hands under his armpits, wrenched him around and straightened her arms with a shove. Arnza's head broke the surface and she heard him sputter and gasp for air. Elissa moved him onto her shoulder and thumped his back with her palm. Arnza coughed and spit out another mouthful of water.

Quick footsteps sounded on the tiles.

"What happened?" Messia's voice cut across the atrium. It was high with alarm.

Elissa rotated slowly with Arnza still on her shoulder. "I'm so sorry, Messia. We were playing and he fell. I…I got him out as quickly as I could."

Messia ignored her and hurried toward Arnza, whose eyes were welling with tears. She bent down by the pool and pulled him from Elissa's arms. Elissa let her hands fall heavily to the water and watched as Messia wrapped her arms around Arnza's body. She nestled him close to her chest and walked slowly across the atrium, murmuring in his ear. The language was smooth and lyrical, and it quieted Arnza's crying to a whimper and then a soft snoring.

Elissa waded to the side of the pool and hauled herself out. Beads of water dripped from her dress onto the stone tiles as she retreated across the atrium. Her cheeks flushed with shame as she passed Messia near the entrance. Arnza was asleep in her arms, but she was clearly reluctant to put him down. Elissa kept her eyes on the ground.

She returned to the empty atrium some time later. She'd changed into a simple dress of undyed wool, with a hem that fell nearly to her ankles. Her remorse felt even heavier than the gown. Elissa lowered herself onto a bench and resolved to wait until Messia returned. She would apologize profusely and offer to find alternative boarding at once. She could worry about Taanit later.

The shadows had grown slanted when Messia came back. Arnza was no longer in her arms, and her dress, which had been wet from his body, had dried. She stopped directly across from Elissa and placed her hands on her hips.

Elissa leaned forward and studied the floor. "I'm so sorry, Messia."

Messia dropped her hands and strode across the room toward her. To Elissa's surprise, she lowered herself onto the bench next to her.

"I'm glad you were with him."

Elissa looked up, stunned. There wasn't a hint of accusation in her voice.

"Really?"

Messia nodded. "That boy has much worse in store for us than an unplanned swim."

Elissa hesitated. She didn't know what to say, but it

seemed they were on the verge of an amiable moment. "Was that Etruscan you were speaking?"

"Yes. Not like Latin, is it?"

"No. It's much softer than Latin."

Messia barked a short laugh. "Can't say the same for the Etruscans. Tough as nails we are. Tough, and unlucky."

Elissa couldn't think of the right words to respond, so she said nothing.

"A lot like your people, come to think of it."

Elissa's head jerked up. Taanit wouldn't have said anything, would he?

"Oh, don't look so concerned. You don't have to worry about us. We can keep our mouths shut. Been doing that a long time."

Now Elissa was truly at a loss for words. "Did Taanit tell you…" she started cautiously.

"He fed me some garbage about you being a relative from Greece under his protection. I'm not going to ask questions when someone's pressing a bag of bronze pieces into my hand."

"So you don't believe I'm Greek," Elissa continued slowly.

Messia raised an eyebrow. "Oh, you pull it off well enough to fool someone who doesn't know better. Your complexion is lighter than most of your people. But no, I don't believe it. Those round eyes, that dark hair, not to mention your distinctly African companion. There's only one place you're from."

Elissa shifted uncomfortably on the bench. She didn't want to lie to Messia, nor did it seem likely she could deceive her, but she had to remember where she was.

Messia must have sensed her unease and didn't press further. Elissa realized belatedly that her silence was probably confirmation enough.

"I'm a long way from home," she said finally.

Messia turned to face her. "Why did you leave? There are no friends of Carthage in Italy, especially not now with war coming."

Elissa tensed at the mention of her city and immediately regretted her body's reaction. She was a Mago; her family was as much a part of Carthage as the sand that made up its walls. No Roman could change that.

"It was a bad time to leave, and I have only one friend in this land. But it seems that was more than I had at home."

Messia smiled, but the light didn't reach her eyes. "You remind me of my daughter-in-law. Proud. Too proud to believe that Fortuna had turned on her."

Elissa started to protest, but she could see Messia's sadness in her sagging shoulders. "What happened to her?" she asked instead.

"She was taken by Romans. Sold into slavery for my son's defiance of Rome."

Elissa's eyes widened. "Oh, gods, Messia. I...I'm so sorry. But what about your son?"

Messia's voice was hard. "He was killed fighting with the Gauls against Rome. My son was born seventy years after our people last fought Rome under the banner of a free Etruria, but he grew up on the lore of those men's bravery. Laris's fault really. Long after the yoke of Roman subjugation had stopped feeling so heavy, my son and Laris kept fighting. An Etruscan is quickly spotted among Gauls, and it was easy enough for the Romans to find his family after he was killed. Roman vengeance is as limitless in its thoroughness as its severity."

Elissa reached for Messia's hand but pulled back when Messia continued.

"My daughter hid Arnza when the Romans came. Laris was near their town on business and stopped in for a visit. He found Arnza in the chicken coop, too weak to even cry. It had been three days since they'd taken his mother."

Elissa covered her mouth with her hand. The thought of sweet Arnza starving and near death was horrifying.

"He's all we have left."

Elissa felt the grip of anger tighten inside her, and she spoke fiercely. "Messia, my people don't fight Rome only for our sakes. We fight for the Italian people, too. For all those under the heel of Roman oppression."

Messia's eyes blazed and she took Elissa's hands in her own. She squeezed them tightly.

"Child, listen to me. There is no defeating Rome. The gods have already shown me that. Rome is a colossus spreading its fingers across the world until the word Rome means master in a thousand different languages. It is best to accept, and to stay out of the way."

CHAPTER 5

"Arnza learned to count to one hundred in Greek
yesterday," Elissa boasted to his grandparents one
morning. "He's really very quick."

"I'm just glad he's reading instead of running around the
house knocking things over," Laris said as he grabbed a fig
from the table in the *triclinium*.

"It's true, he certainly never took to his studies before you
came along," Messia added.

Elissa beamed as she reached across the table for more
honey. "I'm happy to help."

It had been three weeks since the incident with the pool,
and Messia and Laris had warmed to Elissa almost overnight.
They'd taken to having breakfast together every morning,
sharing casual conversation about everything from life in
Etruria to the day's weather. Even better, they appeared to
trust her with Arnza completely. Elissa spent most of her
days playing with him in the garden, or trying to make him
sit still long enough to go through a few lessons. Elissa had
resolved to contribute to this little family. She wanted to be
useful to them, and she wanted to prove to them that her
people were different from the Romans.

Elissa spread another layer of honey across her bread.
"Arnza is certainly no worse a student than I was."

Elissa blushed at the sound of Messia's barely stifled laugh. No doubt she was remembering when Elissa had decided to help with the cooking. In the span of one afternoon, Elissa had broken a bowl, let five hens escape the coop, and nearly set the *culina* alight, all while trying to roast a goose. Elissa had only a little more success at washing linens the next day. Messia had promptly replaced her at the basin and conveniently left no room for an extra pair of hands.

Laris chuckled and kindly changed the subject. "What did Taanit say when he came here yesterday?"

Elissa glanced at the wall behind him. "That business is slow but steady. They've had to travel as far as Arretium to find buyers, but they only have twenty horses now."

"Good, very good," Laris said, nodding. "They should try farther south, as well. The demand for battle-ready horses is increasing near Rome."

Elissa looked at Laris sharply. Taanit had seemed uneasy yesterday. When they'd sailed from Carthage nearly a month ago, the war with Rome seemed likely to break out any day. But Taanit had been tight-lipped on details when she'd pressed him for developments. He'd barely stayed a quarter of an hour before riding off to the next city that had a prospective buyer. He did mention that he'd sent word to her father of her whereabouts. And he'd certainly made time to reiterate the importance of staying indoors and out of sight.

"What's going on, Laris? Has the war in Iberia already begun?"

"No, no, nothing like that. It's just rumors."

Elissa pursed her lips and her eyes flicked to Messia. She needed a new tactic if she wanted to learn what was going on.

"Arnza's reading has been progressing very nicely. In fact, we've nearly run out of new books to read. Laris, I was hoping to accompany you to the market today to pick out some new ones."

"I'm not going to the market. I need to go to the port today to settle an account."

Elissa gave a small nod and dropped her eyes to hide her disappointment. She'd only left the house twice since coming to Vetulonium, and that was during her first days here, when Laris hadn't let her venture more than an arm's length away. She had hoped his opinion of her trustworthiness had changed over the past few weeks.

"Maybe it would be fine if Elissa went to the market alone today, Laris. She wouldn't be gone more than an hour and she'd stay on the main streets." Messia narrowed her eyes at Elissa.

"Yes, I promise," Elissa agreed hurriedly. "You'd hardly notice I'd stepped out."

Laris shook his head ruefully. "How is it that I wound up trying to say no to two charming women?"

Messia and Elissa exchanged a conspiratorial look.

"Perhaps you shouldn't try so hard," Elissa said sweetly.

Laris chuckled. "All right, Elissa, but one hour, no more."

Elissa breathed deeply as she walked down the cobbled streets of Vetulonium. The crisp November air cleansed her lungs of the weeks of inactivity. She stretched her legs with each stride and glanced around curiously. It felt good to walk where she pleased.

The streets of Vetulonium were already busy at this time of morning. She could hear the indistinct cacophony of a market up ahead. It sounded the same in Carthage—buyers and sellers bartering, friends gossiping, politicians campaigning at the forum. All cities must be similar.

Elissa rounded a corner and the mass of people increased

substantially. The sides of the street were crammed with bulging stalls pushed against rickety tenements. The vendors shouted their wares for everyone to hear—figs from Africa, wheat from Egypt, fine silks from Asia. Each stall had its speciality. The market was an explosion of color and smells originating from every corner of the world. Rome dominated the seas now, and clearly the prospect of war had done nothing to dampen its trade.

Elissa shelved her bewilderment and strode purposefully into the milieu. She needed to find a bookseller. She had already used up a quarter of her time getting here, and along with a book for Arnza; she needed to find someone with information about Carthage. Elissa stepped around a merchant holding fistfuls of colored shawls and nearly collided with a small boy in tattered rags.

"Your pardon, Lady!" the boy sputtered in heavily accented Latin. Clutching a loaf of bread, he ducked to Elissa's left and around a street corner without breaking stride.

"Gods take that little thief!" a portly man shouted from behind his stall. He gestured rudely after the boy.

Elissa turned in the opposite direction so the merchant couldn't see her stifled laugh. She rounded the next corner and spotted the distinct yellow of papyrus at a stand midway down the street. She hurried up to the elderly man standing behind the stall. He was pulling a heavy set of tomes from a sack and piling them on the counter.

She glanced at their titles. They appeared to be arranged by place of origin. She pointed to one of the scrolls. "Herodotus should be with Homer, I think."

The elderly man looked up and peered at her curiously over his long nose.

"Ah, right you are. The Greeks do belong together. I must say, Herodotus is quite unusual for a philosopher, but I suppose it's never too early to consider the implications of history." He rearranged the scrolls before looking back at Elissa. "And you, Lady? A Greek? Or just an admirer?"

"The former," Elissa assured him quickly. "But I'm looking for something lighter today. Perhaps there?" She pointed to a few slim volumes with Latin titles.

"Yes, yes, excellent choice. These deal with Rome's most glorious victories over the barbarous Samnites."

Elissa frowned. That wouldn't do. Messia wouldn't like her telling Arnza histories of the other Italians Rome had *gloriously* conquered.

"How about that instead? The chronicles of Romulus and Remus," Elissa said, reading its title. The story of Rome's founding. Messia couldn't fault that, and every boy loves a good tale.

"A Greek won over by Rome's brightness then?" the shopkeeper said with a wink. "That'll be 10 bronze pieces, Lady."

Elissa handed him a few of the coins she'd managed to smuggle from Carthage.

"Indeed. But she must be careful not to burn herself with all that light." Elissa began walking back the way she'd come, carrying the scrolls under her arm.

As she turned down the main street, she noticed it was markedly less busy than when she'd been here earlier. She looked down an adjoining street and saw people packed tightly between the buildings on either side. A dense crowd had gathered in the central square, and a man in a white toga stood on a raised platform in the middle. He was gesticulating wildly at the throng around him. The people were working themselves into a frenzy, shouting back at him in encouragement. Elissa guessed it had only been half an hour since she'd left home; surely she had time to hear what the man was saying. She turned down the next street and began weaving through the outer rows of people.

"Raping our women, pillaging our land!" The man's deep voice boomed above her head in Latin.

Elissa stood on her tiptoes to see over a shorter woman in front of her. The man was still shouting. His olive skin and well-starched toga suggested he was Roman. Elissa pushed her elbows out and squeezed in between two large men in front of her. She needed to be closer to hear him clearly.

"The barbarians descended from the wilds of…"

Who was he talking about? Gauls perhaps? They were always causing trouble in Northern Italy.

"What's he saying?" Elissa asked the woman beside her.

"Shh!" came the reply.

Elissa reached the center of the square where most of the people were gathered. The crowd was packed even closer here. Their bodies pressed into her on all sides. Someone shoved her from behind and her chest flattened against the back of the man in front of her.

"The eastern fools with their hired savages. Too soft and cowardly to fight with their own hands!" Spittle flew from the man's mouth as he shouted.

"African tricksters who dare to come into the lands of Italians and challenge us! It's true they surprised us, but now we will let them see how silk fares against steel. We will let them see what strength does to wiles, honor to avarice. We will let them see how Rome destroys Carthage!"

The crowd roared its approval. "Rome! Rome! Rome!" they chanted as one.

Elissa's body began to pulse with the crowd as they raised their fists and punched the air in unison, but she barely noticed. Her head was whirling to catch up with the man's words. Carthage! Carthage at war with Rome! She'd known it would happen eventually, but now? Winter was nearly upon them. It was the time for the armies of Carthage to solidify their positions and ready their garrisons for winter, not invade Italy! And surely the war was happening far away in Iberia. But he'd said they were fighting in the lands of the Italians. How would the Carthaginian army even have gotten to Italy? Rome ruled the seas now, so there was no way for Carthage to sail a fleet to Italy. Besides, the armies of Carthage were in Iberia, led by the Barca son. The young man was still relatively unknown, but his father was renowned for his intrepidness, not his recklessness.

Elissa's racing thoughts were interrupted by a shriek.

"The Romans are here!"

Elissa didn't look. She knew the Romans were here; she was in Italy for the gods' sake!

"The Romans! The Romans!"

The crowd shook, and Elissa could feel the frenzied energy rising. People's heads turned frantically as they looked for an opening to escape.

Now Elissa looked, too. "Wha…what's going on?"

No one answered. They didn't have to. The unmistakable red plumes of a dozen Roman helmets rose over her neighbor's shoulder.

The dam of people broke.

The man in front of Elissa turned and bulled into her stomach. She dropped the scrolls and skittered to the side, grabbing onto the woman next to her to stop herself from falling. The woman shook her off and flailed wildly to get past the person ahead of her. The crowd had morphed into a hysterical mob. The Roman legion was coming, and no one wanted to be caught in the open when they got here.

Thump. Thump. Thump. The rhythmic tapping of steel on stone reverberated across the square. Orders were shouted in crisp Latin. The stomping shook Elissa from her stupor. Roman boots. In Vetulonium. The legion was here. Carthage was in Italy—at war with Rome. She had to get out of here!

Elissa moved in the same direction as the fleeing people around her. An army could turn from an orderly unit to a pillaging horde in an instant. Everyone wanted to get back to their homes before they found out which these soldiers were today. Elissa tried to run, but people swarmed so close together, her feet hardly touched the ground. Amid the shouting and stomping, Elissa heard a weak cry come from below her. She looked down and saw the boy from the market, lying faceup on the ground, surrounded by dozens of feet. His mouth was shaped in a perfect O, a silent scream of terror frozen on his face. She reached her hand down to him. He needed to get up or he'd be trampled to death! But the crowd of people had already borne her past the boy, and she was as helpless to turn around as a tide in the sea.

Elissa reached the end of the square, where it opened into a street. She clawed her way to the edge of the mob until her shoulder ground into the wall of a tenement on the side of the street. She thrust her hands out and latched onto a protruding piece of wood, then hauled her body away from the mob and into the protective cover of a doorway.

Elissa's chest heaved from the effort. People were everywhere. The Romans were coming. She turned to the door behind her and pushed. It was locked. She slammed her shoulder into it, but the door didn't budge. Elissa bit her lip to stop herself from crying out. She whirled back around to face the mob. People still thundered down the street, but thankfully, the mass of bodies was lessening. The square must have nearly drained of people. She leaned forward and cautiously peeked out from behind her doorframe. The square was nearly empty now, except—

She gasped.

The chaotic mob had been replaced by an orderly column of men. Roman legionaries with iron chests and red cloaks marched in lockstep. The first row was already halfway across the square and marching straight toward Elissa's street.

Elissa swore and jerked her body back. It was too late to bolt down the street after the mob. She pressed herself against the closed door and prayed she'd disappear. The doorway was thick enough to conceal her body from the side, but if anyone turned their heads when they were across from her, she would be utterly trapped. A young woman caught out in the open would be a desirable prize for any legionary. Rape might not even be the worst of it if she let her Greek facade slip.

The pounding grew louder, and the stones reverberated under Elissa's feet with each step. They had nearly reached the mouth of the street. She turned so she was facing the closed door and sank onto the ground. She shrugged her shoulders so her shawl was covering her neck and the back of her head, praying she'd look like nothing more than a mound of gray fabric piled in a corner.

The Romans were across from her now. She held her breath as the hobnailed boots of the closest man approached her. They moved past without stopping. Elissa took a shallow breath and did the same as the next row of men passed. Breathe, hold, breathe, hold, again and again. Judging by the measure of her breathing, at least a dozen rows must have gone by. No one had stopped to look closer at the mound of wool huddled in the doorway. Elissa began to inhale less sharply. As soon as all the legionaries were through, she'd run back up the hill to the safety of Laris and Messia's home. Please the gods Laris hadn't left the city before the legion had come!

Something blunt and hard rammed into Elissa's back.

She started to squeal but managed to bite her tongue before any sound came out.

"Up." The demand came from a gruff voice behind her.

Elissa clenched her fists but didn't move.

"Up," the voice said again. A second kick to her back accompanied it this time.

Elissa flushed with anger. This man was actually kicking her! She barely resisted the urge to whirl around and sling profanities at the thug. She forced herself to slowly bring her feet underneath her instead. She stood, but remained facing the door.

A rough hand snaked in from behind and latched onto her wrist. It pulled, hard, and Elissa was spun around. A tall man with a bronze-scaled breastplate and a large red crest on his helmet—a centurion—stood in front of her. She lowered her eyes immediately.

"Slave," the man said.

Elissa's body responded before she could stop it. Her shoulders straightened and her shawl fell from the top of her head. She met the centurion's eyes directly, but recoiled slightly when she noticed their color. They were a striking gray. If he pulled his sword from the hilt, she was sure they would match its color exactly. His hand tightened around her wrist.

Implausibly, a hint of amusement seemed to tilt the corner of his mouth. But his square jaw was still set and his long aquiline nose turned up in contempt.

"Let me go." Elissa jerked her arm back to break free of his grip.

The pressure on her wrist increased. "I don't think so."

Elissa's eyes darted to the sides. She tried her only remaining option. She dropped her left shoulder and lunged for the street, aiming for the only part of the doorway not covered by the centurion.

He stepped in front of her with a quickness that belied his size. Instead of escaping, Elissa crashed headfirst into the bottom of his breastplate. The bronze scales bit painfully into her shoulder. His icy grip never left her wrist.

"Gracchus!" someone shouted from behind him.

The centurion sent her a ruthless glare that dared her to try that again, then turned stiffly toward the voice. Hooves clopped on stone behind them. Elissa saw another red-plumed helmet behind his hulking mass.

"Gracchus," a voice barked with authority. "Take your band of savages and drain every granary in this city. I don't want a single kernel remaining, you hear? Do whatever you need to get it."

The centurion's hand moved to the sword at his hip.

Thugs, Elissa thought. But there was no time to sneer because the centurion had inadvertently let go of her wrist, leaving her momentarily untethered.

Elissa darted around his back before she could rethink. Her bare arm grazed his as she passed, and she felt the centurion turn toward her in surprise. His fingers grasped for the shawl around her shoulders as she started to run. There was no brooch fastening the shawl, and it pulled clean off her body. Elissa dashed out of the doorway and toward the street corner. She didn't dare look back, but if she had, Elissa was sure she would've seen a very angry centurion holding an empty shawl.

She ran blindly down the next street. Her breath was rapid with fear as her legs pumped and her feet pelted over the flagstones. She wheeled around the corner and raced down a narrow alley behind a large tenement. Elissa had no idea where she was going; she knew only that she should aim for the temple at the top of the city, and that Messia and Laris's home would be nearby. She could just see the tip of its pointed roof over the nearest building. If she could get there, she'd be safe.

Elissa was half-crazed with fear. There were no footsteps behind her, so she assumed the centurion wasn't following her, but she expected an army of legionaries to be waiting on every street. She careened around another corner, eyes closed, and kept running. All she could hear was the pounding of blood in her head and the slapping of her sandals on stone. Surely every Roman in the city could hear it, too. Why had no one jumped out from a shaded alcove to grab her? Maybe the legionaries hadn't reached this part of the city yet. She could almost make out the inscriptions on the temple roof now, and running like a madwoman down the streets was probably attracting more attention than it was avoiding.

Elissa forced herself to slow to a walk. Other than the sound of her breathing, the street was silent. The white temple stood stoically at its end. Elissa ducked to the right and down the final street to Messia and Laris's home. It was empty, too. The door to every *domus* was shut, and any window with shutters was closed. Elissa forced her searing lungs to quiet and hurried down the side of the street where the midday sun cast a narrow lane of shade. She spotted the plain wooden door to Messia and Laris's home and broke into a run for the final few steps, sending up a silent prayer of thanks to the temple's god as she knocked frantically on the uneven wood.

The door swung open to reveal Laris's white face. He grabbed Elissa's shoulder and pulled her wordlessly inside. Laris bolted the door back shut as soon as she was over the threshold. Messia let out a strangled cry and rushed toward Elissa, pulling her into a tight embrace that crushed Elissa's face against her shoulder. Elissa heard her speaking rapidly in Etruscan.

Laris responded in his rough Latin. "Come. We have to hide you. They might force us to house some of the legionaries. And if a Roman finds out where you're from, he'll rape you and sell you before you can scream."

Elissa was frozen where she stood. Her calves ached from her frantic dash, and her limbs suddenly felt too heavy to lift. Realization crashed over her with violent force. The Romans were in Vetulonium. They were at war with Carthage. She was trapped far from home and far from help. Dear gods, she'd been stupid to leave.

Laris saw her expression and forced her hand into his. He dragged her to the *culina* and pushed open the door to the tiny storage room at its end. He didn't let go until she was standing amid the pots and dishes. The square of light from the *culina* shrank to a sliver and then disappeared altogether. The door shut with a click, and Elissa was left mute in the darkness.

CHAPTER 6

Elissa paced through the darkness. Four steps down the long ends, two along the short. She had to lean inward on the middle step to avoid a large pot that jutted out from the shelf. She was well acquainted with all the objects in the small storage room by now, nearly two weeks after Laris had unceremoniously dragged her in and locked the door with an apologetic glance. Messia had come later that night to hurriedly pass her a blanket and a few loaves of bread while hushing away all her questions. Elissa had spent the past two weeks alone in the darkness. Inventorying the cooking equipment had long since grown boring, but she refused to panic. Her nerves had gotten the better of her when the legion barged through the gates of Vetulonium, and she resolved not to let that happen again. She needed to be brave, not hysterical. Especially since the general of the legion, also known as the Roman Consul, and a dozen of his tribunes and aides were now occupying Messia and Laris's home along with her.

Consul Gaius Flaminius and his retinue had arrived shortly after Elissa, *requesting* accommodation, food, and free use of the *domus* for planning the war effort. "As allies of Rome, it is the duty of the citizens of this city to house and supply the legions that are here to protect them," one of his tribunes had announced before marching in uninvited.

The near-constant sound of orders being dictated, officers disciplined and scout reports discussed filtered through the thin walls of the *culina* and into the storage room. From the sentences she could catch, it sounded as though the war was not going well for Rome. There had been a battle at the foot of the Alps on the river Trebia, and the Romans had fared disastrously. Almost 40,000 thousand Romans had marched onto the battlefield that day, and only 10,000 had marched off. Endless debate about a cold river and hidden ambush inevitably followed any reference to that calamity.

Elissa knew she might be helpless, but her city certainly wasn't. The Carthaginian general, Hannibal, must be quite the chip off the old block. His father Hamilcar's hatred of Rome was legendary. Some said he made his three sons swear a blood oath of vengeance after the Carthaginian Council forced him to surrender to Rome during the first war. Barro had spoken glowingly of the young Hannibal's vigor and leadership while serving under him in Iberia, but Elissa had assumed his claims were exaggerated, since the Barcas were always spinning tales to shore up support back home.

The thought of Barro caused Elissa to sink down to her blanket on the floor and hug her knees to her chest. The glory and freedom of Carthage mattered, of course it did, but not more than her brother's life. She pictured his dark hair and warm eyes, and imagined him barging through the door and whisking her to safety. She sent up a silent prayer to her gods to make it so. Was it truly such an unreasonable request? After all, they were likely just a few days' ride apart. Elissa dropped her head into her hands. In truth, it might as well have been the width of the world for all the chance she stood that Barro would find her. But what about Taanit? He'd undoubtedly learned of the legion's presence in Vetulonium by now. Would he come here looking for her? Elissa changed the subject of her prayers. She hoped he wouldn't come. Numidia was allied with Carthage, and Taanit was an enemy of Rome as much as she was.

But without Barro or Taanit, how was she going to get out of here? There was no ship to flee on this time. Helpless laughter bubbled up in Elissa's throat and she clenched her lips to stop it from escaping. Maybe she was starting to lose her mind. Two weeks of silence, the impossible darkness— would marrying Merbal really have been worse? A month ago, she would've said that nothing could be worse, but now, she wasn't so sure. Merbal was greedy and self-absorbed, but he probably wouldn't have been cruel. Still, it wasn't just marrying him that she couldn't abide; it was giving up. Giving up the chance to be something more than a silent wife.

Elissa snickered at herself derisively. What a noble sentiment. See what good her defiance had done her? Apparently a girl who didn't want to marry deserved the same as a kitchen pot. Trapped in an unwanted marriage or trapped in a storage room, either way she was no better than property. Perhaps that was the fate of all women in this world. There was no real freedom for those who couldn't defend it with a sword.

Footsteps padded through the *culina* towards the storage room. Elissa froze.

The lock rattled.

"Why is everything locked in this gods damned house?" a masculine voice muttered. The door shook on its frame.

Hurried footsteps sounded from behind.

"Can I help you with something?" Messia's cool voice calmed Elissa's racing heart.

"The consul is unhappy with the food and has asked his personal cook to prepare the meals from now on. I'm to retrieve the pots."

"I see. I pray the consul will forgive me for my cooking. If you tell me what the cook needs, I would be happy to assist him."

"Two large pots for the broth and a shallow one for the oysters."

The door settled back into its frame.

"Why is this door locked anyway? Kitchenware can't be that valuable."

Elissa slowly stood and tiptoed to the small space behind the doorway. If Messia had to open the door for him now, that would be the only place to hide. As Elissa shuffled backward against the wall, the corner of one the shelves struck her skull. Two drinking cups bounced once on their platform, and then tipped over, hitting the ground. The terracotta shattered on impact.

"What's in here?" the man asked sharply. The door rattled in its frame again.

"Nothing, nothing." Messia walked quickly to the door. Her voice was placating. "Rats is all, we have terrible problems with them in the city."

The man paused. "The consul will punish both of us if he finds out that vermin are crawling over his plates."

"Best not tell him then," Messia said quietly.

Elissa couldn't tell if the man agreed, but she heard footsteps grow more distant as they crossed the *culina*. Her back was flattened against the wall, and she counted her breaths to calm herself. She reached sixty before the metal lock turned and the door creaked slowly open. Messia closed the door quickly behind her, then turned to face Elissa in the dim light filtering under the door.

"Messia, I'm so sorry," Elissa started. "That was awful, I…" Her voice was hoarse from disuse.

"It was too close." Messia's whisper was high-pitched. "If that slave had discovered you, there's no telling what he'd do."

Elissa lowered her eyes. "I'm so sorry, but Messia, I don't know how much longer I can do this. The darkness alone, it's enough to—" She cut herself off. She knew she had no right to make demands. She was putting the whole family at risk by being here, and they'd already suffered so much from the Romans.

"I know, Elissa, I know." Messia reached for her in the dark, and Elissa squeezed her hand when it found hers. "But there's no telling when the consul will leave. I'm afraid he'll be here as long as the legion is in Vetulonium. He steals food and wine from us every day, and then complains to Laris about how it tastes every time he sees him."

The thought of being trapped here indefinitely caused some of her hysteria to bubble to the surface again, and Elissa quickly changed the subject. "How is Arnza faring?"

"We're keeping him out of sight as much as we can. This consul does not seem the sort to tolerate a nosy boy asking questions about Rome. I heard him punish a centurion yesterday for letting a legionary off sentry duty because he was too sick to stand."

Elissa thought of the centurion who had cornered her in the doorway. She hoped he was the one who'd been punished.

"I must go now." Messia wrapped her free arm around Elissa's shoulders and pulled her into an embrace. Elissa pressed her nose into Messia's gray hair and inhaled the sweet smell of honey. She let some of her desperation escape.

"Messia, I can't do this to your family, and I can't stay here forever. I need to get out of Vetulonium, find Taanit and go back to Carthage. I need to get away from the Romans!"

Messia moved back and met Elissa's eyes in the semi-darkness. "I know that, but you can't leave now. The streets are crawling with legionaries and sentries are posted at every gate out of the city. We have to wait until the Romans have left."

"But we have no idea when that will be!" Elissa whispered fiercely. "There must be a way out now. What about the Numidian horses, do you think they're still there?"

Messia shook her head. "I don't know, Elissa. Laris could check tomorrow."

"Yes, yes, ask him to check."

Elissa's mind was already running through the possibilities. If she could get a horse and make it out of the city, no one would be able to catch her. She could head for the coast, maybe find Taanit, and take a ship back home. Or if that failed, she could ride north to her brother and pray that an army of 50,000 Carthaginians was enough protection from Rome.

"And have him find out which gate is most lightly guarded," she added.

Laris had checked the next day, and he'd whispered through the door that a dozen Numidian horses were still in the stables where Taanit had left them. A light guard was stationed at a granary nearby, but it seemed the Romans had yet to realize the value of the horses they had in their possession. The gate out of Vetulonium, on the other hand, was another issue entirely. The Romans must truly have no clue where the invading Carthaginian army was, because they were on high alert. A centurion had charge of every gate out of the city, and by Laris's count, ten of their men stood guard at the entrance to each gate, and several more watched from ramparts on the walls. Getting a horse out of the stables and past all those legionaries seemed an unlikely prospect. Laris had noticed something, though. Vetulonium was a cramped town, and half the legion had been forced to set up camp outside the south walls of the city. To accommodate the coming and going of the legionaries, the south gate stayed open day and night. The guard was doubled there, but if a handful of legionaries could be fooled into thinking that Elissa was a camp follower, there to pay some of the men a visit, she might stand a chance of escaping the city.

She mulled over Laris's information in the hours after he left, and soon became convinced that the south gate was the only way out. Elissa was no great actor, but with the right disguise, the guards might not need an explanation. They were unlikely to suspect a single woman with no baggage of trying to escape. She would have to think of a reason for bringing a horse along, but then again, it wasn't entirely unusual for the wives of low-ranking officers to follow their husbands on campaign. They would stay in the baggage train behind the legion, each woman cooking and cleaning for her husband and his men. At least, according to what Elissa had heard, that wasn't unusual. She'd never seen a Roman legion on the march, of course, but what other choice did she have than to believe the snatched fragments of stories? She was going on her third week locked in this storage room, and Elissa had resolved that waiting indefinitely for the Romans to leave was not an option. She had said as much to Laris when he had come to bring her dinner that night.

"It seems risky, Elissa. What if one of the guards doesn't believe you, or worse, decides you're a whore instead of an officer's wife and isn't interested in listening to any explanations to the contrary? And what will you do once you're outside the gate and in a camp of 2,000 Romans? You'll have neatly delivered yourself to the enemy!"

Laris was right, and she could only pray for the best with the guards, but if she could get a horse to the outskirts of camp, there'd be no stopping her. Elissa had seen the land around the city; it was filled with rocky crags and rolling hills, interspersed with patches of forest for cover. It was exactly the type of terrain the Numidians bred their horses for. Numidian horses were smaller and stockier than most, and they could be outrun in an open field, but no horse was more surefooted and levelheaded. A Roman infantryman couldn't catch them on this land, Elissa was convinced of that.

Laris had acquiesced quickly when she argued the point. Truth be told, he'd seemed relieved at her persistence. Elissa couldn't deny that stung a bit, but she could hardly blame him. His family had suffered enough at the hands of Rome, and Elissa could not have them punished further on her account. The plan was set for the next night; Elissa would slip out of the house, steal a horse from the stables, then pass through the gate and out of the city.

Elissa paced in anticipation all through the next day. Time seemed to have slowed to a crawl. The Romans in the next room bustled about in their usual routine—patrol reports, supply inventories, quarrels over whether the consul had asked for duck or mollusks for the second course. Their voices felt magnified in Elissa's head, each syllable bouncing around inside her skull before expiring. She had a bad headache by nightfall, and had managed not a minute's sleep.

Nevertheless, she was ready when Messia came for her after the house had grown silent that night. She'd fastened her hair in a braid that hung down her back and was secured at the bottom with a leather thong. Messia brought the plain wool dress that Elissa had arrived in, but she'd added long sleeves and a sturdy hooded cloak. Elissa tugged on the dress and pulled the hood over her head so none of her hair was showing. Cloaked in gray from head to toe, she looked like a shade in transit between worlds. No half-sober Roman would be mistaking her for a loose woman. Messia stepped back and surveyed her handiwork.

"Good. But that's the easiest part done." Messia's forehead creased with worry. "Elissa, I think you should stay here. There's so much that could go wrong. We'll find a better way to get you out."

She felt her resolve waver at the sincerity in Messia's brown eyes. She wondered if her mother's eyes had ever looked like that. Barro had said her eyes were the color of amber, like warm honey softened in the sun.

"Elissa?" Laris's whisper came from behind Messia. "It's time."

Elissa took her small satchel from the ground with shaking hands. *It's time*, she repeated silently. She had gotten herself into this mess; it was time to get herself out of it. Elissa started to move toward Laris, but Messia still stood in her path.

"Take this, Elissa. It will remind your gods to protect you no matter where you are."

Messia pressed something cold and metallic into Elissa's hand. Elissa lifted the object toward her face and saw it was an amulet of some sort, but it was too dark to make out any details. She brought the thin leather strap over her head and tucked the amulet under the folds of her dress.

"Messia, I…" Elissa's throat felt tight.

Messia shook her head and squeezed Elissa's hand, then stepped to the side and gently pulled her toward Laris. Elissa nodded at Messia gratefully and followed Laris across the *culina* and into the small garden that ringed their house. The wooden gate separating Messia and Laris's home from the streets of Vetulonium opened silently, and Laris and Elissa slipped out.

Elissa followed Laris down the narrow side streets and alleys of Vetulonium, and her head began to clear. Three weeks locked in a storage room was decidedly three weeks too many. A full moon shone brightly overhead, but without any stars to match it, the sky was still dark. A gust of wind whipped the fringes of Elissa's hood around her face. It had an icy edge that made Elissa shiver through the thick wool of her cloak, and her breath lingered visibly in the winter air. Her head might have cleared but her stomach was still tied in knots. Every errant sound caused her stomach to lurch and the knot to wind tighter. Elissa touched the amulet through her dress. Maybe it was a window to her gods.

"Astarte, goddess of love and war, protect me. Guide my horse's feet tonight," she whispered. Her gods had no priests here; she should make a sacrifice to Astarte herself when she could.

Laris halted before turning a corner and Elissa nearly crashed into him. She squeezed her lips to stop from crying out and stepped back. Laris peered around the corner to look down the next street, then quickly withdrew. He pressed his body against the wall behind them. Elissa followed his lead. Two legionaries came into view on the street in front of them, weaving and laughing as they walked, clearly drunk. Elissa willed herself and Laris to disappear into the rough bricks.

"That redhead was so impressed, she let me have the hour for free!" one of the men said.

The other legionary gave his companion a hearty shove and chortled with disbelief. "More like she couldn't charge you 'cause you didn't have anything to poke 'er with!"

The offended man responded with his own shoving and assurances of the uncommonly large size of his member. They stumbled on down the road slinging profanities at each other.

As soon as they rounded the corner, Laris moved away from the wall and started in the direction from which the legionaries had come. Elissa followed, and they stayed as close as possible to the buildings lining the street. A few lights shone from the rare unshuttered window above them, but except for the pair of drunk legionaries, the streets were empty. Empty, but far from quiet. The sounds of a tavern rang through the street. Men laughing, drinks banging on tables, wood cracking as a brawl broke out. The legion wanted grain and whores from Vetulonium, and it seemed they'd found both.

Laris stopped again once they reached the end of the street. A shrouded square opened in front of them and Elissa recognized the familiar rectangular shape of the stable. The walls of the city loomed large behind the stables, and a dozen horses grazed quietly in the adjoining corral—exactly where the Numidians had first left them.

Laris turned to look at Elissa meaningfully, then nodded in the direction opposite the stables. Four legionaries stood outside a square wooden building, and unlike the two drunk men they'd encountered earlier, these men were rigid and at attention.

"The granary," Laris whispered into Elissa's ear.

She nodded. The punishment for allowing grain to be stolen must be severe.

The square separating them from the stable was in full view of the legionaries at the granary. It was dark, but Elissa would need to move quickly. Thankfully, she'd be sheltered from the guards' eyes once she reached it.

Elissa started forward; she knew from experience that waiting would only add to her fear. Laris's hand came to her arm and stopped her. Elissa faced him, and she suddenly noticed how weary he looked tonight. The lines in his face seemed to have deepened; they pulled his skin downward and caused his eyes to droop. Elissa knew immediately that this was as far as he'd go tonight. He dropped his hand from Elissa's arm and held up a finger instead. *Wait.* When Elissa followed his gaze back to the granary, she saw that a guard no longer stood at each of its four corners. Instead, the men had moved to the front of the building and were beginning an orderly march around its circumference. Elissa understood

Laris's meaning immediately. Soon the legionaries would be behind the granary and completely out of sight. Elissa turned to Laris once more. His finger was still suspended in the air. Elissa caught her breath and closed her eyes, a moment of tranquility before she launched herself on a new path, as uncertain as the one that had brought her here.

She thought of Barro, imagined him charging into battle with his sword drawn, shield raised, Romans falling to either side of him as he bellowed a ferocious battle cry. She could be brave like that.

Laris dropped his finger and Elissa ran. She burst from the street and into the square, staring straight ahead at her destination, refusing to look toward the granary for fear of what she might see. She reached the stables, dropped to a crouch and immediately turned back to Laris. She couldn't see his expression through the darkness anymore, only his outline. He nodded once, turned away slowly, then disappeared down the street.

Elissa swallowed. All alone now. She pushed the fear back down to her stomach and crept along the side of the stable. Her feet moved silently on the soft grass. She could see the corral around the corner of the stable, which meant the closest horse, was only a dozen paces away. Elissa passed the corner and halted. There they were, a dozen horses scattered across the small corral, chewing softly on the few remaining sprigs of grass. The bare ground was a jarring reminder that she'd been in Vetulonium long enough for the horses to strip the corral of its greenery. Had it really been two months since she'd left home? When she'd run onto her father's ship, she thought she'd be gone a few weeks, a month at most. Elissa shook her head ruefully. It would be a miracle if her father hadn't already disowned her.

She took a deep breath realizing that was only one more reason she had to escape tonight. She brought her focus back to the horses in front of her. It was difficult to do more than distinguish each horse's shape, but that should be enough to get an idea of their ability. She eyed each of them appraisingly and had more or less settled on a tall gelding in the corner when a familiar white star came into view. The willing mare she'd ridden into Vetulonium moved in front of the big gelding to nibble at a weed. The mare was at least a hand's width shorter than the gelding, and not as powerful, but she was steady and brave. She would also be far less likely to attract attention than the flashy gelding. It was a good omen, and the knot in Elissa's stomach loosened slightly.

She cast a furtive glance to either side and moved quickly from behind the stable to the wooden fence that surrounded the corral. She squeezed in between two planks and dropped to a crouch beside the closest horse. The horse twisted its head to sniff at her curiously, then resumed shuffling dirt with its lip. She wound in between the neighboring horse's legs until she reached a familiar pair of black ones. The Numidians hadn't bothered to remove the rope from the mare's neck, which made it easier for Elissa to grab onto her and pull her toward the gate. A few horses snorted indignantly as they moved aside. Elissa pushed the gate lightly at first and then harder when it opened silently. She led her mare out of the corral and closed the gate behind them. Elissa paused to run her hand along the mare's sleek neck. No sleepy protests from this one.

She led the horse away from the corral and down the narrow road she and Taanit had taken when they rode into the city. The city walls stood tall on her left side, and the red roofs of houses rose up on her right. Elissa stayed in the center. She was about to walk into a group of armed Romans and demand passage through their gate; there was no point in being secretive now.

The din of moving metal and laughing men grew louder as Elissa approached a sharp turn in the road. She must be close to the south gate. She forced her legs to slow to a more casual pace as she approached the corner, but as soon as the gate came into view, she stopped moving altogether. More than a dozen Romans milled about in the wide dirt road that led through the opening in the wall. Four men stood erect and serious in front of it. Warm torchlight glinted off their steel helmets and heavy breastplates. The rest of the men were seated around a campfire; relaxing in their armor and passing a wineskin back and forth. One of the men laughed heartily at something his neighbor said.

Elissa looked behind her at the mare. The horse dropped her head, waiting for instructions. She tightened the hood of her cloak and straightened, then turned toward the gate. She put one foot in front of the other, then repeated the action, each step bringing her closer. The men by the fire seemed perfectly unconcerned with her, and she'd just about reached the entrance when the nearest guard's head jerked toward her.

"Stop," he commanded.

The guard moved out from beside the gate to stand squarely in her path. Elissa was close enough to see the dark stubble shading the lower half of his face. He smelled of sour wine. His helmet hooded his eyes, but she could still feel his hungry gaze piercing the thick wool of her dress. She looked over his head and sucked in a breath. Just a few quick words to convince him.

"I'm returning to camp. Let me pass."

The man's head lifted in surprise at the authority in her voice. "What's your business there?"

Elissa sighed audibly in what she hoped sounded like exasperation. He needed to think she was accustomed to being questioned by guards. She tried to make her voice brusque. "To return to my husband, of course. I came into the city to find some decent meat for dinner, but as you see, I'm empty-handed." Elissa let go of the mare's lead and spread her hands.

The guard snickered.

"Now if you'll excuse me," Elissa pressed, wanting to end this conversation as soon as possible. "Meat or no, I still have a dinner to make, and I must hurry if I'm to have it ready for my husband in time."

Elissa started to walk forward, hoping it might dissuade him from thinking too carefully.

The guard remained where he stood. His forehead was creased, as if he wanted to ask another question. But then he moved aside, and there was only an open gate in front of Elissa. She stepped over the threshold and out of Vetulonium.

Her relief lasted for all of two breaths, because as she passed through the gate and out of Vetulonium, the entire Roman camp came into view. The knot in her stomach tightened again and cut short any reprieve she'd begun to feel. Thousands of campfires dotted the slope below her, each one with a single tent arranged neatly beside it. Crisp right-angled roads cut through the tents into an open square in the center of the camp. A high wooden palisade separated the edge of the camp from the meadow beyond; the entire city of Vetulonium could have fit between those wooden walls. This was supposed to be only half a legion? The campfires looked like a thousand orange eyes, all glinting at her wickedly.

Elissa knotted her hand in the black mane at her shoulder. *Keep walking, keep walking,* she whispered to herself. Surely she was far enough from the guard by now to slip onto the mare's back. She could skirt the Roman fence and head for the forest past the meadow. And then she could run. Gods, she wanted to run from here.

"Wait!" the guard's voice rang out.

Elissa kept walking. He might believe she was out of earshot and not bother following her.

"Woman! I said wait."

Curse that Roman! Elissa stopped and turned stiffly back toward the gate. She gripped her mare's mane tightly in case she needed to make a quick escape.

The guard hadn't moved from his post, but several other legionaries were looking in her direction to see what he was yelling about.

"Who is your husband?" he called.

She said nothing.

"*Who* is your husband?" he repeated. The guard started to move toward her. He was clearly annoyed at the attention they were attracting.

He'd passed through the gate and was rapidly approaching. She had to make him stop. "What do you mean?" Elissa called back, her voice cracking.

"Your husband! You said you were returning to him. What's the man's name?"

Elissa's entire body tensed with the effort of forcing herself not to flee. Dear gods, give her a name, something common, but not so common that someone else, someone in the camp, might share it. Her mind was completely blank. Countless hours of Roman history lessons, and not a single name came to mind when it really mattered. Hard gray eyes suddenly flitted across her vision. Aha! That dreadful centurion who'd nearly caught her on the street. What was his name?

"Gracchus!" Elissa spat out. "Gracchus! That's my husband's name."

The guard stopped immediately. He looked surprised and glanced at the man behind him. The second man shrugged in response. The guard nodded briefly at Elissa and quickly turned back to his post.

Elissa unclenched her fist and exhaled a long sigh of relief. That was too close. She slid gratefully onto the mare and pushed her into a trot. If she could just get out of the camp now, she'd never have to see another Roman again.

"Didn't think that cold bastard was cut out for marriage," the guard said to the man next to him as he returned to the gate.

The other guard shrugged his shoulders but made no response. That was odd; hadn't he heard the woman say _Gracchus_?

"And which cold bastard might you be referring to?" he responded icily—except that his lips weren't moving.

Dread crept up the first guard's spine. He turned slowly in the direction of the voice, already knowing whom he'd see. Even though he was prepared, he still jolted when he saw Centurion Marcus Gracchus standing behind him. The centurion held his hands loosely at his sides and regarded him with cold disinterest. Gracchus wore full armor despite not being on guard duty, and carried a javelin. Firelight caught in the polished bronze scales of his breastplate and colored them red. He looked like something from the underworld. But maybe that was only his reputation.

The guard might not have been under the centurion's direct command, but everyone in the legion knew who Gracchus was. He commanded the largest maniple in the legion, a hundred and forty of the fiercest soldiers, who always formed the center of the first line in battle. The fighting was the heaviest there, and most commanders didn't last a campaign season before either being killed or moved back to the second line. But not Centurion Gracchus. His men were always the first to break through the enemy line; they were never flanked, never seemed to tire, and Gracchus invariably led them from the front, painting the battlefield red with his sword. He'd been in the legion for more than a decade and had never once taken up a safer position in battle. He'd fought with the same men his entire career, and all were now veterans in their prime, and loyal to their centurion, above the rotating line of aristocratic consuls and tribunes.

"Cornelius, is it?" The icy voice cut straight to his spine again. Gracchus was in front of him now.

"Y...yes, sir," the guard managed to stammer.

Gracchus's mouth tilted upward in a half-smile, and the guard thought he might have seen a hint of amusement flash across his clear, gray eyes. Best to assume not, though. A man didn't earn such a savage reputation for nothing.

"Well, Cornelius, I'd rather not repeat myself, so I suggest you untie your tongue and tell me why I heard a distinctly female voice shouting my name, and why it led you to contemplate my fortunes in matrimony."

Gracchus folded his arms across his chest lazily, but the guard could practically see the energy pulsing through them. The centurion's weight was tipped forward onto the balls of his feet, one ear tilted in the opposite direction, as if he was listening for an attack that could come at any moment.

"No. sir, I wouldn't dare question..."

Gracchus's mouth tightened. He was growing impatient.

"The woman," the guard continued quickly. "She passed through the gate: said she was your wife."

Gracchus's hands were around his throat in an instant. The centurion pressed tightly on the soft skin around his neck and lifted his weight off his feet. "What did you say?" he growled.

"Your wife—is she? Is she not?" the guard managed to stammer, but he knew the answer before he'd finished. Gods, of all men to accidently cross, why did it have to be Centurion Marcus Gracchus!

But the centurion merely shoved him aside and started toward the gate. The guard brought his hands to his throat and staggered back against the wall.

Gracchus turned toward him. "Get me a horse," he said gruffly. "Now!"

Open meadow stretched ahead of Elissa. Finally. She'd carefully skirted the edge of the Roman camp, keeping the mare to a slow trot so as not to make any noise. The orderly rows of tents, the spiked palisade, the thousands of guttering fires—they were all behind her now, and no more Romans were left in front of her.

Elissa squeezed her legs and the mare sped to an easy canter. The full moon loomed large and blanketed the grass in pale gray light. There was a road to her right that cut through the center of the meadow and led out from the Roman camp. It looked like a silver snake in the moonlight, winding out from the camp and into the distance, where a row of shadows marked its far end. Elissa wanted to race her mare along that road. She wanted to dash madly for the forest at its end and get as far as possible from the sleeping legion behind her. But it would take the rest of the night to reach the sea, and she needed to conserve her horse's energy. She'd escaped Vetulonium, thank the gods. What was next? A whole ocean still lay between her and home. She might be able to return to the port where they'd arrived, but how she'd find Taanit and get a ship to take her across was another matter entirely.

Elissa turned her head to look back at the city and something flickered in the corner of her eye. A lone rider was galloping along the road at full tilt. He was crouched so low that horse and rider were nearly indistinguishable. It must be a messenger with urgent news of the war. Elissa angled her horse away from the road; she should take care not to be seen. She glanced at the road once more, but no movement caught her attention this time.

Her skin prickled under her cloak as she heard hoofbeats again. She turned on the mare's back to find the source. There was movement directly across from her. The messenger.

He'd slowed to a canter so his torso no longer blended with his horse's back. Elissa squinted to see through the dim light. The man seemed to be looking for something, too; he turned his head back and forth as if scanning the dark meadow. A dim red flicker caught Elissa's eye—a bronze-scaled breast-plate. She felt a twinge of pain in the shoulder that had collided with it.

A strangled cry escaped her lips. The centurion!

The man's head jerked swiftly. He was staring straight at her; she felt his eyes bore into her like a knife slicing through her disguise. It was as if the sun had already risen and she was hopelessly trying to hide in plain daylight. The fear that had twisted her stomach as she crept through the city and lied to the guards was replaced by terror, icy and numbing as it paralyzed her in its cold grip. *He had found her.*

The centurion was under no such spell. He turned his horse and galloped directly toward Elissa. The mare must have felt her terror, or the other horse's movement, because she sped to a gallop as well. She understood instinctively that they mustn't be caught by the hulking shape hurtling toward them from behind. Soon they were flying over the grass. The mare dropped low, fully extending her legs as she reached for every inch of ground, then coiling them tightly back so she could launch out again. The wind blew away some of Elissa's terror and she leaned over the mare's neck. She gritted her teeth; it wasn't over yet. If she could just reach the forest before the centurion got to her, she would have the advantage of the tightly packed trees.

Her mare flew over the murky grass below, trying valiantly to keep the larger horse at bay. But the centurion was closing the distance between them with every stride, and as short trees started to appear sporadically around them, he was only a few paces behind. Elissa could hear his horse's ragged breathing and feel his furious stare. She stole a glance at him under her arm. Terror shot up her spine as her enemy took shape in the darkness. Muscles bunched his arms where he gripped the reins. His scarlet cloak flapped behind his dark horse, and his eyes were steel pits in a shrouded face. He was the boatman of Hades come to take her soul across the river.

Elissa's heart pounded in her ears but she forced herself to look away. She still had a chance to avoid the approaching doom behind her. She kicked her heels into the mare's sides and begged for more. The mare responded as best she could. They streaked through the dappled light and tangled branches of the rapidly thickening forest. The ground changed from grass to dirt and crackling leaves. They leapt over a fallen log without breaking stride. Her mare's speed was closely matched by the larger horse behind them. Elissa steered into a clump of trees so dense the gray moonlight didn't reach the ground. A branch appeared in front of her and she ducked quickly to avoid colliding with it. Instead, it caught her cloak and tore it clean off her back. A few strides later, they stepped in a patch of soft ground and the mare fell forward onto her knees. She scrambled wildly to right herself and they continued on.

"Stop, woman!" the centurion's voice erupted like lightning through Elissa's panicked mind. "You'll kill yourself and that horse if you keep running!"

His words had the opposite effect to what he intended. She'd barely heard him over the din of their thrashing through the bush, and a quick glance back confirmed that he was falling behind. The mare lurched into the air and they cleared another ditch.

"C'mon, girl, we've almost lost him. Just a little longer…" Elissa's murmured to her horse's sweat-darkened ear.

All of a sudden, the trees around them disappeared and the ground in front of the mare's hooves lightened from black to gray. Elissa jerked her head up and saw the ground fall away into black nothingness a few strides ahead.

Elissa gasped and wrenched back on the mare's lead with all her might. The mare sensed the chasm ahead of them at the same time and locked her front legs instantly. Her hind legs skittered to the side as she fought for purchase. They skidded to a stop mere inches from the edge. Elissa blew out the air she'd been holding in her chest. Dear gods, that was close! She sucked in a few shallow breaths, then let fly a string of curses. How many foolish, reckless decisions had she made to wind up nearly dead at the bottom of a cliff with only one hateful Roman even knowing she'd gone?

Her nerves were at their breaking point, but the distant beat of the centurion's horse pounded ever closer. Elissa leaned to the side and peered over the edge of the chasm. It was really more of a steeply sloped ravine than a sheer cliff. The incline was almost vertical at its top, but the angle lessened as it approached a wide river that cleaved the worn earth far below. Elissa pushed the mare a step closer. A chunk of rock fell away in front of her hooves and bounced down the long slope, gaining momentum until it hit the river with a faint splash. Elissa screwed up her eyes to try to see through the dim light. The ravine was steep, but apart from a few bands of rock that cut across the slope, the ground was mostly soft. If she could ignore her trepidation, she might be able to weave a careful path through the steep sections at the rim to reach the lower angled ground below. The centurion was having enough trouble with the dense forest behind them; he would never follow her down.

The crashing behind Elissa was growing louder. It sounded as though the centurion was going to burst through the trees at any moment. At his slower pace, it was too much to hope that he'd miss the ravine and go hurtling into the river below. Elissa looked back over the cliff, and apprehension flooded her body. If the mare slipped, there'd be no surviving the fall down to the river. The sounds of thrashing brush suddenly stopped. The centurion had broken through the trees, his face dark with fury. He wasn't just going to catch her. He was going to murder her.

Elissa turned toward the cliff. The blood of the Magos flowed through her veins. Old blood, undiluted since the founding of Carthage six hundred years ago. She heard the Mago words as Barro had said them the day he left for the army. *Victory in life, or freedom in death.* Those were the only ways. Elissa shut her eyes and squeezed her legs.

Her mare was so brave; she barely hesitated as she took the first step over the edge, and then another. Her back tilted to near vertical as they began the descent. The dirt fell away in chunks under her hooves and cascaded down the slope below. Elissa leaned back as far as she could to help them gain purchase. The ground was much steeper than it had looked from the rim. The sound of rushing water filled Elissa's head, but she saw only darkness below them. They were going to fall. They were going to fall and they wouldn't stop until their heads were driven into the dirt and their mouths were full of water. She should never have tried to ride down this. The mare came to the same conclusion a moment later and stopped abruptly. A vertical stretch of rock jutted out below her hooves. The step wasn't large, probably not even as tall as Elissa, but it stretched clear across the slope and offered no way around. If they wanted to keep going, they'd have to jump over it and hope to stop their momentum on the flat ledge below. If they couldn't stop in time, they'd fall, and it would be exactly as Elissa had imagined.

"That's enough!" The centurion's voice rang through the still air from above. "There's nowhere left to run. If you come back now, I might be merciful."

His dark silhouette was even blacker than the sky. She imagined what he'd do if he got his hands her. He would grab her arms, bind her wrists behind her back, and then spread her legs and take his captor's rights. He would take her freedom and her dignity. Who would she be without them? Elissa didn't want to find out. She touched the amulet around her neck and squeezed her legs a second time.

The mare hesitated a moment, as if she wanted to give Elissa a chance to change her mind. Elissa held firm, and the mare coiled her legs underneath her and launched into the air. All four hooves left their tenuous hold on the earth, then slammed back onto the ledge below.

Her brave mare tried desperately to stop from pitching forward off the ledge and falling into the abyss below. But the momentum spun her hind legs out from under her and sent her careening outward. Elissa dove off the mare's back toward the ledge, which was rapidly slipping away. She hit the ground hard and her head jerked painfully to the side. She rolled to a stop against the rock step and quickly turned around to see where the mare was. The terrified shriek of a panicked animal ripped through the air. It cut straight through Elissa's heart as she heard a heavy body thud mercilessly down the ravine. Elissa dragged herself back to the edge in time to see her beautiful, black mare hit the riverbank with a sickening crack. Her bones snapped like twigs and her head burrowed into the dirt. Her body broke under the unrelenting force of the earth.

"*NO!*" Elissa screamed.

She tore her eyes away from her horse and emptied the contents of her stomach onto the ground. Bile stung her throat, and her tears melted into the dirt. Elissa pulled herself backward and slumped against the step. *She had killed that brave, beautiful horse*. Elissa had killed her!

Dirt rained onto her back from above. Elissa half-turned her head without caring what she saw. The centurion was climbing down the ravine on foot. He faced into the slope and carefully planted each boot before lifting the next one. He moved slowly and meticulously—exactly what she should have done. Elissa's face burned with self-loathing.

Her selfishness, her recklessness, had brought her here. She had humiliated her father, endangered Taanit, Messia, Laris, and Arnza, and now killed her horse. Let the centurion take her. She deserved whatever he did. Elissa rested her head against the rock and closed her eyes. She couldn't bring herself to care what happened next.

CHAPTER 7

When Marcus finally reached her, he didn't approach at first. He stood at the far end of the narrow ledge and watched her instead. Her knees were held tight to her chest and her forehead rested on top of them. Dark hair fell in heavy waves over her legs. She seemed taller than he'd initially guessed. She had looked so small and lithe perched atop that horse's bare back, riding like mad. Marcus gritted his teeth. He didn't need the reminder of that reckless chase over treacherous ground just now, or he was liable to do something he might regret. He wanted to scare her, not hurt her.

But Marcus had been nearly apoplectic with anger as he watched her inch down a slope he would never have dreamed of taking on horseback. And to think the little harpy had nearly pulled it off! Nearly, but not quite. The dying horse at the bottom of the ravine was a reminder of that. This girl had escaped from Vetulonium by claiming to be his wife, and then led him on a wild chase that had very nearly gotten them both killed. And now she dared to huddle in the corner like a woeful victim?

Marcus's building indignation stirred him from the side of the ledge and he strode purposefully toward the girl. He wrapped his hand firmly around her arm and wrenched her to her feet. The girl rose but didn't look up from the ground.

Her unexpected acquiescence only enraged Marcus further.

"Oh, now you'll come willingly? After you've lied to my guard, torn through my camp and killed what was obviously one of my best horses?"

Her head snapped up at the mention of the horse. Marcus inhaled sharply, unprepared for what he saw. Her skin was as light as her hair was dark, and inset with a pair of glowing green eyes. She seemed ethereal under the silver light of the moon. On the other hand, there was something decidedly more sensual about the generous lips that curved between her rounded chin and delicately upturned nose. Marcus let his eyes roam freely over the rest of her body, hoping for some clue as to what she looked like under that shapeless gray dress.

"She wasn't *your* horse," the girl shot back fiercely.

The centurion smiled wryly; outrage seemed more in keeping with her nature. But it was late, and he was in no mood for games.

"Who are you?" he demanded.

The girl's mouth clamped shut.

Marcus tightened his grip on her upper arm. "I don't like asking twice."

The girl focused her eyes on the ground. "I'm Athenian. I was in the care of a relative in Vetulonium while we waited for passage home."

She spoke softly, but her voice never quavered. The firm edge under her otherwise feminine voice stirred his memory. Marcus rocked back on his heels as he recollected a doorway and a certain nimble girl who had narrowly avoided his grasp. It had annoyed him to be eluded like that, but he'd been distracted and tired from the long march. More pressing concerns had soon wiped away any intention of tracking the girl down. Besides, she had seemed too lean for his tastes, not to mention wily and quick-footed. Marcus preferred his women buxom, and they were the ones who chased him, certainly not the opposite. Still, he nearly asked for her name before stopping himself. The name of a runaway didn't matter.

"I don't believe this is the first time we've met," Marcus said finally.

Elissa glanced up at that, and her eyes met the centurion's. She was surprised to see that he appeared younger than his deep voice suggested—perhaps barely into his third decade. His eyes were still his most striking feature. But what she'd initially thought was simple gray was actually more of an icy blue, the color of a new blade just pulled from the forge. His dark hair hung carelessly about his ears, much longer than the typical close-cropped style of Roman legionaries. His skin looked tanned and roughened from years of marching under the sun. Even through the thick wool of her dress, she could feel the strength and virility of his grip. Elissa barely resisted the urge to spit on that hand. He was the Roman archetype, from his scarlet cloak all the way down to his bronze greaves.

"I see you're planning to be as unwieldy as you were before." The centurion let go of her arm and spread his hands out on either side. "Go ahead, try to run again."

Elissa clenched her jaw at his arrogance. She desperately wished she still had the courage to test him.

He smiled confidently when she didn't move. The realization that he was gloating over her misfortune jolted Elissa out of her temporary resignation. She was about to tell him what a brutal Roman thug he was when the faint sounds of something moving below caught her attention. She moved to peer over the ledge at the same time as the centurion. As she stared into the murky darkness of the river below, her heart split open all over again. The mare was still fighting for life on the riverbank, trying desperately to rise onto two front legs that jutted out at the wrong angles. Dark liquid stained the ground all around her, and her eyes were wide with terror as she tried to heave her broken body into motion.

Elissa heard a strangled cry of horror before she recognized it had come from her own mouth. Her horse was in agony, panicking as she fought for a life that had already gone. It was terrible to watch, but Elissa knew she didn't deserve to look away.

Elissa felt the centurion move beside her and suddenly a smooth, metal point arced gracefully across her field of vision and struck her horse. Elissa was about to turn on him in fury when she noticed the black mare now lay flat against the ground, still at last. The shaft of the centurion's javelin protruded from the mare's neck, immediately behind her head, where the flow of blood was greatest. It took a few minutes for Elissa's mind to register that the centurion had granted the mare an act of great mercy, and with a level of skill and precision Elissa would not have thought possible. She turned toward him, unsure of whether she should, or could, thank him.

His eyes were unreadable when she met them, shrouded in the darkness of this endless night. The centurion jerked his head to the side, motioning her to follow him up the ravine. Elissa lowered her head and started after him. There was nothing else to do.

The centurion's outstretched hand waited for her at the top of the ravine. Was he offering to help her over the final lip? Or did he want to make sure she didn't attempt a run for it once they were on flat ground? He needn't have worried on the latter score. Elissa's legs shook with the effort of holding up her body as she took the last few steps. The night's ordeal had taken its toll on her physically and mentally. She longed for those days spent hiding in Messia and Laris's *culina* when all she'd felt was boredom. Elissa only had a few errant strands of pride left, but they held firm as she pulled herself up and flopped inelegantly over the edge without the centurion's help. He raised an eyebrow at her and turned away, not offering his hand a second time. Elissa crawled to her feet and followed him to his horse.

The centurion rode a large bay stallion, which he had neatly tied to a tree before starting after Elissa on her doomed escape down the ravine. She approached the stallion and laid a quivering hand on his neck. She needed to calm down, think her way out of this mess. He was a beautiful horse; it was no wonder he'd outrun them on the meadow. Suddenly, the centurion's hands closed around her waist and Elissa felt her feet leave the ground. Her stomach connected with the saddle as the centurion slung her over the horse's back like a sack of grain.

"Of all the undignified, awful things!" Elissa squealed as she quickly pulled her leg over the horse's side. She glared down at the centurion spitefully once she was properly seated.

His mouth twisted into a mocking smile and he looked meaningfully at her leg. Elissa glanced down and saw white skin from her ankle all the way to the hem of her dress, which had been yanked halfway up her thigh. She felt herself blush and scrambled to yank it back down. The centurion chortled, which prompted Elissa to shoot him a second glare. He merely arched his eyebrow again and looked away. If her attempts at modesty amused him, it might be because of what he planned to do to her when they returned to camp.

The centurion moved behind Elissa's leg and prepared to vault into the saddle. In the moment before his legs left the ground, Elissa briefly considered snatching the reins from his hands and taking off with the horse. But the moment passed before she could act, and the centurion kept his fingers wound tightly around the reins as he swung into the saddle behind her. Elissa frowned with disappointment. This man was no fool.

Marcus didn't need to read thoughts to know that the girl contemplated running. Her body was tilted off to the side, and it was clear she was considering whether she could duck under his arm and dive off the horse. He locked his arms tightly on either side of her and held the reins firmly in his hands. There would be no more escape attempts tonight.

They made their way back through the forest at a walk. His horse moved carefully over fallen logs and weaved in between trees they'd raced through at breakneck speed not an hour before. Marcus couldn't help being impressed by the girl's audacity. Escaping a Roman camp and galloping bareback through a forest like this was not for the faint of heart. Even some of his fiercest legionaries might have balked at the prospect. She was brave, all right—brave and a liar. The story she'd fed him about her origins was obviously false. It was true that she looked passably Greek, but there was no reason for an Athenian to be fleeing a Roman occupation, and Marcus had developed a keen eye for deception during his decade in the legion.

He broke the silence abruptly. "False words are not only evil in themselves," he said in Greek.

The girl jolted, obviously startled, but she responded quickly, and her Greek was as flawless as his. "False words are not only evil in themselves. But they infect the soul with evil." She turned her head so Marcus could catch the corner of one of her green eyes. "Socrates."

Marcus certainly hadn't assumed that a moralizing philosopher would convince her to tell the truth, but her unaccented Greek had given nothing away.

When he spoke again some time later, it was in Punic, the

language of his enemy. It was the sound of the invaders, the speech of the Carthaginians. He wasn't exactly sure why, only that something about her dark hair and angular face made him think of that not-so-distant city that had outgrown its borders.

"After we crossed the river Trebia, when the battle still hung in the balance, we faced a line of Carthaginians. On the sides, they fought Gauls, Iberians, Numidians. But in the center, *we* fought your people. We carved them up with our swords. The river ran red with the blood of the sons of Carthage. The air was saturated with the screams of your father, your brother, your friends. We killed them and then we stepped over their bodies to kill more. Because the life of a Carthaginian means nothing to us."

As he spoke, Marcus felt her stiffen between his arms. He heard her breath catch in her throat at the word "brother" and he knew who she was. She was a Carthaginian trying to flee Rome. She was the enemy.

Her eyes were misted with tears when she turned to look up into his face and ask simply, "What will you do with me?"

They rode through the streets of Vetulonium several hours later, and the centurion had yet to answer her question. Elissa shifted uncomfortably. She felt exposed and vulnerable in the full light of morning. She leaned forward on the horse to try to add more space between them. She succeeded in removing the centurion's breastplate from her back, but his thighs still hugged tightly to hers. Elissa moved her legs forward and perched atop the horse's withers. It was awkward, but at least he was no longer touching her.

He chuckled quietly behind her. He moved his arm to encircle her waist and tugged. She fell swiftly back into him. Elissa resisted the urge to growl as her shoulders collided with his metal chest again. This man refused to give her even an inch of freedom. She ought to turn around and just— Elissa shook her head to stop her thoughts. She was his prisoner now, and she still had something to lose. She tried to distract herself by turning her attention outward.

The horse's hooves clapped rhythmically over the flag-stones on Vetulonium's narrow streets. The city was exactly as she'd left it yesterday, evidently unaltered by her transition from free woman to captive. A pair of brightly clad young girls spilled out from the bustling market beside them. They laughed loudly as they dodged a pair of groggy legionaries. One man turned to watch them pass and stumbled into his friend, clearly still feeling the effects of last night.

Elissa looked away. Freedom was such an interesting thing, so elusive and changeable that you scarcely noted its presence when you had it. It was only in contrast to captivity that freedom could truly take form. Freedom was the ability to dismount from this horse, find a ship home, apologize to your father for not listening to him. Freedom was not being forced to tell a bloodthirsty Roman legionary the names of those who had sheltered you in Vetulonium. Not to have to pray they wouldn't be punished.

Elissa had initially refused to tell him anything, of course. She'd sat tight-lipped and rigid when he'd simply asked, "Where?" She no longer trusted her voice or body not to betray the truth.

She'd worried he would hurt her or try to use violence to extract an answer. But he didn't touch her. He did something more cruel instead.

"If you don't tell me, I'll be forced to assume that the whole town was complicit. You may recall from our first meeting that I was put in charge of Vetulonium's granary. It was a good harvest this year, and I had intended to take only enough to feed the legion and leave the rest to get the city through the winter. But a city full of traitors to Rome does not need to be fed. A city full of traitors can be left to starve." He paused. "Have you ever seen a person starve to death?" Elissa couldn't move to respond; her whole body had been frozen in an icy, numbing dread.

"I have. Many times," the centurion responded casually. "The people of Vetulonium will still have meat on their bones when the first snows come. They'll be worried, of course, but they'll still have hope. They'll think they might just be able to make it through the winter. But the cold is long and deep, and the weak cannot survive on only the meager stores in their *culinae*. When the snow disappears again, the dogs and livestock will have fallen quiet, and the young and elderly will be buried under their houses. Only the rats will be left roasting on the fire."

Elissa had felt her world grow distant as she imagined the people's suffering. How could anyone be so cruel as to condemn a whole city to such a terrible fate? She didn't want to believe him, but she couldn't ignore his threat either—not when he'd put Messia and Laris on one side of the scale, and all of Vetulonium on the other. She was sure that was exactly what he'd intended.

Elissa turned on the horse to face the centurion. Revulsion clogged her throat and made it difficult to speak.

"Fine, I'll tell you," she spat.

She knew it was dangerous to bargain, but fury had made her try. Damn his macabre game.

"If I tell you truthfully, and of my own volition, will you swear to me that no one else will be punished? That you'll believe me when I say no one helped me escape or knew of my origins?"

The truth, at least part of it, was all Elissa had to trade for Messia and Laris's safety without damning their entire city.

The centurion had pressed her shoulder in response, forcing her to look up into his face. His blue eyes held hers for a long moment. Elissa wanted to scream and hit him, but she felt powerless to turn away.

"If you tell me the truth, the *whole* truth, I swear that anyone you name as having helped you will be granted the same justice as a citizen of Rome."

Elissa pushed aside her anger with a ragged breath; she needed to think clearly. Citizens of Rome were entitled to a fair trial to defend themselves against any accusations. They were innocent until proven otherwise. Perhaps that was the best she could do.

She nodded reluctantly. "Swear to me on whichever god you hold most dear."

If he lied, Elissa wanted to be able to appeal to a god to curse him.

"War is the only god that matters," the centurion replied, still not releasing her from his icy gaze.

"On Mars, then. Swear to me in the name of Mars."

His eyes stayed cold but the faint shadow of a smile crossed his lips. "I swear it then."

Elissa allowed herself a moment's reprieve before launching into her story.

"An Etruscan family was housing me in Vetulonium before the legion came. My Numidian companion told them I was the daughter of an Athenian merchant, and that I needed shelter and protection until he'd concluded his business selling horses in Northern Italy."

Elissa stopped. She tried in vain to push down the surge of guilt she felt at the memory of the mare. This wasn't the time to be thinking about her horse when so many lives hung in the balance. The centurion's offer had not been enough. The rights of a citizen of Rome would not protect Messia and Laris if he knew the truth. The punishment for treason was death. She couldn't abandon them to that fate, no matter his threats.

"The family believed my story. They were simple village

folk who probably couldn't point to Carthage on a map. When your army came I hid in a tiny room in the *culina* that I knew was seldom used. I escaped last night without them ever knowing I'd been there."

The centurion made no response after she finished speaking, but his body seemed to stiffen behind her. He'd broken his silence only once since her confession, and that was to ask where the family lived. Elissa had told him truthfully, because she had no other choice. If she lied and they went to a home Elissa had clearly never been inside, her whole story would unravel, and who knew what terrible fate would befall Vetulonium as a result. Which was why they ended up standing on the street outside Messia and Laris's home. Elissa regarded the familiar stone walls in front of her with dread, wishing they could protect its occupants from the assault about to be launched on them.

Marcus dismounted and then turned to help the girl down. An old habit, he supposed, because she certainly didn't deserve his assistance. The girl ignored his outstretched hand and dropped to the ground without touching him. He felt the heat of anger rise up his neck. The nerve of this girl knew no bounds. *First she runs and then, once caught, she turns every word out of her mouth into a lie.* She was a wily Carthaginian whore—unexpectedly, she lifted her head, and Marcus saw hope filling her wide, green eyes. Hope, over a flickering fear. Suddenly she seemed quite young—young, and rather inept at lying. Which might suggest she wasn't very accustomed to it. As Marcus stared down at her, a faint tingling raised the hairs on his arms. Her eyes were interesting. They weren't the bright, ostentatious green of a polished jewel. They were the color of a turbid sea after a storm, and delicately interwoven with amber. No, her eyes didn't believe the words that came from her mouth, but they begged *him* to.

Marcus handed the horse's reins to the legionary guarding the entrance. He turned his eyes from the girl and studied the man's face instead, but didn't recognize him. Probably the man was one of the new military tribunes recently arrived from Rome. Marcus hated those pompous boy-men. They came from the city to *command* the legion, while they were really here only for political advancement. No one truly fought for the glory of Rome anymore; they fought for their own careers, and to win the next step on the *cursus honorum*, the ladder of political offices that culminated in a consulship. Marcus would have begun his military career in the same manner had he not begged his way into the legions at the tender age of 16, a full four years before he was eligible to stand for election. He had started as a common legionary instead, earning every promotion on merit, not the purity of his blood.

Marcus set out on the path to the entrance; he didn't need to look back to know the girl was following. He'd been proud of his decision, proud of his achievements. He could have relied on the name Sempronius Gracchus, grandson of the Consul of 238, whose success had marked his descendants as *nobilia* forever after. Or the name of his father, Publius Sempronius Gracchus, a stalwart in the Roman Senate. But he hadn't done that. Marcus had dreamed of serving Rome on the battlefield—not at the *rostrum*—like the heroes of old. But a decade of battle and a river of blood had washed away all his idealism. His brother, Tiberius, had been the politician. Tiberius had tried to serve Rome in a way that truly mattered, in a way that would benefit her people and add to her greatness. But his blood had only joined the torrent, spilled by self-serving demagogues who shook your hand with one of his and stabbed you with the other.

Marcus clenched his fists as he took the few steps to the door. He realized his jaw was locked tight and his teeth were grinding together, and reminded himself that now was not the time to think about Tiberius. That was best done in battle where there was an enemy to unleash his fury on. Marcus took a placating breath and tightened his lips into a frown. He turned to the girl. She stood beside him on the threshold, looking determinedly ahead, but Marcus could see dread twisting the side of her face. She was afraid. He turned back to the door and strode purposefully into the house.

CHAPTER 8

The Romans had the peculiar ability to mark everything with their presence. From a land as large as Italy, to a small *domus* in Vetulonium, you knew when the Romans ruled. It was rarely a physical presence, only a vague sense that the order of things had changed, and that whether you were the loftiest of kings or the lowliest of slaves, you had shifted down a rung.

So it was no surprise to Elissa that the once-familiar atrium in Messia and Laris's home felt different. Potted roses still dotted the corners, the little blue pool still waited in the center, but Elissa was aware as soon as she entered that she shouldn't be here. The comfortable home where Messia and Laris had sheltered her no longer existed. The hushed shuffling of servants she didn't recognize and the gruff Latin voices coming through the closed door of the *tablinum* echoed like drums in her head. *Get out, get out*, the rhythm boomed, and Elissa's heart sped up to match its beat.

Elissa was standing beside the centurion at the entrance to the atrium. She took a tentative step toward the door. He thrust his hand behind him and took hold of her arm. Elissa stepped forward again with a glare directed at his set jaw. But he didn't bring his cold stare down to meet hers as she'd expected; his attention was focused on the corner of the room instead. Elissa turned slowly in the same direction. Messia was standing in the far corner of the atrium, her hand tightly clasped to Arnza, who was looking up at his grandmother in confusion. Momentary relief flickered through Elissa at the sight of them, but it was replaced by dread as soon as she remembered who was standing next to her. If Arnza looked out at the room and saw her, he'd probably run to greet her like a missing older sister. He was too young to understand that Messia's tight grip and blanched face were begging him not to betray his recognition. Elissa's chest tightened with panic. She had sworn to the centurion that this family hardly knew her, that they hadn't questioned her origins or protected her because she'd merely been a boarder. Would he really do as he'd threatened and accuse them of treason when he found out that she'd lied?

The centurion released his grip on her wrist. Elissa felt his whole body harden beside her and he moved his hand to the hilt of his sword. Elissa stared at him in horror. His reaction was so much worse than she'd imagined. Her mind was already filling with vivid images of the punishment he'd promised to exact. She looked up at his cold, cruel eyes and realized that he wasn't watching Messia and Arnza at all. The fury on his face seemed to be for someone else. Elissa heard chatter, and turned in time to see a small group of Romans emerge from the *tablinum* behind Messia.

Messia also saw the men entering the room and quickly pulled Arnza to the opposite corner where they wouldn't be noticed. The four Romans ambled toward the pool, their heads bent together in quiet conversation. Three of the men wore the typical uniform of a legionary—scarlet cloaks and feather plumes atop their helmets—but the man in the middle of their circle wore a toga. That man was of medium build. A mop of thinning brown hair topped a round face with ruddy cheeks. His appearance was entirely unremarkable, but the man's companions seemed to hang on his every word. They twisted their necks toward him in an ostentatious display of attention.

As they neared the pool, Elissa noted the purple trim on the borders of the man's toga. That meant he was a senator of Rome, and very powerful indeed. The Senate was the most important political institution in Rome, and only men of sufficient means and lineage were afforded entry.

"Flaminius." The centurion's voice rang out across the atrium and the scene Elissa was observing abruptly came to a halt.

The senator looked up immediately. His eyes locked on the centurion, who turned rigid and motionless. Even his chest seemed to cease rising and falling. It felt as though all the air had been drained from the room as the two men stared at each other.

"Marcus Sempronius Gracchus," the senator enunciated slowly. An odd smile crossed his face. "How is your father?"

Elissa didn't think it was possible for the centurion to appear more menacing than he already did, but the Senator's question pushed him from silent fury to a more potent, verbal kind.

"What are you doing here, Flaminius?" Elissa could hear the venom in his deep voice.

"Now, Marcus, that's no way to address your new consul."

The centurion blinked. He seemed to take a moment to comprehend and then sucked in a breath. "Tempting fate, isn't it, Flaminius? To rush north before the auguries have been read? The Senate must be angry. I imagine the gods are, too."

A slow smile spread across Flaminius's face, but instead of lightening his rounded features, it made him look snide. He spread out his hands, palms facing the open roof. "Ah, Marcus, some of us do not rely on the gods to decide our fate. We decide our own—" he inclined his head meaningfully toward the centurion "—and the fate of others."

The centurion's jaw twisted with malice. "And yet, such men often meet their fate at the end of a sword."

The smile on Flaminius's face grew even wider until it looked sickly sweet. "Now, now, Marcus, threatening your new consul will get you nowhere. We have a horde of barbarians to crush, remember? We're fighting on the same side of this battle."

Elissa twitched reflexively beside Marcus. The consul's eyes shifted away from him and landed on her. Elissa managed to keep her face neutral but her hands curled into fists.

"What do we have here?" Flaminius purred as he circled the pool and walked toward her.

Elissa dropped her eyes. This was the leader of the Roman legions, of those thousands of men gathered around the guttering fires she'd seen outside the city walls. Now was no time for pride.

Flaminius stopped when he was less than an arm's length away. Elissa kept her eyes on the ground. He smelled of lavender. She wanted to melt into the gray tiles at her feet.

Flaminius reached out his hand and slid his fingers under her chin. He tilted her head up so she was forced to meet his eyes.

"Pretty thing, aren't we, girl?"

His eyes were dark, rounded beads above drooping cheeks. Elissa tried to turn her head away but he held her firmly. Bile rose in her throat; she knew what this man wanted from her.

"I'm afraid I—" Elissa started to say. She needed to think of something that would get him away from her!

The centurion suddenly grabbed her arm. He squeezed so hard that Elissa turned toward him in shock, which forced Flaminius to drop his hand.

"She's mine, Flaminius," Marcus said sharply. He pulled Elissa behind him so his body now stood between her and Flaminius.

Flaminius raised his eyebrows in surprise. Another slow smile curled his lips in a poor imitation of happiness.

"I see. Well, I would be happy to buy her from you, Marcus. Say, at twice the market rate? I know your family has hit a rough patch financially."

Elissa reacted without thinking. She tightened her fists and took a small step toward the consul. She was no slave! And she was *not* going to be this man's whore.

Marcus stepped in front of her, blocking her from Flaminius's eyes.

"I said she's mine. If you so much as touch her, you'll wake up with a knife in your throat. I don't care who voted you consul."

The smile left Flaminius's face instantly. His mouth straightened and pulled his skin taut. He spoke quietly this time. "Make no mistake, Gracchus. I am your consul now, and you will afford me all the obedience that office entails. If you cross me, I will not hesitate to punish you as I did Tiberius."

Elissa saw fury ripple across the centurion's body. His sword hand twitched in anticipation. But instead of reaching for the hilt, he straightened to his full height, which towered over the stocky consul. A muscle in his jaw pulsed and he raised his chin to look over Flaminius's head. Then he turned abruptly and strode out the door. He gave Elissa a withering stare that ordered her to follow.

Flaminius shifted his eyes back to Elissa, who was no longer protected from view by the centurion. Hot fear slid up her spine. Her eyes flicked to the corner of the atrium where Messia and Arnza had been. Arnza was no longer there, but Messia was. Her back was pressed to the wall and her lips were a thin white line. She began to step forward, but Elissa stopped her with a subtle shake of her head. The centurion knew she was Carthaginian, and if her lie had failed, he also knew that Messia and Laris had helped her. She couldn't risk giving him another reason to punish them. And then there was this consul, who looked as though he might enjoy devouring Messia on his way to Elissa. No, this was not Messia's fight anymore. Elissa belonged to the Romans now, and if she had to choose between two hateful Roman men, she'd rather cope with the unpredictable centurion than this consul, who had left no uncertainty as to what he wanted from her.

Elissa nodded at Messia and tried to hide her fear behind a brave smile. She whirled around and followed the centurion out before Flaminius could say another word.

The centurion was waiting for her outside the entrance, his back still rigid with tension. Elissa stopped with her shoulder across from his chest and filled her eyes with as much contempt as she could muster. Damn this Roman.

He leveled an impassive stare at her. His eyes had gone back to gray, and there wasn't a flicker of warmth in them. Lifting his hand, he motioned for Elissa to move in front of him. She stood still for a moment longer before she complied.

As they walked away from Messia and Laris's home, Elissa had the unmistakable feeling she would never see it again. She glanced back at the simple stone house that had protected her for nearly two months. Its place in her life had been as bleak as its walls, neither leading back toward home nor forward to whatever was next. It was a halfway point between worlds, and although Elissa was terrified of what came next, she was also tired of standing still. Someday she would find a way to repay Messia and Laris for their kindness, but for now, leaving was the best she could do to thank them.

A sad smile on her lips, Elissa forced herself to look away. *There are good people in this land.* The centurion brushed past her and continued briskly down the street. *And bad people.* Elissa directed her thousandth glare at his back and willed her feet into motion. Her legs ached with stiffness as she started after him. It must have been more than a day since she'd slept.

The sun was at its highest point now. It banished some of the winter chill to the shadows still lingering at the edges of buildings. The centurion turned down a succession of streets without hesitating. He seemed to know the city well. The streets gradually narrowed as they walked, which caused the shadows to reach farther into their center. They turned down another street, this one so narrow Elissa could have touched the rickety tenements on either side were it not for the constant stream of people. An older woman with a basket of laundry hurried past on Elissa's left. A young man in a filthy tunic weaved in front of her, his hand trailing against the building beside him for support. Elissa peered through an open doorway and saw a dozen men sitting on stools in a room brimming with wine casks.

The centurion reached the end of the street and went down an alley. Elissa followed the outline of his tall figure around the corner. The shadows had completely won their battle with the light here, and the bustle of the busy street behind them grew fainter. Elissa's arms tensed. She had assumed he'd take her to the Roman camp for questioning. Why where they nearly alone in this dark corner of Vetulonium?

The centurion stopped in front of a heavy wooden door. Elissa eyed it warily as she caught up and briefly considered whether walking right past him was a viable escape plan. It took a few extra strides to force herself to stop, and then she nearly rolled her eyes at her naiveté. No, she'd need to come up with something better than that. She turned back to the centurion and watched him open the heavy door. He stepped aside so Elissa could enter. She shuffled cautiously forward and leaned in to look inside the darkened doorway. She couldn't see anything. Her eyes flicked to the centurion's face. It was stony and unreadable. His hand twitched. Elissa inched ahead to placate him while she considered what to do. She really did not want to be in a confined space with this man, but it was obvious that he was about to haul her inside regardless. Suddenly the name Tiberius popped into her head. Elissa hadn't understood what the consul had meant when he'd said it, but that was the name that had nearly severed the centurion's self-control. Perhaps if she mentioned it now, it might distract him from whatever he had planned.

"Who is—"

The centurion pulled her inside. Elissa squealed and then gritted her teeth in anger once she'd recovered from the shock. This was the most barbaric, arrogant man, and she would—Elissa let her lip curl into a sneer—later, she would make him regret every single injustice he did to her now.

Her thoughts were on revenge when she entered the room behind the doorway, but she stopped in surprise when she crossed the threshold. This place bore no resemblance to the quiet, seedy street outside. Warm light from a full hearth flooded the room, and dozens of men sat around long wooden tables. The room was bustling with occupants, and hearty laughter rang out from the tables. Men of all sorts sat atop the scattered stools. There were some Roman legionaries, but others were clearly foreign, and still others probably lived upstairs. What they seemed to have in common was the tankards of wine in their hands and the women perched on their laps—and that no one seemed to have noticed Elissa's arrival. She nearly smiled at the welcome prospect of anonymity.

The centurion had reached a table at the far end of the room and drew out a stool for himself. He looked back at Elissa expectantly. She sighed and moved toward him. As much as she didn't want to show her exhaustion, she really did need to sit down. The centurion nodded when she pulled out a stool across from him, then abruptly stood and headed for the bar. Elissa breathed a shallow sigh of relief. She let her attention wander to her neighbor a few stools down. The man wore no armor, but he had the sun-hardened skin and broad shoulders that were a soldier's giveaway. Not that he appeared threatening just now, because his attention was completely diverted by the buxom redhead straddling his lap. Elissa peered curiously at the woman. Her gown revealed far more of her ample bosom than was modest. The legionary appeared to have the opposite thought. He suddenly submerged his face in her swelling bust and shook his head with ferocity, which set the woman off on a hearty chorus of giggles.

The centurion's voice called out clearly above the din. It commanded silence without his having to ask.

"Friends! Next round is on me." He pointed at Elissa. "Courtesy of my companion." All eyes in the room slowly turned to her.

Elissa shrank on her stool, trying in vain to regain some anonymity. There was a moment of silence before two dozen tankards were raised in salute. "To your companion!" the men chorused.

The centurion strode back to the table as the rest of the room busied themselves draining their tankards so they could be promptly refilled. Elissa narrowed her eyes as he lowered himself onto the stool across from her with a cup of wine in each hand. He pushed one towards her. Obviously this was some sort of trick. He probably wanted to mark her as his in case she tried to escape from the crowd.

She layered her voice with resentment. "*Companion* hardly seems the right word."

The centurion merely shrugged.

Elissa blew out air, exasperated. His stony silence was

even worse than his threats. "Whatever you plan to do with me, can you get on with it? It can't be worse than sitting here pretending to share a drink with you."

He leaned back on his stool and moved his leg to his opposite knee. He eyed her with a touch more curiosity but still didn't speak.

"You know what?" she snapped. "Fine. Why don't I solve both our problems and leave? And this time I'm taking *your* horse."

The centurion smiled an easy smile that suggested genuine amusement. He ran his hand casually through his hair, and Elissa noticed hints of copper underneath the dark mass. He stood up suddenly, reached for his cup and drained it in one gulp.

"Let's go then."

Elissa remained seated. She glanced at him cautiously; surely he wasn't about to actually let her leave.

"Go where?"

"Upstairs."

Elissa's eyes widened. She stood and pushed the stool aside with her foot. She began slowly backing up, the way Barro had told her to if she ever encountered a lion in the wild.

"No—no, please, I'm fine here."

The centurion cocked his head. "I thought nothing could be worse than this?"

Elissa cursed her sharp tongue; it had clearly succeeded in rousing the beast.

"I... I, please," she begged. "Anything but that."

The centurion lifted an eyebrow at her—obviously a favorite gesture of his—but then seemed to relax. "Come," he said after a pause. "Your innocence is not in jeopardy today."

Elissa stopped moving backward, but she was still unconvinced.

The centurion sighed and seemed to be growing impatient.

"Come," he repeated. "Or I'll pick you up and carry you, and everyone in this room will assume you're the newest lady of this establishment."

Elissa glanced around quickly. *So* that's *what this place is*. She'd never been to a whorehouse before—why would she have been—and she'd been too preoccupied to consider what it meant that he'd taken her to one. The realization did nothing to assuage her fear.

The centurion's patience broke. He closed the distance between them in two long strides, wrapped his hands around her waist and tossed her over his shoulder.

Elissa squealed in response, and kicked her legs so forcefully—and so close to his sensitive region—that he put her back down immediately.

Elissa landed on her feet and thrust her chin up. She refused to have her dignity squashed by this brute.

"Fine. I'll follow," she snapped.

The centurion shrugged and started for the stairs at the edge of the room. Elissa hesitated, but then lowered her head and followed him. What other choice did she have? They walked along a narrow hallway upstairs, and stopped at the final door on the right. He opened it and stood to the side without entering. Elissa took another step forward while keeping a careful distance from his quick hands. She peered around him into a spacious room. It was well equipped, with a washbasin, table and mirror, and clean sheets on a high feather bed. Elissa straightened in surprise and looked up at the centurion.

"Is this for me?"

He remained in the doorway. "Wait for the food I ordered and then lock this door." He jiggled the door handle.

Elissa frowned; she didn't know what to make of this. Was the centurion merely being decent or was he going to assault her while she slept? She knew she needed to remain vigilant, but the prospect of a fresh bed was overwhelming. She forced herself to turn back and regard the centurion more carefully. He watched her from the doorway for a moment, then nodded curtly and shut the door behind him.

Exhaustion hit Elissa like a wave. Her legs shook, threatening to give way. It was all she could do to drag herself to the high, feather bed and collapse into it. She didn't even bother trying to remove her dress. The last thing she thought before sleep took her was that she'd forgotten to lock the door.

Elissa heard the muffled sounds of movement in the distance—soft footsteps, metal grating against wood, the click of plates. She knew she should open her eyes to investigate, but the noises sounded far away. Too far to be of concern to her now. If the footsteps got louder, then she'd definitely force herself to open her eyes.

"Is she awake, ma'am?"

A man's voice. That was more troubling.

"Not yet, sir. To tell you the truth, I couldn't be sure she was even breathin'," A woman responded.

Were they talking about her? Perhaps she should open her eyes right now. Then again, she wondered, could whatever they planned to do to her truly be worse than having to leave this bed? Elissa melted deeper into the feather mattress and felt the blanket tickle the bottom of her chin.

Something pressed against her shoulder uncomfortably. Elissa groaned. The pressure increased and she started to rock back and forth. She let a sliver of light through her eyelids and a dark shape materialized. Her eyes flew open in alarm. A round face solidified in front of her. It appeared to be an older woman's face, but she was so close Elissa could scarcely see anything other than a flat nose and a lined forehead.

The woman straightened, which allowed Elissa a slightly wider view of her surroundings.

"Well, what do you know, she's not dead, after all!" the woman called to an unseen person behind her. She spoke in the heavy syllables of a central Italian.

The presence of a second person—possibly the man Elissa had heard earlier—finally convinced her that further sleep would be unwise. She forced her elbows underneath her and pushed her body upright. The abrupt change in position made her head spin.

"Who are you?" Elissa croaked at the woman who was already moving away from the bed.

"I work here," she replied, not looking back at Elissa, "and I ain't got no business but with your chamber pot. It's the man out there that wants somethin' from you." She thrust her ample chin in the direction of the doorway.

Elissa stared at the door with alarm.

"Oh, gods help me. I do not want *that* from her. At the moment all I want is to know that the lady is dressed so I can enter this room!"

The woman gave Elissa a meaningful look with her eyebrows raised, plainly telling her how much she believed him. But seeing that Elissa was still wearing yesterday's dress, she bustled to the door to open it.

Elissa hurriedly pulled her feet beneath her and pushed herself to a stand in time to see a tall Roman enter the room. The woman met him in the doorway with the same appraising look she'd given Elissa.

"I've got another for you if this one doesn't work out." She jerked her thumb in the direction of the door across the hall.

The Roman didn't respond. He took another step into the room and shut the door on her overeager face. The woman merely shrugged as she disappeared behind the closed door, and Elissa focused on this new man instead.

Like the centurion, he was unusually tall, but he didn't have the frame to balance his height, so he only succeeded in looking imperious rather than imposing. The Roman paused with his back to the room for an extra moment after he'd closed the door. Elissa took the opportunity to quickly straighten her dress and run a hand through her dishevelled hair.

"I'm sorry to wake you at this ungodly hour," he said still facing the door. Then he turned and strode quickly into the center of the room. "Please, have some breakfast to make the dawn a little more bearable."

Elissa tore her eyes from the strange Roman to glance out the window on the far side of the room. The sun had just crested the horizon. She looked back at the Roman. He'd already taken a seat at the small table, which was now laden with bread, cheese and two cups of honeyed water.

"Please, please, have a seat." He motioned to the chair across from him. "We'll talk as you eat. You must be starving."

Elissa eyed him warily as she moved to the open seat. But she decided she'd think better on a full stomach and grabbed one of the plates, helping helped herself to a thick slice of bread. The Roman smiled and pushed a plate of goat cheese toward her. Then he pulled a wax tablet from his bag and became engrossed with the writing on its other side. His long nose wrinkled in concentration, he hunched forward to mark something with his stylus. He seemed so accustomed to this position, it was easy to forget that he was wearing an iron mail shirt and had a sword belted around his waist. He certainly didn't look the part of the Roman menace.

Unexpectedly he lifted his eyes to her. "Not the most impressive legionary you've ever seen, am I?"

Elissa froze with her next slice of bread halfway to her mouth. He'd said it with a smile, but maybe that was some ploy to trick her into insulting him. She glanced at his thin and undefined arms; surely he must know they appeared more accustomed to holding a stylus than brandishing a sword. The Roman caught the direction of her eyes and broke into a wide grin.

"You seem as concerned as my father was when I told him that! Well, never mind, impressive or no, I *am* a legionary, and we must all make the best of our lot in life, eh? Now, remind me of your name?"

He sounded genial, but his question made her head throb. He was likely to keep asking questions Elissa didn't know how to answer. Should she give him her real name? Or did he think she was Athenian? Perhaps she should make her name sound more Greek.

Her whirling thoughts must have shown on her face. The Roman carefully placed his tablet on the table and then straightened to look at her directly.

"How about if I go first?" he suggested.

Elissa nodded hopefully.

"My name is Quintus Arvina, and despite being ill-suited, I am a Roman legionary. Thankfully, Marcus Gracchus knows a born bureaucrat when he sees one, and he made me his *optio* rather than sacrificing me to the front line."

Elissa stiffened at the mention of her captor; she should have guessed this seemingly innocuous man would be doing his bidding.

Quintus noticed her response and smiled sympathetically. "I know the centurion can be a bit, er, rough, but he's sent me to see to your—" he paused, searching for the right word—"comfort."

Elissa's eyebrows shot up at that. Her comfort had hardly seemed to be the centurion's top priority yesterday when he dragged her off a cliff and into a whorehouse.

"True, comfort was not the word he used," Quintus admitted. "But nevertheless, I will see to your safety and do the best I can for your comfort. Although I'm afraid I must say the same for the 120 sacks of grain, 100 shovels, 950 stakes." Quintus picked up his tablet and continued reading. "53 pots, 10 spare water skins—"

Elissa took another slice of bread as he prattled on. Born bureaucrat indeed. Quintus corrected a few tallies, then cleared his throat and tore his eyes away from the tablet.

"Forgive me, I get carried away," he said sheepishly. "What I meant to say is that I'll ask you to travel with the rest of the supplies under my purview. I realize it's not the most luxurious accommodation, but I'll ensure that you ride in the wagon with the spare cloaks so you'll stay warm and comfortable."

He was kind to be concerned, although associating her with the legionaries' supplies was hardly flattering.

"And will I be as free to leave the wagon as the rest of the goods?" Elissa asked with a hint of acid in her voice.

Quintus tilted his head and met her eyes intently. "I'm afraid so, but I will not bind you unless it proves necessary."

Elissa looked away. This man might be kinder, but he was still acting on the centurion's orders and collecting her like all the other baggage. In truth, she had no choice but to obey.

She bit her lip and nodded in acquiescence.

Quintus smiled gratefully at her response. "Now then, I'm afraid I have a very busy morning, and I must run to the granary to ensure no greedy *optios* are dipping into our share. I'll return at daybreak to collect you for the march. In the meantime, I've asked that crass woman to see to your needs for the journey." Quintus shook his head ruefully, apparently still distressed by her crude references. The fact that they were in a whorehouse seemed lost on him.

He stopped shaking his head and watched Elissa more carefully. "I'm afraid I must remind you that I may be only a bureaucrat, but I am an exceptionally diligent one. While Centurion Gracchus wants you in his company, you'll find no easy escape from me." There was a surprising intensity in his mild brown eyes.

Elissa shifted in her seat, suddenly uncomfortable under his direct gaze. She really needed to become better at hiding her thoughts. She'd never survive this ordeal otherwise. She arranged her features in what she hoped was an impassive expression and nodded once more.

"I understand," Elissa said truthfully as she tried to keep her features level. Of course, she knew escape wouldn't be easy; that didn't mean she wasn't going to try.

Quintus smiled genially and collected his wax tablet. He was already adding more marks as he headed out the door. Elissa saw him say a few words to the Umbrian woman as the door closed, then the woman took up a position outside her door. Elissa rolled her eyes. He needn't have gone to the trouble of paying a guard. The Umbrian woman had filled the washbasin with hot water earlier, and its steam was wafting invitingly toward Elissa. She longed to soak in a warm bath, although she felt dirty in a way no water could clean. She was at the mercy of Romans now, forced to plot escapes and pray they wouldn't hurt her. She'd brought shame to her family, her people and, most of all, herself. She'd fought for the freedom to choose a husband, but in the process, had lost the freedom to choose her life.

CHAPTER 9

Quintus returned exactly one hour later to collect her. Elissa had used the time to wash thoroughly, comb, and then replait her knotted hair. She asked the Umbrian woman for a clean dress and a new cloak, and the woman had produced a thin cotton shift and a forgotten legionary cloak. Elissa took the shift and left the cloak behind. The cotton shift wouldn't be as warm as her wool dress, but it was something clean to sleep in. Finished ahead of time, Elissa waited impatiently for Quintus to arrive. She was anxious to leave Vetulonium. She was tired of hiding in the dark corners of the city, suspicious of every shadow. At least with the legion, her enemy would be in plain sight, and the open road certainly held more opportunities for escape than a tiny storage closet.

However, Elissa's hopeful sentiment took a sharp turn toward despair when she actually saw the legion she was about to march with. She followed Quintus through the same gate she'd escaped through two nights before, but the world outside the city walls had completely transformed. The endless tents and guttering fires of the Roman camp had turned into a single column of men. Most of the legion was already marching away from the city, and the men at the front were only just visible among the distant hills. Their red cloaks and bobbing spear points stretched into the horizon like a great, venomous snake. The last of the men waited where the camp had been, which was now completely dismantled into its component logs and stakes, ready to be carried away and set up in a new location tonight.

"Quite a sight, isn't it?" There was awe in Quintus's voice.

Elissa glanced at him quickly. She guessed he was more inspired by the staggering logistics required to feed and equip the Roman army than he was by their might. She looked away; it was definitely their might that terrified her.

Quintus directed Elissa toward the meadow she had so fatefully raced across. It had transformed into a chaotic jumble of animals and overflowing carts, with wives, children, slaves and merchants filling the spaces between wagons. The baggage train could not have been more different from the orderly legion it followed. But these overburdened animals, bursting crates and weathered people were as much a part of the legion as the red-cloaked legionaries. The baggage train followed the legion wherever it went, and it formed a procession that was nearly as long as the legion itself. Elissa took in this visible evidence that the men marching in the distance were not only instruments of Rome, but husbands and fathers, people who were loved and relied upon. The realization, which was somewhat jarring to Elissa, made it slightly harder to hope they were marching to their deaths. But just slightly. Husbands and fathers fought for her city, too, and they were the ones she should feel for.

"It's not that bad, is it?" Quintus asked. He stood in front of a large wagon with his brow furrowed. He had pulled back the thick leather sheet that covered the wagon so Elissa could see inside, and he must have mistaken her preoccupation for dismay at her new accommodation.

"Of course not." Elissa peered inside the bare interior and gave Quintus a reassuring smile. "It looks comfortable," she said truthfully.

Quintus's eyes crinkled appreciatively and he offered his hand to help her into the wagon.

"Thank you," Elissa said as she took his hand. He might be her de facto guard, but it simply wasn't in her nature to meet kindness with anything other than reciprocity.

Several dozen sacks of grain were stacked at the end of the wagon and, as promised, spare cloaks were piled up high. But the interior was otherwise uncluttered, and spacious enough for Elissa to stand and walk several paces in either direction. It was certainly no smaller than her storage closet.

Quintus had already closed the door flap and was starting to leave as he called back, "I'll return after we halt for the night!

Elissa heard him leave some muffled instructions for the driver before hurrying off. The centurion certainly wouldn't be able to accuse him of being remiss in his guard duties. She sighed, missing Taanit; she really needed a friend who wasn't also her jailer. Elissa faced the towering pile of grain and heaved a sack out from the side. She dragged it to the center of the wagon to create a makeshift seat. Then she returned to the stack of cloaks. She had to rummage through nearly all of them before she found one that didn't match the bright scarlet the Roman legionaries wore. She tugged a burgundy cloak out from the bottom of the pile and held it up to the dim light. The wool must have been left in the dye too long, which had made it a much deeper red than intended. Elissa wrapped the cloak around her shoulders with a smile; it suited her just fine. The wagon lurched into motion as she settled into her seat. She pulled a few extra cloaks around her to protect her from the cold air seeping in through the wagon cover. The wagon began to sway with the gentle rhythm of slow movement. Elissa could see the hunched outline of the driver at the front of the wagon, carefully guiding his ox along the road newly beaten in by the boots of 30,000 men. As far as prisons went, this one truly wasn't so bad—as long as the centurion wasn't nearby.

Elissa dozed on and off as the day passed. She occasionally drew back the flap to watch the hills pass away in the distance. It was full winter now, and most of the trees had long since lost their leaves to the carpet of crisp, brown grass below. Only the evergreens still held their color, and they dotted the hills with tidy splashes of green between the dormant fields. In the baggage train, it wasn't so hard to forget the endless columns of Romans marching to war against Carthage. The people following the legion were as eclectic as the army was uniform. There was a woman across from her who walked with her child perched atop an ancient mule, and a merchant was inching past them with a caged carriage waiting to be filled with loot bought from the soldiers. Occasionally, Elissa caught a glimpse of a Roman matron peering out from her litter, probably an officer's wife dragged along in the rising tide of war. Elissa smiled to herself; a lone Carthaginian girl wasn't so terribly out of place here.

As if he'd somehow been called to her attention by her fleeting sense of comfort, Elissa caught a glimpse of the centurion in the distance. He was riding a great black warhorse at the head of one of the columns. He wore the red-fanned helmet that marked his rank, and his flaming bronze armor contrasted sharply with the dull iron of the other men. Elissa squeezed her arms around her chest and pulled her cloak tighter. She badly wanted to shut the flap and retreat into the wagon, but she knew she should stay put. She needed to observe her enemy, and she would learn the most when he didn't know he was being watched.

Marcus rode at the head of a line of men that was more than two dozen rows long, with five men per row. The men who formed his maniple were positioned near the end of the legion, where the Romans tended to put their most experienced warriors in case of an attack from the rear. And his men looked experienced indeed. Their broad backs bobbed up and down in the distance, and many of them were bare-armed despite the cold. Other parts of the legion had lost their closely packed form, which caused the long line to waver in places, or sections to be missing altogether. But Marcus's maniple marched in the identical rectangle they'd started off in, each man lifting his boot and setting it down at exactly the same time.

Without any change in tempo, the centurion's men suddenly raised the shafts of their spears and brought them crashing into their shields. Elissa swivelled her head to look on either side of the column. Was it a signal of some danger she couldn't see? The men took another step and brought fist to shield again. As they repeated the process with every stride, they created a rhythm as crisp and clear as a drumbeat. But what was its meaning?

"*Roma o Roma!*"

A man's deep voice rang through the air in answer to Elissa's question. Even from this distance, Elissa recognized it as the centurion's. She looked back to where she'd last seen him, in front of his column of men. Instead of calmly leading from their head, he'd wheeled his horse around and was galloping toward the rear of the maniple. His spear point was raised high and his red cloak streamed over his black horse. A few men on the sides turned to watch as the great stallion tore through the earth mere feet from them, but most kept their heads pointed forward, although Elissa saw their backs straighten slightly and their chins lift.

"*Roma o Roma,*" the men repeated in unison. Their voices merged into a single, booming reply.

"*O Roma o Roma,*" the centurion called back. Then he continued: "*Your streets may smell like shit! And the food may come in fits!*"

Elissa chortled in her wagon far behind him, and her eyes widened with disbelief. What kind of marching song was this? Was her cruel and serious captor truly making jokes about his city for all his men to hear?

His men apparently did not share her surprise. "*Roma o Roma!*" they sang even more loudly than before. Elissa didn't have to see them to know their weathered faces were split by wide grins.

The centurion whirled his horse around and galloped back to the head of the maniple. "*Your politicians don't know a whit! And the—*"

"*Woman have tiny tits!*" one of his men interrupted suddenly.

The centurion threw back his head and laughed along with the rest of his men, who repeated the chorus in agreement with their comrade's assessment.

Then he thrust his spear in the air and boomed to the entire legion, "*But Roma, to your legions, the whole world will submit!*"

The air shook as the men roared their approval. They beat their spears against their shields in a cacophonous response. The centurion brought his horse back to walk at the front of his maniple and resumed the march exactly as before. Throughout the whole display, his men had never broken stride.

Elissa scrunched her face up in distaste. Only the Romans could couch an inch of humility in a mile of arrogance. The world had truly been a more enlightened place when the Greeks ruled it. She shuddered involuntarily. And her world had certainly been a safer place before the centurion ruled it. And as if his obsessive attention to her wasn't bad enough, it appeared that his men adored him. Escape would've been much easier if she could have relied on his men hating him as much as she did.

Elissa sighed and sat back on her heels. She let the flap fall closed and returned to her makeshift seat with her thoughts on Barro. He was probably marching through similar hills not far away. He'd always dreamed of leading men like this centurion did. When Elissa was very young and still in Zama, she'd often had trouble falling asleep, and Barro would sometimes come to her room and soothe her with a story. His stories were always about one of the great warriors of old. Achilles, Alexander, Pyrrhus of Epirus, he knew their lives by heart. Elissa found the stories sad; the violence those men had wrought seemed to outweigh any glory they'd gained. So instead of listening to his words, Elissa would watch Barro's eyes glaze over as he spoke and hear his voice deepen with emotion. She saw him yearn for the respect those great warriors had commanded. He, too, wanted to rule the lives of other men—of foes, because they were forced to give their lives up to him, and of friends, because they loved him.

Elissa shut her eyes against the memory. She hadn't seen it then, but she knew it now. Barro wanted power, the same as all men. They preferred power over other men, but they'd take it over women if need be. This centurion had the power of life and death over hundreds of men and at least one woman. Her throat constricted involuntarily; she hated giving that to him. But what else could she do? She was forced to give him her obedience for now, but she would withhold everything else for as long as she could.

The legion halted an hour before dusk, and the men began their nightly transition from soldier to builder. Each man set down his shield and picked up a shovel, spade or stake without needing to be told. The tents went up first, each in its exact position according to rank and maniple. There was one tent for every eight legionaries and a single tent for officers. When a sea of leather and wood stood over dirt and grass, the Romans started on the defenses. A ditch was hacked from the earth around the camp, its width never less than two body lengths across. The spiked stakes the men had carried all day were driven into the earth around the ditch, and a tall palisade was formed. Ramparts and turrets rose up from behind the palisade to provide a vantage for the sentries. Once fully erected, the Roman defenses were so dense it seemed as though the sun had set on the camp prematurely. Torches were lit along the walls and the wide roads that ran at regular intervals through the camp. Even darkness had to be kept at bay. By the time stars peppered the night sky, an idyllic Italian hillside had become a fortified war camp set to withstand a yearlong siege.

Quintus had come as promised once the march was over. He brought Elissa a tent of her own, and gave her instructions to erect it in the corner of camp where several officers' wives were staying. He'd quickly shown her the spot and then left on some urgent errand. Elissa sighed. She was left under the supervision of the wagon driver once again, and he showed no desire to help her with the heavy poles and leather that comprised her tent.

It was well over an hour before her tent was up. She'd spent most of her patience, a bit of sweat and more than a few curses in the process. Elissa winced as she straightened, and directed a sour glare at the wagon driver. He'd already lit a fire and cooked his dinner, and at the moment he was too preoccupied with finishing his stew to notice Elissa's indignant scowl. She dropped her neglected glare and shivered. The sweat on her neck was beginning to chill. She knew she should probably light a fire to stay warm, but since she had nothing to cook over it, there was really no sense. She crouched down and ducked into her tent, then she unrolled her bedding on the grass beneath its triangular roof. She found it hard to believe that eight fully grown men were meant to share this space, which was far too small to stand up in, and Elissa wouldn't even have room to lie horizontally across it.

It was still early and the sounds of eating and laughing filtered through the thin walls of the tent as the men enjoyed their precious few hours without duties. Elissa wondered if she'd be offered a meal, but just now—if she had to choose—she'd rather sleep than eat. She lay on the woolen blanket Quintus had given her to sleep on and listened to the men talk. Her cloak was wrapped tightly around her and tucked into her chin to keep out the cold.

No sooner had Elissa closed her eyes than she heard a great whoosh and felt the roof of the tent rush down on top of her. She hardly had time to choke out a cry of alarm before it covered her mouth. The tent pole followed shortly afterward and hit her skull with a crack. Sharp pain spread quickly across her forehead. Elissa squirmed frantically to push the tent off her face, but it was difficult to extract her hands from the tangled leather. Suddenly, her back was being dragged against the rough grass. Her shoulders were pulled backward out from the debris. The sky lightened from black to gray, and then she was lifted into the air and her feet were forced underneath her. The world righted itself—sky above, ground below. There was an arm wrapped firmly around her hips, and a second arm was under her shoulders, doing the job her legs were meant to. Elissa snapped her head around too quickly, and her sight blurred as she looked at the figure supporting her. A pair of dark-blue eyes floated in the center of her vision. The olive skin around them was stretched tight, giving them a clouded look of concern. The centurion. Elissa's skin prickled everywhere his body touched hers. Her words of reproach caught in her throat, and her cheeks flushed with heat. Of course, the tent would choose the exact moment the centurion was walking by to fall on top of her! Did she really need such a glaring signal of her obvious lack of ability? Elissa started to say something again but tasted blood on her tongue. She must have bitten down on her lip when the pole hit her.

The centurion noticed her embarrassment and stepped backward so his body was no longer pressed against hers. But he kept his hand under her arm for support. Elissa shifted her weight back onto her feet and directed a sheepish gaze at her crumpled tent.

"I really thought I had it right that time," she muttered.

"Quintus should have been here to help you," the centurion said reproachfully. "Even the men take several tries to learn."

"He said he was busy, but it's fine. I must've..." Elissa shook her head. "Never mind, I'll fix it." She bent down to pick up the offending pole—blasted tent—maybe she'd just sleep in the open tonight.

Marcus moved to the far side of the tent and lifted one of the wooden pegs that had been yanked from the ground.

"You have to put in the stakes first." He placed one in the ground and buried its tip with the heel of his boot. "And they have to be deep."

Elissa bent down again and picked up the closest peg to avoid his eyes. She drove it into the ground as he had, and then repeated the process for the next two. They had the whole thing up in five minutes. Its sides were tight where they'd sagged last time. Marcus stared at her from the other side of the tent.

"You're bleeding."

He walked over to her and unwrapped a strip of cloth from his wrist. He held it out to her with an outstretched hand. As Elissa reached to take the cloth, her palm brushed his fingers and an odd heat crossed her hand. She brought the cloth to her face and dabbed at her swollen lip.

"Have you had dinner?"

Elissa shook her head.

"Come join me then."

She briefly considered refusing, but her stomach had begun to growl an angry protest. She looked around. Her tent was up, and the centurion was being downright civil; she really had no reason to refuse. Elissa nodded and fell in behind him as he led the way through the camp.

The number of tents was truly breathtaking. In some places they were lined up so close together it was difficult to pass between them. They were identical, endless rows of brown triangles stretching between distant ramparts. Their spacing grew wider as they walked toward the center of camp, and the tents grew larger as well. At some point, they seemed large enough for a man to stand in and walk around.

The centurion came to a stop in front of a midsized tent at the very corner of the officers' section. He pulled the flap aside and ducked through the doorway. Elissa followed behind reluctantly. A plain room greeted her on the other side. A bed, a trunk and two wooden tables were arranged at opposite corners. All the furniture was constructed of simple wood, and built for ease of assembly. The only nod to luxury was the thick pelts that covered the bed; they would be warm on a cold winter's night.

These certainly weren't the opulent quarters she would have expected for a Roman officer.

"You quickly learn the true value of possessions when you're at war." Marcus's deep voice resonated between the leather walls. He strode to the table in the middle of the room and poured a cup of wine. He held it out to Elissa.

Elissa approached him and took the cup. She brought it to her lips and drank deeply, hoping the liquid would soothe her tight throat. The first sip was hardly in her mouth before she started to gag. She clamped her lips shut and swallowed hard to prevent it from coming back up.

"What is this?" Elissa sputtered.

The centurion barked a laugh and took the cup back. "More water in the wine then?" His eyes were dancing with laughter.

Elissa choked down another cough. Dear gods, that was

wine? Everything she'd had before tasted like honey compared to this stuff.

Marcus poured most of its contents into a second cup for himself. He filled the empty space in Elissa's cup with water. He returned it to her just as a slender boy entered the tent with a steaming tray of meats.

"Thank you, Alba." Marcus nodded at the boy as he set the tray on the table.

The boy gave him a shy smile, then hurried to leave.

The smell wafting from the meats was making Elissa's mouth water, and she didn't hesitate to sit when Marcus pulled out a chair for her. Nor did she wait for his permission to tuck into the appetizing spread. She pulled a rib off the rack of lamb and scooped a few wilted carrots onto her plate. She was halfway through the lamb before she stopped to look up at the centurion seated across from her. He was regarding her with a mixture of surprise and amusement.

Elissa stopped chewing and set the rib down slowly. She leaned back from the table and took a deep breath. Dear gods, here she was, probably in for some sort of interrogation, and she was happily throwing herself into it as long as there was food? If there was ever a time to think before she acted, it was now.

She regarded the centurion more carefully. He didn't look as though he was trying to appear threatening. Her eyes left his face and perused his wide chest and wiry arms. The man positively brimmed with power and aggression. Inexplicably, the worried expression on his face when he'd pulled her out of the tent crossed her mind. And she remembered how he'd forced himself between her and Flaminius's prying eyes. Elissa shook her head; this man's unpredictability only made him more dangerous.

The centurion smiled slightly and grabbed a leg of roasted pheasant from the table. "What's your name?" he asked as he cut into the bird.

"Elissa."

"Last name?" He raised his head and his eyes met hers.

She hesitated. Would he have heard of her family? Would it be better or worse if he had? Her head throbbed, whether it was from the knock it had received or his questions, she couldn't be sure.

The centurion's eyes never wavered.

"Mago," she said, defaulting to the truth.

The centurion exhaled sharply and set his knife down on the table. "That's bad."

Elissa furrowed her brow in confusion.

He leaned forward in his chair and scrutinized her closely while he spoke. "The Magos are well known in certain circles of Roman society. Before the wars, your family would've been more recognizable to a Roman than Hannibal and the Barcas. If the wrong people find out who you are, your fate will be completely out of my hands." He lifted his palms to emphasize the point. "You're a marked woman, Elissa, and you're going to need my help."

Her momentary confusion gave way to anger. "Your help?" she sputtered in disbelief. "What I *need* is for you to let me go, you overbearing brute!"

Marcus didn't react to her insult. He merely sighed and tipped back in his chair. "And where exactly will you go?"

"Home."

He shook his head. "How will you get there, Elissa? No ship is going to Carthage from Rome, or from anywhere else in the Mediterranean for that matter. This is war, and I don't think you realize which side you've ended up on."

Elissa looked away. She didn't want him to see the desperation his words had caused. She really did have no idea how to get out of here.

"Stay with the legion, call yourself a Greek, and don't let anyone convince you to tell them otherwise. No matter how they threaten you." He raised his eyebrows meaningfully.

Elissa tried in vain to swallow the lump that had risen in her throat. "Until when?"

"Until the war is over. Until Rome wins and allows Carthage to receive merchant ships again."

His confidence in victory renewed some of her desire to fight. "And if Rome doesn't win? If Carthage is imposing her will on Rome instead?"

"Then you won't have a problem getting back," he stated simply.

Elissa frowned, somewhat startled by his frankness at the possibility of a Roman defeat.

"Listen," he said, spreading his hands across the table. "I will not reveal your identity and I won't press you for information that I don't believe you have. You may stay with my baggage until the outcome of this war is decided, and then you may go home."

Elissa stiffened. How she wanted to slap that square jaw of his.

"Centurion. I am not a part of your baggage, and I am not here because of your *kindness.*"

Elissa stood and moved toward the door, not waiting to see his response to her outburst. As she walked by the table, the centurion's hand latched onto hers. His hand was warm, and her wrist fit neatly in his large palm.

"Why did you leave?" he asked, watching her intently.

"To escape overbearing men," she snapped at him.

His hand left her wrist and he ran it through his hair, its copper tones catching in the candlelight. He turned his head up to hers and met her challenge with a rakish grin.

"Well, don't let yourself go hungry." He picked the thickest loaf of bread off the table and held it out to her.

Elissa paused. *Think before you act*, some blessedly rational part of her brain reminded her. She snatched the loaf from his hand and strode out the door.

The next morning's activities began at dawn in the exact reverse of how the day before had ended. The men took down their tents first, and then disassembled the ramparts and turrets until only the outer palisade was left. Only when night had fully given way to the diluted winter sun were the thick trunks of the outer wall taken down.

Elissa carefully disassembled her own meager defenses that morning. She made sure to remember where every peg and strap had been placed so she'd be able to replicate the tent tonight. As she was finishing, Quintus stopped by with a heavy bag of bread, figs and dried meat, along with his profuse apologies for not having brought her dinner the night before. Elissa reassured him that she'd barely been hungry, but Quintus was having none of it and was obviously distressed by his uncharacteristic oversight. He escorted her to the wagon with a solemn promise to check back in a few hours. Elissa smiled as Quintus left; he was so mild-mannered and bookish, it was still a shock when she remembered he was wearing armor.

Elissa settled back into position for the march and was grateful again for the lack of attention she seemed to attract in the baggage train. Even the unhelpful wagon driver had his nonchalance to recommend him. But as the hours passed with the slow clop of the oxen's feet, Elissa learned that although anonymity was safer, it was also rather boring. The brown hills in the distance seemed stuck to the horizon, never coming closer or moving farther away.

Elissa was nibbling on a fig when the sound of approaching hooves rose above the pedestrian din of the baggage train. She pulled back the flap to investigate and saw the centurion and his black stallion making a straight line to her wagon. Elissa dropped the flap and bolted to her seat. With any luck he hadn't seen her and would have to spend the afternoon searching through the long line of similar wagons before he found hers. But the hoof beats only grew louder. They slowed to a walk right outside her wagon.

"Elissa." The centurion's deep voice passed easily through the walls.

Elissa froze. Maybe if he couldn't see or hear her, she might actually disappear.

"Elissa, I just saw you looking out of the wagon. I know you're in there."

Heat rose in Elissa's cheeks. She took a deep breath and pulled back the flap. Then she stopped breathing entirely. The centurion was seated on his magnificent stallion, so much bigger than the bay she'd been impressed with the night she'd tried to escape. His bronze breastplate glittered spectacularly in the sunlight, catching the yellow rays and throwing them in every direction. His face was in profile; his hair still tussled from the gallop. Muscles bunched in hard lines across his upper arms and ran like thick cables to the leather bands around his wrists. Elissa's breath wedged in her throat. This man bore about as much resemblance to the silk-wrapped Merbal as a lion to a mouse. When Elissa finally forced herself to meet his eyes, the centurion's expression was triumphant. He'd clearly noticed her reaction. She groaned and let the flap fall closed. Dear gods, why couldn't she keep her head around this man?

"Come now, Elissa," he said with laughter in his voice. "I thought you might like a ride."

Elissa's ears perked but she didn't move. "You would give me a horse?"

"Yes." A large hand reached into the wagon and pulled open the flap. "I would accompany you, of course." He leaned down on his horse to peer inside the wagon.

Elissa tried to ignore him by studying the second horse trailing behind the stallion. It was a young chestnut gelding, fully tacked and ready to be ridden. Elissa's gaze flicked between the horse and the centurion's expectant face. She ground her frustration between her teeth. As much as she would've loved to disappoint him, the prospect of an afternoon ride in the sun was simply too appealing. She retrieved her cloak as the centurion called for the wagon driver to stop. The oxen lurched to a halt and Elissa stepped out into a brilliant winter's day. The air was crisp and dry, and the sun bathed the countryside in pale rays of light. The centurion led the chestnut over to her and Elissa mounted easily. The horse pranced on the spot as she relaxed into the saddle. Elissa turned to face the centurion, who was staring at her with a directness that reddened her cheeks.

"Shall we go then?" she asked, averting her eyes.

The centurion bowed his head and held out his hand in exaggerated courtesy. "Where can I escort you, my lady?"

"To the sea?" she asked hopefully.

"I'm afraid we're packed a bit light for that journey."

Elissa smiled with a hint of sarcasm. If he wanted to pretend she wasn't his captive, that was fine with her.

"Then how about those hills over there?" She pointed to one of the flat hills in the distance. It would feel good to go somewhere with only one Roman instead of thousands.

The centurion smiled and set off at a brisk walk. Elissa reined in beside him and settled into the pace. Grass crackled pleasantly under their horses' hooves. If she closed her eyes, she could almost pretend she was in Zama. There was a meadow like this outside their villa. The lush smell after a summer rain tickled her nose, and the African sun warmed her skin. Elissa sighed nostalgically and tilted her face up to the cloudless sky. How lucky she'd been then. Whole days when she'd forgotten her father's disapproval in the blissful abandon of a horse flowing beneath her. Home. A place she'd always felt safe, if not exactly loved.

"What are you thinking about?" The centurion's question sliced through her reverie.

Elissa glanced over at him. In the bright sunlight, and

away from his fearsome legionaries, he looked more like a young aristocrat out for a ride than a battle-hardened killer.

"Home."

"Tell me about it."

It sounded like a command. Elissa stayed silent.

Marcus looked down at his hands. He could understand her reluctance. If she'd asked, he would have told her not to trust him. But for some reason, it still stung. Marcus shook his head in frustration. He should be with his men right now, marching in formation with the rest of the legion in case they were ambushed. Instead he was here, taking an afternoon ride with his Carthaginian captive and acting as if he were courting her. Why could he not get this girl out of his mind? He kept seeing her as she'd been last night, her dark hair illuminated by the fire, defiance blazing in her green eyes. He'd nearly grabbed those curving hips and pulled her into his lap. When he gazed at her now, it was all he could do to stop himself from leaning over and pressing his mouth to her full lips.

"What are you thinking about?"

Marcus's head jerked up in surprise. She was teasing him. The realization diverted his attention from any thoughts of his men. He smiled in response. Maybe he should tell her exactly what he'd been thinking. She was liable to find out soon enough. But he wanted her to be a willing partner when the time came, and he knew he was likely to scare her if he was too forward now. She was brave, but also undeniably innocent. Marcus took in Elissa's rosy cheeks and the shadow of her breasts underneath her cloak. Yes, she would be worth waiting for.

Elissa cleared her throat and Marcus's eyes shot up to hers. He shifted uncomfortably in the saddle and glanced down in shock. Had he really been aroused merely by thinking of her? Good gods, that was a first.

"I was thinking." Marcus coughed to clear some of the hoarseness out of his voice. "I'd like to hear about where you grew up. Is Carthage very hot?"

Elissa's mouth twitched and Marcus recoiled. Gods, had he really just asked about the weather?

"I didn't grow up in Carthage. I grew up a day's ride to the south, in Zama."

"I'd like to hear about it," Marcus said, quickly recovering his decorum.

Elissa hesitated, but seemed to relax again as soon as she started talking. "Well, it's very beautiful. Rolling hills like here, but in some places the ground is sand rather than grass. There are lots of trees, but different types. Trees with giant leaves and scales for bark, and shorter ones that are prickly to touch but have the juicy inner core of a melon. The sea is darker on the coast, more of a deep blue than the turquoise waters I saw here. The people in the country are farmers, simple and kind. It's easy to be generous when the harvest is always plentiful." Elissa went on describing her neighbors, the olives and figs they grew, the animals they kept, the yellow color of their homes.

Marcus watched her as she talked, listening to her voice as much as her words. A faint smile played at the corners of her lips as she lost herself in memories.

"Sometimes I miss my home, too," he said some time later.

Elissa jolted at the sound of his voice. She seemed to have forgotten he was there.

Marcus laughed with a hint of bitterness. "Yes, Elissa. I do have a home."

She stared at him for a moment before asking, "Would you describe it to me?"

Marcus found himself hesitating. He never spoke of

home. He did his best not to think of it, either. These days, it only made him angry. His fury was useful in battle, but outside of war, it made him dangerously rash.

"My family lived in Rome." Marcus began tentatively. But she was asking no more than he'd asked of her. "It is a dirty, crowded mess of a city. But we had a villa outside the city in Veii, and we spent the summers of my childhood there."

"What was that like?" She sounded genuinely curious.

Marcus smiled, but he felt a new tightness around his eyes. "I could've asked for no more."

"Do you miss it?"

"Yes."

They let the silence hold, and it had long since grown comfortable by the time Marcus broke it again.

"Why did you run, Elissa?"

He'd asked her the same question last night, but now he felt she was more ready to answer.

"To escape." Her voice was hollow.

"To escape men?"

"Yes." She paused. "And to escape myself." She looked at Marcus a bit uncomfortably. "My expectations of myself, I mean. Or rather, the expectations everyone had of me. I felt I needed to be more than the little they thought of me."

Marcus turned to stare straight ahead. "You thought your fate should be different from the one laid out for you."

Elissa's head swung toward him. "Yes. And I suppose the weight of knowing, and expecting it to be different can become heavy."

Marcus smiled, a small private smile that wasn't meant for her. Yes, he knew what it was like to stray from the beaten path. To feel as though your feet marched to a different beat than your heart did. When he looked at Elissa again, it was with admiration in his eyes. He had not been able to do what this woman had. He didn't have the courage to leave the ruts of routine and see where the wheels rolled.

"Have you…have you ever felt that?" Elissa asked in response to his silence.

"I—" Marcus stopped himself. He wasn't about to tell her what he'd been thinking. She wasn't his enemy, despite where she'd been born, but she *was* his captive, and he could hardly admit his doubts to himself, never mind anyone else. No, he had taken her on this ride to entice her into his bed, and that was what he'd get back to doing.

"I think I approve of this wind." His eyes fell on Elissa's bare thigh, which had just been revealed when a particularly strong gust of wind blew her cloak aside.

Elissa caught the direction of his eyes and blushed. She hastily rearranged her cloak.

"I'd like to go back now," she said brusquely.

"Very well." Marcus turned his horse in the direction from which they'd come.

Elissa's silence only grew icier as they rode back, and Marcus found himself regretting his comment. If anything, she was even further away from joining him in his bed than she'd been yesterday. Marcus glanced over at her to confirm his assessment. Her jaw was set firmly and her lips were pulled into a tight frown. Her hips, on the other hand, were more agreeable. They were perched sumptuously on her horse's saddle, and her rounded backside was displayed to great effect. Marcus smiled. This woman was made for passion, and sooner or later she'd grow tired of fighting it. Or better yet, she'd be willing to take the fight into his bed.

Marcus felt a rumble in the back of his throat. A night spent with her was sure to surpass any of the ones he'd spent with the jaded camp followers or Roman socialites he'd been with before. Sex with them was as dispassionate as a market transaction; they serviced his body, and he offered them protection or pleasure, whichever they preferred. He used to think of these unattached couplings as encounters of mutual convenience and benefit. He certainly never thought he'd be spending time and effort to win over a woman who clearly had no interest in him. But then, many things that used to satisfy him were disappointing now. Fighting was the only thing that simplified his world enough to give it purpose. He'd fight to defeat Rome's enemies, and he'd fight to win this Carthaginian girl's virtue. Maybe he'd even find that victory worthwhile in itself. When Marcus finally deposited her back at the wagon, it was with renewed confidence that he said he'd see her again soon. After all, he'd never yet been defeated in battle.

Elissa stared up at the night sky. The camp was still and quiet. Only the occasional crackle of a banked fire or the snort of a sleeping horse broke the silence. One would never guess that this was a war camp, and the purpose of the night's peace was to prepare for battle. Thousands of stars were scattered across the black sky. How many people had watched them, trying to identify their patterns and decipher their meaning? The astrologers said the sky was a tablet for the gods, and that humans lacked the ability to read it. Elissa wasn't sure she believed that. Why would the gods communicate with man in such confusing ways, so that only a few could understand? Maybe the sky had no meaning, no purpose beyond its existence. Was that comforting or frightening? She looked away. Frosted grass brushed against the tips of her toes and chilled her feet. She glanced toward the nearest rampart on the palisade. The sentry's torches flickered from up high; they would stay guard through the night. War never ended.

Elissa started in the direction of her tent. She figured midnight walks were fine, so long as no one caught her. But instead of cutting a straight line back, her feet took her to the nearest wall. She would need to follow its length to reach her tent, tucked away in a corner of the camp. She walked easily and without fear through the cool night. She felt safer in this darkness, protected from unwanted eyes. Elissa reached out her hand and ran her fingers along the palisade as she walked. Her fingers rose and fell as they traced the poles that made up the wall. The wood vibrated as a man walked along the rampart above. Elissa wondered what it would be like to be one of those legionaries, defending this wall rather than trying to escape from it. Each one of them was a tiny but essential cog in a massive wheel. Would you feel dwarfed by your smallness or comforted to be part of something greater than yourself?

Elissa stopped walking. The wood no longer vibrated here. She took several steps back so she could see to the top of the wall. A torch flickered in the turret above her, but there was no guard standing next to it. That was interesting.

She began moving again. It was probably only the angle she was looking from that obscured the guard. But when she'd walked a complete semi-circle around the base of the turret and still no guard appeared, she grew suspicious. Elissa scanned the smooth wall in front of her, and her eyes stopped on the faint outline of a rectangle. It was a door so narrow a person would need to turn sideways to pass through. It was probably invisible from the outside, a secret exit meant to be used in a siege.

Elissa tiptoed silently up to the door. There must be a legionary standing guard on the other side. She pressed her ear against the wall and let the rough bark bite into her cheek. She stopped breathing, expecting the sound of shifting feet and clinking metal to fill the silence. Nothing. Elissa pulled back and nudged the door with the tips of her fingers. It didn't move. She tried again with the palm of her hand and it creaked. Elissa took a deep breath, closed her eyes and threw her shoulder into the door with all her weight. It gave way suddenly, and she hurtled through the door and landed on the other side. Elissa rolled off her back and scrambled to her feet in time to see the door to hit the wall behind her with a resounding thump. She cringed and hurriedly pressed her back to the wall. Her breath was rapid with fear; surely a legionary would have heard the noise and come running. But there was nothing. No footsteps, only the gentle rustle of the wind blowing through the tall grass.

Elissa's breath began to deepen. Maybe no one was coming. She glanced hesitantly toward the sky. Perhaps the gods would smile on her tonight. The thought that they might not have abandoned her—that she might not be completely alone, propelled her feet back into motion. She kept as close as possible to the wall, knowing it would be more difficult for the sentries to see her if she was directly below. A ditch had been cut into the ground across from her, and it appeared to run the length of the wall. Elissa couldn't see how deep it was, but she suspected it was too deep to climb up the other side without help. The Romans were nothing if not precise in their defenses. The idea of getting stuck at the bottom of that ditch and having to wait until morning to be found was nearly enough to stop her altogether. And truly, what *was* she doing? She had no horse, no food and no plan—except to keep going forward unless, or until, she was stopped. What if she was caught? Would she be treated like a deserter? Killed and left in an unmarked grave?

She suddenly felt lightheaded, and reached out to steady herself against the wall. Her breathing was becoming shallow, and Elissa struggled to pull in enough air through her clenched teeth. Oh, gods, she was panicking. *Breathe*, she told herself, *just breathe*. What if this really was her moment, her one chance at escape? The unguarded gate, the empty turret, the convenient door—when would she be so fortunate again? Her eyes flicked up to the stars. Maybe this was what fate looked like.

Her feet seemed to move on their own. She would go at least far enough to see if there was a break in the ditch at the corner of the wall. If the ditch continued uninterrupted, she would go back through the door and return to her tent as if nothing had happened. Elissa slowed to a shuffle as she approached. She stopped at the corner and leaned forward to see around the wall. She squinted at the ditch, trying to distinguish any difference in its depth. Elissa inhaled sharply. There! Only a dozen or so paces ahead, it looked as though two separate ditches converged. Loose earth was piled higher there, and the distance between the ground and the rim seemed less than a body's length.

Elissa turned her eyes up to the stars. "Thank you," she whispered.

She took a step forward, and then another, and then everything fell apart. The world condensed in a flash of excruciating pain. Hot, searing agony started at the top of her head and then exploded over her whole body. Elissa's legs crumpled like twigs. Sticky warmth flooded the side of her head. Her mind grew distant, as if she were watching someone else's body. They last thing she remembered before it all went dark was a pair of boots in front of her face.

Sensation came back slowly. Her mind had departed her body at the first rush of pain, and it seemed reluctant to return. Elissa noticed her wrists first. Something rough and scratchy was biting into the skin. She tried to twitch her fingers. Nothing moved. Either her hands were bound, or she'd lost the ability to use them. Neither alternative was good.

She could still see only black. Perhaps it was just that her head was pointed in the wrong direction. Elissa tried moving it. The pain burst open again and a surge of nausea welled up in her throat. The black went fuzzy and Elissa fought to maintain consciousness. She pushed her chest out and forced her lungs to fill with air. A bead of color appeared in the center of her vision; she took in another breath and the bead expanded. After ten more breaths she'd pushed the blackness to the edges of her eyes, and the pain had receded somewhat. She seemed to be in a tent, a very large tent. Rectangular blobs of color were scattered across the room. Shimmering squares of gold were clustered in the middle of the tent, and tiny dots of green and red hovered on top of the gold. Tables. Gold tables. And plates of grapes? She couldn't be sure. But those larger blobs of blue must be couches. There were a lot of them.

Something moved off to her right, and Elissa jerked her head in its direction. Too fast, she thought as the world spun around her. But it solidified more quickly this time. She was indeed in a tent, a very opulent one. Pitchers of wine and bowls of multicolored grapes had been placed on every available surface, and the ground was covered in soft carpet rather than bare grass. A servant moved into view. He circled the room, checking to make sure every plate and pitcher was full. He stopped when he noticed Elissa watching him and stared at her for a moment. His pupils were tiny dots in wide brown eyes. He looked afraid. A kernel of dread took root deep in Elissa's chest. *Where exactly was she?*

"Ah, our guest has risen."

Elissa tried to turn in the direction of the voice and realized it wasn't only her hands that were bound. She was seated on a straight wooden chair, and her arms had been pulled around the back and cinched together at the wrist. Her ankles were forced apart and tied to two legs of the chair.

"Servant, bring our guest to the table. I imagine she's quite hungry after the evening's exercise."

Dread rushed through her veins, turning them to ice. The voice was high and acidic. She recognized it. Elissa's chair was lifted off the ground and she was carried through the air with remarkable ease. The chair was set back down in front of a wide table; its legs were gilded and it had elaborate claw feet. The surface was covered in food—exotic fruits, stewed vegetables, salted meats. There was enough here to feed a dozen people. The smell was overwhelming.

Hot breath tickled her neck.

"Remember me?" someone whispered in her ear.

Elissa yanked her head away so quickly her chair tipped over. A hand pushed her chair back into place, then reached over her shoulder and put two fingers on the bottom of her chin. His skin was warm and moist with sweat.

He turned her head to face him. She swallowed and nodded slowly. Flaminius.

"Good," he purred into her ear. "Because I remember you."

His fingers traced the line of her jaw. They moved up her cheekbones and around her ears until they rested on her forehead.

"You're bleeding."

His fingers suddenly turned to lead weights on her skull. He pressed his thumbs into the soft wound on her head and squeezed.

The air left Elissa's lungs and she cried out in pain as warmth spread across the top of her head. The table seemed to spin in front of her and her vision went black.

"Now, shall we eat?"

Flaminius moved out from behind Elissa and walked to the table. His thumbs were coated in blood. He brought one of them to his lips and pushed it into his mouth, then smiled at her. His front teeth were smudged with red.

Elissa's fear was hot as it surged through her body and melted the cold terror that had come before. She forced her vision to clear. She had to get out of this tent. Right now.

"I...I need my hands to eat." Elissa tried to make her voice sound pleasing but it came out too high.

Flaminius's smile grew until all his teeth were showing, as though he might devour her in a mouthful. "No. I think I'd rather you eat from my hand."

Flaminius fished an olive from a nearby dish and turned to Elissa with his hand outstretched. She didn't move. He pressed the olive to her closed lips; it felt oily and cold against her mouth. Elissa looked up at him. She could take those stubby fingers in her mouth and bite down until she tasted blood. Flaminius moved his fingers to the back of the olive and pushed harder. Elissa kept her eyes on his as she took the olive in her mouth. He leaned back on the table in front of her and spread his legs wide. Elissa shuddered as his tunic hitched higher on his thighs.

"Now, why don't you tell me who you are. We won't have any interruptions this time."

Elissa forced her voice to stay pleasant. "My name is Elissa."

"Ah, Elissa." He said her name slowly, as if he wanted to savour its taste in his mouth. "Elissa. How did you come to be in Centurion Gracchus's possession? He is not usually the type to keep slaves on campaign."

Elissa's brain felt sluggish and disconnected. She pinched her hand behind the chair to force herself to focus. What story could she possibly give that would convince him to leave her alone?

"I was taken from Vetulonium," she began.

Flaminius's black eyes narrowed. "Taken as the lawful property of an Italian owner? Or from an enemy of Rome?" Flaminius leaned in closer. His breath was sour. "Or did you escape?"

Elissa squeezed her back against the chair to maintain the space between them. "I… I was taken lawfully."

Flaminius raised his eyebrows, then turned and reached for something on the table. When he faced Elissa again, he held a serrated knife in his hand. Her eyes widened. He wouldn't really use that on her, would he?

"How much did he pay for you, then?" He ran his fingers along the edge of the knife as he spoke.

Elissa's brain whirled. Whatever amount she invented needed to believable, but also high enough that he wouldn't threaten to buy her.

"He, he paid—" Her voice trailed off as her thoughts grew frantic. She stopped herself. There was no good answer. She needed a different tactic.

Elissa drew her body up as tall as her bonds would allow. "Consul Flaminius. I am the lawful property of Centurion Marcus Gracchus and I demand an audience with him. As my owner, it is his right to hear my sins and decide my punishment."

Flaminius straightened in surprise, but then leaned back on the table again.

"Well, aren't you the little orator. But I'm afraid I rather outrank your centurion. If I decide to transfer your ownership to me, he will have no choice but to comply."

Elissa sensed that they were nearing a decision point, and time was running out for her to influence the outcome. She took a deep breath, leveled her chin and directed the full force of her fear, frustration and anger at this hateful man.

"The centurion will not comply. And if you insist, he will take his men and mutiny, leave your command. I very much doubt you want to deal with a rebellion in the middle of a war."

Elissa knew it was a lie. As obvious as the centurion's hatred for Flaminius was, Elissa couldn't imagine him risking capital punishment on her behalf. But she also knew she had to match Flaminius's strength, and as she had none of her own power, she'd have to use the centurion's.

Flaminius's face flashed with anger and he shoved the knifepoint into the table.

"You think I fear your centurion?" he spat, his face nearly purple. "The Gracchus family are nothing but overreaching plebeians. I consider it my personal duty to force them back into the gutter they crawled out from."

He came for her now, his eyes glowing with intention and fury. He straddled her legs with both of his and hovered over her. His sweat was acrid, and the perfume he'd used to mask it was sickeningly sweet. Flaminius crouched down until his eyes were level with her knees. Elissa felt his hands brush her ankles. She heard fabric tearing near her feet, and cool air rushed against her calves, then her knees, then her thighs, and then the space she'd prayed he wouldn't go. Elissa looked down and saw her dress ripped from the hem all the way to the base of her stomach. Flaminius put his hand on her thigh. His touch was hot. He pushed his fingers up, higher, and to the center of her body.

Elissa screamed. No, no! This couldn't be real. This couldn't be happening. Flaminius traced the line between her leg and pelvis with his fingers. He brushed his palm against the hair between her legs and tugged on a curl. He moved lower until his fingers were pressing against her virgin skin. Then he pushed inside her. Elissa screamed again and thrashed wildly, but all she could move were her head and shoulders. She was helpless to make him stop. Flaminius pumped the tip of one hand inside her and used the other to hitch his tunic over his waist. Elissa slammed her eyes shut. She begged her mind to leave her body again, and this time, to never come back. It obliged, and Flaminius's looming shape grew foggy. The pressure inside her dulled. She became dimly aware of some new commotion behind her, but she didn't have the will to make sense of it.

A shock ran through the room like lightning, and the thunderclap that followed shook Elissa from her daze. She opened her eyes. Flaminius was gone. Fingers were working quickly, unbinding her wrists and ankles.

The centurion's voice boomed across the tent. "You touch her again, Flaminius, or even think of stopping me from taking her, I'll run you through with my sword. I'd give my life to end yours in an instant."

There was a long moment of stillness before Elissa felt her body being lifted from the chair and draped over the centurion's warm back. Night air filled her lungs, and she saw his strong legs moving quickly over the dark grass below. She lifted her head slightly. Quintus was behind them. His brow was knotted and his eyes were grave.

"I want a double guard posted outside my tent tonight. No one passes through without my permission, understood?"

Quintus nodded quickly, then hurried away without looking at Elissa.

Marcus didn't set Elissa down until they were inside his tent. He placed her on the bed, and his right hand snapped back to the hilt of his sword. He left the tent again and Elissa heard him barking orders outside. She felt removed from her body. Her mind was still stuck on an alternate course in which it was more than Flaminius's fingers that had violated her. Flaminius, Consul of Rome. His fingers inside her, moving, pumping. Her body helpless to expel the intruder.

Her mind eventually registered that Marcus had re-entered the tent. He stayed in the corner by the door, his chest heaving as if he'd just run a mile. Sweat glistened on his cheeks, and his chin was dotted with dark hairs that he'd surely planned to shave off in the morning. He wasn't even wearing armor, just a gray sleeping tunic with his sword hastily belted around the waist. Elissa saw all of it, and cared about none of it. It was only his eyes that managed to penetrate her frayed consciousness. His fury had condensed them into a deep gray; rolling black storm clouds that charged the air with energy and purpose; an onslaught that showed no signs of breaking.

Suddenly Elissa became aware of the dishevelled state of her dress. The tear in its side ran up to her waist and her entire thigh was exposed. She scrambled to cover herself with the furs on the bed and managed to pull several thick pelts over her lap before Marcus reached her. She could smell the musk from his exertion—an earthy mixture of sweat and pine. So unlike Flaminius's sickly floral smell.

"Hands," he growled.

Elissa's arms lifted involuntarily. Marcus held both her wrists in one hand and wound a thick length of rope around them with the other. Elissa winced as he tightened the knot. He dropped her hands heavily.

"If you want to act like a prisoner, I'll treat you like one."

Elissa kept her eyes down and her mouth shut. For once, she didn't have the will to fight.

Marcus turned away and started pacing the room. He drew the tent flap aside to check on his men. Their backs were straight, their hands on their swords. He turned back inside. His arms were vibrating with energy and desperately needed release. He imagined Flaminius coming after him and Elissa, and the siren hum of his sword grew louder. He longed for the encounter; he'd tell his men to stay back so he could face him alone. It would be a quick fight. Flaminius was a politician, not a warrior. But his death would be no less satisfying. Marcus would let all his anger and vengeance flow through his arms until they ripped Flaminius's body apart.

He heard Elissa shifting on his bed and glanced down at his sword. His knuckles were white against the hilt and he'd pulled the blade halfway out of the scabbard. He looked over at Elissa. Her knees were curled into her chest and her eyes were squeezed shut. Her lips were working furiously but no sound came out. He was terrifying her.

Marcus took a deep breath and pushed his sword back into its scabbard. She deserved to be terrified. The haphazard escape she'd attempted tonight was unforgivable.

It had jeopardized her life and those of his men. But he forced himself to continue watching her. She was reckless and thoughtless, and also small and scared. His mind flashed back to the scene he'd just witnessed. Flaminius hovering above her, the tops of his thick thighs exposed, one hand reaching inside her, the other fumbling at his breeches to release himself. Marcus's vision went red again. He would kill that man a thousand times over if he could. His breath quickened and his hand moved back to the hilt of his sword. He squeezed his fist until his veins felt like they'd burst from the skin and the rage had temporarily leached out.

He strode quickly across the room to Elissa. Probably too quickly. She seemed so small sitting there below him.

"Elissa——" he began.

Her eyes flew open; the amber flecks alight with fury, threatening to consume the cool green around them in wild flames.

"Just do it," she hissed. "Kill me. At least I would die honorably in the fight against your people. And you would have nothing from me."

The force of her anger caused Marcus to step back. He had expected her to repent, certainly not to beg, but at least to ask for leniency. Instead, she was challenging him, asking to be martyred like a warrior. His own fury, his boundless fury, was matched only by hers. The realization knocked Marcus's thoughts of Flaminius off course. For the first time tonight, he truly saw her. She was like water poured on his fiery need for vengeance. It extinguished the tallest flames, but the embers underneath burned even hotter. He no longer wanted Flaminius dead; he wanted her—alive and in his arms. Having her would be like the euphoria when a ferocious battle has just turned for your side. Exhaustion and fear grow liquid in your veins, and your body is flooded with an aura of invincibility. Strength and confidence rule your every movement; every step is perfect and exact. Marcus took a deep breath and felt his body fill with new purpose. He held out his hands and took a step closer.

"I'm not going to hurt you, Elissa."

Her brow tightened with suspicion. "I…I told you. I don't care what you do to me."

Marcus stepped forward until his knees were touching her legs. "Oh, really?"

Elissa's eyes widened but she stayed where she was. "Yes, I—"

"You'll sleep in my bed tonight," he interrupted.

Her eyes darted to the sides as she searched for an escape. Marcus brought his hands down to the bed and trapped her body between his arms. He leaned down so his chest was barely above hers.

"No, I won't," she said more firmly this time, but she didn't move her body away.

Marcus lowered himself until his torso was against her chest. His face hovered an inch above hers. He could make out the subtle curve of her lips, the delicate turn of her nose, the downward tilt of her eyebrows. Something flared in her eyes, and it wasn't fear. That was all the excuse he needed.

He dropped his weight onto his elbows and then his wrists as he lowered himself on top of her. She followed his progress in reverse until her back was flat against the bed and their stomachs pushed against each other. He took her wrists in one hand and held them above her head. Two perfect circles swelled the middle of her dress.

"No, no, stay back. You're no better than *him*." Her voice was reedy, her eyes wide with alarm, but her body was motionless.

"Oh, I'm very different from him." Marcus moved his lips down to the base of her long neck and pressed them into the hollow at her collarbone. "Do you know why?" he whispered against her skin.

Elissa shook her head slightly, in disagreement, he guessed.

He could feel her neck burning where his lips brushed against it. She jolted as if a current had run through her. He sensed her growing desire and extended his tongue to taste the desperation on her skin—soft and deliciously salty. She wanted more. A growl rumbled at the back of his throat, and his lips rested more firmly against her as he spoke.

"Because, Elissa." He paused, hovering over her long, perfect neck. "Because you're going to love what I do to you."

Then he descended, and his lips and tongue took up the onslaught with twice the vigor. Elissa gasped in his arms. But instead of pulling back, she lifted her chest closer to his. Marcus shut his eyes as pleasure overtook him. Her breasts were soft against his body, her hair thick and floral against his face. He buried his face in those silken strands, searching for the tiny, rounded ear he knew he'd find there. He wanted to trace its outline with his tongue, kiss it until she only heard his mouth, only felt his skin, only smelled his need. And he knew she wanted that, too. Her mind had lost its fight with her body, and now she arched into his hands, pushed her hips into his stomach. She was finally his to take.

"Centurion!"

Marcus's head shot up, but he didn't move away.

"Centurion!" the voice called again. "Someone's approaching!"

Marcus grunted as the meaning of the words penetrated his consciousness.

"Flaminius," he growled.

He raised himself onto his elbows and off Elissa. His limbs felt heavy and slow, as if they were moving through water. Elissa didn't stir below him. Her eyes were closed and her cheeks flushed with heat. Marcus could tell she already regretted their coupling. As soon as Marcus was free of the bed, she brought her knees to her chest and curled up in a protective ball. Marcus felt a surge of tenderness as he looked down at her. He wanted to lay a gentle trail of kisses across her hands and arms until she forgot her fears and came back to him. He found himself reaching for her hand, but shook his head vigorously. There was a fight waiting for him outside, and an unfocused mind led to delayed reactions, and delayed reactions led to death. He grabbed a fur from the bed and laid it over her instead. Then he turned and strode briskly out of the tent, belting his sword back onto his hip as he walked.

His men were in fighting formation outside his tent. They had arranged themselves in a phalanx; their shields were locked together to form a protective wall in front of the entrance. Marcus drew his sword and walked to the side of their line. His veterans were positioned at the ends, and one of them glanced at Marcus as he came up beside them. A brief flicker of surprise registered on the man's face, and Marcus realized he was still in his sleeping tunic. The linen had twisted around his body and was pulled up rather high. He grinned and winked at the man, then stalked out in front of his line, assuming a battle-ready crouch.

It was only a single man on horseback who approached, and Marcus could tell that it wasn't Flaminius. His jaw tightened in frustration. He sheathed his sword and crossed his arms. The legionary slowed his horse to a walk and halted a few paces in front of him.

"Centurion Gracchus?" The legionary's voice shook slightly and rose at the end.

"You know who I am."

Marcus noted a slight tremor in the plume on top of the legionary's helmet. He looked terrified. And young. Probably a new tribune hardly crossed into manhood. What was Flaminius doing, sending someone like this to confront him?

"I...I...," The boy cleared his throat before continuing with slightly more confidence. "I have a message from Consul Flaminius."

"I gathered."

Marcus showed the boy his back. His men stepped forward as one to protect him; they were less dismissive of the threat the tribune posed.

Marcus heard rummaging behind him and turned in time to see the boy toss something small toward him. He snatched the object out of the air and closed his fist around it. The thing felt cold in his hand. He uncurled his fingers—a simple iron ring lay against his palm. Marcus took the ring in two fingers and held it up to the moonlight, noting its scratches and the places where it had been tarnished and re-polished. He flipped it over to read the inscription on the inside, although he already knew what it said.

Pro familia Romaque. For family. For Rome.

Marcus slammed his fist shut and tightened his fingers until the ring bit into his palm. The man who'd last worn this ring had believed in both of those things. He had lived to bring honor to their family and had died fighting for justice for the people of Rome.

The dam Marcus had so carefully built groaned and then broke, and he was flooded with memories. They nearly knocked him over with their force. Tiberius at their family's villa in Rome, his face lined with determination as he donned the toga of a senator for the first time. Tiberius speaking at the rostrum, pumping his fist in the air as an overflowing crowd chanted his name. And then the memories that made Marcus's throat tighten until he was gasping for breath. Tiberius sitting across the table with a game of *latrones* assembled between them. He'd reached toward Marcus and rearranged the pieces, demonstrating how he'd bested him so that Marcus might win the next round. Tiberius—the beloved brother, the eldest son, the second father.

Then came an image Marcus had never seen but pictured whenever he closed his eyes. Tiberius, surrounded by men in dark cloaks, his body suspended in their lethal embrace, his head dangling lifelessly on his shoulder. That first cold knife as it slid through his cloak and into his skin. Was it deadly? Or did it hit somewhere like his stomach, painful but not lethal? Marcus had never seen the body. His family had never cremated Tiberius or performed the funeral rites. The assassins had dumped his body in the Tiber as though he was some kind of criminal. His soul gone. His body never to be respected, never to be loved, never to be held again.

Marcus's head jerked back up. *Flaminius.* Flaminius had done this. There hadn't been enough evidence for a trial, but Flaminius was the leader of the conservative faction in the Senate, the man who had the most to lose from Tiberius's policies, and the most to gain from his death. The law Tiberius had died trying to pass would have taken fertile farmland away from the rich aristocracy and given it to the people— the people who fought and died for Rome's wars and lived like peasants in her streets. The old, greedy men who ruled them like kings had called Tiberius a populist and a radical and killed him for wanting something better. And Flaminius had led them. This ring was the final evidence of his guilt.

"Please, no."

Marcus looked down. He hadn't even realized he'd moved, but somehow the tribune was underneath him now. The tribune's horse stood nearby without its rider and the boy was on the ground. His eyes darted frantically to the sides and his arm was outstretched in supplication. Marcus growled and pushed his boot into the boy's shoulder until he lay flat. Marcus drew his sword and brought its point to the center of the boy's neck. He would send his own message to Flaminius. Let him know that vengeance would find him, and it would be his own doing.

"No!" The shout was high-pitched.

It wasn't the tribune. Lips frozen in place, he was completely immobile in what he must be sure were his final moments. Then there were hands on Marcus's skin. They ran up and down his arms, gently pulling them away from the boy's neck. Marcus whirled around to this second assailant. He would take him down and then finish with the boy.

Elissa stumbled backward at his shove and landed on her rear. She rolled over onto her knees and spoke quietly. "Please don't kill him. I don't know what he gave you, but he's only a boy. It would be dishonorable to do this."

The sound of Elissa's soft voice cracking with fear broke through the haze of his anger. He came back to the present. He saw her. Her face was crumpled and pleading. Her hands clutched at the earth as if she would draw strength from it. He didn't know how she'd gotten around his line of men but he could see them shifting uncomfortably behind her. Her submission was more convincing that any defeat could be. She was begging for the life of a boy she didn't know, a Roman boy who, by all rights, should be her enemy. Something flickered in his chest, something shifting and uncomfortable. It was jealousy.

Marcus sheathed his sword. He was stunned silent by disbelief. He'd been seconds away from murdering this boy, and now he felt *jealous* of him? His hand shook as he placed it on Elissa's cheek and guided her up to a standing position. He held her eyes for a moment as he tried to adjust to the utter possessiveness that now gripped him. He took her hand and turned back to his tent, leaving Flaminius's tribune on the ground and quaking with relief. He didn't let go of her until they were back inside his tent, and even then, it was only for the time it took to slip Tiberius's ring on his finger.

CHAPTER 10

"Elissa. Elissa. Elissa!"

Elissa jerked her head toward the man riding beside her, having finally heard him calling her name. Quintus was watching her with a curious expression on his face. His head was tilted away from her and his brow was furrowed. He looked as though he wanted to say more, but repeated himself instead.

"I asked whether you'd ever seen the temple to Ba'al Haamon in Tyre. I've heard it rivals Jupiter's in Rome."

Elissa shook her head and kept her eyes fixed on her horse's mane. The day dawned a murky gray, and the sun barely penetrated the thick clouds above. It suited Elissa's mood perfectly. She didn't want to talk, and she didn't want Quintus to ask what was distracting her. She certainly didn't want to reveal that she'd been searching for Marcus in the line of men ahead. Above all, she did not want to even *think* about Flaminius and what he had done to her last night. She was fortunate it hadn't gone any further, and that was where her thoughts on the matter began and ended.

She was riding with Quintus behind Marcus's maniple. The line of red cloaks in front of them moved as rhythmically as ever, except that today they were no longer just a solid block in the distance. Elissa could distinguish the individual shapes of men now. Marcus had decided that morning that it was no longer safe for her to travel unprotected in the baggage train. From now on, she would be given a horse and would ride with his maniple at the back of the legion. Elissa had been too exhausted to protest at the time. She'd hardly slept last night. Whenever she shut her eyes, she became acutely aware of the man sleeping next to her. She was in a man's bed, and a Roman centurion's no less. She'd wanted so badly to simply turn over and roll off the bed with one of those furs, to forget about the centurion and Flaminius and rest. But Marcus had said he would only unbind her if she swore not to leave the bed, and Elissa was quite sure any quick movements would have him changing from fast asleep to battle-ready within seconds. So she'd stayed put and kept her eyes fixed on the ceiling to stop it from spinning.

All night she'd prayed to Astarte that he wouldn't touch her. She didn't understand the sensations he'd awakened in her last night, but she was determined not to lose control again. She'd been terrified and hurt by Flaminius and she'd let her guard down. That could not happen again. So she searched the column of men in front of her until she located Marcus. He was astride his great black stallion a safe distance away. Only then did she turn back to Quintus.

"Where are we going?"

Quintus smiled kindly. He seemed to understand her lack of interest in the small talk he'd taken great pains to maintain all morning.

"Chasing a shade, it seems." When Elissa regarded him quizzically, he continued. "We know Hannibal spent the first part of winter at the foot of the Alps in Cisalpine Gaul. We assumed he'd be heading south to march on Rome afterward. That's why we've been blocking the mountain passes through the Apennines. But we don't actually know where his army is, and none of our scouts have been able to locate it. We're traipsing across Etruria, trying to be everywhere and nowhere at the same time." Quintus shrugged. "Maybe they're gone, disappeared back across the Alps as quickly as they came."

Elissa was skeptical. He didn't really believe that, did he? It was much more likely the Carthaginians had kept out of sight because their scouts were better than the Roman ones. Which meant they had local help.

It appeared that Quintus's thoughts ran along the same lines. "We think several large Gallic tribes may have joined them," he added quietly.

Elissa heard the fear in his voice. It was well known that the Romans were terrified of their northern neighbors. The Gauls had been the last people to sack Rome nearly two hundred years ago. Rome had been just another Italian city with outsized ambitions then. Now, they were the masters of Italy, and it was strange they hadn't outgrown their fear of the nomadic warriors to their north.

"I hope they'll come to battle quickly," Elissa mumbled.

Quintus looked at her sharply with his intelligent eyes. "Me, too, Elissa. But we're planning for any outcome, and if it does come to battle, you need to be nowhere nearby."

"What do mean?" Her voice grew higher in pitch. "Quintus, you have to return me to my people!"

"I think so, too, Elissa," Quintus's tone was placating. "But nothing is certain in war, and even if we do lose the battle, there may not be a way for you to switch sides safely. Blood-drunk soldiers do not follow codes of honor when it comes to unprotected women."

Elissa understood the truth in that, but she couldn't accept that victory for Carthage wouldn't also mean victory for her. She would switch sides and then find Barro immediately. He would protect her. Elissa looked over at Quintus. Somehow, she felt she owed him an explanation for last night. She wanted him to understand that she'd *had* to attempt an escape.

"I have no choice but to try, Quintus. Every day I stay

here, I risk being found out. And I don't believe the centurion plans to let me go as he says he will."

Quintus was silent.

Elissa lost her patience. "I'm sorry, Quintus, I didn't mean to hurt—"

Quintus held his hand up to cut her off. "I understand why you did it, Elissa. I don't even blame you. And I'm truly sorry about what happened to you as a result." He winced, and then nodded in Marcus's direction. "But you've misjudged him. If he says you'll be safe until the outcome of the war is decided, then you'll be safe. The centurion keeps his word. Surely you must believe that after last night."

Elissa shook her head. "I don't think he needed much of an excuse to go after the consul."

"Then you're blind, Elissa," Quintus scoffed. She started to object but he pressed on. "I never wanted to join the legion. I'm not really an ambitious man, and I've certainly never shown a talent for fighting. I only ever wanted to live a comfortable life, and occasionally serve Rome in my dull, bureaucratic way."

Elissa was grateful for the change in subject and did her best to encourage him. "But people need dull bureaucracy, Quintus. Carthage was built by the sharp minds of men like you. We promote intelligent men, not beat them away."

Quintus smiled. "Yes, I've heard that. But Rome is not Carthage or Greece. We value the sword over the stylus, and we're fiercely competitive. Thankfully, there are some Romans who don't believe it's an aberration not to fit the mold."

Elissa shifted uncomfortably in the saddle. She didn't like where the conversation was turning. Or rather, to whom.

"I used to own a vineyard in Campania," Quintus continued. "It was a beautiful property. Steep hills striped with orderly lines of grapes and ringed with marble white cliffs. I made the best wine in Latium, just like my father before me. The days were long, but it was honest work, and provided there weren't too many wars to interrupt trade, I did well for myself."

It wasn't hard to imagine Quintus on a vineyard—managing disputes between workers, organizing supplies, running distribution channels, and doing it all with his quiet competence.

"Yes, it was a good life," Quintus said wistfully. "But one for a different time, I'm afraid."

"Why? Can't you go back?"

"There's nothing to go back to. The days of a single man owning a modest farm are long gone."

Elissa frowned, not understanding.

"All across Italy, wealthy nobles have been buying up plots like mine and consolidating them into massive farms that are worked exclusively by slaves." Quintus shook his head. "No one can compete with them, and even if we could, they'd just find other ways to take the land from us."

"But that's not fair," Elissa protested. "Where will the farmers go when they lose their land?"

"To the slums of Rome."

"Surely not! They must at least have the money from their farms."

"They would if they were paid a fair price for them. But men with power don't need to pay fair."

Elissa watched Quintus carefully. His features were level, but there seemed to be a new sadness in the lines on his face. "What happened to you, Quintus?"

Quintus sighed. "It's not a story I like telling."

"I'd like to hear it," she said quietly.

"Well. My debts were mysteriously called in at precisely the time I couldn't afford to pay them. We were nearing the end of a three-year drought and most of the smaller farms like mine had already folded. I was struggling to get by when some wealthy senator happened to look at a chart and notice that my plot was the only blank space that prevented him from owning the whole valley. Unfortunately for me, the senator was a patron of my lender, and seeing as I owed three times as much as I had, my options were limited. I could either work as a bond slave until my debts were paid or fight in the legions for twenty-five years and have my debts forgiven."

Elissa stared at Quintus with her mouth wide open. His story was tragic, and that he could tell it with such calm resignation astonished her.

Quintus reached over and patted her shoulder with a smile. "It could have been worse, Elissa. I may have lost my vineyard, but I kept my dignity. That's more than most in my situation have been able to say."

Elissa lowered her gaze. He might be willing to accept the Romans' greed, but she could not. "How many years do you have left in the legion?"

"Fifteen."

Her eyes went wide again. "Fifteen years of this…misery? How could the gods be so—"

Quintus cut her off sharply. "I said I kept my dignity. That opinion of the legions is your own."

Elissa recoiled at the ice in his tone. "I just meant, well, war is a far cry from farming."

The corners of his lips creased. "I know what you meant," he said apologetically. "And it's true that the adjustment was difficult. A man of three and one learning to hold a sword for the first time is no glorious sight. Particularly when you're sparring with honor-mad patricians finally out from their father's thumb."

"And that wasn't misery?"

Quintus chuckled. "Oh, to be sure, it was miserable for a while. But I met Marcus soon enough."

Elissa turned away quickly, and her hands tightened on the reins. She should have known the conversation would return to the centurion.

"I know your thoughts on the man, Elissa. But hear mine." When she didn't protest, he continued. "I was having a particularly bad time with a cruel man twice my size. We were sparring one day, and the man had me on my rear and still wouldn't let up. He swung until the shield was out of my hands, and then he just kept swinging. I was sure my bones had cracked under the force of his blows. I think a couple did, actually," he added.

Elissa was horrified. "That man was the centurion?"

"No, of course not! That man is long since dead. Marcus was the one who threw himself in front of me to stop him. Then he threatened him and all the other recruits with violence should they ever act so dishonorably again. Marcus was still practically a boy. Just one and eight, I believe. But the other recruits were already afraid of him." Quintus shrugged. "The only unfortunate effect of my special treatment was that I never did learn to spar. All the other men avoided fighting with me once they realized I was under Marcus's protection."

Elissa stayed silent for a few minutes. This was not the centurion she knew. "Why...why would he do that for you?"

"Well, he did have a price."

"What was it?" she asked reluctantly. She thought of the price the centurion had extracted for rescuing her last night. She shuddered. At least he'd let Quintus live. Unlike that poor boy he'd nearly killed.

"He wanted me to teach him the ledgers. He said a lesson every night was the cost of his protection."

Elissa was incredulous. "*That's* what he wanted in return? For you to teach him the ledgers?"

Quintus turned in the saddle so he was looking directly at her. "Well, yes. What did you think he'd want? He knew he'd be an officer soon, and that a well-run logistical operation often decides the battle before the field is even set. Of course, he learned everything I could teach within a year, and our arrangement quickly grew one-sided. But he is a loyal man, and he kept me around anyway." Quintus faced the column of men ahead of them, and his eyes lingered on the man leading it.

"I would give my life for that man. And so would everyone up there. That's why we never lose in battle. It's true we drill harder and longer than any of the other maniples. But that's not it. We go into battle knowing that if we don't come out, our lives will have served a greater purpose. We'll have died not only for our country but for someone who knew us, cared for us, sacrificed for us. Someone who would gladly have died for us in turn."

Silence hung in the air for a long time afterward. Quintus stayed in his own private thoughts, and Elissa stayed in hers. She believed that Quintus loved Marcus, and the centurion had acted nobly in protecting him. But how could she reconcile his story with the facts of her own? The man had prevented her from returning home, taken her captive and treated her like his property. She'd been humiliated, terrified and assaulted, and she blamed him for all of it.

"Why couldn't he have just let me go, Quintus?"

Quintus jumped in the saddle, obviously startled by her abrupt return to the present.

"I…Elissa." He stopped himself and seemed to regain his footing. "Are you sure the alternative would have been so much better? A lone woman travelling across a country at war is not in an enviable position. What honorable man would leave someone to that fate?" He paused, and then said the truth Elissa was unwilling to hear. "Besides, if you're so desperate to get back, why did you leave in the first place?"

She closed her eyes and let the familiar feeling of regret wash over her. What *did* she think she was returning to? Her father's anger at her escape was unlikely to be blunted by relief at her return. His humiliation would probably be doubled when he found out she'd been captured by Romans.

She would be labeled a traitor. A reckless girl who'd brought ruin on her family by daring to question the fate the gods had laid out for her. Hers would be a cautionary tale mothers would whisper to their daughters if they were reluctant to marry.

The tears she hadn't cried after Marcus had captured her, after she'd left Messia and Laris, after Flaminius had attacked her, all came in earnest now, and she was helpless to stop them. Was there no escaping this life of sadness and misery? Could she truly only exchange one pair of chains for another?

Elissa's shoulders sagged as tears ran down her face. There was no going back to what her life had been before. She pictured her father—tall, austere and utterly unreachable. She thought of her escape and the galloping horses that had nearly crushed her. She had risked everything that morning—her safety, a comfortable life, the tenuous acceptance of her father. She had gambled, and she had lost. This was her true fate.

Elissa was numb the rest of the morning. She cried until her eyes were dry, and then she felt nothing. No more fear for the future, no more longing for the past, only the empty present. Her horse's withers rose and fell beneath her. She was so distracted she didn't even notice when Marcus rode up to her.

When she finally saw him, she noticed the accusatory glare he levelled at Quintus. He lifted his eyebrows, obviously demanding an explanation.

Quintus shrugged. How was he to know that one comment would have spun her off tilt?

Marcus pulled his horse up beside Elissa and looked down at her.

"Come, Elissa," he said quietly. "I will lunch with you."

Elissa glanced up at him, uncaring. She didn't agree or protest, but let her horse follow when Marcus turned back to his maniple. His men had stopped marching and were sitting on their packs, breaking bread and passing it among them, snatching a few moments of rest in the middle of another hard day. As they approached, Marcus slowed his horse so Elissa's was walking beside him. The men seemed to notice their centurion immediately, and Elissa faintly registered the shock on some of their faces. Several stood and reached for the shields they'd set down. Marcus ignored them and moved his horse closer to Elissa's.

"Ey, Centurion! Who's the foreign broad?"

Marcus didn't turn to look. "Sit down, Julius." His voice rang with authority.

The man dropped like a heavy sack, his legs bending as quickly as if Marcus had pushed him. It was a clear signal to the rest of his men that they were not to question him. Marcus rode into a forest of widely spaced trees. The sun was high in the sky and the pine trees cast short shadows. The dry grass and needles crunched under their horses' feet. A light blanket of snow against the tree trunks would have completed the scene perfectly.

Marcus led them a bit farther into the forest before he dismounted. He walked around to Elissa's horse and held the reins. She slid from its back without thinking and walked to the trunk of a large tree, resting against the rough bark. She closed her eyes. She didn't know why they were here or what he planned to do, but she couldn't bring herself to care. Elissa sank down by the trunk and pulled her knees to her chest; it was all she could do to hold herself together.

Marcus walked up to her, paused for a moment, then lowered himself onto the ground. He crossed his legs in front him like a school boy.

Elissa lifted her head to look at him and immediately

caught sight of the new ring on his finger. "Is that Tiberius's?"

Marcus's hand jerked to the ring protectively. He held it between two fingers and squeezed. "Yes."

"Flaminius killed him?"

Marcus's face grew dark and Elissa could feel the cloud of anger condensing around him. Good. She wanted his anger palpable; she wanted to reach out to it and pull herself back to caring.

"Yes," he replied tightly.

Elissa nodded curtly. "That's too bad."

Marcus seemed startled by her response. Perhaps he'd been expecting more compassion. But what was the use? The gods didn't care how you felt, so why should she?

"Do you have a brother, Elissa?" Marcus asked slowly.

"Yes," she replied, not even bothering to consider whether she should lie.

"Is he alive?"

"I hope so."

"Where?"

Elissa sighed and turned to the forest around her. Her eyes hardly registered what she saw. "Maybe here."

Marcus frowned.

Elissa nearly laughed. Was he listening for signs that her brother was about to burst from the forest? Wouldn't that be a nice surprise? "I mean in Italy," she said, deciding to spare him the trouble. "If he's alive, he's with Hannibal."

Marcus's body relaxed and he nodded shortly. "You are fortunate then." He seemed mildly annoyed.

Elissa felt a jolt of indignation. "Am I really? I didn't consider it fortunate when you kidnapped me. And a dead mother and resentful father weren't exactly Fortuna's blessings, either." She had a right to bitterness, didn't she? Despite all her mistakes, she'd been damned from the start.

Marcus straightened and studied her. His mind passed over her familiar anger and went straight to her second remark. Her mother was dead? That was quite a loss, especially for a young woman. An image of his own mother came unbeckoned to his thoughts. Aurelia, as she'd been in his childhood. Tall and distinguished, with only a few strands of gray peppering her dark hair back then. A small smile often played on her lips, and her eyes twinkled with laughter. But those hints of humor were only for her sons and her husband. To everyone else, she was the implacable Roman matron they expected.

"What was her name?" he asked quietly.

Elissa was quiet for so long, Marcus thought she might not have heard him.

"Jezebel," she said finally.

Marcus nodded gently. "How did she die?"

Elissa lifted her eyes. Marcus's heart skipped a beat as he peered into those twin pools of pain.

"Me."

He shook his head in disapproval. "Elissa, if she died during childbirth, that's not your fault—"

"She didn't." Elissa cut him off. "She gave birth to me easily enough. But afterward, when she saw what she'd made, she killed herself."

Marcus pushed himself onto his knees and closed the space between them in an instant. He wanted to reach into that deep well of sorrow and rip it out, and he wanted to cause physical harm to whoever had given her the idea she'd just told him. He leaned over to touch her cheek, but she turned her face away. Marcus reluctantly sat back on his heels and took a deep breath. He had to know who had hurt her. But he needed a different tactic.

"I, uh, maybe I know what it's like to blame yourself," he said haltingly while staring over her head.

Elissa looked back at him. Her mouth was tight with one

eyebrow raised. Not encouraging him, but not saying no, either.

"I, well—" Marcus stopped and forced himself to meet her eyes. If he was going to do this, he would do it right. "It's my fault Tiberius died. I could have stopped it if I'd been there." Marcus blinked hard a few times. He hadn't admitted his guilt to anyone but his parents.

"How?" Elissa slanted her head to the side and a thick strand of hair fell over her shoulder. Some of the animation had returned to her voice.

"I was supposed to be a politician like him. Our grand-father's wealth and fame were sufficient to buy all future Gracchi sons the right to be senators. Had I taken that path, maybe I could've stopped his murder. He would at least have had another ally in the Senate to support his cause."

"Do you think that would've changed anything?"

Marcus sighed and shrugged his shoulders. "I don't know. I would've made a lousy politician. But I would've known he was in danger. And then I would never have left his side."

"And then you'd have been murdered, too."

"Probably," he said, uncaring.

"Would that have been better?"

Marcus turned his attention back to Elissa. She was leaning forward now, her focus on him. He'd brought her back to the present.

"Maybe. Not for my family. But perhaps for me. It certainly would've been simpler."

Elissa leaned back until her head was resting against the trunk. "Death is always simple."

"Is it?"

"For the dead."

Marcus smiled humorlessly at the truth of her words. "It was complicated for you," he stated.

Elissa shut her eyes before she spoke. Her voice sounded strained, as though she had to force the words around some obstacle. "There's supposed to be a reason you commit suicide. Honor, duty and the like. Giving birth to a healthy girl is not one of them." Her voice cracked. "Unless there's something very wrong with that girl."

Marcus jumped up; he grabbed her by the wrists and lifted her onto her feet. His arms had closed around her before she could make a sound. He buried his lips in her dark hair and whispered fiercely. "Elissa Mago, there is nothing wrong with you! If I even heard a man suggest otherwise, I'd kill him on sight."

Elissa pulled herself from his arms and took a step back, her eyes wide with surprise. Then her mouth turned up in a dry smile. "Well, thank you, but I can't have you killing my father."

Her dark humor did not have the intended effect on Marcus. He straightened his shoulders and his jaw tensed with anger. Her *father* blamed her for her mother's suicide? What a terrible, immoral—

Marcus stepped forward again, and this time he took her face between his hands. She tried to move away, but he held her firmly. He looked down into those shining jewels and said very clearly, so he could be sure she heard him, "It was not your fault, Elissa."

Then he dropped his mouth onto hers. He didn't care that he was shocking her. He needed her to feel the truth of his words. To press them into her body with his tongue and twine them in her hair. He needed her to believe him, just as he needed her to want him.

Elissa was in a familiar position—flat on her back with the roof spinning above her. The furs lying over her body felt itchy and she shifted her shoulders. Marcus twitched beside her; he probably wasn't actually asleep. Elissa closed her eyes and tried to force the memory of their kiss that afternoon from her mind. She brought her palm to her cheek and traced the outline of her lips with her thumb. He had kissed them with alarming urgency. His palm had cradled her cheek like this, and guided her mouth closer to his. Had she really let that happen? She'd been too numb and preoccupied to recognize his intensity for what it was, and she'd already lost the will to stop once she realized where it was going.

The worst part of the whole thing was her body's reaction. When he finally did let her go, her body had protested resentfully. Her lips had stayed parted long after she should have closed them tight. Even now, Elissa found herself wondering what it would have felt like to allow his tongue the entrance to her mouth it had so desperately desired. If she'd thrown her head back and given herself over to him, would his hands have moved from her back onto her breasts? Would he have lifted his knee and pushed it into the spot that burned at the pit of her stomach?

Elissa's fists tightened with shame. She bolted upright and shoved her legs out from under the furs. As soon as she got her feet on the ground, she was going to march straight out of this tent. Damn the consequences. Anywhere was better than here. She'd hardly managed to sit up before he clasped her arm. Elissa looked down and saw the centurion's olive hand against her pale skin. She groaned and let him pull her back down to the bed. Now her body was facing his and his hand was on her arm, even closer than before.

"Elissa," Marcus said softly.

"Don't," she said harshly. "Just don't." She jerked her arm away from him but her body stayed in place.

Marcus didn't move to take back her arm. It was too dark to see more than the outline of his face. A lock of dark hair flopped across his forehead. One arm was bent over his head and the other rested on the furs. It was the dead of winter, and he still slept uncovered. His bare chest seemed massive next to hers; the hard lines of his arms curved into rounded muscles at his shoulders, with the broad expanse of his torso below. His skin was stretched tight over muscles that looked as though they'd been cut from granite. Some sensation flickered in Elissa's stomach as she watched him, and she groaned a second time. She drew up her knees into her chest and turned away. The way her body was behaving was the furthest thing from acceptable. She was a Mago, a daughter of Carthage, and she was sleeping with the enemy. And even worse, part of her was enjoying it. Elissa's breath caught in her throat and a strangled sob escaped her lips. She squeezed her eyes shut to keep the welling tears at bay. Gods, this could not be happening here!

"Elissa," Marcus said again. His voice was hoarse.

A second sob wracked her body, and before she could stop it, her shoulders were shaking and the tension at the back of her throat had dissolved into tears. Marcus reached across the bed and pulled her into his chest. He slid his arms around her back, and her cheeks rested against his warm skin. The soft, steady pressure of his hands on her back was comforting. He whispered softly in her ear as he soothed her. Elissa couldn't remember ever being held like this. She shut her swollen eyelids and let the sadness take hold. She felt lifeless. As though she'd lost her hold on the world and might drift away like a leaf in the wind. She had no past to return to, no future to hope for, and no more fight to prevent her from caring. She was bare skin over bones.

Marcus moved his hand to the center of her back, and even through her tunic, Elissa could feel the heat coming off his body. There was so much vitality pulsing under his skin, it was a shame she couldn't take some of it for herself. Elissa freed an arm from his embrace and placed her palm below his shoulder. Her hand curved around his bicep, then moved down to his elbow. She felt the skin roughen and his muscles constrict under her touch. She shifted her hand up to his shoulder, and then back down again. She did that a few more times until his skin grew noticeably hotter. His whole arm had become taut.

It was curious, she thought, that someone like her could have such an effect on someone like him. She moved her hand across his arm and onto his torso. His chest tightened as she trailed her fingers across it and down the ridges of his stomach. She let them fall to the side to feel the faint outline of his hip.

Marcus groaned and pushed his hip deeper into her hand. Elissa's eyes went to his face for the first time. His eyes were closed, his lips parted. His brow was furrowed as if he was deep in concentration. Elissa hesitated and then started to take her hand away. She didn't know exactly what he was feeling, but it looked too similar to this afternoon's intensity for her comfort. But as she shifted to pull her hand back, her arm brushed against his stomach. Elissa gasped. The male length of him rested there—rigid, hard and shockingly large. Elissa yanked her hand back as if burnt, suddenly understanding the source of the vitality and animation that had fascinated her moments before.

His eyes were still closed and he grunted indignantly and rolled toward her. Elissa's legs shot in front of her and she launched herself out of bed, taking most of the furs with her as she went.

"No!" she sputtered, searching in vain for words that would be both apologetic and reprimanding.

Marcus sat up in bed with a pained expression on his face. "Elissa, I was sure we were past this. I'm not going to hurt you."

Elissa took a step back. Her eyes were wide and her whole body tensed for flight. Disbelief and loathing ran through her mind faster than she could attach thoughts to them. What was she doing? Seducing the enemy? Inviting him to take her virtue?

She stepped back again and her whole body began to shake. The ground felt so unsteady, her knees threatened to buckle. Elissa reached out a hand for something to balance herself, but her legs gave out too soon and she crumpled to the floor. Her side hit the ground and her momentum carried her onto her back.

Elissa looked through her hazy vision at the tent's roof, which had begun to spin. Here she was again, staring at something that shouldn't be reeling, and helpless to make it stop. Marcus's face appeared above her and she was dimly aware of his hands around her back. She tried to ignore the sensations, seeking the sweet blankness of her overwrought mind instead. She needed the release of oblivion.

CHAPTER 11

Entering a new city was always chaotic. A legion this large stretched out over miles as it marched, and although they maintained a tight formation, there was room to move about if you were a centurion. Marcus could ride up and down the line of legionaries, talking to his men, assessing their fitness. He could feel the hills fall away under his horse's strong legs as he scanned the horizon for danger. Sometimes, when the day was long and uneventful, he would imagine a line of barbarians appearing atop the nearest hill. He would race to sound the horn, but his men's feet would already be moving before he could get there. They would close ranks in a tight rectangle, each man exactly an arm's length from the next. The *hastati* would form the front. They were the young men who could only afford light armor; Marcus would never put them in much danger. That was for his strongest fighters—the *principes*, who would arrange themselves behind the *hastati* in a wide triangle to plunge through the barbarian line. Behind them were the *triari*, the unflappable veterans and the wall of steel behind his troops. They would give the younger men courage and shelter should they need to break ranks and regroup.

But that was battle; and battle was not for today. Today, Marcus watched quietly as his men made their way through the high walls of Arretium. They were quartering in the city for the time being. If battle should find them here, there would be no carefully orchestrated formations or clash of opposing lines. It would be a siege. A long, drawn-out exercise in suffering as they waited for reinforcements they would never know for sure were coming. Marcus shuddered as he watched the walls grow taller ahead of him. He hated cities.

He twisted in the saddle to look at the back of his maniple instead. He'd told Quintus to ride there with Elissa. He couldn't pick them out from the thickening throng of bodies, but he didn't need to see her to know what she looked like. Exactly the same as when she'd fainted in his tent three days ago. Pale and drawn, like she was living in a tomb. Marcus sighed. She'd gone somewhere he couldn't reach, and as much as he would have liked to, he couldn't use her simmering desire to bring her back. The conflict between what she thought she wanted and what she actually wanted had brought her to this place. Her mind was at war with itself, and with her willfulness turned inward, she was finding the only opponent she couldn't best. He'd left her with Quintus during the day and taken to sleeping on a rolled-up mat on the ground during the night. Let her have her war. He needed to focus on his.

The tops of his horse's ears bobbed evenly as he trotted between the stone walls of Arretium. At least his horse was comfortable following the thousands of men who'd already entered. Marcus looked around at the shoddy wooden buildings on the outskirts of the city. Worn dirt paths weaved between structures, the dull monotony of its citizens' lives stamped into the earth. Not that his life, traipsing around Italy after an enemy who refused to give battle, was much of an improvement. Mass hysteria followed mass derision as predictably as the tides whenever reports of Hannibal's army came in. Allied tribes joined him, then defected, then joined again. One day, the Carthaginians were pathetic merchants taking up arms; the next, they were vicious soldiers with an army of wild beasts ready to tear the Romans apart. Marcus knew better than to believe half of it. It was all the same to him anyway. The Roman army would fight no matter who was on the other side. And they would live or they would die, and it didn't much matter which one.

Marcus lowered his eyes as one of his men appeared in front of him. If they only knew how their commander really felt. This whole cause was hopeless because they fought for a side with a rotting heart. Its consul was a murderer, its Senate was corrupt and self-interested, its, well, its centurions harbored enemy fugitives within their ranks—fighting Rome's enemies with one hand while stabbing her in the back with the other. Marcus winced. Thank the gods his noble grandfather wasn't alive to watch him drag the Gracchi name through the mud.

His horse's head suddenly shot in the air and he leapt to the side. Marcus swerved dangerously off-center but managed to right himself by pulling back on the reins. He forced his horse to a stop, then straightened to see what had spooked him. A man had jumped out from the scattered people who lined the street. He stood in the middle of the road, directly in the way of the thousands of legionaries still to pass. He was staring at a point somewhere behind Marcus.

Marcus spun his horse in a tight circle to bring the man back in front of him. The man's dark features were contorted in a look of shock.

"Watch it!" Marcus growled.

The man's eyes immediately met his, and his alarm seemed to double. His focus returned to whatever he was watching over Marcus's shoulder. Marcus whipped his horse around in the direction the man was staring.

Elissa. He was staring at Elissa. She had closed the distance between them while he was distracted and now rode only a few lengths behind. Elissa's eyes flicked up to Marcus's face. She stopped. Her gaze moved to the man behind him and any remaining color drained from her cheeks. Marcus's hands tightened on the reins. This man must recognize her. Or maybe he knew a Carthaginian when he saw one. A single word from him, and Elissa would be exposed. Marcus would be helpless to stop it. Or to save her.

He drove his heels into his horse's sides with all the urgency of battle. The stallion snorted and bunched his hind legs. Marcus twisted the stallion's head around so the man was positioned between his ears and then kicked a second time. The stallion leapt.

They landed on empty ground instead of on the man.

There was a commotion as several people along the road scrambled aside to avoid his horse.

Marcus halted and spun toward the crowd. The first line of people had scattered, revealing a shop door swinging behind them. Marcus started toward it but stopped when he realized the door was too short. He'd have to go on foot. He hastily pulled his leg over the saddle. Quintus's hand was already on the reins.

"Marcus." Quintus's voice was low in warning.

Marcus ignored him and glanced at Elissa. She had stayed beside Quintus. Her back was straight as a rod, but her face was impassive.

"He's gone, Marcus." Quintus's face pleaded with him to stay calm.

Marcus looked at his friend. He hesitated, then took a deep breath and brought his leg back over the saddle. Maybe he was overreacting. He really had no idea who the man was or what he might do. Jumping off his horse and giving chase was likely to attract more attention to Elissa than it would deflect. Marcus clenched his jaw as logic returned to him. Gods, he really was acting like an idiot. *A strange man merely looks at Elissa and he goes wild.*

Nevertheless, he watched Elissa more carefully as he settled back on his horse. Her lips were pulled tight and she still looked pale, but she'd definitely lost the deadened expression she'd worn before. The skin on Marcus's arms prickled. There was something off about that man. He glanced at the door the man had disappeared behind. He was probably long gone by now, safely hidden in the anonymous milieu of the city. Perhaps nothing would come of it. He told himself it was farfetched to believe Elissa knew someone else in Italy, and even more unlikely that she'd managed to hide her recognition. She must've only been afraid to see an African, probably a Numidian with the Carthaginian army, and worried about what would happen if her identity was revealed.

Marcus pushed his horse to a walk and motioned for Elissa to fall in beside him. He wouldn't let her out of his sight until he was absolutely certain this man wasn't a threat. It would be disastrous if Flaminius learned the truth about her. The only thing he knew for sure when it came to Elissa, when it came to anything really, was that Flaminius could not have her.

Taanit.

Taanit was here. In Arretium. She'd hardly believed it when she first saw him. She'd looked away to examine a modest temple to Juno, and then there he was, standing in the middle of the road with Marcus staring angrily down at him. Elissa had frozen, and panic had arrested her face in a blessedly impassive mask. Joy and relief were quickly replaced with terror as she watched Marcus kick his massive stallion into a gallop. She was sure it was a race that would end with her oldest friend trampled beneath the horse's feet.

By some miracle, Taanit had noticed the danger at the same moment and ducked into the crowd. By the time

Marcus had spun back around, Taanit was gone, and there was nothing left for Elissa to do but quell her pounding heart and ride up to Marcus. She must have been moderately successful at hiding her reaction, because after carefully scrutinizing her, he'd left the question unasked. Although he hadn't let her out of his sight for the rest of the day.

Elissa was tired of lying, tired of hiding. She considered simply telling Marcus who the man was and that he could bring her safely home. Marcus was so unpredictable; he might actually let her go with Taanit. These past few days it seemed that she distressed him as much as he distressed her. She couldn't understand the simmering intensity she felt when he was nearby, the guilt she felt afterward, and the resentment overlaying it all. So she'd tried to simply tuck it all somewhere she couldn't feel. Marcus, in what seemed a genuinely selfless act, had helped her by staying away. So why did that only make her feel worse?

Elissa forced her eyes to open. She made herself examine the room around her instead of the confusion inside her head. It was beautiful. Richly-colored tapestries hung on the walls, and the sleeping couch in the corner was laden with thick furs. A small table with wine and grapes waited unobtrusively off to one side. But the best part was that it was hers. Marcus had assigned her private chambers in the wing of the *domus* he'd secured for himself and some of his men. This home was much richer than Messia and Laris's had been. Its wings spun outward from a cool, green garden at its center. A glass window in Elissa's room overlooked a bubbling fountain in the corner of the yard. Arretium was a rich city, and one of the largest in Etruria, but it, too, would be left barren by the growing legion that had entered its walls.

Elissa stood and walked to the pitcher of wine in the corner of the room. She poured herself a cup and took a measured sip. It was well watered, but her lips still puckered at the memory of the last wine she'd tasted. The warm liquid ran smoothly down her throat and into her belly. By the time she'd finished the cup, a tingling calm had descended over her. Elissa poured a second helping and sat on the couch, turning her mind back to Taanit with renewed calm. She needed to find him and get word to him about where she was staying. But how? Marcus wasn't about to let her roam the streets alone, and she didn't have any friends to carry a message.

A succession of quick taps sounded at the door.

"Come in," she called, grateful for the distraction from her intractable problem.

A large man with a head of white-blond hair walked into the room. He was dressed in a worn tunic and carried a tray of food.

Elissa blinked several times as she stood. He was a Gaul. His blond hair and light features were indisputable. She'd never seen one before. Elissa had always thought the Romans' fear of their barbarian neighbors was overblown, but seeing the barrel chest and massive arms of this Gaul, she was no longer so sure. He set the tray of food down on the table and waited by the door. That was odd. Perhaps he wanted to see if she needed anything else? Elissa turned quickly toward the food, not wanting to upset the man by staring. As she reached for a fig, she noticed a tiny white triangle poking out from underneath one of the bowls. She frowned and lifted the bowl. A small square of papyrus lay in the middle of the tray.

Elissa whirled toward the Gaul with a dozen questions on her lips. But the man was already gone. She turned slowly back to the tray and reached for the papyrus with trembling hands. It was rough against her fingers as she unfolded it. She let her eyes dart quickly over Taanit's loose, slanted scrawl.

Elissa.
Meet me on the southern road outside the domus.
Two hours after dark.
I'll explain then.

Elissa shut her eyes tightly, then read it again. There could be no mistaking Taanit's writing and his clipped tone.

Tonight. He was coming for her tonight. Elissa felt dizzy with relief as she lowered herself back onto the couch. Taanit was safe. He would take her home. Back to Carthage. Back to her father. Elissa winced, thinking again of her uncertain welcome. She took a deep breath and tried to relax. Being humiliated in Carthage was better than being a traitor in Rome.

There was a second round of knocking at the door.

Elissa stood, and then sat back down. "Who is it?" she called.

"It's me, Elissa." Quintus's level voice came from the other side of the door.

Elissa bit her lip as her mind moved quickly. It was several hours before dark, and Marcus and Quintus would probably dine before nightfall. There was no chance she'd be able to hide her imminent escape from Marcus. He would know something was wrong as soon as he saw her and then refuse to let her out of his sight.

"Elissa!" Quintus called again. The door rattled in its frame.

"Don't come in!" she blurted. "I'm unwell and I wish to sleep."

The door stilled as Quintus took in this new piece of information. "May I still see you? Perhaps there is something I can do for you," he said more quietly.

Yes, Quintus, there is so much you can do for me. Show me the way out of the villa for one, bring me two horses for another, and tell Marcus I'm sorry, for lying, and…everything else. I hope he avenges his brother.

"No, Quintus," she said instead. "I'm very tired, that's all.

I'd like to rest now." She let her voice trail off as if sleep could claim her at any moment.

There was a pause on the other side of the door. "I hope you rest well."

Elissa heard him turn from the door. His footsteps grew faint as he walked back down the hall.

"I'm sorry," she whispered. For what, she didn't really know.

The light dimmed slowly that evening. The sun hovered on the edge of the horizon and cloaked the city in a dark gray, neither light nor dark—a protracted period of uncertainty. But night came eventually, as it always does, and Elissa started counting as soon as she could no longer see the fountain beneath her window. *Two hours.* The moon would be well along its worn track across the sky by then.

Elissa had half-expected Marcus to come barging into her room despite her request for privacy and rest. She imagined him banging on the door, demanding to see her, and some of her old indignation returned. Gods, that man was overbearing. She was no one's prisoner! Unwelcome reminders of her previous escapes strayed across her thoughts. This would be her third attempt. The first had ended in the death of her horse, and the second had nearly gotten her raped. Was she crazy to believe this time would be different? No, she told herself firmly. This time she had help. And besides, it was Taanit, so she had to try.

"Maybe that's all I can do," she said to the silent darkness outside her window. Maybe it was enough to know she'd fought against her shackles, and whether she'd succeeded was beside the point. Elissa smiled in spite of the growing knot in her stomach. She was already starting to sound more like her old self.

Elissa waited until the moon was in its appointed place before leaving her room. It would be safer for Taanit to wait than for her to. She grabbed her cloak from where she'd thrown it on the couch. She hesitated for a moment, rolling the fabric between her fingers. The burgundy coloring was deep and rich, beautiful, precisely because it wasn't what it was supposed to be. She tossed it over her shoulders. It was less visible in the dark, too.

Elissa put her fingertips on the door and slowly pushed it open. She poked her head out and looked down the hall in one direction and then the other.

Empty.

She opened the door fully and stepped out of the room. The door closed with a soft click. Elissa paused, listening for sounds of movement. Footsteps rustled on the bottom floor, pots clanged in the *culina*, but there was no muffled hum of low voices, no chiming of cutlery as someone reached for another dish. Elissa breathed a sigh of relief. The evening meal was over. *Good.* It would've been much more difficult to get out to the street unseen. But that also meant she didn't know where Marcus was.

She tiptoed down the hall and paused at the entrance to the *tablinum*, thinking he might be spending an evening at the ledgers. But the edges of the door were dark, and it was too late to be working without candlelight. He must be with his men. Elissa had heard several legionaries grumbling about late-night drills this morning.

She stopped. Her distracted thoughts had carried her right past the stairs and back down the hall she'd started from. Elissa nearly groaned when she saw the door to her room reappear up ahead. She needed to concentrate on how to get out of here, not thinking about the centurion's whereabouts. Elissa renewed her concentration and directed her wayward feet to the wooden stairs leading to the atrium. She placed a foot on the top stair and slowly eased her weight down.

Silence. She placed her other foot on the stair below. Again, there was no grating creak to give her away. Elissa repeated her steps until she stood on the tiled floor of the atrium. She was protected from view by a small alcove that led out from the stairs. Leaning forward, she carefully peeked around the corner into the atrium.

She jerked back instantly.

A man was staring right at her.

Leather soles padded along the tiles toward her.

Elissa backed up until her calves were against the bottom stair. She could either try to run up the stairs and into her room before the man caught her, or she could have some legitimate pretext for being downstairs hiding in dark corners. She had just decided on the former option when the light from the atrium suddenly dimmed. A man stood at the entrance to the alcove. He was so large he completely blocked the room behind him. Elissa's eyes widened, and then she whirled around, intending to dash up the stairs before the lumbering giant could catch her. Unfortunately, her legs weren't as quick to react as the rest of her body, and her toe caught on the lip of the bottom stair as she turned. Her hands shot out to break the impact of her imminent fall. Inexplicably, she halted in midair with her arms straight out in front of her.

Elissa looked over her shoulder and saw the man with his arm outstretched, clutching a fistful of her burgundy cloak. The scream was halfway out before she noticed the man's other hand. His finger was on his lips, below a shocking mop of blond hair. The Gaul. The one who'd given her Taanit's note. The scream died in her throat. The Gaul released her cloak but kept his other hand on his lips.

Elissa let her arms fall to her sides. "Will you take me to him?" Her voice trembled.

The Gaul nodded slowly. He turned and walked into the atrium. He didn't stop until he was halfway across and Elissa still hadn't moved. He looked back at her and gestured with one hand.

Elissa stared at him for another moment. Then she dropped her head and followed. At some point, a person simply had nothing left to lose. The Gaul led her across the atrium and into a narrow hallway off the main room. Elissa hesitated again. The light was much dimmer here, and it was difficult to see where the hallway led. She heard a door open in front of her. Cool night air flushed the passageway, and she needed no more convincing. She forgot her trepidation and hurried down the hallway. She didn't stop again until her feet were on hard dirt instead of colored tiles.

Someone stepped out from the shadows surrounding the *domus*.

Taanit.

Elissa nearly shouted with happiness. She launched herself into his outstretched arms and pressed her face into his slender shoulders. His arms automatically closed around her waist and she squeezed him back tightly.

"Taanit," Elissa murmured into his shirt.

"Elissa." Taanit brought his arms to her shoulders. "Elissa," he repeated, gently pushing her away so he could hold her at arm's length. His eyes roved over her, looking for signs of damage. "Are you all right?"

Elissa's throat was rapidly becoming clogged. It was all she could do to frantically nod her head. She hadn't realized how desperately lonely she'd been until now. Taanit was part of her home, and he was here in front of her, greeting her lovingly.

Relief filled Taanit's familiar hazel eyes. He drew her back against the wall of the *domus* where they were protected from view of the street. Elissa suddenly remembered the Gaul and glanced around to look for him.

"He's over there." Taanit pointed his head toward the street. "Waiting to take you to safety."

"What do you mean, take me away?" She shook her head. "Wait, Taanit, where have *you* been? What happened to *you*?"

Taanit released Elissa's shoulders and gestured in the direction of the Gaul.

"I need to get you out of here, now." He took Elissa's hand and began to pull her down the road.

Elissa jerked her hand back and planted her feet. "Taanit. Tell me where we're going," she said firmly.

"Back home, Elissa," he replied earnestly. "Listen, I've known you were with the legion since the day after they caught you. I was afraid you were dead." Taanit gazed down at his feet. "Up until yesterday. When I saw you riding with that Roman centurion. I was so worried, I thought about trying to rescue you right there. But then I looked at you, and you seemed...comfortable." When he raised his eyes, his expression was reprimanding.

Elissa met Taanit's eyes. He was so different from Marcus, so unsure. She felt an inexplicable need to protect him. Her fear of returning home, her nagging sense of guilt about lying to Marcus and Quintus—he didn't need to hear any of that. "I want to go home," she said clearly.

Taanit looked relieved. "I'm going to get you there. But—I can't take you myself." He held a hand to his dark brown cheek. "I'm too conspicuous, especially with you."

Elissa frowned. "Taanit, it's just as dangerous for you in Italy! We'll go together."

Taanit shook his head. "I'll get myself back, but I can't protect you, too. The Gaul will take you. He's been a Roman slave for years, but his tribe fights for Hannibal now. He wants to fight the Romans, too. He's going to take you as far as the Tiber. I managed to get word to your father before war broke out in earnest, and he said there's a place you can stay outside Rome. There's a senator he's been bribing for years. He'll help you cross the sea."

Elissa turned away so Taanit wouldn't see the fear on her face. This was a bad plan. Too many things could go wrong; she'd have to trust too many people.

"Taanit—no, we don't even know if we can trust the Gaul."

"He delivered my message, didn't he? And I'm paying him the entire sum I made from the horses. Your father's share too."

Elissa's hand flew to her mouth. "Taanit, I'm so sorry. This is all my fault and I'm—"

She fixed her eyes on the ground. "I'm so sorry."

Taanit's shoulders sagged. "It's done, Elissa. All we can do is try to get you back home."

Elissa wanted to cry. She wanted to scream and stamp her feet like a child until everything was resolved. Look what she'd done to Taanit, her oldest and only real friend. He was born a slave and she was born free. He'd tried to make a life for himself as a freedman, he went into a trade. And she'd shown up on his boat demanding his help. Complaining about her father and the husband he'd chosen for her, insisting that she deserved better. Now they were trapped in Italy at constant risk of being killed or enslaved. She'd impoverished Taanit, put his life and freedom in danger. And after he'd spent months searching for her, she wasn't even sure she wanted to leave? She was as evil as a Siren, luring the men who tried to help her into a tempestuous storm and then dashing them against the rocks.

Elissa forced herself to meet Taanit's eyes again. She'd hurt him enough already. "You're right. I'll do whatever you ask."

Surprise flashed in his eyes, followed by relief. He reached for her hand and squeezed her palm. "This is the best way, Elissa, trust me."

She smiled back weakly. "I do trust you, Taanit. And I'm sorry. For everything."

Taanit seemed about to say more, but he changed his mind and clasped her hand instead. He guided her away from the *domus* and down the road. The Gaul was waiting for them on the side, his arms crossed. Outside, he didn't appear quite so large anymore. Elissa gave him a brief smile as he looked her over. His frown never wavered.

Taanit pulled a bag from under his cloak and held it up to the Gaul. "The sum we agreed on."

The coins clinked together as the bag changed hands. The Gaul tucked it away quickly, then started to walk off.

Elissa turned to Taanit. She was suddenly flush with desperation. They'd only just found each other again! Taanit's face crumpled and he drew her into a tight embrace. He pressed his face into her hair and inhaled deeply.

"I'm sorry, Elissa. This was the best I could do."

Elissa's heart constricted in her chest. She forced a hand between them and gently pushed him back. Her voice was thick when she spoke.

"Taanit, you've done more than I should ever have asked for. You and Barro, you've been everything to me. Please, I'm begging you, think of me no more. I'll be safe. I only want the same for you."

Taanit's eyes flew to her lips and she could have sworn he wanted to kiss her. She stepped away swiftly, and after giving his hand a final squeeze, she followed the Gaul down the road.

They were going the wrong way.

They were definitely going the wrong way. They should have been heading to the outskirts of the city, not farther into its center. But when Elissa mentioned this to the Gaul, he merely grunted and replied with one word.

"Horses."

Elissa shook her head in frustration. The horses were stabled on the outskirts of the city. They certainly weren't going to find any in the villas that had risen up around them. This was a very wealthy part of the city. Fortresses of stone and brick spiralled upward from the road. The moon illuminated their clay roofs far above. The streets were quiet at this time of night; respectable inhabitants knew better than to be out after dark. Denied their prey, the criminals and whores clustered in the seedier parts of town. And where the whores went, the legionnaires followed. Elissa found herself wondering again where Marcus was. She thought of him spending an evening with one of the buxom women she'd seen in Vetulonium. The image made her angry.

When they rounded the next bend in the road and there was still no sign of a stable, Elissa's attention snapped back to the man in front of her. She would not follow him blindly.

The Gaul took a few more steps and then stopped. He slowly turned around.

Elissa placed her hands on her hips and stuck out her chin. If they were travelling all the way to Rome together, they'd better learn to communicate.

"No horses," she said, pointing in the direction they were walking.

The Gaul's scowl deepened as he moved back toward her.

"Where are we going?" Elissa lifted her shoulders and brought her hands out to either side.

The Gaul didn't answer. He continued toward her without slowing. He placed his massive palms around her waist, hoisted her in the air and tossed her over his shoulder.

Elissa screamed.

The Gaul put his hand on her back and pushed. Any remaining air was forced from her lungs.

"Quiet," he grunted. "We're meeting someone."

Elissa went limp. *Meeting someone?* That could be good or

bad; it depended on who they were meeting. Perhaps it was the senator Taanit had mentioned. Elissa opened her mouth to ask, but the Gaul released his grip and let her slide to the ground.

"Walk or I carry."

Elissa shut her mouth and walked.

They hadn't gone far before the Gaul stopped again. They were outside an inconspicuous beige villa. The building was large and windowless, with only a narrow entrance opening onto the street. Two legionaries stood there. The butts of their spears pierced the ground and the brims of their helmets hooded their eyes.

Elissa glanced at the Gaul. He motioned to the entrance and the two legionaries stepped aside. Were they expected? Elissa's eyes darted back and forth from the Gaul to the legionaries and the darkened entrance. She didn't know which was more threatening. But if the Gaul wanted her to go in there, she wasn't going to have much choice in the matter. So who were they meeting? Surely they must be Roman if legionaries were guarding the entrance. But was it a bad Roman or a—not bad Roman? Elissa shook her head in disbelief. Did she really consider some Romans "not bad" now?

Something hard pressed into Elissa's back. The Gaul's hand was behind her, firmly pushing her through the doorway. She spun her head around and pinned him with her most vicious glare. He didn't seem to notice. Elissa let him direct her into the villa. The hallway was dark, but she could feel hard marble under her feet as the Gaul's footsteps thudded loudly behind her. The light brightened as she walked, and the low drone of conversation filtered through the hall. Elissa slowed and then stopped.

A large atrium opened up in front of her. The room was packed with Romans. Legionaries of every rank were clustered together, deep in pensive conversation or raucous with laughter.

Tribunes with wobbling stacks of papyrus scurried between them. A group of Roman matrons stood in the corner, as still and silent as the Corinthian column that partially obscured them. Elissa took a step backward. This was no place to meet someone. Not someone who would help them. She collided with the Gaul's solid chest. He reached around and locked one of his massive hands around her wrist.

"Come." He gave her wrist a sharp tug that forced her back into motion.

He pulled Elissa between couches and dining tables to the largest cluster of people in the middle of the room. The Gaul didn't slow as they reached the crowd; instead, he cut a path straight through. The men skittered out of the way, and a chorus of grumbles rose up around them. Elissa trailed in his wake, trying to keep pace with his larger strides. Her cheeks grew redder and redder as every person they passed stopped talking to stare at her.

The Gaul halted. He jerked on Elissa's arm to propel her out from behind him. Elissa slowly lifted her eyes from the floor. She took in a gilded serving table, a silk dining couch and, belatedly, a man sitting in its center. She saw his untarnished greaves, his decorated belt and the slight bulge at the bottom of his breastplate. Thick, ruddy fingers curled around a gold cup. She didn't need to see any more.

Elissa turned and ran.

Right into the Gaul. He grabbed her wrists and rammed his knee into her stomach.

Elissa crumpled to the floor. Her knees crashed into the cold marble and her head fell forward onto her neck.

His breath was hot against her ear.

"Got you."

Elissa's arms were wrenched painfully overhead. Her body was forced to follow to keep her arms in their sockets. A hand wrapped around her chin and shoved her head up, and Elissa's hair fell back from her face.

Flaminius.

He took his hand off her chin, opened his palm and struck it across her cheek. Elissa cried out in shock. Tears sprang to her eyes as the stinging cascaded down her body.

Flaminius grabbed her hair and yanked up to keep her from sagging to the floor. "Little bitch," he growled in her ear.

He raised his voice to the whole room. "Behold, honored guests!" He paused until every face in the room was turned toward them. "Behold the enemy of Carthage!"

Flaminius's hand shook as he yelled, and Elissa's head flapped lifelessly in time to his voice.

"And not just any Punic slut," Flaminius continued to the rapt audience. "This bitch is a Roman's whore!"

There was a rapid shuffling of feet as people prematurely tried to distance themselves from anyone they thought might be accused.

Flaminius dropped his voice so the room had to strain to hear what he said next. "Centurion Marcus Gracchus has not only been protecting our enemy, he's been bedding her!"

There was a collective gasp of shock and the room was briefly stunned into silence.

Flaminius tossed Elissa carelessly back into the arms of the Gaul. "Give her to a slaver," he said, turning back to his couch. "And don't accept anything for her. She's worthless."

Elissa shut her eyes. It was over. There was nowhere left to run. No place to hide. The Gaul's hands closed around her waist. Her stomach slammed into his shoulder as he lifted her, but it wasn't painful. An odd sense of relief washed over her. She didn't need to be afraid anymore. The worst was already here. Taanit had trusted this man to bring her home, and she had trusted Taanit. They'd both been betrayed.

The crowd's shock changed into anger, then vengefulness. Elissa hardly felt the splash of wine on her leg or the tug of her cloak as it was ripped from her body. She barely heard the calls of "bitch" and "whore," "Punic slut." As the Gaul lumbered out of the villa, it was only the call of "traitor" that caused her a twinge of regret. Marcus was finished now, too. He didn't deserve that. He should have let her be that night in Vetulonium. He should have let her ride away into the silver moonlight.

But Elissa didn't dwell on what could have been. She'd retreated inside herself, gone to the small space pain couldn't reach. She had crossed an ocean in search of freedom, attempted audacious escapes, and tried to lie her way to getting it. But it was in a crowd of jeering Romans, her clothes torn and sullied, her pride wounded beyond repair, that she discovered the truth that had been there all along. *Freedom isn't something you find, it's something you take.*

CHAPTER 12

The sun was on Elissa's face. She closed her eyes and let the warm light caress her. It felt like a hand pressed to her cheek, fingers running lightly through her hair, lips brushed against her forehead: a golden lover.

A baby cried.

Elissa opened her eyes. Wooden bars cut dark lines into the ray of light, smothering her fantasy. The bottom of the wagon lurched as they drove through a rut in the road. The baby, who was across from Elissa, held in the mother's arms, cried out again. The mother twitched but didn't open her eyes. The baby was hungry.

Elissa put her hands on the floor and shifted her weight onto her other leg. Her feet tingled from being trapped underneath her all day. She closed her eyes again.

It was night. She was freezing.

Elissa shifted her legs so only her ankles were uncovered. She still wore the woolen dress Messia had given her in Vetulonium. The intervening months had not been kind to it. The hem was frayed beyond repair and the seam on one side had split. Cold air seeped in through the opening; it closed around her legs and soaked into her bones. She missed her cloak. But that wasn't her most pressing concern at the moment.

Gods, she had to pee. And she wasn't sure she could wait until morning. Caeso, the slave trader who now owned her, allowed them a short break from the wagon at dawn. Most of the slaves used the opportunity to relieve themselves, but Elissa had been too humiliated to expose herself in front of the other slaves and Caeso's four brutish guards. She regretted that now. There was no way her bladder would make it through the night.

Elissa glanced around the wagon. The walls were solid wood on three sides with a covered roof. The narrow slits between planks let hardly any light through. The end of the wagon consisted of ten vertical wooden bars, which were slightly more generous with the light, but not at all with the prospect of escape. A person's hand would barely fit between the bars, and a heavy chain was wrapped around the door to prevent it from opening. It didn't matter. There was nothing out there for her anyway—nothing but monotonous road and endless land. This wagon and its fifteen slaves were her world now. Elissa stared into the darkness until she could distinguish each person's outline. They were leaning against the wall or sprawled on the floor to sleep for a few hours. A light layer of straw had dusted the floor when Elissa first arrived, but the more experienced slaves had since piled it into a corner. The straw was already wet and reeked of urine.

Elissa forced her stiff legs to move. A thick length of rope was wrapped around her ankles and between her legs. Elissa struggled to pull her feet into a crouch. She fell forward onto her knees. New pain met the remnants of old, and she swore under her breath. She slowly pushed herself back up and straightened her legs, then started to shuffle into the corner, slowly picking her way around prostrate bodies and jutting limbs. Something moved under her foot. She pulled it back and the floor groaned. A man shifted onto his side and curled around his injured stomach. Elissa kept moving. She reached the corner with the straw pile. The smell was rancid. That was probably why the mother had chosen it. She was leaning against the side of the wagon with her baby cradled in her arms. They looked eerily still, but it was hard to be sure in the dark. Elissa crouched and hitched her dress up to her hips. She swivelled her head to see if anyone was watching, but it didn't really matter.

With the sudden release of pressure, she felt the best she had in two days. She closed her eyes and enjoyed the moment. When she was finished, she let her dress fall back to the floor. Her arm brushed against the mother's, and she felt the reassuring movement of air from her chest. Elissa leaned in toward the baby, who still hadn't moved.

Dread crept down her spine. She lifted her hand and held her fingers to the baby's mouth.

The slight rustle of air tickled her fingers.

Elissa exhaled with relief. She brought her fingers to the infant's tiny cheek. It felt so cold.

She shifted to the mother's side and lowered herself to the floor. The slave next to her muttered but moved aside. Elissa gently took the baby from the woman's arms, which fell limply to her sides. Elissa brought the baby, swaddled in a threadbare rag, to her own chest.

She reached out a finger and pushed the sides of the rag back from the baby's face. Thin brown hair peeked out from under the blanket. A little girl. Elissa brought her closer and pressed her lips to her fragile forehead. Her skin was soft and so pale it seemed translucent. Elissa couldn't help but think of her own mother. Had she ever held her like this? Had she cradled her against the cold, fought to protect her from the cruelty of the world?

Elissa leaned down to tear the hem of her dress with one

hand. The sound of ripping fabric cut through the silence and cold air rushed up to her knees. When she was finished, her dress only covered half her legs, but the baby was wrapped in a thick wool blanket. Messia would have approved. Elissa traced the little girl's cheek with her thumb, then leaned back against the wall and nestled the baby deeper into her chest. She wished she could feed her, too, but only the mother could do that. Elissa would give the mother her ration of bread in the morning. And then she'd ask Caeso for a second to eat herself. The trader was greedy, but he knew the mother was worth more to him with her baby alive. Born slaves were always more compliant than ones who'd been bought. Elissa closed her eyes.

The rain hammered down. Pulsing waves of water fell from sky to earth. The road had turned to thick mud that sucked at the wheels of the wagon, and the donkeys strained to make progress. The mud pulled at hooves and boots. Down, down, down, to wherever the water went.

One of the brutes following the wagon had gone down, too. He'd stepped in a rut and his leg had disappeared up to his knee. It had taken a ruthless tirade from Caeso and several of the other guards to get him going again. Elissa had watched from the wagon, grateful for the skinny wooden planks that blocked out most of the rain. She'd started laughing when the second pair of hands had latched onto the guard's leg to pull him up. She hadn't stopped until well after he was trudging behind the wagon again, now missing his left boot.

The brute had heard her laughing. He'd glared at her throughout the ordeal, his thick features twisted with loathing. He'd come up to the wagon afterward and clenched his heavy fists around the bars. He'd stared right at Elissa as he ran his tongue over his rotting teeth.

Elissa hadn't looked away. Caeso wouldn't let him touch her. She was worth too much.

The rain kept falling, the brutes kept grumbling and the wheels kept turning. She didn't blame Taanit for what happened; the Gaul had betrayed them both. Perhaps Taanit should have known better than to trust a Roman slave, but she was the one who had put him in such a desperate position to begin with. So why was it here, in a filthy wagon with her life no longer her own, that the cool balm of forgiveness began to settle deep within her? She had used Taanit and lied to Marcus in her desperate fight against fate, and she was sorry for it. But her only true crime had been her innocence. Nothing really changed, no matter what she did. She knew that now. The past was set, the future unknowable. All that mattered was surviving the present. Surviving with her spirit intact. Whatever that took.

Elissa brought her knees to her chest. The mother was feeding her baby in the corner. That was good.

The clouds darkened and the hills faded into the night. Trees lining the road turned to black spear points that pierced the hovering clouds. Liquid poured from their wounds.

Elissa had relieved herself in the open with the rest of the slaves that morning. Dignity was a tenuous thing.

"Out! Everybody out!"

The slave beside Elissa groaned and pushed himself to his feet. Elissa forced her legs to straighten and did the same, then moved to the back of the line of slaves waiting to exit the wagon. They made a sad procession. Slumped shoulders under worn rags, bound feet shuffling methodically forward. The slaves snatched their ration of bread as they stepped out of the wagon.

Elissa finally got to the front.

The brute she'd laughed at was waiting at the entrance. He held her piece of bread in his hand. He put it in his mouth as she stepped out of the wagon.

Elissa ignored him and limped to the side of the road. A group of slaves had congregated there; they chewed on their bread and stretched their cramped bodies beside the worn dirt. Elissa nodded at the nearest man without looking, then moved off to the side and squatted. Her shortened dress was making this much harder to do discreetly. The brute who had eaten her bread left the wagon and walked down the road. No, he was walking toward her.

Elissa stood.

The brute walked straight through the line of slaves up to Elissa. He grabbed the front of her dress and jerked her away from the road. His breath reeked of rotting meat.

"Caeso! Caeso!" she screamed.

"Shut it," the brute growled.

"Caeso! Caeso!"

Elissa's voice didn't falter because she wasn't afraid. The morning after her capture, she'd told Caeso the truth—she was a Carthaginian aristocrat, one and eight years old, and a virgin. The trader's eyes had bulged and he'd practically licked his lips with greed. She was worth more than all the other slaves combined.

Caeso stumbled out from the front of the wagon. He saw Elissa, her dress pulled up past her knees, and the guard who hovered menacingly over her. He started running. No one stole from Caeso.

"Ey! Guard! Out, out, out!" Caeso gesticulated wildly. "And the rest of you, on him!" He waved an arm at the other guards and thrust a finger at Elissa's assailant. "I'll have the lot of you thrown in the Tiber if he takes that one!"

The brute still gripped Elissa, and his head swivelled back and forth as he took in the changing situation. The other guards were moving quickly toward them. Elissa could practically see his mind turning to keep pace. He took his hand off Elissa a moment too late.

A long wooden stick sailed through the air and crashed down across the brute's back. He roared in pain and whirled around. Caeso skittered backward away from him. The brute lunged after him but pulled up short as the other three guards arrived. They stood behind Caeso protectively. He was the one paying their wages, after all. Caeso's mouth twisted into a smile and he pointed his stick at Elissa.

"You want her, you pay for it."

The brute grunted and twisted his neck to glare at Elissa. His face was red and bulging with fury. He didn't want to rape her anymore; he wanted to kill her. Elissa turned and trudged back to the wagon. At least he'd have to pay for the privilege.

The rest of the morning passed the same way as the last three had. Hills, trees and rutted road passed slowly by through the bars of the wagon. The hills seemed flatter now, and there was more level ground between their slopes. The trees had changed, as well. The dark pine needles had fallen away, and bare branches and gnarled limbs took their place, reaching to the sky in search of their lost leaves.

The procession was definitely headed south.

Squelch, squelch, squelch.

The guards' boots stuck to the mud as they trudged behind the wagon, the road still wet from yesterday's rain.

Squelch, da dum, squelch, da dum.

Elissa angled her head. That second sound was new. She surveyed the wagon, listening to the other slaves. But there was nothing out of the ordinary, only the soft rustle of tired bodies.

Da dum, da dum, da dum.

It sounded like a spear thumping against the ground or a horse galloping. Elissa glanced back at the guards. They didn't seem to have noticed anything. When the wagon lurched to a stop, they were obviously surprised.

"Ey!" Caeso yelled from the front of the wagon. "Look alive, you lazy sods! Someone's coming."

The guards shifted their feet and glanced nervously at each other. They could hardly look less alive if they tried. Most of them seemed like they'd fought before, and Elissa thought the brute and one of the other guards might even be former gladiators. But they were tired, underfed, and far past their prime. The glow of any former glory had long since faded, and nothing but cruelty was left.

Da dum, da dum, da dum.

They were definitely hoofbeats, and they were closer now. The guards formed a line outside the entrance to the wagon. Caeso came up behind them and stood on the wagon to peer over their heads. Elissa couldn't see anything but their backs through the wooden bars. Whoever was coming was coming fast. The hoofbeats grew louder and the guards straightened. Caeso growled something and they pulled their swords from their scabbards.

The hoofbeats slowed to a walk.

"Keep riding!" Caeso called. "There's nothing here for you."

No one answered. The horse kept walking.

The brute growled and stepped forward. Elissa could hear his fist tighten on the hilt of his sword in warning.

A sword she couldn't see left its scabbard.

"You're a slaver." She recognized the voice.

Elissa screamed.

Caeso looked at her through the bars. Then he whirled back around and the world exploded.

The guards shouted and scattered. Caeso jumped down from the wagon and pulled a knife out of his belt. The hoofbeats quickened to a gallop. Steel whistled through the air. One of the guards went down; his body arcing through the air as he fell. His hands were on his stomach, and his fingers were painted scarlet.

Elissa rushed to the end of the wagon and brought her face to the bars. It widened her field of view, but only a little. Caeso shouted orders frantically, but no one was listening. One of the guards dove to the side and came up in a battle-ready crouch beside the wagon. He lifted his sword over his shoulder; his body was intent, but his hands trembled. He started to swing. A massive black object blurred Elissa's eyes. She blinked and looked back at the guard. He lay on the ground, motionless.

Something yanked on Elissa's waist. She tore her attention away from the battle and saw that the rest of the slaves had joined her at the bars. They were pushing and pulling at the front row as they jostled for a better position. Elissa curved her hands around the bars and squeezed. She refused to move.

The brute backed into the wagon. He was breathing hard and one of his arms was covered in blood, but he still had a chance. He only needed to protect his flank. He kept moving until the backs of his legs were pressed into the wagon. He held his sword in front of his face.

Four black legs walked slowly toward him. They stopped. The assailant dismounted. Elissa saw his bronze greaves, a red tunic and mud-spattered thighs. *Marcus had come for her.* She didn't think. She rammed her arms through the narrow bars and lunged for the brute's head. She yanked back on his hair as hard as she could and pinned him to the wagon.

"Marcus!" she bellowed.

Marcus lunged. The brute twisted around and wrenched his head free of Elissa's grip. He froze. Metal flashed on the wrong side of his back. The sword withdrew and his blood flowed out. The brute fell from view.

Elissa was being dragged backward. Her hand broke free of the bar and she was forced away from the door. The wagon shook as the slaves threw themselves at the exit. They sensed freedom and their chains had become intolerable. Elissa couldn't see anything through the mass of frantic bodies; she only heard the muffled sounds of struggle through the walls of the wagon. She hit the back wall and slumped to the floor. She put her head between her knees and prayed.

Please, please, please, Astarte, Melqart, Ba'al Hamon.

Then she tried the Roman gods. *Please Jupiter, Mars, Hercules.*

Feet moved quickly outside the wagon. They lunged and thrust. Metal clanged against metal. There was a loud thud. A whistle as air parted. Then the unmistakable sound of metal cleaving bone.

"Marcus!" Elissa screamed again.

He didn't respond. Elissa bolted upright and rushed to the side of the wagon closest to the fight.

Footsteps were headed to the front of the wagon. Metal clanged. The chain holding the door snapped and fell away.

Elissa sank to the floor with her eyes closed.

"Thank you," she whispered. Whether she was thanking a Roman or Carthaginian god, she didn't know.

The pressure of bodies against the door had already lessened, and only the last few slaves were still trickling out of the wagon. Elissa pushed herself up and followed them on shaking legs. Her feet sank into the mud as she stepped onto the road. She blinked at what she saw—most of the slaves were scattering into the forest. They had apparently decided that fleeing from their mysterious Roman saviour was safer than thanking him.

Marcus had remounted his horse and stood on the side of the road. His black stallion was blowing hard, and Marcus was muddied up to his knees. Blood ran halfway down one of his legs.

Elissa walked toward him. She would have run, but her ankles were still bound.

He didn't move. His face was set as stone.

Elissa reached him and placed her hand on his knee.

His eyes were cold as he looked down at her.

"Thank you," Elissa whispered.

Her tongue felt thick in her throat. He'd come for her. No matter why he'd done it or what came next, he'd come for her. After everything she'd done.

A baby cried out.

Elissa tore her eyes from Marcus and turned around. She'd forgotten about the mother. Marcus had freed them, too.

Elissa froze.

In her hurry to get to Marcus, she hadn't fully comprehended the battlefield she'd walked through. The guard who'd been trampled under Marcus's horse lay face up in the mud. His eyes were open, but unseeing, his face frozen in silent horror. The brute lay lifeless and bloodied at the foot of the wagon. She must have stepped over him and not even realized it. Another guard was sprawled on the side of the road. Caeso was closest to Elissa; he'd been disarmed, and Marcus had finished him with a heavy slice to the neck. He lay on his side near Elissa's feet. Blood trickled from his mouth into the mud, as the last remnants of his life flowed away.

Elissa turned back to Marcus. "I'm so sorry," she breathed.

There was a commotion behind her, and Marcus raised his head. The mother was at the front of the wagon, desperately grasping for the reins to one of the donkeys. Another slave was half-mounted and trying to snatch them back so he could ride away.

"Get off her!" Elissa shouted to the man. She shot Marcus a pleading glance, then hurried over to them as quickly as her bound feet would allow.

By the time she reached them, the slave was fully mounted and had both reins in his hands. He kicked savagely at the donkey's sides. Elissa lunged forward as they started to pull ahead. She caught a rein with one hand, but couldn't get her feet underneath her in time to stay upright. She smacked face-first into the mud.

"Piss off!" the slave screamed at her. He wrenched the rein from her hand.

"Let. Go." The icy drawl came from above her.

Elissa looked up. Right at the belly of Marcus's stallion. A sword stretched across the space from the horse's back to the slave's neck.

The slave blinked. He slid off the donkey and ran.

Elissa slowly managed to stand. Her dress, already pathetically small, was now sopping with mud. She shuffled lamely over to the mother and shoved the loose reins into her outstretched hand. Elissa focused on the baby in her mother's arms. She reached for the leather strap around her neck and took off the amulet that Messia had given her months ago. It was a gift meant to bring Elissa good fortune, and she'd held onto it, praying that the gods would heed her blessing. She draped it over the baby's tiny body. It would not change the mother's fate or the child's, but at least it would bring them some money.

As she turned, Marcus held out a hand to her. She grabbed it and he helped her onto his horse, then leaned down to slice the rope between her feet with his sword. He locked one arm around her waist and held the reins in his other hand. Elissa wrapped her fingers tightly around his wrist. She wouldn't let go again. They rode north at a walk. Both Marcus and his horse were exhausted; the stallion's head hung low and Marcus's arm drooped onto his thigh. His chest tilted forward to rest against Elissa's back.

Elissa finally broke the long silence. "Marcus, perhaps we should stop for the night. I could tend to your wound." She glanced down at his thigh. Blood no longer trickled from the gash, but his thigh was now coated in a thick, dark paste.

Marcus ignored his leg. "We keep riding."

Elissa twisted her body toward him. His square jaw was covered in dark, coarse hair she hadn't seen before. The corners of his eyes were creased with fatigue, and his skin, usually so warm and virile, was gray. Elissa had been taken nearly four days ago, and it looked as though Marcus had been riding for nearly all of that time and when he'd found her, he'd fought and killed five Romans to set her free.

He'd killed five *Romans*. They might well have been former slaves and lowlifes from the slums of the Suburra, but they were still Roman. He had killed his fellow citizens for her. The realization must have flashed in her eyes because Marcus glanced away and pushed her shoulder, directing her to turn around. Elissa shook her head. She covered his hands with her own and pulled back on the reins. The stallion halted. She brought one leg over the horse's neck and the other in front of her so she was facing Marcus in the saddle.

Marcus Sempronius Gracchus. Her enemy, her captor, her tormentor, and her saviour. She had felt many things for him—hatred, fear, uncontrollable attraction. But now, overlaying it all, she felt gratitude. She had betrayed this man, and he had saved her, and given up part of himself to do it. So she thanked him the only way she knew how. She gave him what he'd wanted since that first night in Vetulonium. And what she'd wanted so badly, denying it had nearly driven her mad.

Elissa brought one hand up to his shoulder, and buried the other in his sweat-dampened hair. She strained her neck until their lips met. His beard prickled against her cheek, and she pulled at him with her hands and with her lips until he let go of the reins and wrapped his arms around her waist. He opened his mouth and Elissa slipped her tongue inside. She traced the line of his lips and followed the curve of his mouth. She tilted her hips until the aching pit at the bottom of her stomach rested between his legs. She felt his hardness as he rose to meet her. The pressure turned hot and tingling, and it melted the ache with its fire. Elissa kissed him with a wanton abandon she'd never felt before, because at that moment, there was nothing in the world but him.

CHAPTER 13

Marcus's head felt stuck to his shoulder, as if someone were holding his ear down to prevent him from looking to the other side. His arms were lead weights that seemed detached from his body; he had to rest his hands on his knees just to hold the reins. The wound on his thigh stung painfully. If he'd had any wine left, he would have poured it over his leg to clean the gash. Then again, he'd rather pour it down his throat to soothe his swollen tongue. And all of that was nothing compared to his horse.

The poor beast was ruined. Its breathing was rapid and irregular, even though they were moving at a slow lope. The black stallion tugged down at the reins. Marcus held them tightly to keep his head up. He occasionally delivered a sharp kick to the horse's sides to keep him from collapsing to the ground. His brave, valiant horse had run for nearly four days, and now, at the end of the fourth night, Marcus knew he would never run again. He looked accusingly at the woman between his arms. Did she know what she'd cost him? Her dark hair was nestled in the pit of his arm, and she rocked rhythmically back and forth with the horse's stride, her eyes comfortably closed. Marcus wanted to shake her, wanted her to wake up. She should feel his horse dying beneath them.

But he didn't move. He stared at her instead. She had lied to him, run away *again*. And for what? What had he done to deserve this? The stallion stumbled and Elissa's head fell off his chest. Marcus tightened his arm around her waist protectively. She grunted and brought her head back to his arm. Marcus closed his eyes. He wanted so badly to sleep, to stop moving for a few minutes and stretch out on the ground. Just to stop.

He saw Elissa as she'd looked when he rescued her. Her hair matted, her dress torn to shreds, her ankles chafed and bound. Marcus reached down to his knee and felt the ghost of her touch. The feel of her hand on his body was only a feather of sensation, but the raging fury that coursed through his body had slowed to a trickle. The pounding in his temples lightened to a drumbeat. She was safe. Gods help him, but she was safe. He'd wanted to yell at her, to curse her for her insolence. But she'd thanked him, submitted to him, and then she'd kissed him with breathtaking desperation. He still felt a stirring between his legs as he remembered the way her tongue had traced the lines of his mouth. Never, in all his years of experience, had a woman abandoned herself to him like that. It had felt like jumping in a cold lake after a lifetime of thirst.

Marcus shook his head and cursed. This woman would be the death of him. Probably soon. Elissa pulled her head from his chest and shifted in the saddle. She was perched over the stallion's withers in a position that would have unseated a less expert horsewoman. Sleep rumbled in her throat.

"Marcus—"

He didn't reply.

"Marcus," she repeated. She turned to glance sleepily over her shoulder. "Where are we going, Marcus?"

Marcus kept his gaze straight over her head. "To the legion."

Elissa's eyes widened but she didn't protest. She turned

to face forward again. She didn't speak for a long time, although her head no longer rested on his chest so she must have been awake. Her next words were quiet.

"I don't know what you plan to do, but I think I should be bound when we get to the legion. Flaminius told everyone that I…I was your bedmate…" She trailed off hesitantly.

Marcus was well aware that Flaminius had told an assembly of the highest-ranking officers in the legion much more than that. It was the other things he'd said that had resulted in Marcus being accosted in the city that night. A group of men from another maniple had jeered when they'd seen him on the street. They'd called him a traitor and an enemy of Rome. His men had nearly killed them on the spot for slandering his honor. Marcus had forced them apart in time to hear the truth on the men's lips. He'd known immediately what had happened. He'd been suspicious when Quintus had said Elissa was unwell and wished to retire early for the night. But he'd decided to let her be. It was better for her, he'd thought. Marcus snorted humorlessly, regretting that now. It had been sheer luck that he'd found her. He'd saddled his horse as soon as he could and fled Arretium, praying that whatever slaver had taken her was headed to Rome on the main road.

"I know what he said. Do you care to make it true?" he taunted her bitterly.

Elissa didn't rise to the bait, and they went back to passing the night in the silence of the stallion's faltering feet. They stayed on the road where travel was quickest, making good time despite the exhausted horse. The darkened outline of hills had already grown jagged, and the occasional gray cliff split through the thick blanket of pine. Provided they weren't accosted by bandits or brigands, they should reach the legion by morning. Marcus winced as he imagined the encounter. When did men who had been his family for a decade suddenly become his enemies?

"I need you to know something." Elissa interrupted his dark thoughts. She turned her head so she could peer into his eyes. "I think, in a lot of ways, being captured was harder for me to accept than dying. I just—I felt so lost." She sighed and turned away. "You should've let me go, Marcus. But you took me instead. And then you saved me from rape and from slavery. So let's not hurt each other again. If we go to the legion, we'll go as captor and captive. I give you my word never to lie to you again. My honor may not mean much to you anymore, but it's all I have. I give it to you freely and whatever else you think is fair payment for my life."

Marcus closed his eyes when she finished speaking. His brain whirled and his heart pleaded, but he was too exhausted to make sense of whatever message they were sending. She was right, wasn't she? The score was even. At first he'd told himself that he'd taken her because she was the enemy and he was Roman. When that had proved untrue, he'd said it was because she was a challenge to conquer, and that was enough in itself. The truth was he'd taken her because he wanted to, and he'd kept her for the same reason. She had given him something to hold on to when everything else was falling away.

Shame washed over him, hot and itchy under his skin. It was his fault, wasn't it? He might have saved her from rape and slavery, but he'd also put her there. And now his punishment from the gods was revealed. The whole legion would see him as he was on the inside—a traitor and a liar. A man without honor.

Elissa shifted her shoulders and half-turned her head to gauge his reaction. She seemed calmer than before, and more resolved. The amber in her eyes no longer glowed like flames. The yellow had melted into green, like the canopy of a thick forest absorbs the sunlight.

"Do we have a deal?"

Marcus dragged his head away. There was too much to say, so he said nothing at all.

They rode through the night without seeing any sign of the legion. An army of 30,000 should have been hard to miss. If you couldn't spot them in the flesh, then the torn-up roads and overnight cities they'd left behind should tell you when you were close. But dawn had come and gone hours ago and still they'd seen nothing. Elissa could tell that Marcus was growing more nervous by the minute. He shifted uncomfortably and glanced down at their horse every time they rounded a bend in the road and no legion appeared on the other side. Elissa was not as anxious to rejoin the legion, but he was right to worry about the horse. The stallion was truly on his last legs now. Marcus had slowed him to a trot to conserve the last of his energy, but he was dragging his hooves and tripping every other step. The poor beast deserved a *triumph* for his bravery; he was likely to get only a merciful death instead.

They crested a hill in the road and suddenly, they'd arrived. A long line of red weaved in between craggy brown hills that stretched into the distance. The first of the legionaries were visible on a mountain pass, but the thick forest running up the hillside obscured most of the other sections of the line. They were headed east, back toward the sea. Marcus exhaled loudly behind her, and Elissa felt his chest tighten with anticipation. She glanced at him out of the corner of her eye. His jaw was tight and his face drawn. Even after all the time she'd spent with him, Marcus was still completely unreadable to her. After their passionate kiss, he'd withdrawn from her, and despite their close proximity, Elissa had no sense of what he was about to do—which was terrifying, because she had no idea of what was waiting for them down here. Even if Marcus's maniple had stayed loyal to him, how would a hundred of his men stand against a whole army that thought him a traitor?

"Bind me, Marcus." They could at least make his treason less obvious.

His hand twitched, but didn't move. Elissa held up the rope that had been attached to her ankles.

"Marcus."

He took the rope from her.

Elissa held up her wrists.

He fastened one end around her wrist. Elissa nodded encouragingly. He moved his hands and did the same to the other wrist.

At least, now she'd look like a captive. Elissa didn't dwell on the question of whether she actually was or not.

Marcus dug his heels into the stallion's sides one last time and they started down the hill toward the legion. The road was rutted from the many boots that had already marched over it, and the stallion bounced awkwardly over the depressions and mounds of dirt. She could feel Marcus's body changing behind her as they drew nearer. His shoulders relaxed and his chest tilted up. He slowed the stallion to a walk as they approached the first men at the back of the legion. Romans respected confidence and authority, and Marcus could still show both.

As they rode past, row upon row of men swivelled their heads to stare. The even rhythm of the march was interrupted by the smattering of extra steps as the legionaries turned to get a better look. A ripple of whispers ran through the lines, and then abruptly died out. Elissa hunched her shoulders and tried her best to disappear.

Marcus's maniple was the second to the last. His men's backs were perfectly straight; not a single man turned around to catch the whisper of the person behind him. Their bodies stayed rigid, and they stared directly ahead. Quintus was riding at the front in Marcus's usual place. He sat with an awkwardness Elissa hadn't noticed before. In fact, all of Marcus's men were marching with a new stiffness. There were no spontaneous songs or lewd jokes to be heard.

Marcus's peered into each man's face as they walked past. Halfway down the line, he stopped abruptly and stiffened his shoulders. Elissa resisted the urge to look at what he'd seen. Marcus kicked the stallion into motion once more; the horse faltered, but Marcus held him up with the reins, and they trotted to the front of the maniple where Quintus was riding. As they reined in beside him, Elissa chanced a quick glance at her friend. He stared determinedly at Marcus and away from Elissa.

"Take her," Marcus said in a tone that brooked no argument.

Quintus started to protest.

"Quintus." Marcus's voice was low with warning.

Elissa raised her head to look more closely at Quintus. He seemed to have aged ten years in the past four days. Purplish circles were set under his eyes, and his forehead was creased with worry. There was something off about the way he was sitting in the saddle that Elissa couldn't explain.

"I'll walk," Elissa said quietly. She swung her legs over the horse's neck and let herself slide off. Her legs wobbled dangerously. She couldn't remember the last time she'd eaten.

Marcus ignored her. "I need another horse," he told Quintus. He spun the stallion around to face his men.

"Halt!" His voice boomed with the authority Elissa remembered from their first meeting.

His men stopped immediately. A murmur of dissent came from the maniple behind them, but they halted, too. Marcus paused to change horses; mounting the new one Quintus had brought him. A legionary held the reins of the black stallion, whose head drooped nearly to the ground now that they'd finally stopped. Marcus pushed his fresh horse into a trot down the line. Elissa knew he held a tight grip on the reins to keep himself upright, but she doubted it would be visible to his men. To them, he would be the same unflappable leader he'd always been.

"Men," Marcus called out clearly so every one of them could hear. "I know you've suffered through no fault of your own. I brought a Carthaginian into our midst, I protected her, and it's all of you who've been punished." Marcus dropped his head, displaying his shame for his men to see.

They shuffled their feet awkwardly.

Marcus continued. "I apologize to each one of you. I apologize to your fathers and to your sons, and I humbly submit to your will."

His proud Roman nose pointed at the dirt, and his powerful arms sagged limply. To see his towering body in such a meek posture seemed ludicrous.

Sounds of protest rose through the crowd, and the men glanced at each other in confusion.

"Ey, Centurion, was only a few lashes," a legionary yelled from the center.

"Not so bad." Another agreed.

"We 'ated that snub-nosed consul anyways!"

Murmurs of agreement mixed with grumbles of protest.

Marcus paused, then lifted his head. His body radiated intensity, a tumultuous mixture of shame and anger that transfixed every man he passed. He spoke quietly, but his words carried the same weight as if a thousand men had shouted them.

"You are each your own man. You are free citizens of Rome. If you choose not to fight for me, I will not blame you. I will release you from service and ask no more of you."

Some men glanced at their neighbors, but no one moved.

"However, if you choose to stay, I can promise you this. I fight for *you*. Only for you. I will fight the enemies of Rome and the enemies of Romans." He looked meaningfully at the center of the legion, where the consul usually rode. His voice was louder when he turned back to his men. He kicked his horse into a canter. "I will fight until they hack my arms from my body and they fill my chest with arrows! I will fight until I am old and grizzled and too weary to hold a sword! I will fight until the enemies of Rome are dead and vanquished, so irrelevant even history won't remember them! Let the gods hear me now and remember my words. I will fight for you!" Marcus raced to a gallop as he shouted, punctuating each word with the thrust of his sword.

The men beat their shields in unison and a war cry rang out.

Marcus slowed his horse to a walk and waited for them to quiet again.

"Men. Our enemies are upon us, and this is no time to be divided from within. If we stand together, we will stand strong. There is still glory to fight for, and honor in dying for it. Let Hannibal hear us call his name. Let them come, and let them learn. We are Romans, and we will never die!"

"Hurrah! Hurrah! Hurrah!" his men shouted as one. They pumped their spears in the air and stomped their feet. Their chests swelled with renewed pride. Even a few men from the maniple behind them joined the battle cry. Not a single man stepped out of line, gathered his belongings and turned for home. They were Romans. To live as a coward would be a fate far worse than death.

Elissa looked up at Quintus. He had straightened in the saddle and a smile played on his lips. His eyes shone as he watched Marcus riding among his men. Marcus stopped every few feet to clasp a hand or beat an outstretched shield with his blade. He grinned as he reached down to his men. He loved them. That was why he fought for them and why he would die for them. And he'd been willing to do the same for her. Flaminius said Marcus's loyalties were divided—that he had a Carthaginian's heart inside a Roman's body. But as

Elissa watched Marcus among men who were more like brothers, she realized those two parts of him might not be so different after all.

Elissa marched at the head of the maniple for the rest of the day. She did the same on the day after, and the day after that. Winter unfolded into spring as she marched. Green buds sprouted at the ends of bare branches, and pines shook off their winter frost. The roads stayed soft even in the morning, so they were no longer forced to walk through the frozen depressions of yesterday's footsteps. They marched over mountain passes too high for trees to grow, and through valleys with forests thick enough to blot out the sun. They walked and they walked, and the whole time, no one seemed to know where they were walking.

Elissa marched in the space between the first row of Marcus's maniple and the last row of the next one. Quintus rode beside her most of the time. His anger had gradually thawed into a comfortable silence, and at some point, Elissa realized their lack of conversation was more out of habit than bitterness. Quintus wasn't the type to hold grudges, but she'd betrayed his trust by trying to escape again, and she deserved his silence. She would apologize to him when he was ready to hear it.

The silence from Marcus's men was different. They were clearly unhappy to have her marching with them. They said nothing for the first few days. But when Elissa's eyes wandered, she would catch one of them staring at her with hatred in his eyes. The taunts eventually started. It was only a few of the veterans at first. They took it upon themselves to invent some creative nicknames for her, most of them involving "Punic" and "whore." The men's confidence grew, and then some of the younger ones began to take rather insulting liberties with her parentage. Marcus appeared suddenly, steaming mad.

His glower sent them into a silence that lasted for days. His men quickly learned that the best way to maintain their tenuously re-established order was to ignore her completely. Besides, with her hands bound and clothes tattered, she at least looked the part of a captive now. Elissa was happy to oblige them in pretending she didn't exist.

Marcus stayed as far away from her as possible while still within shouting distance. He rode in the center of the maniple most of the time, and even marched with his men on foot when the going was especially difficult. That was when he seemed happiest—sharing a bawdy story or complaining about the endless hill they were climbing. When he came near Elissa, his face clouded over and he turned edgy and irritable. He would usually ride off as quickly as he'd come. Marcus offered her a horse to ride every morning, and every morning she steadfastly refused. By the end of the first week, he stopped asking.

The going was tough, but she wanted for nothing. Marcus gave her food enough for two men, and he kept her provisions in his saddlebag so she wouldn't have to carry anything on her back. He'd even found her a new cloak and a sheet of finely spun wool to fashion a dress. His abrupt departure spared Elissa from having to explain that she was a lousy seamstress. She'd spent the night alone by the fire, repeatedly trying to shape the recalcitrant fabric into some-thing resembling a dress. She ended up doing little more than cutting a hole for her head and bringing the fabric in at the sides, but she was pleased with her efforts nonetheless. The next day, as she marched in her new cloak and billowing dress, the blisters at the bottom of her feet turned to calluses, and the pain in her calves receded to a dull ache. Even Marcus's black stallion seemed to have survived their ordeal. Elissa glimpsed him being led by a legionary at the back of the maniple. She smiled with relief, knowing it must have been Marcus's decision to spare him.

The days passed quickly under her rapidly strengthening legs. Her world shrank to the heels of the men in front of her, and the steady clopping of the horse beside her. But it also grew. For the first time since the ride to Vetulonium, Elissa noticed the beauty around her. She noticed the way the trees thinned as they climbed up the side of a mountain. How green grass merged seamlessly into gray rock. She noticed the clouds that gathered at the tops of mountains, as if to remind mortals not to peer too high into the domain of the gods. The path they marched along was difficult and unforgiving, but not inhospitable. Just as they crested a high mountain pass, they would descend into a lush valley with vineyards and farmers' huts bordering a worn road. Elissa had no idea where they were going or what was next, but she felt oddly at peace because she'd never really known what the future held, and there was nothing more to do than put one foot in front of the other.

They were halfway up a long mountain ridge when the feet in front of her stopped moving. Elissa halted and looked over at Quintus. He was riding a few paces ahead, and he had stopped, as well. Quintus rose in his saddle to see over the heads of the maniple in front of them. Marcus's men shifted impatiently behind her. It was only mid-morning, and they weren't expecting to stop for the midday break for another few hours at least. Hoofbeats sounded behind them, and Elissa turned to see Marcus riding up to them. His attention was fixed farther up the ridge, where the rest of the legion had nearly finished the climb to the mountain pass. He reined in his horse beside her.

"What's going on?" she asked.

Marcus glanced down distractedly. "I don't know. Flaminius doesn't send reports back here." He reached into his saddlebag and pulled out a loaf of bread and a hard chunk of cheese. "Here. Eat this while we wait."

Elissa nodded and took the food. Marcus trotted away again.

By midday they still hadn't moved, and the men were growing more and more restless. Even Quintus, normally so calm, nervously scanned the ridge every few minutes. The sun was past its halfway point in the sky, and although the days were growing longer, it would still be many hours before they could finish the climb and find a more hospitable place to rest for the night. Quintus was sitting tensely on his saddlebag when he suddenly jumped to his feet.

"What is it, Quintus?"

He ignored her and walked to the side of the ridge where the view was better. Elissa pushed to her feet and followed. The ridge was mostly grassy, other than a few bare outcrops of rock. The ridgeline was long and broad, and the angle was gentle for most of its descent to the valley floor. About half-way down, a large cliff caused the mountain to abruptly fall away, which afforded a clear view of the valley below. Most of the men were clustered where the ground began its slow curve toward the valley. They jostled for position, craning their necks to see better. As Elissa joined them, she was initially struck by the brightness of the trees speckling the distant valley grass. Red and orange mixed with deep gray and black. It seemed like the middle of autumn, not the beginning of spring, and the brilliant leaves would soon fall from the trees.

A legionary next to Elissa growled and stomped his spear on the ground. His neighbor swore under his breath and brought his hand to his sword. Elissa looked back to the valley.

Her hand flew to her mouth to stifle a gasp.

It was the Carthaginian army. What she'd initially thought were trees were actually men—thousands and thousands of men. The Iberians in their bright armor, the Numidians, dark-skinned and mounted, and the Gauls, bare-chested except for the thick furs on their backs. And there, in the center of the great mass of warriors, was Hannibal. From a distance he looked almost Roman, except that he wore a purple cloak instead of a red one. He was astride a massive African war elephant. The great beast lumbered over boulders and trees as if they were no more than sticks on the ground. Hannibal's men marched around him in a great mob, with no attention paid to rank or structure. They were enemies of Rome, and that was all they needed to have in common.

"Care to join the rabble?"

Elissa whirled around. She'd been so transfixed by the army of Carthage that she'd failed to notice the twenty Romans who had ridden up behind her. The legionaries next to her had seen them arriving. They were tripping over themselves in their hurry to move away from her.

Flaminius. His eyes traced her body and his upper lip twisted in a snarl. She'd only caught glimpses of him since returning to the legion. She much preferred seeing him from afar. Up close, she could see that he marched in full consular regalia. A long plume on the tip of his helmet signified that here was the Consul of Rome, the unquestioned leader of the legion. And if that didn't do it, the twenty *lictors* surrounding him would. His armed bodyguards carried the *fasces:* a bundle of sticks fastened together and topped by a single axe-blade. The strange weapon signified a consul's authority over all Romans—and his power over life and death.

Elissa's breathing grew shallow as she watched him. He had come for her. No, she couldn't go back to slavery! She took a step back, and then another. Where was Marcus? Why hadn't she seen him since morning?

Flaminius jeered and closed in. "Don't fret, little whore, I have no more use for you. In fact, you've been more helpful than you could imagine."

"Flaminius." Marcus's voice cut through the charged air.

A crowd had gathered around Flaminius and Elissa, and now they stepped aside to let Marcus pass through. Marcus stopped his horse directly in front of Elissa so she was protected from Flaminius's view. He sent her a deliberate stare that warned her not to do anything rash and then turned back to Flaminius.

"Shouldn't you be busy finding more incompetent scouts? Surely there's another foolish position we could rush into."

Flaminius snickered. "Funny you should mention that, Gracchus, because I am indeed looking for more scouts."

Elissa kept her feet rooted to the ground, but she craned her neck to see around Marcus's horse. She had learned to fear the ominously quiet tone Flaminius had used.

Marcus scoffed. "Perhaps you should ask Hannibal to spare some of his. They seem to know exactly where we are, and they've had no trouble maneuvering around our supposedly impenetrable blockade on the mountain passes leading south."

Flaminius's smile didn't waver, but anger burned in his eyes. Marcus's men must have noticed because they moved in closer. Two of his veterans came to stand on either side of his horse's withers. Another five moved behind his horse, all but blocking Elissa's view of him.

Flaminius's *lictors* responded in kind. They closed around Flaminius in a tight semi-circle. Several of them moved the reins to one hand to free up the other arm for their weapons. The *fasces* might seem peculiar to non-Romans, but the lethal axe-blade at its tip begged no questions.

"Now, now." Flaminius motioned to his men. "Let's not be rash. I came to you with a job, not a fight, centurion."

Marcus didn't respond.

Flaminius held up a hand to his *lictors*. "You were right to criticize our scouts. They performed abysmally. Now Hannibal is ahead of us rather than behind us, and the Carthaginians have an open path to Rome. That is obviously unacceptable."

Marcus pushed his horse forward until its head was nearly touching the larger horse in front of them. Flaminius's horse moved his neck to the side to avoid contact.

"Tell me what you want from me."

Flaminius narrowed his eyes and hauled on his horse's neck. "I order you to take your whore and five of your men and follow Hannibal's army. Find out where they're going, and how to head them off and force them into battle. You will send one of your men back to the legion each day to deliver your report." He flashed his white teeth. "You can send your whore on the sixth day."

Elissa listened with increasing concern, and now realization cut through her like a whip. So this was it—Flaminius's punishment for Marcus's treason. It had taken him weeks to find just the right combination of humiliation and finality, but he'd done it. He would banish Marcus on an impossible scouting mission, but one a consul was nevertheless justified in ordering. With him gone, Flaminius would be free to disband his maniple. He could force Marcus's men never to fight together again. The brother-hood that Marcus had worked so hard to create would be shattered. And without any chance of revolt, Flaminius would damn whatever vestiges of Marcus's reputation were left. It would never be safe for him to return to the legion. His home for over a decade would be lost to him.

Elissa's feet felt heavy as she forced them to move. She couldn't let this happen to Marcus. The price was too great. She had to stop this. She stumbled around the line of legionaries in front of her and pushed straight through the one after that. She had a clear view of Marcus now. She would beg him to stop. She would give herself over to Flaminius if that was what it took. She wasn't worth such a sacrifice. She had nearly reached the back of Marcus's horse when a pair of arms encircled her from behind.

Elissa struggled to break free as Quintus shushed in her

ear. "Shhh, Elissa, it's okay. It's over now." He wrapped his arms tightly around her and pressed his cheek to the top of her head. "It's over."

Elissa started to protest but Marcus interrupted her.

"I accept."

The men around them recoiled in shock. The legionary nearest Elissa glanced at his neighbor and stamped his spear on the ground. Elissa's arms fell limply to her sides.

"On one condition."

Flaminius scoffed. "You're in no position to be dictating terms, Gracchus."

Marcus kicked his horse into a trot and spun him in a tight circle around Flaminius. Flaminius's head swivelled to keep pace with his progress. Marcus stopped once they stood side by side. He leaned over to Flaminius and winked, as if he were giving him a particularly juicy morsel of gossip. "A man is only lost once he admits defeat." Then Marcus straightened, and boomed for all his men to hear. "If you do not agree, my men and I will fight to our deaths here today, and the enemy below will see how divided we truly are!"

Marcus's men shouted their agreement and banged their spears against their shields. The few standing closest to Elissa pulled their swords from their scabbards. Flaminius's *lictors* stepped toward him in defense. The air thickened with tension. Every man was rigid, weight tipped forward, poised to attack. Elissa clenched her own hands—she would fight, too, if she had to. She eyed the knife on Quintus's belt. She could grab it before he noticed and draw a few Romans away by running. Elissa's mind faintly registered the astonishing turn of her loyalty. The enemy centurion had disappeared, along with her innocence. She'd left them both behind on the long march from naïve aristocrat, to slave, to—whatever she was now. She looked at Marcus. He was leaning over Flaminius boldly. A dark lock of hair fell across his forehead, and his grin made him seem almost boyish.

Flaminius stiffened and his eyes darted to the sides. Elissa could see that he had only twenty *lictors* against a hundred of Marcus's men. The rest of the legion would surely come to his aid, but they'd be hesitant to fight fellow Romans. And would they get here quickly enough to save his life? Flaminius's shoulders suddenly relaxed, as if he'd released a chest full of air. He smiled and said with exaggerated courtesy, "What can I offer you, centurion?"

"My men stay together in one maniple. Under the command of their new centurion, Quintus Arvina."

Quintus's arms dropped from Elissa as quickly as if he'd been struck by a bolt of lightning. All eyes moved to him, and Elissa immediately stepped aside to get out of their way.

"Centurion—" Quintus started to protest. His face was blank with shock.

Marcus held up a hand to silence him. "Those are my terms," he said, this time to Quintus.

Flaminius raised an eyebrow and smirked at Quintus. "Fine, let your men die with your *optio*." He looked at Marcus once more, and the smile fell from his face. "You leave now."

Marcus kicked his horse forward so Flaminius was left staring at his back. "Done. Bring me five—" his gaze went to Elissa "—six horses."

"Go," Flaminius growled to his *lictors*.

His twenty bodyguards turned and galloped away. Flaminius kicked his horse to follow, but then changed his mind and hauled back on the reins instead. When he faced Marcus again, his eyes were shining with hatred. "You're finished, Gracchus. Just like your brother. I'll write to the Senate and have you tried for treason. Your family will never hear your name without the word *traitor* in the same breath. All your life, your battles, your victories—it will be as if they never existed."

Marcus calmly turned his horse around. "And you,

Flaminius, will live a long and peaceful life. You'll die at the age of ninety. Taking a shit on the latrine."

Marcus's men roared with laughter as Flaminius's face colored purple. His mouth flapped as if he wanted to say more, but no words came out. He stuttered, and then kicked savagely at his horse to speed off after his *lictors*.

Marcus ignored him. He rode up to Quintus and dismounted, then brought his palm to the older man's cheek. "Old friend, I know I ask too much of you, but heed this last order. Take my men and lead them. Lead them as you've always led me."

Quintus's mouth opened and then shut. Tears welled in his eyes. He placed his hand on Marcus's shoulder and pulled him into a tight embrace. Marcus hugged him back fiercely. When Marcus eventually moved away, he kept a hand on Quintus's arm.

"I will see you on the other side, my brother."

Quintus only nodded. His eyes were glazed with unspent emotion. Marcus stepped back and turned to another group of waiting men. They slapped him on the shoulder and clasped his hands. They shouted out their past victories and the names of their fallen brothers. They thanked him and they said goodbye, their eyes filling with tears. Elissa's cheeks were wet, too. She did not know these men, and most of them probably hated her, but she knew love and she knew loss.

Quintus was still standing where Marcus had left him. Elissa walked over and slipped her hand into his limp one. "Quintus, I…" She paused and swallowed. A lump had swelled in her throat.

Quintus rotated to look at her. His eyes cleared as if he were seeing her for the first time. Elissa recoiled, terrified of what he might say.

Quintus drew her forward and wrapped his arms around her shoulders. Elissa's breath caught in her throat as she stepped into his embrace and let her cheek rest against his shoulder. "I'm sorry, Quintus," she mumbled against his neck. "It's all my fault and I'm...I..."

"Shh." Quintus cut her off. He raised his hands to her shoulders and pushed gently back until he was looking at her again. "You're a handful, Elissa Mago, I'll be the first to admit that." He leaned in close until his soft hazel eyes were inches from hers. "But Elissa, I know you can give him more than you can take."

Elissa felt as if someone were ripping her apart and squeezing her back together all at once. She watched Marcus. He was still walking among his men, shaking hands, pausing for a quick embrace. She looked back at Quintus. His brow was creased, his face alight with something unnameable.

Elissa's heart broke open. She held Quintus close as tears streamed down her face. "Thank you, Quintus."

Quintus flattened his hand on the back of her head as he clutched her against his chest.

"I know," he whispered.

CHAPTER 14

The horses were delivered to Marcus before the sun had crept much closer to the horizon. They weren't lame or starving ponies, either. Six fit warhorses with muscled hindquarters and sturdy legs were led down the ridge. Marcus might be exiled, but he still had one last duty to Rome. Elissa could tell from his thorough preparations since Flaminius had left that he was intent on discharging it with as much honor as he had the rest.

Soon after the horses reached them, Elissa, Marcus and his five chosen men set off down the ridge and back toward the valley. The men were all weathered veterans, accustomed to being alone in the field with an enemy nearby. They studiously avoided looking at Elissa as they loped briskly away from the legion. Their orders were to follow the enemy, predict his path through the mountains, and determine where he could be intercepted. Not a job that required five days, but this was only a convenient pretext for exile. Even if Marcus did gather useful information, who knew what Flaminius would do with it. Elissa glanced over at Marcus, who was riding next to her. His mouth was set in a straight line and his brow was drawn tight. He looked intent, but not unhappy. Was it too much to think that part of him might be as relieved to be leaving the legion behind as she was?

Elissa winced. She shouldn't fool herself. He was still

Roman, and the enemy they were scouting were still her people. Elissa found herself staring into the valley that Hannibal had so recently vacated. Had Barro been there? Was he even still alive? She closed her eyes and pictured her brother as she had last seen him. He'd cropped his dark hair short before leaving for Iberia to join the army. He wore his new armor, a shining shirt of mail over a bright purple tunic. The armor had been commissioned specially for him as a parting gift from their father. Elissa tried to remember Barro's face. Had it been clouded with anxiety or alight with excitement at the prospect of adventure? She shook her head. No, he'd been solemn, his jaw set with resolve, his amber eyes hooded. He had looked so much like Hanno that day.

Elissa's thoughts lingered on her brother as they entered the long valley Hannibal's army had passed through. The Carthaginians had already disappeared over the low pass at its head; it would likely be dark before they had a vantage high enough to see them again. Elissa relaxed into the comfortable rhythm of her loping horse, and the hours passed in steady silence. It had been weeks since she'd enjoyed the pleasure of moving forward without the effort of having to place one foot in front of the other. The valley made for easy travel. The ground was mostly bare grass, with only the occasional boulder or stunted juniper to weave around. They could still see the legion on the ridge above them, tiny shapes moving imperceptibly up to the skyline.

Elissa breathed deeply and filled her lungs with mountain air. It was refreshingly empty. No sounds of war, no smells from thousands of nearby men, only the subtle tang of her horse's sweat mixed with the nearby pine. Marcus was riding ahead when he broke off a conversation with one of his men to glance back at her. Elissa's smile came easily when she met his eye. Marcus hesitated, and then he smiled in return.

The shadows had grown to cover all but the far edge of

the valley by the time they reached the pass. They slowed their horses to a walk and surveyed the land beyond. The high mountains and rocky cliffs fell away, and low hills and wide valleys stretched out toward the darkening horizon. The forest was a thick blanket of green, sporadically interrupted by cleared patches of farmland. The pass ended in a wide valley, and at its bottom, one of the rectangular patches flickered with firelight—Hannibal's camp. Marcus turned back to face his group.

"We'll find shelter and stop for the night."

He found a suitable place at the edge of the forest on the far side of the pass. The ground was still soft and grassy here, and a small stream trickled out from behind a boulder. No one had more than a blanket to sleep on; they left them in their packs for now and set about their tasks for the night. One man hobbled the horses; three more set out to hunt for dinner, and the last started on the fire. Elissa, having never caught more than a hare with a slingshot, resolved to help with this last task. She walked toward the forest with eyes trained on the ground, looking for small sticks to feed a new fire. She had only passed the first few rows of trees when Marcus's hand circled her wrist.

"Where are you going?"

Elissa lifted her eyes from the ground. It was too dark to see more than the angular outline of his face. She hesitated before answering. Now more than ever, she desperately wanted to know what he was thinking. Was he angry with her? Might he even hate her? He had hardly spoken since rescuing her, but still, Elissa didn't sense that his silence had grown hostile. He seemed to want to say something now. She just didn't know what.

"To gather wood for the fire," she finally replied.

He didn't let go of her arm.

"Marcus." Elissa grew exasperated. "I gave you my word not to lie. I only want firewood."

Marcus didn't let go. He slid his grip down her arm so he was holding her hand rather than her wrist. He squeezed and she felt a familiar heat creeping up her arm. Marcus hadn't touched her since the day of her rescue, and she was embarrassed at how pleased she was to feel his skin again. Leaning forward, she closed her eyes and imagined throwing her arm around his shoulders and letting her body melt into his. He would slide his hand down her waist and trace the curve of her back. He would cup it around her bottom and hoist her into his arms. She would bring her lips to the side of his neck and follow it down to the point where his skin softened at his collarbone. Her stomach ached from wanting him, but she still didn't move.

It wasn't guilt that stopped her. Marcus was so much more than a Roman to her now. He was the man who had climbed down a cliff to find her, who had mercifully ended her horse's damaged life. The man who had teased her and fought for her, and had awakened a passion inside her that she hadn't known she possessed. He had sacrificed his men and his home for her, too. But it wasn't the cold weight of guilt that made her want him now. And it wasn't the blazing fire of passion. It was something softer. Something that started in her chest and warmed her veins as it filtered through her body. It flushed her skin and whispered in her ear.

"Come," he said. "I want to scout the Carthaginian camp tonight."

Elissa clamped her mouth shut. Her feet didn't move. Marcus tugged on her hand. She blinked. Marcus stared at her for a long moment, but the darkness once again masked his expression. He squeezed her hand and took another step into the forest. Elissa hesitated, then let herself be pulled along.

The trees were bunched more closely together here, but their new leaves were still too small to block out all the light from the stars. Elissa could feel the ground sloping steadily downward into the valley below. Hannibal's camp was somewhere at the bottom of this forest. And maybe Barro would be there. The thought of seeing her brother made Elissa's heart beat faster. But she shouldn't deceive herself. The Carthaginians would have scouts positioned at every entrance to prevent intruders from getting too close. It was unlikely she and Marcus would see more than trees tonight.

He was walking slightly ahead of her, and now he pulled his hand to retrieve it from Elissa's grip. Elissa held firm. Marcus's step faltered, but then he slowed so they were walking side by side, hands still clasped. Their feet fell quietly on the soft forest carpet. They walked quickly without any deadfall or obstacles to slow them down. Elissa took two steps for every one of Marcus's. Their shoulders brushed together as they moved, and Elissa found herself leaning even closer to him. It felt good, safe, to have him so near.

But Elissa's apprehension grew as they neared the camp. She heard Quintus's words of warning in her ear. An army at war could hardly be expected to receive a young woman graciously, especially an unwelcome visitor like her. Besides, most of the soldiers in Hannibal's army would be as foreign to her as the Romans. Carthaginians were merchants—they paid for their army, but didn't fight in it. Apart from the few Carthaginians in the officer class, the rest of the men were mercenaries—infantry from Libya, cavalry from Numidia, Gallic and Iberian auxiliaries; none of these men could be expected to show allegiance to the daughter of a Carthaginian aristocrat. By the time they reached level ground at the bottom of the valley, Elissa had all but convinced herself that Marcus had been right when he'd said that waiting for peace to sail home was the only safe choice. Elissa could see herself on that ship—the sand walls of Carthage rising up around her as they entered the harbor. The tangled mess of brick and wood would unravel in front of her as she strode past the city walls. Why did that thought make Elissa's chest tighten? As if someone had a hand around her heart and was squeezing. She looked up at Marcus. His shoulders were rigid and square, his head was cocked to the side, carefully listening for errant sounds. He raised his hand, telling her to stop. Elissa's attention returned to the present, and she glanced to either side. A breeze rustled the grass, an owl hooted, but nothing moved. Marcus let go of her hand and pointed to one side. Elissa nodded and bent into a crouch. They crept quietly across the grass and through the scattered trees. With their footsteps now muted, Elissa could hear what had stopped Marcus. The sounds of crackling fires, metal banging, and gruff voices echoed through the trees. Even the dim forest light now contained a tinge of orange. Thousands of campfires were burning nearby.

Marcus set his hand on her back as he angled her off to the left side and closer to the camp. Elissa turned to look at him.

"We have to find somewhere we can see," he whispered in her ear. His breath felt warm against her neck.

Elissa nodded. So they weren't about to go barging in. That was a relief. They continued walking until they reached the bottom of a steep embankment. Rock and hard dirt rose up the hill in front of them. The slope was littered with stunted trees and brambled shrubs that would be distinctly unpleasant to crawl through.

Marcus took her hand again and led her along the base of the slope. The ground was more uneven here, and more than once they were forced to climb over a fallen log or around a muddy patch of ground. Every time, Marcus would stop, surmount the obstacle, and then hold out his hand to help Elissa over. Her fingers were still wrapped tightly around his palm when he stopped her with a touch to the shoulder. He nodded at the steep hill in front of them.

"We should be able to climb up here. I'll go first to make sure it's safe and then come back for you."

Elissa shifted nervously in place. It was dark here. The narrow trunks of the trees jutted into one another, their limbs tangling as they reached toward the ground. The branches were a ghostly gray in the dim light.

She looked back up at Marcus. "I'm coming with you."

Marcus shrugged, but she saw the hint of a smile on his lips. They turned toward the hill and began climbing it slowly. The dirt was too hard-packed for Elissa's sandals to get much purchase. She made use of the scruffy vegetation instead, which had roots just deep enough to offer a secure hold for a hand or foot. Elissa pulled herself awkwardly between shrubs and the slender stalks of trees, burrowing her feet in the dirt as best she could for added security. Her cloak seemed to catch in the thorns of a shrub every other step, and she kept having to retrace her steps to untangle it. Marcus was having markedly less trouble. He hardly needed the vegetation, preferring to kick steps into the dirt and carefully walk his way up. He stayed close to Elissa, though, and was always there to offer his hand when a crucial hold was missing.

Elissa didn't bother finding the last thorny shrub to pull herself over the hill. As she rolled ungracefully over the top, her back crunched painfully on a submerged root. She bit her lip to stop from cursing. Marcus joined her along the edge and motioned for them to stay close to the ground where the grass would hide them. Elissa nodded with her teeth still digging into her bottom lip. The uneven dirt clawed at her knees and elbows as she crawled forward. The sounds of the Carthaginian camp were much louder here; Elissa could even start to make out distinct conversations. She badly wanted to bring her feet under her and stand. Perhaps she'd catch sight of the Carthaginians. But it was too risky; there would surely be someone watching this close to the camp. Marcus slowed until he was across from her. Because of his greater height, he had to shuffle on his stomach to stay hidden. His grimace suggested he was enjoying the experience no more than she was. He reached toward her and clasped the top of her arm. *Don't move*, his grip said.

Marcus pushed himself off his stomach and slowly straightened until the top of his head was hovering above the grass. He paused, listening. Elissa stayed where she was. Her heart beat fast; she dreaded the awful whoosh of an arrow as it sliced through the air or the cry of a scout who had spotted them. But the night was still. Marcus rose slowly to his feet, and Elissa's heart sped again. He motioned for her to stay. And then he was gone. The grass rustled as he merged with the night.

Elissa closed her eyes and forced her heart to slow. No one had seen them, and she wasn't about to let her fear get the better of her. This wasn't the same as when she'd tried to escape. She was with Marcus; she wasn't alone. Elissa rolled onto her back and opened her eyes. There were no trees to obstruct the sky here, and the stars shone brilliantly above. She looked to the far edge of the sky and started counting, hoping it might distract her from her fear. She quickly lost track of her tally; there were too many stars to count. Elissa thought back to the night she'd tried to escape the Roman camp. She'd wondered then if the stars held some meaning for her, some message from the gods that might help her make sense of her life, of everything that had happened to her. That night she'd been recaptured, beaten and nearly raped. She'd decided then that if the sky did hold a message, it wasn't for humans to read. But as Elissa stared at the stars tonight, the edges of the sky framed by silver stalks of grass, the world seemed less malevolent to her. Maybe those innumerable pinpricks of light did have meaning. They gave man some sense of the scale of things. They were beautiful, and that was enough.

The ground reverberating under her shoulders broke Elissa's trance. She rolled back onto her stomach just as

Marcus's boots reappeared beside her. He held his hand down to her. Elissa reached up and let him pull her to her feet.

"We can see from over there." Marcus gestured across the meadow to a point where the ground began sloping down toward the camp.

Elissa hesitated.

Marcus squeezed her hand. "No one's watching."

She nodded, only somewhat reassured. Marcus tugged gently and Elissa started to walk. The light grew brighter, almost orange as they crossed the meadow. They could hear an axe chopping wood, poles thumping together, fires crackling, metal clanging. The world was busy and alive beyond the meadow. But up here, it was eerily still; there was only the sound of swaying grass as their feet brushed it aside. They reached a lone oak tree at the edge of the meadow, an old, proud tree, with thick limbs that forked close to the ground. Marcus squeezed Elissa's hand a second time and bent to whisper in her ear.

"We need to climb up to see."

Elissa stared at him instead of the tree. His rich hair was swept back across his forehead, and his blue eyes shone in the dim light. His face was level and perfectly calm. Elissa realized in that moment that she trusted him completely. She stepped forward and stood on her tiptoes to reach the lowest branch, then curved her palms around the smooth bark and lifted her feet off the ground. She thought she could hear Marcus chuckling behind her as she threw her leg over the branch and turned her body so she was sitting on top of it. This wasn't her first time climbing a tree.

"That's it, Elissa, keep going," Marcus encouraged, his voice ringing with laughter.

Elissa obliged him. She climbed until the branches shrank to the width of her wrist and she had to stand right at the base to be confident in their strength. She'd heard Marcus following, but now he'd stopped. She looked down and saw him sitting on one of the thicker branches below. He met Elissa's eyes and then pointed through the broad leaves of the tree.

Elissa gasped.

The ground fell away beyond the tree, concealed by the high walls of the Carthaginian camp. The walls formed a large wooden rectangle around the flatter land, and thousands of domed tents glowed within it. The camp was bursting with men, and Elissa could make out the shapes of those nearest to her. One led a horse, several more laughed around a fire, another walked briskly between tents with rolls of papyrus in his arms. Elissa couldn't help noticing the similarity to the Roman camp she'd just left—the spiked palisade, the ramparts for sentries, the flickering campfires. But the order of things was completely different. The Romans placed their tents in tight lines, with open pathways leading to common areas at crisp right angles. There was an order to the Carthaginian camp, too, but it was in circles rather than straight lines. Distinct clusters had formed within the wooden walls, and within each cluster, the men looked more similar to each other than they did to their neighbors.

The Numidians were in the nearest corner. The smooth backs of thousands of horses shimmered in the orange half-light. The horses had been tied to stakes in the ground or left to roam freely in small corrals. The men who walked between them were dark-skinned and wore a length of hide around their shoulders rather than armor. A few still carried the rounded shields or spears that they fought with, but most had replaced their weapons with an axe or a pot.

Next to them were the Libyans. They were more heavily armored than the Numidians, and with their plumed helmets and leather breastplates, they could almost be mistaken for Romans. But the colors they wore were far more eclectic than the uniform scarlet of the Romans. The purple of

Carthage mixed with the green and blue dyes of Egypt, and then bled into the exotic turquoise and violet of the Far East.

The Africans made up the nearest half of the camp, and beyond them it was more difficult to pick out each cluster. Or maybe it was only that Elissa was less sure of their origins. There would surely be Iberian and Gallic tribes Hannibal had enlisted in the Carthaginian cause, but the men sitting around the fires in tight groups all appeared the same to Elissa. Their long hair and bare chests marked them as distinctly barbarian, but Elissa could only guess where they lived or which tribe they came from.

"The Carthaginians."

Marcus's voice was hushed, and yet it nearly startled Elissa off her branch. He'd moved farther up so he was now standing on the branch below her. His arm was thrown over the branch behind her for balance. Elissa followed his gaze to the center of camp. There, amidst the Numidians, Libyans, Iberians and Gauls—a thousand different tribes from a thousand different places—were the Carthaginians. Their tents were larger and positioned in tidy rows rather than the haphazard clusters of the rest of the camp. Fewer men milled about between tents, but those Elissa could see wore full armor. Their breastplates were smooth sheets of metal or the same segmented copper that Marcus wore. Gilded standards stood outside their tents, with sickle-shaped crests and depictions of Ba'al Hammon, patron god of Carthage. Elissa shifted forward along her branch and squinted to narrow her vision. A large gold standard with trailing ribbons of white was moving through the camp. She followed its progress between tent rows and crackling fires. She wanted to see the man holding it. She wanted to see someone she could imagine she knew. Maybe a butcher she'd walked by in the market, or a harried mother on her way to the temple at Byrsa—a face she could give to someone she missed.

The standard carrier obliged her at that moment. He circled around the back of a high rectangular tent and came to stand by a large fire with several men gathered around its warmth. Elissa leaned in closer, trying to see the distant man better. He was tall and slender. He stood erect, his square shoulders in sharp contrast with the men lounging casually by the fire. He wore a round steel helmet with a long white plume at its peak. He rammed the butt of the standard into the ground and reached up to pull off his helmet. The plume shook as it moved from the man's head to rest by his hip. Elissa traced the white feathers as they swayed methodically from side to side. Her eyes moved slowly from the man's helmet, across his copper breastplate, and up to his face. Orange light danced across high cheekbones and gentle waves rippled through his thick hair. Soft amber eyes were set above straight lips. She couldn't see all that, of course, but she didn't need to see; she knew what her brother looked like.

Elissa closed her eyes as a wave of longing crashed over her. Her body swayed from the force of the feeling. Barro, the man who'd been both mother and father to her almost since she was born. Barro, the brother who used to hug her to sleep when she was sick. Barro, who'd always made time to scold her when she missed a lesson with one of her tutors because she was playing with Taanit. *Barro.*

She opened her eyes again. For a moment, all she could see were her white hands against the tree bark. Her body had hinged forward at the waist, as if she were leaning into her brother's distant embrace. Elissa tensed her legs. She could leap from the tree and run to him. She would scream his name as she ran up to the walls. Surely he'd hear her call! Surely he'd come to her. He would protect her as he always had.

Something warm covered her fists. Marcus's tanned hands rested on her pale ones. He'd walked farther out along the branch so he could turn and face her, and he stared up at her with eyes that glowed silver-blue in the moonlight. His lips were slightly parted, as if he held a word between them. But he glanced down instead, and his jaw pulsed.

"Not here." His voice was tight.

She didn't understand what he meant.

Marcus cleared his throat and tried again.

"We can't do this here." He jerked his chin in the direction of the camp. "The sentries will shoot anyone who gets close enough to shout. Your brother is a standard-bearer, which means he rides at the front of the army. We'll come back tomorrow. First thing in the morning as the army begins to march. That way we'll be able to go to him directly."

Elissa was stunned into further silence. How did he recognize Barro as her brother? And what did he mean "go to him"? He didn't intend to hand her off himself, did he? No Roman could possibly expect to approach an army of Carthaginians and return alive.

Elissa looked at their joined hands, and then back up at Marcus. She started to say something but the words were trapped in her throat. She prayed that her widened eyes were saying what her tongue could not. Did he really expect her to trade his life for the chance to return to Barro? Elissa thought of herself riding next to Barro in the middle of the Carthaginian army. She pictured Marcus's back filling with spears as he tried to ride away.

"No," Elissa said with a firmness that surprised her. "I will not exchange your life for my home." Her throat abruptly closed. "It...it would be a hollow happiness." Elissa drew in a shallow breath and forced herself to swallow.

Marcus lifted his hand to her cheek, smiling sadly. "You are nothing if not unexpected," he murmured. "But that decision has already been made. I promised my men I would fight the enemies of Rome until my dying breath. And so I will. But you, Elissa, you are not an enemy of Rome. You are a brave woman caught in impossible circumstances. And I—" Marcus glanced down and shook his head. "I will set those circumstances right."

Now Elissa shook her head and covered Marcus's hand with her own. "Marcus. You would die for this?"

Marcus's lips curved in a smile but the light did not reach his eyes. "Elissa, do you know why my men accepted me back? Deserting the legion to rescue you was treason, and yet, a few shouted words and I was back to being their beloved leader?"

Elissa shook her head again. She truly did not understand the hold Marcus had on his men. She attributed it to some shared experience that only men who'd been in battle together could understand.

"I gave them meaning," he said with a shrug of his shoulders. "We all die, Elissa. Whether of plague or famine, or some foreign war that we have no choice but to fight. Dying is routine. It's having something to die for that is not. My men would rather accept a traitor as their leader than give up the purpose to their lives. Rome is right, and just, and glorious, and worth dying to protect. That is what I wanted to give to them, the idea they deserve. Because when Rome festers into a putrid and ugly scar in the minds of men, that's when they truly die." Marcus's features twisted into an ugly mask, and then they straightened. "But sometimes we find meaning in the most unexpected places." He levelled his stare at Elissa. "And the most unexpected people." Marcus paused for a long moment, then finished quietly. "To die for you, Elissa Mago, would be a blessing, not a curse."

Tears sprang to Elissa's eyes as she turned away. She couldn't meet those piercing blue eyes. She couldn't tell him what he deserved to hear, what she wanted to say. It was the truth, gods help her, but the words wouldn't leave her throat, not with her mind still whirling with thoughts of Barro, and her father, and the dream of her mother on that pale moonlit night. So she looked away from his clear eyes and upturned face and into the night sky. She tried to lose herself in the innumerable stars.

"Come," Marcus said finally. "Let's sleep for a few hours before morning."

Elissa heard those words all through the rest of the night and into the next day. *To die for you, Elissa Mago.* They went around and around in her head. They rose to the surface as she watched Marcus's tall figure riding in front of her, and then sank back down when she looked into the distance and saw the Carthaginian army marching ahead.

Elissa had spent most of her life trying to fill the hole in her heart that her mother's death had left. How was it that now, in the most unwelcoming of places, she felt the jagged edges of loss start to round, and a feeling other than loneliness take root? It was a whisper of something else, something that felt an awful lot like belonging. But was it enough to sacrifice her brother, her father, her people? No, it was not, Elissa decided as they descended the last of the green mountain valleys into a wide lowland plain. Marcus could no more ask her to give up her family than he could ask his men to rid themselves of Rome. But he knew that, and he hadn't asked, which only made her heart ache all the more. Green-leaved trees gave way to brown grass and small, spindly trees, and Elissa's resolve bent but did not break. She would return to Barro tomorrow, and she would beg him to spare the life of the man who had brought her. She would plead directly to Hannibal if need be.

The day was spent in silence. Marcus rode at the front with at least one of his men, and Elissa stayed behind, sitting listlessly atop her feisty horse. There were only five of them now; Marcus had sent a man back to the legion this morning to report on what they'd seen last night. Elissa hadn't spotted the Roman legion since they'd dropped out of view yesterday afternoon, but she suspected they weren't far behind. Flaminius would want to head off the Carthaginians at a moment's notice. They were getting dangerously close to Rome.

The Carthaginians, on the other hand, were making no attempt to conceal themselves. They marched through the center of a wide-open plain. A distant lake colored the horizon blue, but the land was otherwise dry. Shades of brown were punctuated by lopsided rows of silver-green olive trees, their spiralling black branches reaching for the sky. It was as if the lush lands of Italy were slowly melting into the familiar browns of Carthage. Elissa's present slowly returning to her past—

They stopped for the night next to the massive lake they'd stared at all day. Lake Trasimene, Elissa heard one of the men say. "Lake" seemed something of an understatement. Trasimene was a veritable ocean. Its water was the deep blue of the Mediterranean on a cloudy day, and its shores were surrounded by brown hills. Scrubby brush covered the distance between blue water and blue sky. A narrow road ran between the shore of the lake and the steep hills behind it, but Marcus had insisted they take a higher route instead. He'd wanted to make camp in the hills near the Carthaginians, but they'd been unable to find water, so Marcus had reluctantly led the descent back to the lake. The fires from the nearby Carthaginian camp were just being lit as they'd dropped down to the lake and out of sight.

The water lapped gently against the sandy shore of the lake as Elissa tried to fall asleep that night. A tiny splash cast silver ripples across the inky water. The wool blanket under her head scratched her cheek. Marcus lay beside her; his body was still, but not relaxed. Elissa rolled onto her side to face him, thinking back to the first night they'd met. She'd been huddled miserably on the side of a cliff; he had approached cautiously, with arms outstretched. He should have been the one to run away that night, not her. But selfishly, despite what it would cost him, Elissa was glad he hadn't. She reached across the distance between them and took hold of his hand. She ran her fingers across the roughened calluses on his palm and pulled it into her chest, then brought her lips to his knuckles. Marcus squeezed the tips of her fingers and let his arm relax contentedly to the ground. Elissa sighed and closed her eyes. If only for one night, she could pretend to know what it was to love and be loved.

Marcus and Elissa set out in the gray light of early morning. Marcus told his remaining men to wait by the lake, and if he didn't return by mid-morning, to go back to the legion. The four men glared at Elissa accusingly. Elissa winced as she mounted her horse and turned away as soon as she could.

They climbed steadily up the hillside with the rising sun. Their horses' heads bobbed rhythmically as they picked their way around patches of shrub and uneven ground. By dawn, a thick bank of fog had grown to obscure the lake below. Elissa squeezed the reins nervously. They wouldn't be able to see the Carthaginians until they were over this hill. Once they'd spotted them, Marcus planned to find cover until they located Barro, and then stay hidden for as long as possible before approaching him. It was a reasonable plan, but not knowing whether it would work was even worse than waiting.

The mist thickened around them. It had lightened from gray to white, which must mean the first rays of light had broken free of the horizon. A strong wind picked up as they crested the top of the hill, and it caused patches of white to swirl in and out of view chaotically. Marcus halted a few strides in front of her and held up a hand for Elissa to do the same. She ignored him and reined in her horse beside his. The hills ahead looked identical to the one they'd just climbed—brown grass with scrubby green brush. There was nothing to draw her attention, and the absence of noise took longer to register than its presence would have.

Silent. It was completely silent.

Marcus noticed the absence of sound a moment before Elissa, and he was already filling the emptiness with movement. He whirled his horse in a tight circle as his head swivelled about, searching for a hidden army, immediately alert for an attack.

Elissa didn't move. She leaned forward in the saddle and squinted through a patch of fog.

"There." She pointed in front of them at a flash of orange that had cut through the gray. "I think I see fires."

Marcus stopped his horse and stared in the same direction. His brow furrowed and his dark eyebrows pulled together. A gust of wind rushed along the hilltop; it caught Elissa's cloak and whipped her plait along her face. The cloud faded away and a large meadow between the two nearest hills came into view. Hundreds of fires burned freely along the grass, spewing thick smoke into the clouds. But there were no ditches dug into the earth, no leftover logs from the palisade, no signs of a camp having been anywhere near this place.

"Shit!"

Elissa's head jerked to Marcus.

He looked afraid.

"What...what's wrong Marcus?"

A sharp cry pierced the murky air. Elissa's horse startled and skittered to the side. Elissa swerved dangerously off the saddle and had to haul back on the reins to right herself. There was a second shout, followed by the unmistakeable clash of metal. Elissa glanced frantically to either side. The thick haze of smoke was making it impossible to tell which way to run. The air whistled behind her. Its tenor got higher and higher, and then, *thud*. Arrows hitting the ground.

"Over here!"

Marcus had turned his horse down the hill and was crouched low over the animal's neck, preparing to gallop. But why was he pointed back down the hill? It sounded as though that volley of arrows had come from near the lake. Elissa shook her head frantically. Marcus sat back in the saddle and pushed his horse toward her instead.

"Elissa, please. I need to see what's happening. This was a trap. The Carthaginians wanted it to look like they were camped here. And if Flaminius took that road by the lake..." His words trailed off as he struggled to keep his voice level.

Elissa stared at him. Dense fog had blown back in, so all she could see was Marcus. His eyes were alight with frantic energy. Something gleamed within them that made her queasy; it felt like she was drowning, everything slipping away. Water filled her nose and eyes, and fear poured into her. She swallowed them both back down. She trusted him. She nodded once.

Marcus took off down the hill at a gallop.

Elissa's horse followed without her asking. They cut a diagonal track across the hill and back toward the center of the lake. The noise heightened. Men shouted. Metal clanged against metal. A spear thumped as it missed its target. The next one made a squelching sound as it didn't. Dirt fell away in hard chunks under her horse's thundering hooves. They crashed through bushes they'd carefully picked their way around not an hour before. Thorns tore at the leather straps on Elissa's shoes. She closed her eyes and forced herself to lean forward to keep them upright. She struggled to hold her crazed horse, as Marcus drove his even harder.

The fog churned angrily around them. Brown hills and green shrubs mixed together in the swirling white. Elissa's stomach turned; she was going to be sick. The clouds raced up the hill and the lake below them cleared. She threw her body back against the reins, and her horse's hind legs locked and slid helplessly through the dirt. They still nearly crashed into Marcus, who had stopped directly in front of them. Elissa was too transfixed by what was happening below to bother cursing at him.

Chaos. The legion had stalled in a long, narrow line along the shore of the lake. A group of Carthaginian heavy infantry prevented the Romans from moving farther up the road, and a horde of screaming Numidians cut them off from the rear. The remainder of the Carthaginian army surged out of the hills above the legion. Where they met beside the lake, each man's origin became irrelevant. Purple cloaks mixed with red, man with horse, swords with bodies. But the trap was perfect, and there was no doubt the Romans would eventually be consumed within the Carthaginian vice. Terrified men squeezed out of every open space. They only succeeded in running partway up the hill before murderous Gauls fell on top of them. Hundreds of legionaries were jumping into the lake to escape. Unable to swim, they waded into the water until it came up to their chests, then covered their faces with their arms and waited for death.

"Elissa!"

Marcus's voice sounded as if it were coming from very far away. Elissa couldn't tear her eyes from the carnage. It seemed as if a gaping pit to the underworld had opened up to engulf the entire legion.

"Elissa!"

Marcus had moved in front so he was blocking her view of the carnage. But the sounds of death still reverberated in her head. It was like the hilt of a sword banging inside her skull, an incessant pounding that racked her ears and left her disoriented. Something warm clasped her arm and Marcus drew her body firmly toward him.

"Elissa, look at me."

She turned to him slowly. Marcus brought his other hand to her cheek.

"*Cara*, I have to go. I have to fight. Those are my men dying down there. I made them a promise."

Elissa woke from her stupor. *Cara*, beloved in Latin. Her fingers latched onto Marcus's hand. Her head shook involuntarily as the words rushed out. "No, no, Marcus, you'll die down there! You can't go. We need to run. Let's run away from here. We can leave now."

Marcus's brow furrowed and he smiled softly. He reached back to his saddlebag and pulled out his helmet. The tall red fan that marked him as a centurion still jutted from the top. Marcus twined his hand through the feathers and yanked. There was a ripping sound and the bright red feathers slipped between his fingers and fell to the earth. He placed the bare steel helmet on his head.

"Look at those wagons, Elissa." He pointed to the front of the legion.

Elissa reluctantly followed the direction of his finger. Four ornate wagons were pushed together to form a circle of relative calm where the first clash of Romans and Carthaginians had taken place. One of the wagons was tipped over on its side and cushions, scrolls and half-eaten food were strewn across the ground. But most of the objects that shone and weren't bolted down had been removed. The Carthaginians must be confident of victory if they'd already started looting. It was no easy thing to kill a man with your tunic stuffed full of his possessions.

"I want you to go there and hide. Those are the consul's wagons, so they were taken first. Anything valuable is gone, but someone's bound to come back for a second look after the fighting is over."

Elissa's heart was pounding in her head. He wanted her to hide in Hades and wait for him to come back? "No, Marcus, no! Let's escape from here. Let's get away." Her breath was coming in short, rapid bursts as she sucked air in and out of her tightening chest.

Marcus cupped her cheek and brought her close enough that their noses touched. His eyes had hardened to a gray she hadn't seen in a long time.

"I must fight. Not for Rome, but for my brothers. What kind of man would I be if I abandoned them now? They're being slaughtered down there!" His words were coming more quickly. "I can't take you away, not now. And hiding is safer than running. These hills are teeming with battle-crazed men. If you run, they'll chase. And if they catch you—" a muscle pulsed in his jaw "—if they catch you, they'll rape you and tear you apart. At least down there, you'll have a good chance of changing sides on your own terms."

Elissa pulled her head back and straightened. She was terrified, but she was not going to die here with these Romans. She was on Hannibal's side, wasn't she? And he was winning brilliantly. She met Marcus's eyes. Well, *part* of her side was winning. He had a duty to his men, and she had a duty to him, to what she felt for him. Suddenly all of Elissa's inhibitions, her pride, her torn allegiances, her fear—all fell away. In the face of death, she had nothing left to lose.

"If I go down there and hide, it will not be to change sides. You must promise me that you'll return. I will not leave that place without you."

Marcus missed the change in her tone. He gathered the reins in both hands and prepared to drive his horse into the fray. The beast's eyes were wide with anticipation and his front feet danced on the spot. Marcus's eyes were shining as he faced Elissa. "I promise you I'll come back, in this world or—"

"Don't you dare finish that sentence, Marcus Gracchus! You will come back in this life. Because—"

Kate Q. Johnson

Elissa stopped herself. She saw Marcus sitting imposingly on his horse, his broad chest squared to his duty below. He was so loyal, so Roman; even after being banished from the legion, he couldn't run. And it infuriated her.

"I love you, Marcus."

Marcus jerked towards her. His brows shot up, incredulous. His mouth was slightly agape. He reached his hand up to Elissa as if she were a revelation and curled his fingers in the back of her hair. He guided her in closer, then leaned over in the saddle and brought his forehead to hers. He closed his eyes.

Elissa let stillness overtake them. It was an instant of togetherness, a brief slice of time when their bodies matched their hearts. A tear slid down her cheek. She breathed him in—his musky scent, his radiating heat, his devotion. Would this be their moment? The one she held forever in her mind but only felt real in her dreams?

Marcus moved back so he was looking at her. His eyes were wide and earnest.

"I have loved you since I first set eyes on you, a nameless girl in a dark doorway who gave me fire when I was freezing. I would have happily chased you forever, *cara.* Like the moon follows the sun across the sky. You are my love, my life, and I will come back for you."

He reached down to his sword and drew it from the scabbard, then dug his heels into his horse's sides and galloped away before Elissa could respond. She didn't even know what she would have said. Dirt cascaded down the hill as he raced into battle. She saw him hack at a Gaul as he entered the fray. The man spun around after Marcus had passed, then toppled backward lifelessly. Elissa watched Marcus until he was just another speck in the mass of bodies. She followed him until she couldn't tell if he was Roman or Carthaginian, friend or foe, alive or dead. She closed her eyes.

236

Elissa's horse fidgeted nervously. She opened her eyes and looked down at the wagons. They weren't far below. The Carthaginians had pushed the Romans back along the road, and the fighting had dispersed farther from the wagons. The nearest one was turned on its side. Its interior was dark and sheltered; it would be a good place to hide. She'd find herself a weapon and she would wait for the battle to be over. Wait for Marcus to return. She did not doubt his promise, and she would keep hers. Elissa took a deep breath and loosened her horse's reins.

Marcus tore his sword from a man's side. Blood dripped from the metal as he slid it through the air. Something slammed into his foot and nearly jerked the sword from his hand. He spun his horse around at the same time a massive Iberian warrior whirled to face him. The man was shirtless; dirt and blood were smeared across his chest. The Iberian brought his arm up for a high, sweeping slash at Marcus's waist. Marcus raised his sword to parry the blow. The Iberian's arm came down but Marcus's horse shied away from something on the opposite side and sprang into the air. Marcus's thigh slammed into the Iberian's chest partway through his swing. The Iberian's sword fell limply from his hand as he disappeared under the horse's hooves. But Marcus didn't have time to finish the job because his horse had fallen to his knees and was squealing in pain. Marcus glanced down and saw the end of a spear jutting from his horse's shoulder. He hauled up on the horse's head to keep them both upright. He'd lose all his advantage if his horse fell. He grasped the wooden shaft and tugged. The spear came loose from the muscle easily. The horse scrambled to his feet. Marcus adjusted his grip on the shaft and wound his arm back. There was a point of stillness after Marcus had lined up his target and before he released. The putrid smell of sweat and blood and stomach contents receded. The sounds of swords tearing through flesh, spears clanging against shields, arrows whistling nearby, were all silenced by his concentration. The air was alight with terror and exertion; it threatened to burn alive every man who breathed it. Marcus loosed the spear, which landed in the neck of a nearby Numidian who'd bent to retrieve his shield. If the man screamed, Marcus didn't hear it.

Marcus shouted in pain. Someone had opened a hole in his thigh and it felt as if hot water was pouring down his leg. There were hands on his shoulders; they dragged him down, down to the pit of bodies and blood. Marcus hit the ground shoulder first, but he was rolling back to his feet as soon as he landed. The point of a sword came down in the space he'd just left. Marcus brought his own sword up to block the next blow to his head. Steel rang above him and he struggled to keep his elbow up under the weight. He launched himself to a stand as soon as the pressure lessened. The pain in his thigh receded to a distant ache, banished to the recesses of his mind amid more pressing concerns. He lifted his sword over his shoulder, ready to block another strike but it never came. His assailant was gone, lost in the teeming mass of flesh around him. Marcus ducked to the side as an arrow slid past his left ear. A Carthaginian backed up in front of him, lost in his fight with a legionary. They'd both dropped their swords and were hanging onto each other with bare hands, occasionally freeing an arm enough to throw a fist. The Roman shrieked as the Carthaginian locked onto his ear with his teeth. Marcus caught a glimpse of the man's pale and terrified face as he wrenched it free of the Carthaginian's mouth.

"JULIUS!" That was his man.

Blood streaked down the side of Julius's face as Marcus sprinted toward him. Marcus was fast, but the Carthaginian was faster. He saw the glint of steel rush at Julius's ribs. He was still too far away to stop it. Suddenly, the Carthaginian screamed and lurched forward into Julius's arms. Julius sputtered as a new coat of blood painted his face. The man slid from his arms onto the ground. An arrow jutted from his neck.

"Julius!" Marcus shouted again as he reached him. He brought both hands to Julius's shoulders and spun him around so their backs were pressed together and they each faced out in a protective stance. "Where are the others?" he shouted over his shoulder.

"Gone, centurion! Flaminius put 'em back with the baggage train. Said we were only fit to ride with the mules. Quintus made 'em run when he smelled trouble!"

Marcus parried a blow with his blade. He rammed his foot into another man's back to shove him away.

"Get out of here, Julius!" he grunted between sword strokes. He heard a shield ring as Julius blocked a strike to his head.

"Centurion?" Julius sounded surprised.

"GO!" Marcus roared. Julius could live with the shame of running. He could *live*. Marcus jumped forward to avoid a slash of steel that cut between them. Skin tore along his upper arm as he landed. He shouted in pain as he turned back to his assailant. A massive Libyan was bearing down on him. Marcus chanced a quick look over his shoulder to confirm that Julius had gone before focusing on his assailant. The man was heavily armored, which left almost no exposed flesh. Marcus leapt forward again and cut first—a high slash to the neck. The Libyan danced to the side and jabbed low, aiming for Marcus's wounded thigh. Marcus moved too late. The tip of the Libyan's sword caught the torn flap of skin and ripped it farther across his leg. Marcus sucked in air as pain slid up his throat. The Libyan advanced on him; Marcus backed away, trying to buy himself more time. His right arm hung limply from his shoulder, and his breathing was ragged and shallow. His leg was slashed in a long line from his knee to his stomach. Marcus knew he might die. He wasn't afraid. His body burned with battle fever, and that strange euphoria had taken hold. His limbs felt light despite their exhaustion. Awareness diffused through his body. He knew the texture of the ground without having to look. He could tell whether the dying man beside him was likely to reach up and gut him from below, and knew the precise flick of his wrist needed to sever the Libyan's head from his neck. Death was everywhere around him. It seeped into the dirt, leached into the lake, clapped like thunder in the sky. But Marcus was not dead. He stepped forward and used his sword to block a swing at his side. Marcus deftly reversed his grip on the sword and thrust his arm up. The sword point moved across the Libyan's chest and up into his thick, black beard. The man's brown eyes widened until they were circled with white. He stuttered and blew out his last breath. Rivulets of red ran through his black hair.

Marcus stepped back, breathing hard, ready for the next fight. He turned in a circle, searching for an opponent. The crowd was thinning around him, and the scarlet cloaks were growing fewer. This was never a battle; this was a slaughter, and the worst of the killing was nearly over. A few brave legionaries were still fighting, figuring the best they could hope for was to take a few Carthaginians with them on their way out. But the majority were leaving this miserable stretch of road along Lake Trasimene. Those who were well enough to walk were flowing into the lake; some probably hoped for escape, but most only wanted a less painful death.

Marcus started up the road. It was hard with his injured leg. He limped along, trying to fight the tide of people moving toward the lake. He thought about Quintus and prayed his old friend had gotten away. Marcus dropped his shoulder and pushed between two gray-faced legionaires who were leaning on each other to walk. There was only one promise to keep now, and thousands of men lay between him and keeping it. A Carthaginian appeared in front of him, running in the opposite direction, hands clutching his belly. They locked eyes for a moment. The man was terrified. Marcus could see the insides of his stomach through his fingers. Their shoulders brushed as they passed each other. Marcus kept moving. Something crunched under his foot, and he looked down to see a long red plume trampled into the dirt; the line of feathers led to an ornate steel helmet. The inside of the helmet had filled with mud, but the intricate engravings on the exterior were still untarnished. Marcus's fist tightened around the hilt of his sword. He took another step forward and saw pale fingers curled in the dirt. The man lay on his side. A thick arm branched off a wide chest. His breastplate glowed in the mist, a muddy boot print pressed into the gold etchings at its center. Blood trickled out from its side. Marcus reached down to the man's arm and turned him over. Flaminius's round eyes stared back at him. Marcus straightened, unable to look away from those twin pits of black. Here was the man who had killed his brother and banished him from the legion, tried to rape his *cara* and sell her into slavery. Flaminius. Just another anonymous body now, dead in the dirt. His chest and neck were unharmed; the blood pooled from his back. He'd been cut down while trying to run away. A coward to the end. Marcus felt no triumph in victory or glory in vindication. Death was death; it rendered all men the same. Marcus stepped over the lifeless body. He needed to get to Elissa.

Marcus started to force his way through a group of legionaries moving toward the water, but they pushed him aside. The same thing happened again and again. The road along the lake was blocked by a mass of bodies a thousand men deep, and Marcus was being swept to the water with them. The ground began to slope downward, and boot prints instantly filled with mud. He stopped fighting and let himself follow the tide of men. The murky water rose up to his ankles and then his knees. He waded deeper. The shore was marshy here, and reeds poked out between his legs. The water was up to his waist now. Someone pushed at his back, anxious for the release he thought the water would offer. Marcus turned around. The Numidians were behind them, herding the Romans into the lake. They looked like centaurs in the fog. The man behind shoved at him again and Marcus focused on his face. It was grim and pale. He was hardly out of boyhood. Did he think he was escaping? Did he think he'd see his mother again? His lover? Marcus knew that he wouldn't.

When the water rose up to their chests, the Romans started swimming. They spun their arms and kicked their legs to keep their bodies afloat, but succeeded only in churning up waves. Their iron armor pulled at their chests and arms, and their heads sank lower. The screaming started. Water gurgled at the backs of their throats before it ceased. Other Romans saw this and stopped before their feet left the ground. They waited for the death the Numidians would deliver instead.

Marcus took a deep breath and kicked his feet off the muddy bottom. He dug his arms into the water with bent elbows and flat palms. He couldn't bend his injured leg, so he brought his other leg to the center of his body and kicked twice as hard. The water sucked at his chest, but the bronze scales on his breastplate were light, and he could move his arms freely. Marcus heard Tiberius's voice in his ear—*one, two, three, breathe, one, two, three, breathe.* They had often swum together as boys at their family's seaside villa in Baiae.

The water lightened from brown to blue as Marcus swam deeper. The sounds of killing gradually receded. Marcus changed direction to swim parallel to the road. *Stroke, stroke, stroke.* He stopped to tread water for a moment, trying to catch sight of the wagons in the distance. They were still far along the lake but he was making good progress. He couldn't see Elissa among the wagons, but he didn't see anyone else, either. He put his head down and swam faster.

An arrow plunged into the water a hair's breadth from Marcus's hand, followed by another at his feet, far too close to be stray arrows. Marcus filled his lungs and dove under the surface. As he opened his eyes to the darkness, a third arrow streaked through the water in front of him. The white stream behind the arrow wobbled lazily as the water robbed it of its momentum. Marcus stopped diving deeper and angled across the lake. He pulled with his arms and kicked with his leg until his lungs seared with pain. When he could hold on no longer, he turned upward, toward the light. He broke the surface with a splash and greedily sucked at the air, waiting for a volley of arrows to follow, but they never came. A mercifully thick fog clung to the surface here, and it obscured everything but the ripples cast by Marcus's strokes. He was grateful for its cover as he headed for the shore.

His feet touched the ground again under a thick haze of gray. His arms ached from paddling, and his legs protested wearily at having to hold up his body. The last few hours of hard fighting hit him like a fist, and it was all Marcus could do to trudge up the sandy shore in a straight line. He was exhausted, spent, and he still had to find Elissa. What if she wasn't there, what if someone had already taken her? The ground sucked at his feet as he tried to move them faster. His breathing was ragged and shallow. He forced it to calm. He was alive, and the wagons he'd sent her to were just ahead; she would be there.

There were no bodies on this part of the road. The discarded ends of spears and arrows stuck in the sand. Marcus looked up at the wagons he'd told Elissa to hide in. They were arranged in the same square he'd first noticed, but they seemed different. Had there been two overturned before, or only one? And was there more loot strewn about the entrances now? A shadow lumbered past the nearest wagon, and Marcus broke into a run. His injured leg dragged uselessly behind him like an anchor. He heard metal clanging in the open space between the wagons, gruff voices in a language he didn't understand.

Marcus stopped behind the nearest wagon and peered around its end. Three large Gallic warriors stood in the clearing between wagons with a mountain of petty treasure piled in front of them. They seemed to be arguing about it. One of the Gauls had his hands on an ornate golden platter and was pushing it to one side of the pile, while the other Gaul was moving to stop him. The third Gaul was halfway through the entrance to one of the overturned wagons. His upper body was completely obscured by the wagon's dark interior. He jolted back suddenly and whatever he said got the others' attention. The end of the wagon shook slightly. He reached deeper into the wagon and after a short struggle, seemed to grab hold of something. The top half of his body re-emerged from the wagon. He stepped forward and hauled his loot to the entrance. At the end of the Gaul's arm, crouched in the doorway, was Elissa.

He acted at the same time as Elissa. A high, clear scream cut through the fog, and her arm descended in a sweeping arc that could have been mistaken for a welcoming wave if it weren't for the glint of steel in her hand. The knife plunged into the side of the Gaul's neck at the same moment Marcus jumped out from behind the wagon. Marcus's low bellow joined Elissa's scream in a chorus of action. He lunged for the two Gauls in the clearing, his lame leg completely forgotten. The men's heads shot up as Marcus hurtled toward them. He saw the surprise flash across their faces. The gold platter hit the ground, and both Gauls drew their swords at the same time. Marcus pulled up short and dropped into a low crouch. The battle euphoria was long gone; only the animal instinct to survive and protect was left.

The Gauls were massive, one light-featured and one dark, but both barrel-chested and vibrating with furious energy. The darker one stepped forward to Marcus's left, and the other moved around to his right. The man on his left struck first. Marcus met the Gaul's long broadsword with his shorter one at chest height. Marcus swung quickly, aiming high, but the Gaul brushed his sword away as if it weighed nothing. Marcus ducked as the second man's sword whistled above his head, and he scrambled out of their way before they could swing again.

The Gauls circled closer. The blond one bared his teeth; they were black and rotted. He slashed at Marcus's neck. Finally, he'd made a mistake. Marcus moved to duck under his arm and catch the Gaul from behind, but he'd forgotten his injured leg. His toe caught on the uneven ground and sent him staggering forward. He would've had a chance at getting his good leg underneath him in time to stop the fall, but a boot collided with his backside and threw him face-first into the dirt instead. Marcus's neck snapped to the side on impact, and his legs crumpled uselessly behind him. He managed to roll onto his back quickly, but it was already too late. The Gaul loomed over him. He brought the point of his sword to the center of Marcus's neck and pressed. The steel felt cold against his skin. The Gaul pressed harder, and warm liquid trickled down his neck. Marcus brought his shoulders under him and inched his body up, testing to see whether the sword would move with him. It dug deeper into his neck instead. The Gaul set his foot on Marcus's stomach and leaned down, cruelly trapping the air between his stomach and throat.

Marcus knew the instant the Gaul decided to kill him. His mouth straightened and his eyes grew hooded. A man about to make a kill looks nearly drunk, and for a moment, time hangs suspended in the space between life and death. He is the master of another's existence, and he tastes the absolute power of the gods. A flick of his hand, the push of his sword; a life expires. Then he moves on, forgetting the dead man in as little time as it took to kill him.

But that wasn't what Marcus thought of when the Gaul pushed. He saw only Elissa. Her luxurious hair, her alabaster skin, and her eyes—most of all, he would miss her ocean eyes. But why didn't he see love burning in those beautiful green eyes? He saw fury and fear. How could he die knowing Elissa was in pain? The splitting pressure on Marcus's neck suddenly released. The Gaul hadn't moved, but his mouth had gone slack and his eyes had lost their glimmer of rage. His whole body tilted forward, and then he was falling, directly on top of him. Marcus forgot his disbelief and rolled to the side to avoid the hurtling body. When he looked up again, the Gaul was lying beside him and Elissa was standing where the Gaul had been. She held a rock in her hand, and her mouth was frozen in a silent cry.

Someone yelled behind her and started running. Movement flashed across his eyes and Marcus saw the second Gaul rush at Elissa with his sword raised. She barely had time to look before his sword rushed through the air toward her neck. Marcus hurled himself off the ground before his mind had time to fully register what was happening. The Gaul's sword was halfway through its arc when Marcus's body collided with his. His shoulder crashed into the Gaul's stomach. The Gaul staggered backward in surprise; the sword flew from his hand and fell uselessly to the ground several feet away. Marcus drove his body down and forced the Gaul beneath him, pinning him to the ground with his weight. The Gaul brought his hands to Marcus's chest to shove him off, but Marcus felt his protests no more than he would feel a fly. He wrapped both hands around the man's thick neck and squeezed. The Gaul bucked and squirmed. He tore at Marcus's arms and face with his hands; his nails caught flesh and ripped his skin but Marcus only squeezed tighter. The Gaul's eyes bulged and his neck brightened to red, and then darkened to purple. The Gaul eventually went limp underneath him and the light left his eyes, but Marcus kept squeezing.

Marcus eventually became aware of something soft on his shoulder. He turned his head but didn't move his hands. Elissa was crouched behind him. She moved in front of the Gaul's head and placed her hands over Marcus's. Her touch was light and cool. She curled her fingers around Marcus's one by one, and slowly lifted each of them from the dead man's neck. She gently tugged on his hands until he was standing in front of her. Finally, he saw only her. Elissa's eyes were full of love this time, just as he'd hoped. She drew him toward her and wrapped her arms around his waist, holding his head against her shoulder. Marcus closed his eyes and felt her hair tickle his nose, her warm skin against his cheek. They sank to the ground together. Their arms formed perfect circles around each other, and they clung tightly, as if they were all that was holding the world together.

CHAPTER 15

E lissa couldn't let go. She didn't need to hold on to Marcus's hands so tightly; she was more than capable of staying astride their loping horse with only her legs. But still, she couldn't let go. Her hands clutched Marcus's over the reins. The familiar roughness of his skin against her palms was reassuring. She breathed out shakily. They were alive.

Marcus tightened his arms around her shoulders and shifted his weight closer to her. When they had ridden like this the night they'd met, Elissa had nearly fallen off his horse trying to put more distance between them. This time, she leaned back against Marcus's chest and rested her head in the crook of his arm. From the safety of his embrace, Elissa forced herself to examine her surroundings. The brown hills of Trasimene had blurred to green, and tall pines ran in neat rows on either side of the road. The *Via Cassia* was nothing like the rutted trails they'd traversed all winter. This road led to Rome, and even the dirt had to behave itself.

Elissa's heart gradually slowed to match their horse's stride. They had been lucky to find an uninjured mount in the wreckage of the battle. The warhorse had made their escape swift, although no less terrifying. Now that they had left that dreadful lake behind them, some of the tension finally started to drain from Elissa's body. She closed her eyes, and sleep pushed at the edges of her consciousness; Elissa let it take her. Marcus's comforting arms fell away and she heard the screams of dying men again. Fear leached into her skin. The sky filled with arrows. The Gaul's rank odor drifted into the back of the wagon, and his sweat dripped onto her skin. A curtain of red covered Marcus's neck. The end had come.

Elissa's eyes jolted open. The end. It hadn't come, had it? They were alive, and being carried farther away from that terrible battlefield with every stride. Elissa remembered the sharp crack of the Gaul's skull, and the smoothness with which her knife had plunged into the other one's neck. She had killed two men today. Perhaps it was only the shock, but she didn't feel guilty. She felt powerful.

Elissa twisted her head to look up at Marcus. There was a new reverence in his eyes as he looked back at her. She had saved his life now, too. Marcus leaned down to kiss the top of her head. His arms constricted around her waist, as if he needed to be convinced she was really there. Perhaps this was only a cruel dream? That moment of togetherness in the hills above Trasimene stretched out on an alternate course. Would she wake up and be back in that dark wagon surrounded by shining silverware and opulent cushions as the world burned around her.

Alone, once again.

Elissa closed her grip on Marcus's hands and pulled back on the reins. The horse tossed his head but slowed. They halted in the middle of the road. It was silent apart from the rustling of needles. The sun beat down on the red dirt. Nothing moved. You'd never know the world was burning just a short distance away. The Carthaginian army could appear behind them at any moment, bearing down on Rome in its insatiable thirst for destruction.

Elissa swung her leg over the horse's neck so she was facing Marcus. She brought her hands to his wrists, then moved them up his arms. When she reached his shoulders, she curved her fingers around the back of his neck. As she did, her thumbs brushed the cut on his throat, nearly sealed with the remnants of blood. She lifted her hands higher, up to his hair, where she rolled the coarse strands between her fingers. Marcus drew Elissa closer until his legs straddled her hips. He forced his arms between them and pushed her caresses aside, letting her know that he needed more tangible reassurance. His mouth descended and Elissa tilted her face to meet it. Marcus crushed his lips urgently against hers, his tongue probing inside her mouth. His lips were salty from sweat, and the acid tang of fear lingered on his tongue. They'd been so close to losing each other. Elissa opened her mouth wider and boldly pushed her tongue into his mouth. She wanted more. She returned her hands to his shoulders and pulled him down toward her. His caresses came harder, his tongue worked faster. She needed him. Elissa pressed her body deeper into his arms. Her breasts ached for his touch.

Something rumbled in the back of Marcus's throat and his kiss became more desperate. He shoved her cloak aside and slipped his hand through the side of her dress. Elissa gasped as she felt his warm skin on hers. He cupped her breast, kneading it with his fingers, and his thumb brushed lightly against her nipple. Elissa tipped forward until his hardness met the throbbing point between her legs. Even through the fabric, she could feel that he was ready for her. She craved that final connection between them, wanted it *now*. She rotated her hips, shifting deeper into him. She lifted her leg, intending to drape it over his thigh. Suddenly, Marcus jerked back. Air hissed through his clenched teeth. Elissa dropped her arms and leaned back immediately.

"What is it, Marcus?"

"Nothing." His voice sounded strained and hoarse. He quickly shifted his cloak so it covered the top of his leg.

Elissa frowned and crossed her arms self-consciously. She needed the liquid heat of his tongue, the bliss of his hand on her breast, the waves of sensation as she moved her hips against him.

"Don't you want this?" She struggled to keep her voice level.

Marcus's eyes flashed and his hand cradled her cheek. "*Cara*, of course I want this! I want—I *need* you more than anything. But not here." He dropped his hand from her face and motioned for her to look around them.

Awareness returned to Elissa gradually. Their horse shifted restlessly and tugged at the reins. A thin layer of dust coated the air, and an ugly ditch rolled off the road next to them. Admittedly it was not picturesque.

Marcus's voice cracked as he spoke. "I've already waited a lifetime for you, Elissa Mago. I can wait until sundown."

Elissa glanced up at the sun, which was at its peak. Marcus had said they'd reach his villa outside Rome before nightfall. Elissa closed her eyes and couldn't help seeing his neck coated in red again. As she'd run up behind that Gaul, she'd tasted the sour tang of death in the air, and feared she was too late. She'd been so close to losing Marcus. Opening her eyes, she shook her head. They were alive; their passionate kiss had convinced her of that. She drew her shoulders back and levelled her most serious glare at him. "I'll wait until sundown, but not a moment more."

Marcus seemed surprised by her forwardness. Then he smiled. A grin slanted his lips, and soon his head fell back and he started to laugh. It began as a deep chuckle in his throat, but soon it had spread to his stomach, and then his whole body was shaking convulsively.

Elissa was offended by his reaction at first, and then perplexed. But her shoulders were soon shaking along with his. She didn't know what was so funny, only that it felt good to laugh. It had been so long since she'd had a simple moment of lightness, and she'd never shared one with

Marcus. She doubled over and clutched at her stomach, laughing in earnest now. They had run from the jaws of death, and they were alive!

Marcus gradually calmed down and shook his head, still chuckling. "Oh, Elissa. For months I've tried to coerce you into my bed. I've tried charming you and threatening you. I've killed Romans for you and abandoned the legion. And none of it worked. Because in the end, it had to be *you* ordering *me* to your bed!"

A slow smile crept across Elissa's face. "Ordering you to my bed—I like the sound of that."

Marcus sent her that rakish grin of his. He held out his arm and signalled for her to turn back around in the saddle.

"At your service, my lady," he said with mock courtesy. He brought his lips to her ear and whispered, "Now and always."

Elissa's confidence had waned long before they reached the villa in Veii. She became acutely aware of every movement of his body—his chest rocking back and forth in time with the horse, his muscled arms around her. Elissa realized that she knew nothing of his past experience with women. Well, nothing except that he'd had a lot of it. But had those other women traced the hard lines on his chest as she had? Had they tasted his desperation on his tongue? Maybe not, but they'd surely known what to do once the barrier of clothing was removed between them. Elissa hadn't had a mother or female friends to tell her what to expect on her wedding night. What if she was as bad at lovemaking as she was at sewing? Elissa fidgeted nervously in the saddle but stayed silent. She wanted Marcus to think of her as confident and brave.

They branched off the main road to Rome and suddenly

Elissa's silence wasn't forced. An idyllic white villa was perched on a rounded hill ahead of them. Olive and pine trees dotted the gently sloping hillside below the villa, merging with the lush grass at the base. A long rectangular building stood in the middle of the meadow; its shape suggested it must be a stable.

"Welcome home, *mi cara*," Marcus murmured into her hair.

She turned to Marcus in disbelief. "*This* is your home?"

He chuckled and nodded.

"Why did you ever leave?"

"To find you."

Elissa nudged him playfully before focusing on the villa again. It was a simple rectangular shape, with red tiles above light brown walls. But it was also very large, and as they got closer, Elissa took in the proud marble columns flanking the outside walls. Although there was no extravagance in its design, this was clearly a house of wealth. Elissa noticed movement on the front balcony, and it belatedly occurred to her that Marcus's parents might be here. Her hands tightened reflexively. She was not ready to face the whole Gracchi family after such an awful day.

"Marcus, is anyone else here?"

Marcus seemed to understand her apprehension. "No, my father and mother stay in Rome while the Senate is in session. Veii is still a several hours' ride from the city." He paused, and then smiled with a pride she hadn't seen before. "Besides, all of this is mine. It's belonged to a Gracchi son for generations."

Elissa surveyed the sprawling estate with new appreciation. The place was tasteful and remote, and for Marcus, a retreat from the responsibilities of a centurion.

"It's perfect," she said.

Marcus squeezed her hand once he'd dismounted outside the entrance. "It's yours now, too."

Elissa's legs shook slightly as she slid to the ground. The idea of having some claim on a Roman villa was too much to add to the terrors of the morning and the uncertainty of tonight. She pushed the thought from her mind as she watched Marcus walk with a slight limp toward the entrance. A man had come out to greet them. He bowed low when he saw Marcus and then hurried to take their horse. Elissa handed off the reins gratefully and joined Marcus at the entrance. They walked over the threshold together.

Cool marble tiles and wide Corinthian columns waited for them on the other side. The air smelled of fresh grass and the salty tinge of the nearby ocean. Water sprayed from a fountain in the atrium. Elissa wanted to pause and get her bearings, but Marcus grabbed her hand and pulled her down a long hallway that led away from the entrance. Elissa walked quickly behind Marcus, her feet silent against the smooth marble tiles. They stopped at the end of the hallway and Marcus went through a doorway. Elissa followed more slowly as a magnificently large room opened up in front of them. Its floor was covered by rich burgundy carpet, and a balcony overlooked an atrium at its opposite end. Sheer curtains flitted in the evening breeze. Elissa let go of Marcus's hand and walked farther into the room. An oak table stood in the corner, its surface scattered with papyrus and inkpots. A vase of freshly cut pine boughs had been placed among them. Elissa inhaled the familiar smell of the forest as she watched Marcus move toward the large sleeping couch in the center. Although the room was massive, the couch still managed to consume much of its space. Plush white sheets were laid across it, and feather cushions ran along the edges. Elissa glanced nervously out the open window. The sun had nearly disappeared.

Marcus tossed his cloak on the desk and eased himself onto the couch. He reached toward his back and grunted.

"Help me with this?"

Elissa forced herself to walk to the couch and sit down beside him. She moved her hands to his back and set her fingers to undoing the thick strips of leather that held the scales of his breastplate together. Marcus winced as she tugged the last knot free. Elissa paused, not wanting to hurt him, but he nodded for her to continue. She brought her hands to his shoulders and carefully lifted the metal plate over his head and chest. Marcus sighed deeply and his shoulders sagged without the extra weight. Elissa placed the armor on the floor and turned back to Marcus. His cheeks sank heavily, and his skin was tinged with gray. He was exhausted. Elissa forgot her trepidation as her heart overflowed with tenderness. How could she possibly have been afraid of what they might do tonight?

Elissa dropped to her knees and started on the greaves around his shins. These laces were thinner and easier to unfasten. She soon had them on the floor next to his breastplate. She ran her hand up his bare leg. His skin was much lighter where the armor had covered it; above that, it was caked with dirt and grime, and here, a thin trickle of blood fell past his knee. Elissa tried to wipe the blood away with her thumb but it smudged her skin. She frowned and brought her hand up to his stained tunic.

She gasped as she pulled it back over his thigh.

A deep gash ran the width of his leg. The wound was deep and bloody. Blackened blood congealed around bands of muscle and fat underneath the torn skin. A thin yellow liquid leached from the sides.

"Marcus," she breathed as her eyes flew to his face.

He gave her a half-hearted grin. "What, you didn't think I'd trip over my own feet for no reason, did you?"

Elissa blew out her breath. "Why were we riding all day with your leg in such a state? This should've been tended to hours ago!"

Marcus's smile stretched to the other side of his face. "Do

you suppose Hannibal had a needle and thread to stitch me up? We should've stopped to ask!" Elissa hardly heard his teasing because she was already halfway to the door. She poked her head into the hallway and yelled for someone to come right away. She didn't wait for them to arrive before shouting her request for the supplies she needed.

"Wine, warm water, clean linen, needle and thread, something to bite down on!"

She had never actually tended a wound before, but she'd seen enough slave mothers in Zama care for injuries of this kind to have a general idea of how it was done. As soon as she'd given her orders, she turned back to Marcus and kneeled in front of the wound again. It ran nearly as deep as the bone, and old blood and dirt coated the open flesh. She would need to clean it well, and it was going to hurt. She looked up at Marcus. His smile had disappeared and a deep line ran across his brow. He was having the same thought.

"Elissa...have you ever done this before?"

She hardly noticed as one man set a stack of linen down beside her, followed by the needle and thread, and another brought the water and wine. She twisted one of the linen sheets into a tight rope and held it up to Marcus. "Bite on this."

He began to protest, but Elissa was already reaching for the wine. She brought the mouth of the jar over his leg and glanced up at him, eyebrows raised.

Marcus put the gag in his mouth and fell silent.

She took a swig of the bitter liquid for herself, then slowly poured some wine directly into the center of his wound. Marcus's leg straightened and every muscle in his body strained against the pain. She might have heard his teeth grinding through the gag if she hadn't been so focused. She needed the liquid to saturate every open surface. And then she needed to scrub the dirt away. Elissa had seen wounds spoil before; it was dreadful and deadly, and she was not going to let that happen to Marcus.

She worked as quickly and efficiently as she could. Slowly, bit by bit, she turned the skin from black to pink, and the wound from old to new. Several times, Marcus's leg went limp and she stopped her work to glance up at him. But Marcus merely grunted and tightened his leg again. His face had grown taut and pale, but he nodded curtly. Elissa picked up the needle. She'd been an incompetent seamstress when she was younger, and that was before she had to worry about maiming someone with a stray stitch. Elissa remembered her tutor in Zama, an elderly woman whom her father had sent from Carthage to teach her how to be a good wife. She was a stern woman with sharp eyes, and she would watch Elissa poke and prod at the fabric with exasperation. "Not like that!" she'd exclaim. "Keep your elbow high and your hand steady. You're not pricking the cloth with a sword; you're coaxing it to stay together."

Elissa took a steadying breath and lifted her elbow so it was even with her wrist. All she needed was confidence, she told herself. She pinched the needle firmly between two fingers and plunged the tip through Marcus's skin. It moved through his flesh with surprising ease and came smoothly out the other side. Elissa's shoulders relaxed a little. She pulled the thread until the knot caught at its end, and then repeated the process on the other side of the wound. There, one stitch was done. Elissa paused as she considered where to place the needle next. The stitches needed to be close enough to seal the skin, but too many would cause Marcus undue agony. Elissa reassessed the length of the wound and made the next stitch a finger's width from the first. Two were done.

When Elissa was finished, she sat back on her heels and surveyed her work. Twenty neat stitches crisscrossed the width of Marcus's thigh. Each was perfectly centered and evenly spaced. She was certain it was the best work she'd ever done. Maybe she wasn't such a bad seamstress, after all; it was only the material that had been wrong. Or the motivation, she thought as she wound a clean piece of linen around Marcus's thigh. Elissa stood and removed the gag from between his teeth. His mouth immediately fell slack. Marcus's hand shook as he ran it through his darkened hair; his brow was slick with sweat.

"Oh, dear," Elissa murmured. She'd been so lost in her work she hadn't fully appreciated the pain he was in.

She handed him what was left of the wine, then walked to the head of the couch and drew back the sheets.

"In you go," she said briskly.

Marcus paused mid-swig to give her a weak smile.

Elissa let him finish the pitcher before taking it from him. She wrapped her hand around his and hauled him onto his feet as gently as she could. Marcus wobbled dangerously as he straightened. Elissa propped her shoulder under his armpit and grunted as she took his weight. They limped toward the bed together.

"In," she said once they got there.

Marcus scoffed half-heartedly. "Only if you come with me."

Elissa brought her hands to his shoulders and pushed. He toppled over backward onto the couch.

"We're not doing anything until after you've slept."

Marcus groaned but rolled onto his side. She had barely started to clean up the bloodied linens before snores were reverberating from the couch. Elissa smiled wearily. She suddenly felt as exhausted as he was. She gathered the spent supplies and set them out in the hall. None of the slaves had been willing to interrupt them in the Dominus's room. Not that there had been anything to see, Elissa thought as she sat down on the edge of the couch. She glanced back at Marcus. He was splayed on his back in the very center of the wide couch, his head on the cushion behind him. The copper strands of hair caught the last rays of sunlight and colored them red. Elissa lifted her feet off the ground and eased herself onto the nearest cushion. She wrapped the end of one of the blankets around her legs, then leaned her arms against the couch's soft back. Her eyes closed. Surely there was no harm in resting for a few minutes.

Something soft brushed against her skin. It started at her thigh and then moved across her hip. It dipped at her waist and then travelled up to the fold of her breast. The sensation was faint but breathtakingly clear. Her breast was blanketed by a comforting warmness, and then released back to the cold air. Covered, then released. Probing points kneaded her softness. They shifted her skin and awakened a new sensation. Elissa sighed and pushed her chest forward. Her nipples rose and hardened. She rolled onto her back, letting her hands fall to her sides. This was the most delightful dream, and she wanted to enjoy it.

The sensation on her breasts changed. It was warmer now, and more focused on the center of her breast. Something deliciously wet circled the base of her swollen nipple. It teased her as she yearned for more. Elissa brought her hand to her stomach and paused. She ached between her legs, a place that begged to be touched. Elissa slowly traced her fingers down her stomach and onto her navel. She moved lower. Soft curls tickled the tips of her fingers. She paused to twirl her fingers through the strands, tugging them gently. Her fingers were warm, as if they'd been dipped in bath water. She moved them lower and brushed lightly against the inner folds of her body. Elissa traced their outer rim in a slow circle, gradually increasing the pressure with each turn. A tiny bead rolled under her fingers and the aching deepened. Elissa moaned.

There was a rumble in her ear and the sensation at her breasts stopped. Elissa's eyelids fluttered, protesting the end. But it was for the best; she must already have slept longer than she'd intended. Suddenly, her whole body seemed to lift off the bed. Elissa gasped. The throbbing between her legs exploded into a different feeling entirely. Her body snapped tight and heat flooded her skin. She tried to open her eyes but her lashes were stuck to her cheeks. She clenched her fists and gasped for air instead. There was a delicious wetness between her legs. It tugged at her, traced the inside of her folds, then pressed insistently against that throbbing bead she'd discovered before. Elissa's back arched off the cushions and her mouth opened in a silent groan. The knot in her stomach unravelled to trace a viscous line of sensation from the center of her legs all the way up to her neck. Every part of her demanded to be touched. It was as if her whole body were poised on the edge of a cliff. One flick of his tongue and she would hurtle off the precipice into oblivion.

"Marcus—" she groaned.

Her eyes flew open as she realized what she was saying.

Marcus was above her. His shoulders hovered over her hips, his elbows pushed into the cushions on either side of her. His hair fell loosely over his forehead, lips slightly parted, eyes hooded. Oh, gods, what had she done? Heat rose in Elissa's cheeks. Had she truly been touching herself? And in front of him no less!

Elissa rolled onto her side and buried her face in the nearest cushion. She felt Marcus's weight ease down beside her, his arms wrapped protectively around her waist.

"*Cara*," he murmured in her ear, "that was only the beginning. Let me show you what else we can do together."

His breath tickled her neck and she squirmed away.

"What else is there to do after I've shamed us so?" Elissa muttered into the pillow.

Marcus's hand came to her shoulder and forced her around to face him. He was looking at her gravely, his brows drawn over his eyes.

"Shamed us? Elissa, in all my years of—" He paused,

seeming to struggle for the right word "—er, experience, I've never had a woman make me feel so desperate for her body, her pleasure. And I wasn't even inside you!"

Elissa blinked. She was having trouble following what he was saying. "So...you liked what I was doing to myself?"

Marcus leaned in closer until his lips brushed the base of her neck. "Oh, I hated it. Despised you for it. I was half insane with jealousy," he said gravely, but Elissa heard the smile in his voice. Marcus flipped her onto her back and captured her body between his knees before she could protest. "And now it's my turn to show you what *I* can do to *you*."

He pulled his tunic over his head. Dark hair curled over the hard mound of his chest, and straight bands of muscle cut across his stomach. He eased his weight forward onto his hands and the ropy muscles in his arms thickened. The pit in Elissa's stomach began throbbing again. She traced the hard lines of his body down his stomach to where the hair grew thick again. His staff jutted out from between his legs—alert, ready, and shockingly large. Elissa's body tensed and her eyes flicked to his face.

Marcus immediately lowered himself so she could no longer see that part of him. He brought his lips to the hollow at the base of her neck and whispered. "Shh, *cara*. You have nothing to be afraid of. It will only hurt a little this one time, and I am deeply sorry for it. That is, if you want this?" He brought his forehead to her chest and fell silent while he waited for her reply.

Elissa was scared of what they might do and of its implications. For her, for them, the line dividing Carthage and Rome had fallen away long ago, but the line between married and unmarried still held firm. In the long march of irreversible steps away from who she'd been, this would be the final one. There would be no reclaiming her innocence once it was lost.

Marcus shifted and Elissa's attention returned to him. His bare legs extended clear across the couch. His arms were propped up beside her, and the muscles in his back strained to keep his head from resting too heavily on her. Elissa softened. Of all the steps she'd taken, this was the only one where she'd had a choice; Marcus was giving her that. Elissa remembered the feeling of rapturous vertigo she'd had before opening her eyes. She smiled softly to herself. Truth be told, her innocence was in tatters already. And she had a suspicion this was one part of it she wouldn't miss.

Elissa suddenly jolted to a sitting position. "Marcus, your leg!" she exclaimed.

Marcus smiled confidently and shifted so she could see the bandage on his thigh. "No sword is going to keep me from you, Elissa Mago."

Elissa laughed in spite of her nervousness. Sure enough, the bandage was still white, with no signs of bleeding underneath. She brought her hands to his shoulders and pulled him back down to the couch with her.

"I trust you, Marcus Gracchus."

This time when Marcus kissed her, he didn't stop.

Elissa was right to trust him. They spent the night locked in each other's arms. When he pushed his hardness through the delicate folds between her legs, it had hurt at first, as Marcus had said. Elissa had felt a sharp tearing as her body gave way to his. The pain had made her want to scream. Marcus stayed very still, hovering above her, refusing to move again until he was sure she felt ready. When the pain subsided and the hunger had returned, Elissa put her hands on his back and practically dragged him farther into her. He sank so much deeper than she expected, and even when she'd enveloped all of him, she still wanted more. Then they started moving.

They rocked back and forth. Slowly like a boat bumping against the dock in a gentle breeze. Marcus shifted out, and then back in again. Out and back. Each time he returned to her, Elissa's fingers tightened on his back. Soon she was digging her nails into his skin and begging him for more. She threw her head back against the cushions and Marcus set upon her neck. He sucked at her skin and pushed into her with his tongue. Elissa latched onto the top of his shoulder with her mouth and grazed his skin with her teeth. Marcus moaned and his rhythm sped. They were moving toward a new focus of pleasure, this one inside her.

Marcus shifted so his body was tilted forward. The tip of his shaft pushed against her most sensitive place at the end of every motion. Tingling flooded Elissa's body. Their hips ground together, his hands were on her breasts, then kneading the back of her hair. And his mouth, his mouth seemed to be everywhere at the same time. On her lips and on her neck, it traced a wet line across her chest, and then tugged at the tip of her breast.

Her body was pushed closer to its limit with every thrust. She felt like the string of a bow, flayed bare and stretched to breaking. The next time Marcus pressed forward inside her, he didn't pull back. The throbbing multiplied. Elissa gasped. Her chest rose to meet his. Marcus tightened his arms and held her there. She was suspended from the couch, in free fall, motionless apart from the coursing sensation racking her body. Marcus's muscles contracted and then released. She felt his seed flowing into her. It warmed her ragged body and slowly relaxed her muscles. As she inhaled shakily, Marcus carefully lowered her back to the couch and moved his chest down to hers. He bent his neck and leaned his forehead into her shoulder. They held each other in stillness. Elissa gradually felt him soften inside her, and she lost track of his presence. She felt as though she was floating above the couch. The night air cooled her skin, and a breeze came in through the open window to rustle her hair. It was bliss, and it was only the first time.

The sun had hardly peeked through the window when Marcus stirred again. He nuzzled her ear and pulled her toward him under the pale rays of light. This time, there was no pain at the beginning, and the pleasure was just as great. The next time, the sun was high in the sky, and the pleasure was even greater. They hardly left the room that first day. Whenever they unraveled from each other's arms, they'd instantly snap back together again. Elissa's body fit perfectly within Marcus's, and his shape must have been cast in clay to suit hers. Hannibal could have been burning down Rome for all they knew. The world might be on fire, but they were in love.

Finally, Elissa had love. Not the affection of her brother, or the unreachable sentiment of her father. But she had love—burning, passionate love. A love that flushed her skin when Marcus kissed her. It beat against her ear when she lay on his bare chest at night. She saw it in his reproachful looks when she strayed too far from his side during the day. For three weeks, amid the villa's marble columns and water fountains, they had love. The fact that the peace they'd found could never last only made it sweeter. It made them hold each other more desperately, and entwine themselves so deeply they could almost believe that fate would be unable to tear them apart. Only the intervention of the gods could have brought a Roman and a Carthaginian together during the greatest war the world had ever seen. The divine scales had weighed their love against the deaths of thousands. It was a shimmering jewel in a field of ash. But they both knew that what the gods give, the gods can take away.

CHAPTER 16

The end came innocuously enough. It was only a note. There was a rolled-up piece of papyrus in Marcus's hand when he looked up from the scrolls scattered across his desk.

"My parents are coming."

"Hmm," Elissa mumbled. She was curled up in an armchair in the corner of the *tablinum*, poring through a fascinating account of the ancient Pharaohs of Egypt.

"They're coming tonight."

Elissa's head jerked up. "Who's coming?"

The corners of Marcus's eyes crinkled as he regarded her with amusement. "My parents. Tonight."

"Tonight!" Elissa's hands tightened around the scroll she'd been reading. She suddenly felt very alert. "That… that's wonderful," she added quickly when she noticed the happiness in Marcus's face.

His excitement disappeared under a furrowed brow. "Yes, it would be wonderful to see them. But I'm going to send a messenger telling them not to come. It's not safe to be out of the city. Hannibal could still march on Rome any day, and word might get out that they visited me. Flaminius's accusations of treason could have reached the Senate before Trasimene."

Elissa brought her feet back to the marble floor. She

stared at them for a moment before speaking. The thought of meeting Marcus's parents made her stomach twist with nervousness, but she knew it was what he wanted.

"Marcus, surely your father knows that. He must be better informed in Rome than we are out here. He wouldn't come if it wasn't safe. Your parents want to see you. And you want to see them. So let them come."

Marcus stood up from behind the large oak desk. He circled it quickly and strode across the room to Elissa. He reached down and picked up her hand in his, then watched her silently as he ran his thumb along her skin and entwined his fingers with hers. A firm tug and she was out of the chair and in his arms. She laughed and leaned forward against his chest. His arms closed around her waist and he pressed his lips to the top of her head.

"I love you," he whispered.

Elissa pulled her head back so she could look up at him. Even more than their passionate lovemaking, these were the moments she loved most—a simple togetherness that filled her heart with tenderness and a sense of belonging. She lifted her hand to his cheek and the late-afternoon stubble tickled her palm.

"I love you, Marcus. And I'll love your parents, too."

Marcus turned his head to kiss the inside of her hand.

"They'll love you, too."

Of that, Elissa was not so sure.

Elissa flitted nervously around the villa for the rest of the day. She bustled from room to room, deciding what furniture needed to be rearranged—and then rearranged again until it was the same as when she'd started. She tried to help the cook with meal preparations, but was asked to oversee the cleaning instead. She could have gone out for a ride in the afternoon sun, but she didn't know when Marcus's family would turn up, and she didn't want to appear flippant or uncaring by missing their arrival. Marcus had laughed when he'd caught her nervously pacing one of the halls. He was convinced his parents would love her, and in his mind, that was that. He threw her a reassuring smile on his way out to the yard to spar with some of the household boys. Elissa glared back at him. If he ripped out those stitches, she was not redoing them.

Elissa resigned herself to spending the afternoon in the *balneae*. She bathed carefully, then began to painstakingly coax her hair into something resembling the elaborate hairstyles that Roman women wore. As she twisted her dark locks into curls, she asked herself why she was so nervous about meeting Marcus's family. Perhaps it was her resentment at the real world for intruding on the surreal life they'd found here. Or maybe she'd just had a complicated experience with parents. But Elissa couldn't help thinking that the Gracchi would be less willing to accept the sacrifices Marcus had made for her. And could she say anything to convince them otherwise?

As the sun dipped low in the sky, Elissa became progressively more agitated. Her hands shook as she fastened one of the curls to the top of her head. She had fixed her hair in a great mass at the back, with wavy locks hanging loosely on either side of her face. Elissa patted a thin layer of chalk across her cheeks as she stared at the mirror in their sleeping quarters. Pale-green eyes gazed back at her. She leaned closer to examine her reflection. Her skin had darkened from nearly half a year spent outside, but her features appeared the same. Or was that a new line across her forehead? *Something* looked different. Her eyes seemed smaller, perhaps narrower at the corners, as if they'd seen enough of the world and decided to shut out some of the light. They widened again. Marcus was watching her from the doorway. Elissa glanced down at the table self-consciously.

"It's not polite to stare, you know," she muttered.

Marcus didn't respond, but she heard his footsteps moving toward her. She raised her eyes and watched his figure in the mirror. He wore a leather training-breastplate over his tunic, and she could see that sweat still lingered around the neckline. He moved the same as he always had—light on his feet and directly toward his target. His tunic rode high on his legs, and Elissa could see the muscles in his thighs bunch and release with each step. Marcus placed his palm on Elissa's shoulder once he reached her. She turned her chin up to him. The morning's stubble had thickened over his square jaw, and his eyes were gray in the late-afternoon light. Elissa felt a twinge in the pit of her stomach. How was it that her heart still sped whenever he was near?

"I brought you something."

Elissa raised her eyebrows but didn't look away.

Marcus reached into the side of his tunic and took out a small object.

"That's not the needle I'm going to need to redo your stiches, is it?"

"No, *cara*," Marcus replied with mock horror. "I would never ask you to do the same job twice. I have something much better for you." He moved his hands over her chest and then around to either side of her neck. A thin strand of silver stretched between his fingers.

"This was my mother's," Marcus said as he fastened the necklace. He straightened and took a step back to admire her reflection in the mirror.

"Marcus," Elissa whispered as she traced the twisting tendrils of silver with her fingers. "It's breathtaking." She leaned closer to examine its details. Fine strands of silver were woven around hundreds of emerald beads. They glittered blue and green amid the gleaming white. It was stunning, but not ostentatious or large—a beauty that could be subtle, because you were already looking. Elissa's eyes met Marcus's in the mirror. He bent down and touched his lips to the shallow depression at the base of her neck. Elissa closed her eyes and felt his breath float across her skin.

"Breathtaking," he murmured. "Like you."

Elissa hardly heard him. She turned in her chair and opened her arms in expectation of his embrace. Marcus wrapped his arms around her and lifted her out of the seat. His lips moved from her neck to her shoulders, and his hand traveled across her chest to caress the open skin above her robe. Elissa moaned softly and gave up any pretence of keeping her hair intact. She slid her leg around Marcus's bare thigh and pulled him closer. He lowered his hands to her waist and hoisted her in the air. Elissa brought her thighs tightly around him. Marcus carried her to the couch and set her down against the cushions. Their mouths met, and then their bodies. They made love as the shadows outside lengthened and night fell. They could have spent forever like that, secure in each other's arms, drifting slowly through waves of pleasure. But at the sound of an approaching litter being carried down the long road to the villa, they knew that the Gracchi had arrived.

Publius and Aurelia Gracchus stood in the entrance. Cool night air wafted through the open doors behind them as slaves walked into the villa with crates in their arms, moving the Gracchi's belongings out of the litter that had carried them from Rome. They disappeared down one of the many hallways that branched off the main entrance.

Marcus stepped forward to greet his parents, his shoulders still rising and falling with his quickened breath. He and Elissa had only just arrived as the doors opened. She glanced down at her *stola* sheepishly; it was slightly askew at the shoulders. She subtly tugged it straight, then started to reach toward her hair but brought her hand back down.

That was going to take a more serious intervention. Her fingers twitched nervously. As far as first impressions went, this one was less than ideal.

Marcus bowed low and nodded at each of his parents in turn. "Father, Mother. You honor us with your visit."

Elissa stole a look at his father's face. She saw with surprise that he was grinning widely. His light brown eyes twinkled with amusement, and he wore a knowing expression as he regarded Marcus.

"My son, I doubt you've ever acted so deferential! Now, come here so I can see you better."

Marcus chuckled and strode across the hall toward his father. He clasped Publius's outstretched arm and pulled the older man into an embrace. Elissa couldn't restrain a smile. Side by side, they appeared so very different. Publius's hair was short and spiralling, and as white as a dove's. He was much smaller in stature than Marcus, and although he must have been fit in his younger years, he had clearly rounded at the edges. But somehow, they were still unmistakeably father and son. Publius draped his arm across Marcus's back warmly, his senator's dignity immediately forgotten at the sight of his son. Elissa stepped forward, suddenly eager to meet him as well.

A female voice cut across the room. "And you must be the one we've heard about."

Elissa's attention snapped to Marcus's mother. She stood erect and serious behind her husband, watching Elissa with icy gray eyes. It was exactly the way Marcus had regarded her the first time they'd met. Aurelia was tall and lean like Marcus, and a dark red *palla* covered her hair. Elissa didn't have to see to know her hair would be dark brown in color. Aurelia scanned her efficiently, her gaze lingering on the silver necklace around Elissa's neck. If she was displeased, she didn't show it. Her face stayed level, her lips straight and perfectly neutral.

Marcus released his father and turned toward Aurelia. "Mother," he said affectionately as he approached.

Aurelia's austere features lightened. Her thin lips were welcoming as she took her son's hand.

"Marcus. I'm so very pleased to see you."

Marcus lightly kissed the top of Aurelia's head. "And I to see you, Mother." He leaned back and eyed his mother with mock appraisal. "I see you look as beautiful as ever."

Aurelia's smile deepened. "You flatter me, son. I look like more of an old woman every day." Her smile faltered as her gaze returned to Elissa. "Unlike this one—" she gestured across the room "—who appears ripe in her beauty."

Marcus spun to face Elissa. "I forget myself!" he exclaimed. He threw a jesting wink at Elissa and guided his mother across the room to meet her. Publius joined them so all three Gracchi were standing in front of her.

"Mother, Father. Allow me to introduce you to Elissa Mago."

The pride in Marcus's voice only made Elissa more nervous as she dropped into a deep bow. She paused at the bottom and spoke to the ground.

"I'm most pleased to meet you, Senator and Lady Gracchus."

Elissa felt firm hands under her elbows, directing her to her feet. Elissa looked up into Publius's warm, brown eyes.

"The pleasure is ours, Elissa Mago. Anyone who can put up with our son's—" Publius paused and his lips twitched, "—er, temperament is welcome to us."

Elissa choked back a surprised laugh. Marcus was not so reserved. He bellowed deeply and slid his arm around Elissa's waist.

"Well, she's not always so easy going herself," he teased.

Elissa's cheeks flushed and she had to resist the urge to ram her elbow into his side. She glanced at Publius, who was watching them with amusement, and her eyes flicked to his wife. When Aurelia met her gaze, Elissa smiled politely and looked away. There was a keen intellect behind that gray stare; this was a woman you didn't want to cross.

"Come," Publius said with a firm thump to Marcus's shoulders. "Let the women get to know each other. You and I have much to discuss."

Marcus raised his eyebrows at Elissa questioningly, but he'd already pulled his arm from her waist.

Elissa smiled weakly back at him. "Yes, I—"

"Good," Publius interrupted. "Now, remind me where the *tablinum* is, son."

Marcus stepped away from Elissa and motioned his father down the hall.

Elissa waited for them to disappear before facing Aurelia. "May I show you to your rooms?" she asked politely.

"I know where they are." Aurelia replied curtly. She strode briskly in the opposite direction from her husband and son.

"Of course," Elissa murmured to her back.

Elissa stayed in the entrance, unsure of whether she should follow. Joining Marcus and his father was out of the question. They would be discussing the war, and even the most accepting of Roman fathers was sure to chafe at a Carthaginian woman participating in that conversation. Elissa sighed. Marcus would tell her later, anyway. She walked slowly to the garden, where the smell of fresh earth and the sounds of trickling water might soothe her confusion.

Marcus stared at his father from across the large desk in his *tablinum*. Publius was speaking rapidly, and all the levity of their initial meeting was gone. A deep knot had settled in the middle of his father's forehead.

"Thirty thousand men lost at the Trebia. Now the same

at Trasimene. It's a miracle the recruiters could find any new men at all. But find them they have. Thousands of new legionaries. Maybe a hundred thousand men."

Marcus's attention snapped back to his father. "A new legion?"

"Yes, son, new *legions*," Publius said impatiently. "We'll need the biggest Rome has ever seen if we're to finally liberate Italy from the scourge of Hannibal."

Marcus exhaled slowly and leaned back in his chair. "And who is to lead this new army? Who will ensure that its fate is different from the last two?"

"Two new consuls for the year: Lucius Aemilius Paullus and Gaius Terentius Varro. Varro is a hot-headed idiot like Flaminius, but Paullus is steady and experienced. Although with an army this large, you'd hardly expect it to matter who leads it."

Marcus shook his head. "No. With Hannibal, it matters. Where are the Carthaginians now?"

"Tracking the eastern coast down to Apulia."

"He's not coming to Rome, then."

Publius shrugged. "It seems not. For now at least." He rested his arms on the desk. "But what about you, Son? Will you join this new legion?"

Marcus crossed his arms and stared over his father's head. "You must have heard Flaminius's accusations."

Publius leaned back in his chair. "Yes. I heard them. And so did the rest of the Senate."

"Then you know I wouldn't be welcome back with the legion."

"Well, I think that depends." Publius tilted forward and his mild brown eyes seemed to harden. "Are they true? *Are* you a traitor?"

Marcus met his father's stare. Publius's face was oddly blank, as if it were a question of no significance.

"Yes."

There was a flash of something in Publius's eyes, but he quelled it. "Because of the girl."

Marcus leapt to his feet, and his chair clattered to the floor behind him. "No." He placed his hands on the desk and ground his fists into the hard wood. "It was *not* her fault."

Publius held up his palms. "All right, son, all right. I meant no offense. And I never said it was her fault. If the rumors are true, you're the one who's to blame."

Marcus took a deep breath. He removed his hands from the desk and walked to the chair in the corner of the room. Elissa had sat here this morning; she'd looked so charming curled between the armrests with a scroll. Marcus sank heavily into the seat now.

"Yes, it's my fault," he said quietly. His shoulders drooped with the weight of his choices.

Publius stood and walked over to his son, setting a hand on Marcus's shoulder. "These are serious crimes, Marcus. Harboring the enemy, deserting the legion, killing Roman citizens. Any one of them by itself would get you thrown from the Tarpeian Rock."

Marcus lifted his head. His father suddenly seemed old to Marcus, much older than his six decades. In the twelve years since Marcus had left for the legions, his father's hair had thinned and turned white. His skin had become lined with age and his cheeks sunken. His eyes still held the same keen intelligence Marcus remembered, but they'd lost some of their brightness. His father had suffered a long political career, the murder of a son, and now the treason of another. He'd grown into a tired old man.

Marcus glanced at the ground. It was cruel to add to his father's burden. He should tell Publius that he would do whatever was necessary to protect himself. That he could leave knowing his only remaining son would live a long life. But when he met his father's eyes, he became the boy he hadn't been in a very long time.

"I love her, Father."

Publius sighed deeply and closed his eyes. He walked back to the desk and slowly eased himself into Marcus's chair. "Then you must take her away from here," he said finally. "Away from Rome, away from Italy. Somewhere the tremors of our two cities devouring themselves are not felt." Publius straightened and pulled something out from under the folds of his toga. "But first you must give her this."

Marcus stared blankly at the object in his father's hand. It was a folded sheet of papyrus with a circle of wax in its center. A sealed letter.

Marcus's legs shook slightly as he stood and walked over to him. "What's this?"

"Delivered to me from Senator Marcellus. He refused to say how he got it. Only that if the rumors about my son were true, then I ought to give this to you. Well, *give it to the girl* was precisely what he said, but at the time I thought that too odd to mention."

Marcus frowned and took the letter. He stared at the empty outside page. "Marcellus.... why do I know that name?"

"He was accused of taking money from the Carthaginians a few years back. Greedy bastard managed to buy himself an acquittal and walk free."

Marcus's grip tightened, and the papyrus crackled between his fingers. He could feel the blood draining from his face.

Publius furrowed his brow.

"What is it, son?"

Cold stone pressed into Elissa's thighs through the thin fabric of her *stola*. She sat on a bench in the middle of the garden, listening to the night come alive around her. Water trickled through the fountain up ahead, and the leaves of a mulberry

275

tree rustled softly in the breeze. A chorus of crickets undulated through the villa walls. The potted hyacinths were in full bloom, their violet petals glowing in the dark. The summer air was heavy with sweetness tonight; it enclosed Elissa in its warm embrace.

Footsteps padded across the *peristyle* surrounding the garden. They paused, and then crunched along gravel. Elissa sighed and rose from the bench in time to see Aurelia round the garden path. Elissa dipped her head and started to walk away.

"Elissa," Aurelia called.

Elissa stopped. She kept her eyes low and slowly turned back.

"Sit with me a while."

Elissa hesitated, but it wasn't really a question. She returned to the bench and waited for Aurelia to sit first. Elissa's bare arm brushed against hers on the narrow bench. It was hard not to fidget. They sat beside each other in silence, and the night's peace gradually settled over her again. Elissa's breathing slowed; her shoulders relaxed. The floral air wound lazily between them. Aurelia sat so still, Elissa could almost forget she was there. But her thoughts dwelled on the women next to her. She wondered what Aurelia thought of her.

Aurelia's voice blended seamlessly with the low murmur of evening sounds. "I used to come out here on summer nights like this. I would sit in silence and watch the stars. No one ever asked anything of me here. The stars didn't care."

Elissa shifted uncomfortably. Had she not come here for the same reason? She looked over at the older woman. The waning moon lit her face from behind and formed a perfect oval silhouette. Aurelia continued. "But I care who you are, Elissa Mago. And I care who you are to my son."

Elissa's body tensed in anticipation.

"Where do you come from?"

"Carthage," she said quickly.

Aurelia nodded. "Who is your father?"

Elissa answered without hesitating. "His name is Hanno Mago. He is a merchant and a councillor in Carthage."

Aurelia nodded again, seeming unsurprised. "How did you come to be in Italy, Elissa Mago, daughter of Hanno?"

This time, Elissa paused. But the question truly wasn't harder to answer than the one before. "I ran away from my wedding and hid on my father's ship. It arrived in Etruria."

Aurelia's expression was inscrutable, but the silence lengthened. "And my son has fallen in love with you."

The accusation behind the words was too much for Elissa to silently accept. She reached across the space between them and gathered Aurelia's hands in her own.

"And I love him," she said urgently.

Aurelia freed her hands from between Elissa's and returned them to her lap. "My son has given you much, Elissa Mago. And I wonder what you have given him in return."

Elissa's cheeks flooded with shame and she struggled to push her desperation back down. Her skin suddenly felt itchy. She wanted to scream at this woman that she loved her son, and then she wanted to run from this interrogation.

"I love him," she said again.

"That is not enough." Aurelia's voice was sharp with finality.

Elissa gathered her courage and met Aurelia's gray stare directly. "That is all I have to give."

"The time for games of love and freedom are over. This is war. And only one of our people will survive. There is no middle ground for you."

Tears welled in Elissa's eyes. Her throat felt swollen, and she couldn't reply for fear of what would come out.

Aurelia bent down and picked something from the ground. When she straightened, there was a small flower between her fingers. Its petals had wilted in the late-summer sun, and a feathery globe of seeds had taken their place. The pale strands were beautiful, but hopelessly delicate. A light breeze, and it would all blow away.

"Choose a side, Elissa. Otherwise there will be nothing left of him."

Aurelia raised the flower to her lips and blew. The seeds exploded from the stem. A thousand remnants cast off in every direction and floated away with the wind.

"But I choose Marcus!"

Aurelia brought her hand to Elissa's cheek. Her grip was firm and steady, and she held Elissa's eyes with her own.

"Then you forsake your family, your history, your people. You vow never to seek them out again. You are no longer of Carthage. And you can never be of Rome. Only when you are of nowhere, can you have my son."

Elissa's heart felt as though it was folding in on itself, and her happiness seemed to collapse into a deep pit at her core. She tore her cheek from Aurelia's palm. No, it couldn't be true; the choice didn't have to be so stark, did it? The austere lines on Aurelia's face were smooth, but her eyes glowed with intensity. Their brightness nearly matched the moon behind her.

"I ask no more than he's already given to you."

The night suddenly took on a malevolent air, thick and hot. Elissa could taste it on her tongue, saturated and over-sweet. It clogged her nostrils. The trickling fountain roared in her ears. She couldn't hear anything over it. She couldn't think. She needed to get out of this garden.

Elissa jumped to her feet. "I…I'm sorry. I have to go," she stammered.

Then she ran. She tore through the garden and between the stoic columns of the *peristyle*. Her feet flew over the marble tiles at the entrance and down the stairs to the villa. They ground into the tiny pebbles outside and hammered along the hard dirt road. It slanted steeply down from the villa and Elissa lengthened her stride. Her legs pumped harder. Her calves ached from the effort. She was at the bottom of the hill now, and already far from the villa. Her lungs seared painfully as her body struggled to keep up with her mind. Elissa let herself slow to a jog, and then a walk. Her chest heaved as she took in her new surroundings. Tall cypress trees sprang up around her, and rows of shrub peeked out from the open spaces between them. Elissa turned off the main road into the welcome cover of the vineyard. The last thing she wanted was to be found.

She walked between rows of evenly spaced stakes. Swollen purple fruit hung heavily from the shrubs' thin branches. A thin carpet of grass muffled her footsteps, and the moon cast her path in silver light. Elissa reached a fence that cut abruptly across the long line of stakes; thick grass replaced shrubs on its other side, and a hoof print was stamped into a bare patch of ground. It must be the horse paddock. Elissa curved her hands around the rough wood and pulled herself over the top bar. She heard a loud snort and hooves thumping rapidly. Elissa froze with one leg over the fence.

A massive stag faced her from the paddock. His antlers were twisted and forked into a giant ivory crown above his head. His brown hair had thinned from the summer heat, and thick muscles ran visibly along his neck and hind-quarters. The stag watched her in perfect stillness, nostrils flared, one foot held above the grass in preparation for flight. Any movement from her would surely send him bounding away. The stag's moment of decision stretched out through time. His head dropped a fraction, and then another. He snorted again and put his foot back down. Suddenly the threat was forgotten, and he lowered his head to the ground to resume his search for food.

Elissa exhaled with relief and slowly climbed down the other side of the fence. The stag's ears flicked toward her but he kept rummaging. Elissa leaned into the fence and watched him with fascination. What a curious beast—terrified for his life one moment, then perfectly comfortable the next. Maybe she wasn't so different—caught somewhere between fear and happiness—trying to hold onto two opposing ends at the same time. How could she be of Carthage and still be with Marcus? Marcus had fought for Rome while loving her, and it had nearly torn him apart. But as they galloped away from the carnage at Trasimene, it had been her in his arms. How could she not make the same choice now?

The stag's head shot into the air. He paused, listening to something Elissa couldn't hear. Then he turned and ran, and his white tail bounded away into the darkness. It was several minutes before Elissa heard the footsteps behind her. She didn't bother moving. The stag might be gone, but for her, the moment of decision stretched on. The fence sagged beside her and then stilled. Elissa could feel his presence without looking. She could hear everything he didn't say. Didn't *have* to say. The decision was hers, and the silence expanded to fill the night. Then his weight on the fence lifted and he was gone. Elissa glanced behind her in confusion. Marcus's broad shoulders swayed as he walked back through the rows of grapes. His tall figure faded into the blackness.

Elissa looked at the place he'd just stood. There was a single sheet of papyrus there. Its seal had been broken, and the tightly folded letter had sprung open. Her father's tidy handwriting filled the page.

Marcus leaned against the wall and crossed his arms. Thick rays of sunlight flooded the room. The air was warm, but not hot, and warblers crooned a melody outside the window. It should have been a beautiful morning.

Elissa paced back and forth across the room. She gathered

her meager possessions and rapidly shoved them into a bag. A few spare clothes from the dresser, her cloak from the chair. She paused and glanced up at him. Marcus had the sensation of something stabbing him in the center of his chest. She looked away quickly, but not before Marcus caught her expression. There had been pity in those green eyes.

He turned and left the room.

Marcus's stride lengthened as he crossed the hallway. He needed to prepare for the journey. Not that he would need much. A sleeping roll, a few provisions, his armor. They were traveling across Italy, to Arpi. He would rejoin the legion, if they'd still take him. And Elissa would return to her family, what she had wanted all along. Marcus would fulfill his promise; he would take her to Barro.

He reached the atrium and went through the entrance-way. He was practically running now; his feet slammed into the tiles with every step. The sound echoed through the empty villa. His parents had left for Rome in the early morning, and most of the slaves had quickly found chores that took them outside or into the city. Marcus's fists tightened at his sides. He had promised to return her to Barro before he'd known she loved him. Before he'd begun to imagine their life together. They could have gone to Athens or Alexandria. He could have kept them safe. He could have kept them together.

Marcus needed to go to the stable to give instructions for packing the horses. It would be a three days' hard ride to Arpi.

Elissa, come home. All will be forgiven. I only hope you will also forgive my wrongs…

Marcus shook his head in exasperation. He needed to get that man's voice out of his mind.

…It was never your fault. It was only the memory of your mother that made me turn away….

He sank his teeth into his lower lip. He wanted his body to hurt like the rest of him.

Tall cypress flanked the sides of the road on his way to the stables, and pools of shade gathered below them. How often had he lounged against one of their trunks after a hard day of training? He'd even had his first kiss there—a girl from one of the neighboring villas he'd figured was beautiful.

Go to Barro. He will keep you safe; he will send you home…

Marcus ground his teeth as he walked up to one of the trees now. He closed his fist and rammed it into the trunk as hard as he could. The wood gave no quarter, and a wave of shock reverberated up his arm. The bark bit painfully into his knuckles.

Come home, Elissa. I love you.

He turned and pressed his back to the trunk. He slowly sank to the ground and pulled his knees into his chest. His arms flopped uselessly at his sides and his head hung heavily. His knuckles were stinging; they'd started to bleed. The birds sang a slow, mournful tune above him as the sun filtered through the pine needles and dappled the grass. Marcus's shoulders began to shake. His eyes stung with unspent tears. He had given everything for the woman he loved. Now he had nothing.

CHAPTER 17

lissa sat very still. Leather soles clapped against stone. A bowl of ground meal steamed on the table in front of her. She didn't look up from her hands; they wrung and twisted in her lap. Around and around they went. The skin had already turned pink and itchy. She was rubbing them raw.

She took a deep breath and forced her hands apart, then leaned back against the straw cushion and looked blankly around the room for the hundredth time. A second narrow couch faced her from across the dining table. The frayed sheet separating the main room from the sleeping room hung limply in the corner, and white square walls surrounded her on every side. The walls converged at a single point in the middle of the roof, which gave the room a peculiar cone shape. Row upon row of these odd huts lined the streets of Arpi. Marcus had banged on the doors of quite a few of them before finding room and board at this one.

Elissa's hands twisted in her lap again. Marcus. His jaw had been set from the moment she'd told him she wanted to return to her father on the night Marcus had given her his letter. She'd stammered incoherent apologies and begged Marcus to believe that she loved him, but it was no use. There was nothing more to say; she couldn't betray her father, not if he wanted her back. Marcus had nodded silently, and his icy resolve hadn't cracked since. He'd stared straight ahead for the entire journey to Arpi. They'd ridden from dawn to dusk for three gruelling days, and every moment, Elissa had silently begged him to speak. To beg her not to go, to rage at her for betraying him, to do *something*, anything. But he had only looked at her with his impenetrable gray stare, and Elissa had watched his broad back as he rode away.

A small bowl of olives appeared on the table in front of her. Elissa glanced up at the woman who'd delivered it. She was young and slight of stature. Mousy hair hung listlessly behind her ears. Elissa smiled wanly and tried to catch the woman's eye; it would be good to at least learn her name. But the woman turned and hurried away. Elissa's eyes fell down to her hands. She was back where she'd started—trying to befriend a disinterested host and waiting to return home. She had only succeeded in running in a circle.

The front door thudded against the wall, and Marcus bent under its low frame. Elissa surveyed his body anxiously. Her heart sped and then slowed when she saw that he was uninjured. But his skin was gray underneath the thick beard that now covered the lower half of his face, and his shoulders stayed slumped even after he'd passed through the door.

"Tomorrow," Marcus grunted as he took the few steps to the center of the room. "Your brother will meet us at dawn tomorrow."

Elissa jumped to her feet. "Tomorrow?" she repeated numbly. "You spoke to Barro? How did you find him? What did he say?"

Marcus stared at her with leaden eyes. "I paid a Carthaginian scout to deliver the message."

Elissa sat back down. "Marcus…" she croaked. Her throat had squeezed tight and she suddenly felt very cold. "Please, Marcus…"

He turned and walked back through the front door.

Elissa's head fell heavily against the back of the couch. Please *what*, Marcus? What exactly did she want from him? To forgive her, to keep fighting for her? Her hands returned to her lap; she clenched one and dug her nails into the soft skin. All her life she'd longed for her father's love and forgiveness. When it had been offered to her, she'd grasped at it reflexively. Her father had said he loved her, that he didn't blame her for her mother's death. It was the love Elissa had never known, the love she'd always wanted. But what about the love she'd never expected?

Elissa thought of Marcus as he'd just been. Tall, proud and utterly defeated, a captive lion resigned to his cage. Was his love, his life, the price she had to pay for her father? Elissa closed her eyes and let her head fall into her hands. The gods demanded a brutal payment. They had asked, and she had answered. Returning to her father would take her soul.

Thump, thump, thump.

It was her hammering heart. It was time beating away. It was the incessant reminder that it would soon be too late to change her mind.

Thump.

Her horse pawed the ground impatiently.

Elissa took a deep breath and a breeze ruffled the hem of her cloak. She looked down at Marcus. He shifted his weight to his other leg. His hair caught the first rays of light and turned them copper.

Tall grass swayed around them and the tips of the stalks tickled the bottoms of her legs. She was mounted. Marcus stood by her horse's withers with one hand on the reins. He had left his own horse to graze nearby so as not to appear threatening. Wind rustled through an olive tree.

285

The whispers of the leaves rose to a crescendo, and then fell silent.

Thump, thump, thump.

Were those horses in the distance?

She wasn't sure. The world seemed flat and still, with only the occasional olive grove between the endless yellow grass and the rapidly lightening sky. But Marcus was staring intently at the low, grassy knoll ahead of them. He leaned forward, his ear to one side. Then he straightened, and his fist tightened around Elissa's reins.

Thump, thump, thump.

Those were definitely horses.

Elissa glanced frantically about. Her horse tossed his head and started to move, but Marcus held firm. His eyes never left the grassy knoll. Elissa focused on the back of his head. She couldn't see his face; she *needed* to see his face. She dropped the reins and reached toward him. She needed to run her fingers through his hair one more time, to burrow her head in his neck and inhale the scent of pine, to look into those clear eyes and believe that everything would be all right.

Marcus took a step forward. Away from her. He brought his hands to his belt and slowly unfastened the buckle, then removed his sword from his waist and held it in front of him. He threw it aside. He took another step, and then another. Elissa tore her eyes away from him and saw that a line of men had appeared on top of the knoll. There were at least twenty of them, and all were mounted. The sun lit them from behind and turned them into mere silhouettes, black shapes with plumed helmets and long spears in their hands. One of the riders separated from the group. He carried a tall, sickle-shaped standard, its edges glowing orange in the rising sun.

Elissa's hand flew to her mouth.

Marcus turned to face her. "Is it him?"

Elissa didn't take her eyes from the riders on the hill. "Barro," she whispered from behind her fingers.

Marcus nodded once, but didn't turn away. Elissa tore her gaze from Barro to look at him. A question was written on his face. Did she want this?

Elissa's body was frozen; only her head swiveled back and forth. Barro had started galloping down the hill with his line of men. Marcus watched her, waiting for her to decide. Half of her was stuck in time, the other half watched it race on.

She swung her leg over her horse and dropped to the ground.

Marcus was only a few strides ahead, but the distance felt interminable. Stalks of grass whipped against her thighs as she ran to him. His face lightened, and he thrust out a hand. Elissa caught his palm and pulled it to her face, then brought her lips to his wrist and kissed it again and again as tears streamed down her face.

"I love you, Marcus. I love you. I'm so sorry. I don't know how to decide. I can't do this. I can't stop loving you."

Marcus wrapped his arms around her shoulders and pulled her into his chest. "Shh, *cara*, shh," he whispered in her ear. "It's all right, my love. I know, I know." He stroked the back of her head as her whole body shook.

The hoofbeats rose until the horsemen had surrounded them on all sides. Elissa clutched at Marcus desperately. She pushed her fingers into his hair and pressed her head against his shoulder. She needed to feel all of him before it was too late.

"I can't let go, Marcus," she murmured. "I can't."

Marcus brought his hands to her shoulders and gently pushed her backward. He held her chin as he traced his fingers along her cheek.

"Hey, hey." he lowered his head to catch her eyes. His were a clear blue, and they shimmered in the morning light.

287

"Elissa, for us, it's always *amor*."

She quivered and sank deeper into his arms. Marcus held her upright, but he was watching something over her head.

"Elissa?" an incredulous voice said behind her.

Elissa didn't move.

"Elissa!" the voice said again.

She stared up at Marcus. His eyes had hardened back to gray. She took a deep breath and forced her weight onto her feet. Her hands were still locked around Marcus's shoulders; she didn't have the will to take them away.

Barro's voice was colder this time. "Are you the one who took her?"

Marcus's hand tightened around her waist. "Yes."

"Let. Go. Of. Her." Barro enunciated each word slowly. Elissa could tell he was gritting his teeth.

Marcus looked down at her. He spoke to her upturned face. "Yes, I took her. I took her and I will never regret it."

Suddenly, Marcus's hands were on her shoulders and she found herself spinning away from him. "But she belongs with her family," he said. "And that is where she must go."

Elissa whirled back around to him. Her tongue seemed to twist around all the things she needed to say.

Marcus brought the tips of his fingers to her chin. He stroked her trembling lips with his thumb. "I could never ask otherwise of you. Go, *cara*, go to your brother."

Then he released her, and Elissa stood alone in a field between the two men she loved. She slowly turned from Marcus to Barro.

Barro had dismounted and was standing by his horse. He took a step toward Elissa, and then another one. He held out his arms to her.

A strangled sob escaped Elissa's lips, and she began moving toward him.

Barro peeled off his helmet and let it fall on the ground. His rich brown hair flopped loose, and his familiar eyes widened as he watched her. His stern brow lifted, and a welcoming smile curved his lips.

Elissa's stride quickened.

When she reached him, Barro flung his arms around her shoulders and immediately pushed her behind him so his body was between her and Marcus. Then he turned to face her.

"Elissa, Elissa…" He pressed his hands to her cheeks. "I can't believe it's really you. I can't believe you're here. I can't believe you're…"

Barro took hold of Elissa's wrists to keep her pinned behind him, then whirled back to Marcus.

"Take that man," Barro commanded in a voice Elissa had never heard before.

Barro's men started moving. There were so many of them—shirtless Numidians with long spears in their hands, and tall Libyans with steel armor and glinting swords. They all closed in on Marcus.

Marcus stood still. He stared impassively ahead.

Three of the Numidians reined in their horses around him.

Elissa took a step forward but ran into Barro's back. His grip on her wrists tightened.

Her heart pounded. What was happening? Marcus was defenseless! He'd already thrown away his sword, and he was wearing only light armor. He'd given Elissa up. He wasn't threatening anyone.

Barro's men kept closing in.

Marcus's voice cut through the taut air. "Take care of her, Barro. Protect her. I swear to your gods and mine, I will kill you from the next life if you don't!"

Barro clenched his teeth and hissed angrily. He pulled his arm from Elissa's wrist and held up his hand. His fingers flicked backward, then forward. It was a signal—GO.

Elissa screamed.

The Carthaginians attacked.

Marcus dodged the thrust of the first man's spear. He rammed his shoulder into a Numidian's leg and ducked under his horse. He tore a spear from another one's hand and sent it flying in the opposite direction. But there were too many of them. They swarmed him from every direction. Elissa was losing sight of him in the mass of horses and men; she could only see his head. Now she could only see Carthaginians. They thrust and hacked at the center of the circle. Elissa heard flesh ripping. Blood darkened the grass.

"Barro!" Elissa screamed.

She wrenched her other arm free and lunged for Barro's shoulder.

"Stop this! Get them off him! You have what you want. Let him go!"

Barro spun around in shock. He stared at her dumbly, as if he didn't understand what she was saying.

"LET HIM GO!" Elissa roared, this time in Punic instead of Latin.

Anger flared in Barro's eyes. He lifted his hand and cracked it across her face. Elissa staggered backward in disbelief. Tears sprang to her eyes and her cheek stung. Barro turned away from her again.

Elissa hurled her body at him. Her shoulder collided with the center of his back, and his body was shoved forward. His leg shot out to keep him upright but it didn't matter; Elissa had already grabbed the hilt at his waist. She jerked the blade from its scabbard and had the knife at her neck before Barro had turned back around. She pressed the edge against her skin. Blood sprang out from around the cold metal. It trickled down her neck and across her hand.

"Let him go or I push," Elissa rasped around the steel edge.

Barro's amber eyes were furious as he stared at her. But then he straightened, and the disbelief faded from his face.

Something much sharper replaced it.

"Men!" Barro called out. "Leave the Roman scum."

Elissa leaned to the side to see around Barro. She kept the knife at her throat.

The Carthaginians had stopped fighting and were slowly backing away. As the space between them grew, Elissa could make out a dark shape at their center, lying crumpled in the grass, motionless.

She dropped her knife and ran to him.

Barro caught her by the arm as she passed, wrenching her shoulder and forcing her to stop. She turned on Barro, intending to yank her arm free. But Barro already had his hands around her waist and was lifting her onto his shoulder. She kicked her legs and hammered his back with her fists, but it was no use. He forced Elissa, stomach first, onto his horse's back. The impact wrenched her final scream from her lungs. Barro climbed up behind her and pulled her arms around her back to stop her from writhing. The last thing Elissa saw as they rode away was Marcus's cloak. Torn to shreds, it rested on a clump of grass.

They were long past the grassy knoll, and far away from Marcus's crumpled body before Elissa stopped struggling. Barro had moved her so she was sitting in front of him on the saddle, but he'd quickly learned that her arms needed to be bound to keep her on the horse. After that, Elissa had stopped fighting her brother and started fighting the images in her head.

Marcus, motionless in the grass, his blood leaching into the dirt.

Marcus, his lips curved in a smile and his eyes glinting with laughter as he teased her.

Marcus, dead. Marcus.

Elissa cried out in pain. Barro tightened his arms around

her. The rest of his men galloped beside them over the long, flat plain. If they stared at her, she didn't notice.

If Marcus was dead, then so was she.

Elissa let her head loll forward onto her neck. She had no more tears to spill, no more energy to fight with. She watched the grass disappear under their horse's thundering hooves. It blurred to a sheet of yellow, and fell endlessly away.

"Come on, Elissa, we're here."

Elissa didn't look up.

Barro tugged on her leg again. "Come on, now. You can rest in my tent."

She didn't move.

Barro sighed and brought his hands to her waist. He lifted her from the saddle and pulled her off the horse.

Elissa hardly felt her feet hit the ground.

"All right, Elissa, that's enough. You're going to explain a few things first."

Barro struggled to prop her weight on his shoulder. He got her arm around his back and started moving toward the tent ahead of them. He lifted back the flap with one hand and dragged her inside.

Elissa didn't bother looking around.

Barro grabbed a wooden stool with one hand and slowly eased Elissa's weight onto it. He grabbed a second stool and sat in front of her.

"Elissa," he said quietly.

She stared at the ground. The grass in the tent had been flattened by many footsteps, but it was the same color she'd watched all morning.

"Elissa," Barro repeated impatiently. He brought his hand to her face and pushed her chin up until she was forced to look at him.

Elissa covered her cheek.

Barro let go of her quickly.

"I'm sorry, I shouldn't have hit you."

Elissa moved her fingers from her cheek down to her neck. She traced the line of the knife across her skin; the blood was still warm and slick on her neck. She pulled her hand away, holding her fingers in front of her face. They glistened red. She turned her hand over. The skin was pale, but unharmed. She flipped her hand again. Bloody, but unchanged—a never-ending circle.

Barro was watching her closely with his brow furrowed.

"What happened to you, Elissa?" he asked carefully.

Elissa dropped her hand. "Why did you do it, Barro?"

Barro sat back on the stool. His next breath hissed through his teeth.

"Do what, Elissa? Rescue you? Walk into what I was certain was a Roman trap on the off chance that it actually *was* my sister that centurion had? My sister, who last I heard was living in Carthage, engaged to be married! So you tell me why, Elissa. Tell me, why aren't you in Carthage? Why are you in Cannae on the day of battle? And why are you so distraught over the death of some Roman!"

Elissa hardly heard him over the pounding in her ears. Why did he think Marcus was dead? Had he seen something she hadn't?

Barro was standing now. He paced agitatedly across the tent. "Do you have any idea how many Romans I've killed these past two years? I could fill this tent with their heads! And not for one moment have I felt anything but relief. Relief that there's one less Roman on this godforsaken continent who can kill me!" Barro stopped pacing. He walked back to Elissa and brought his face within inches of hers. "This is war, Elissa, and you don't belong here."

Barro stared at her. She stared back. Neither blinked.

Then Barro abruptly pulled away. He walked to the corner of the tent and picked up his shield and spear. "I have to go. There may be a battle today."

He strode quickly to the front of the tent, but paused with his hand on the flap, then looked back at her. "I am a soldier now, Elissa, and I go to my duty. Victory or death, whichever my fate may be." He drew back the tent flap.

Elissa turned away from him.

Barro spoke again, this time to the back of her head. "What is your duty, Elissa? Do you serve your people? Or do you serve yourself? And if it's the latter, then why are you here? Why did you ask me to come?"

He left the tent.

Elissa didn't move. The flap of the tent swished back and forth against the grass. Back and forth, back and forth, a perpetual pendulum. Duty, country, self. Family, honor, fate. A game of fortune the gods played with the lives of men.

What did any of it matter when the man she loved could be dying in a field nearby?

Elissa closed her eyes and saw Marcus lying alone in that field of grass. Thin slivers of yellow cradled his body and held him above the ground. His arm was outstretched as if he were reaching for something, and his head rested lightly on top of it. A thick strand of hair swept across his forehead. His mouth was slack, his lips parted. There was no fear or pain in his smooth features. He looked at peace. Elissa smiled. It was a gift from Astarte. Marcus, her lover, at home with the mother of all things.

But Elissa wanted more than what she could see in her mind. She wanted to take his hand and press it to her lips again. She would lie down beside him and wrap his arm around her waist. She would feel the same heat rising through her body, the twisting sensation in her gut as their bodies merged. She would once again know how it felt to love and be loved in return. Love against allegiance, love against reason, love against fear, against cowardice, against regret. Love, always. *Always amor.*

Elissa jumped to her feet.

"Fuck the gods."

She was going to find him. And if he was dead, then so be it. She would live as she would have lived with him—against it all.

Barro didn't return until well after dark. Elissa had no choice but to wait for him. She'd already scoured the Carthaginian camp for a horse, donkey or even a pack animal—anything that would get her back to that field more quickly than walking. But every animal was gone; every weapon was, too. They'd walked or been carried to the battlefield. Elissa resolved to wait until Barro returned. He would give her a horse or she would take one, and then she would leave forever.

As she waited, Elissa thought mostly about Marcus and prayed that he was alive. But she also thought about Barro. Her brother had changed. He had become the hardened soldier he'd always wanted to be, the leader of men. He was truly their father's son now, and Elissa couldn't help feeling proud of him for it. The history of Carthage, and the glory of the Magos, would live on in him. Elissa was glad of it. But for her, it was the end of family and country. Duty demanded too much of her, and her answer was no.

The hours stretched on and the shadows outside the tent grew longer. It was possible that the Romans and Carthaginians were fighting a colossal battle nearby, but Elissa didn't think so. The screams at Trasimene had carried for miles past the lake, and the din of battle had been inescapable from every direction. If there was a battle nearby today, Elissa didn't hear it; there was only the eerie silence of an abandoned camp. She sat on the same stool where Barro had left her, but this time facing the entrance, desperate for it to open again.

Finally, Elissa heard movement outside the tent, slow footsteps at first, but thundering hooves and shouts in Numidian soon followed. Elissa began pacing the tent. The officers should be close behind the cavalry. She poked her head outside every few minutes, expecting to see Barro striding toward her. The sky dimmed, but the tent flap stayed shut. Hazy orange circles appeared along the walls of the tent as fires were lit around camp. Elissa could hear the din of male voices through the thin walls. She could catch some of the words in Punic or Numidian, but most of the men spoke languages she couldn't understand. Words with long rolling vowels or clipped consonants, and odd grunts. Fifty thousand warriors had united under the banner of Carthage, thousands of tribes with a hundred different languages, all here for one purpose—to vanquish Rome. Everyone but Elissa Mago, who only wanted her brother to return so she could run back to the man she loved.

The voices gradually hushed to whispers, and snoring punctuated the ends of sentences. The last time Elissa had looked outside, stars shone dimly through the blanket of black in the sky. The tent flap opened and Barro stepped inside.

Elissa jumped to her feet. "Barro!"

He looked up and jerked to a halt. His weary expression turned to surprise.

Elissa realized it was probably her dramatic change in demeanor that shocked him, but she didn't waste time explaining herself. "I have to go, Barro. I need to go now. I need a horse and then I need to leave."

Barro shook his head tiredly. "A horse? Elissa, it's the middle of the night." He held up a hand as he brushed past her. "And I'm exhausted."

Elissa trailed him to the corner of the tent. Barro dropped

his shield and set down his spear. He reached behind him, struggling to untie the laces at the back of his breastplate. Elissa inhaled shakily and forced herself to remain still. Another few minutes weren't going to matter; she'd already waited all day. She needed to appear calm and decisive if Barro was going to listen to her.

"Here. Let me help you." She reached over Barro's shoulder and unfastened his cloak, then moved her fingers over the leather laces at his back and untied them one by one. Barro nodded and sighed gratefully as she lifted the heavy pad off his chest. But instead of turning around to her, he walked back to the entrance and poked his head around the flap.

"Boy! Bring some supper, eh?"

Elissa gritted her teeth. She was not waiting until he'd eaten to find Marcus.

"Barro..." she started, but he silenced her.

"Elissa, I'm exhausted. I marched to Cannae and spent all day standing across the battlefield from the biggest army I've ever seen. And then I went to my general and learned that I'm to command the right flank, and if I fail to hold it, the whole war will be lost. I came back to my tent to eat a little, and maybe rest for a few hours before the fight, and I find my crazed sister yelling for a horse and begging to leave. And the worst part is, I'm forced to wonder which Roman she'll run off to and whisper our secrets in his ear."

Elissa's face flushed with anger and her hands tightened into fists. She rounded on Barro, "Which Roman I'll run off to?"

Barro saw the onslaught coming and his face set with determination. But Elissa's anger drained away as quickly as it had come. Barro was right; he had been given a crucial and dangerous command, and he should rest and eat tonight. She was not a child throwing a fit at her older brother anymore; she needed to find the man she loved.

Elissa reached for his hands and took them in her own. "Barro," she said softly, "you have been so much more than a brother to me. You have been a father, a protector and a friend." Elissa stared into his amber eyes. They were the color of honey left in the sun, their mother's eyes. "You are a good man, and a great leader. But this is the point at which our paths diverge. I can no longer be Elissa Mago, daughter of Hanno, sister of Barro, without regret." Barro started to pull away but Elissa held firm. "Give me a horse and let me go," she whispered.

Barro looked at her for a long moment without blinking. Elissa didn't turn away. She wanted to remember everything about her brother—the shape of his brow, the curve of his nose, the way his eyes glinted when he'd made up his mind about something. Whether he helped her or not, after tonight, he would live only in her mind.

He released her hands. "You are too much like our mother, Elissa. Too wilful and independent to be satisfied with this world."

Elissa followed his eyes to the ground and smiled sadly. "That may be, but unlike her, I will die fighting."

Barro raised his head. "She did die fighting, Elissa. She fought as hard as she could against the evil spirit that took her body, and then her mind. She fought for you and me. She fought for us all. But in the end, she wasn't strong enough to overcome her fate." He reached for Elissa's cheek and cradled it in his palm. "I only hope that your fate is different from hers."

Elissa covered her brother's hand with her own and pressed it to her face. Then she pulled it away. "That is not for you to decide."

Barro watched her in protracted silence. He dropped his eyes and walked to the entrance.

"Come. Let's find you a horse fit for a long journey."

"Stand down, man! This is Barro Mago, of the second Libyan company."

The Carthaginian sentry held up his torch and leaned forward. Unlike his Roman counterparts, this sentry didn't have the advantage of a raised post to survey intruders. Barro didn't hesitate. He might not have worn armor or carried his standard, but he was unmistakably a man with authority. He held his swarthy head high and strode confidently past the sentry. Elissa was probably the one to give the man pause. She trailed behind Barro with a magnificent warhorse at her side. Turning, she stroked the stallion's muscular neck to avoid the sentry's stare. Elissa could feel the sentry's wary eyes boring into her back, but he stepped aside to let her pass.

Barro led her through the last row of tents on the edge of camp and into the well-trodden field that lay past it. When they reached a wide oak tree in the middle of the field, Barro stopped. The thick branches twisted and spiralled into a dense canopy that blocked out most of the sky. Standing next to the trunk, they couldn't even see the light of the moon.

Barro pointed at the sky. "Do you see that star? The brightest one?"

Elissa followed his finger to a tiny pinprick of light. It was the only star visible through the oak's leaves. She nodded.

"Stay between that star and the setting moon and you will return to the field you left this morning."

Elissa nodded more rapidly. A lump was rising in her throat, which was going to make it difficult to say goodbye.

Barro squeezed her hand tightly and led her around the horse. He took the reins from her and swung them over the stallion's neck.

"I love you, sister."

Elissa embraced him fiercely. For a moment, their bodies were bound as closely as their names. They shared a history, and the same blood ran through their veins. But when Elissa released her arms, she knew their future had disappeared. She turned to her horse, gripped the saddle and swung onto his back.

"Tell Father that I got his letter. And that I forgive him."

Then she was gone. She galloped out from under the oak tree and away from her brother, away from the Carthaginians and the war, away to Marcus. She closed her legs around the stallion's sides and leaned low over his neck. The wind whipped across her face and sent her hair cascading down her back. The stallion's white neck merged with the night; his pounding hooves blended into the earth. One thought thundered in her head and to the stars above—
I'm coming, Marcus. Coming to you.

Elissa cut a straight path between the moon and the bright star that pointed north. The earth stretched in front of her as long and flat as she remembered from the morning. All that existed were the twin white lights in the heavens and the sea of grass between them. Time fell away under her horse's flying feet. Or maybe it was Marcus, pulling her toward him by the strand of love that connected their lives.

When she reached the grassy knoll, the night was at its darkest, a thick black that was less a color than the absence of light. It was the hour of night that stretches on forever, when the light neither comes nor goes, a darkness that stands in defiance of time. Elissa could make out the twisted shapes of olive trees in the field below, but nothing more. She slowed the stallion to an easy lope down the hill.

She stopped at the bottom of the knoll. It was too dark to tell exactly where they'd met the Carthaginians that morning. The stallion tossed his head and chomped at his bit. Half a night of running and he had hardly broken a sweat. Elissa forced him to be still. She needed to listen.

"Marcus?" she called out.

Her voice rustled through the tall grass and faded away.

"Marcus?"

The night was as quiet as it was dark.

Elissa swung her leg over the stallion's neck and dismounted. She pulled the reins over his head and led him farther into the field. She thought she saw a depression in the grass, but when she arrived there, it was only a dip in the ground.

"Marcus...where are you?"

Her voice trembled. He had not answered her call, and nothing had moved in response. If she found Marcus here, it would be because he was dead.

Elissa pushed that possibility from her mind and kept moving. She trailed her hand along the tips of the grass as she walked. Every step, she dreaded that her next one would take her to his body. It would be cold, nothing but empty flesh. A shudder ran through her and she choked on a cry of despair. What would she do without him in this world?

She would build a massive pyre and burn his body like the Roman kings of old. She would take his ashes and scatter them from a tall mountain. He would live in the wind, and through the trees, he—

Elissa's hand brushed against something wet.

She stopped.

She lifted her hand from the grass and held it up to the meagre light in the sky. Her fingers glistened.

Blood.

Her hand shook as she bent down. She traced her fingers along a stalk of grass. It was slippery and cold. She moved her fingers to another stalk. It felt the same.

Elissa stood. She forced her shaky feet to follow the trail of blood that dotted the tips of grass. She was sure she'd come across Marcus's body at any moment. His path had been sporadic and halting. His blood lay thicker in some places and then absent in others. But where had he gone?

Elissa stopped. The trail had ended. She returned to the last clump of wet grass and walked several feet in every direction. Dry. Elissa frowned, not sure if she should be relieved or more frightened. She paused, then decided to trace a wider circle around the clump of grass. Something sharp caught her finger halfway around. A thorn dug into her finger from the branch of a low shrub. Elissa pulled her hand away and bent to examine it.

She weaved her fingers between the thorns on its stem and felt a soft tickling on the back of her hand. A long strand of wool was twisted around one of the thorns. She tugged it loose and raised it to the sky. It was scarlet, the same color as Marcus's cloak.

Realization hit her in a jolt. He was gone. Marcus was gone. He was bloodied and injured, but he had been well enough to walk, and he'd had the wherewithal to grab his cloak. He must have found his horse and then ridden off. Elissa felt as though her feet were floating above the ground.

She ran back to her stallion and threw her arms around him. She murmured her joy into his neck. "He's alive! He must be. He's alive!"

The stallion bobbed his head but decided to suffer her ministrations. Elisa shoved her face into his mane and inhaled his musky scent. She would see Marcus again, she would apologize and kiss him again, she— Her hands fell from the stallion's neck. But where had he gone? He had taken his horse and run, but where? He was injured and losing blood, so maybe he'd returned to Arpi for help.

Elissa shook her head. No, no, he wouldn't have done that. He believed he'd lost her forever. He'd sacrificed his life for her and been willing to die. But he hadn't died. He'd woken up in an empty field instead. Bleeding, heartbroken, and very much alive. *Where would he go?*

She was already scrambling back onto her horse before the thought was fully formed in her mind.

He would've been certain that he had nothing to live for. So he would go to battle to die.

Elissa heard the trumpets first. Their call pierced the air and then hung in the sky. The short cry stabbed at her heart, and the long bellow filled her with fear. It was the call of battle. There would be no feigned formations today. Death hung in the morning air.

Marcus would die on that field today.

Elissa dug her heels deeper into the stallion's sides. She needed more from him. The stallion dropped his head and stretched his legs even farther across the ground. She begged him to run faster, away from the star that pointed north, away from the setting moon. They ran back through the sea of grass, back to the Carthaginian camp, back to the war of civilizations that caused the earth to tremble.

The wind tore the hair from Elissa's back and flung it in front of her face. There was no fleeting sense of freedom as they ran this time. There was only fear—cold fear that gripped her heart and paralyzed her body. If she didn't find Marcus, he would die. Elissa was sure of it.

She looked to the rapidly lightening sky. Black had changed to deep blue, and then to gray. The stars had faded and the moon cast a pale glow. It was nearly morning.

But she was almost there. The silence between trumpet calls grew shorter, and the ground became less flat. Undulating hills rose up and down, and a silty river snaked alongside her. She thought she heard stomping feet.

Yes, there it was—the distant cacophony of a moving army. But where was the steady rhythm of thousands of boots hitting the ground in unison? The noise was chaotic and random, and growing louder.

They were climbing a long, gradual hill. The ground was nearly bare of grass, and the earth was the color of clay. The stallion's hooves kicked up a cloud of dust behind them.

The screams reached her halfway up the hill. The shrieks of terror were the loudest, but low grunts of exertion soon followed. And between them, the empty moans of dying men.

She was too late.

Tears of horror flowed down her cheeks but were immediately whipped away by the wind. How could she be too late? It was hardly morning and she was so close. The clash of metal was right in front of her, and the air smelled of blood. Marcus was down there; she *knew* he was.

Elissa filled her lungs and let loose a wild scream of anger. It was a long, raging battle cry that sent her stallion flinging himself forward over the crest of the hill. Fear turned to fire in her veins and burned away her hesitation. She raced over the hill and down the other side into the largest battle the world had ever seen.

Men screamed. Swords clashed. Horses reared into the air and crashed to the ground. Rome and Carthage had melded into a scorching mass of flesh and steel and death. Blood flowed through the openings between bodies. Heat rose from the ground, as if the very earth were being reshaped.

Elissa galloped straight toward them. Hundreds of men were dying by the minute. Their lives burst into noise and then dissipated. She was across from the Carthaginians, who'd been pushed back against the hill she was racing down. The Romans were arranged in a massive rectangle in front of the Carthaginian line. They had lost their characteristic spaces between maniples. Instead, each man stood with his chest to the back of the man in front of him—one hundred men deep and a thousand men across. Every Roman pushed or slashed to break through the Carthaginian line. Like the string of a bow, the Carthaginians had bent, but their line had not broken. In fact, the flanks of their line had begun to wrap around the sides of the Roman legions, trapping the first dozen Roman lines between Carthaginians on both the front and sides.

Elissa hauled back on one of the reins to redirect the stallion to the nearest Roman flank not covered by the Carthaginians. She could only pray to the gods she'd scorned that Marcus was on that side. Elissa made herself as small as possible atop her horse, choosing to believe against all odds that every man within spear range was locked in combat and too distracted to take aim at her.

A new chorus of shouts suddenly rose above the rest.

Elissa watched as a massive company of Libyans dislodged itself from the main army and marched out from the sides of the Carthaginian line. How had she not noticed them before? Thousands of men in purple cloaks moved in tight rectangular formation. But instead of lining up beside the Carthaginians who were already engaged, they kept going, past their own men and up toward the center of the Roman army. Elissa frowned in confusion but galloped on. She needed to get to the Romans before the Carthaginians did. She bunched up her knees and flattened her chest against the stallion's neck, asking still more from him.

The stallion faltered, but then dropped lower to the ground and dug harder with his back legs. They were going to make it; they were going to beat the Carthaginians to the Roman flank. She would yell for Marcus. She was a lone woman galloping into battle on a white horse—surely he would see her and come running. And if he didn't... If he couldn't find her, or worse, if he saw her but couldn't get to her, then she would die here, in the same field as the man she loved. Despite the desperation of it all, the improbability that she would live to see Marcus again, she didn't feel terror. She felt hope. It was just as Marcus had said—it was only those with nothing to die for who were truly lost.

A horn sounded in the distance. A second responded. Elissa pushed her chest off the stallion's neck. Something was changing. The unmistakable cry of a horde of galloping Numidians tore through the air ahead of her. The ground quaked as the Numidians came pounding up from behind the Romans to block their escape from the rear. At the same time, the Libyan company that Elissa had run so hard to get ahead of started to turn lengthwise and continued to rotate until the front line of Libyans faced the sides of the Roman legionaries.

Elissa's arms went slack as her brain slowly caught up to what she was seeing. She was no longer running into the side of the Roman army; she was running into the company of Carthaginians about to slaughter them. If she looked to the other side of the legion, she knew she'd see the same thing. The Carthaginians were encircling the Romans. Despite having half the number of men, Hannibal had managed to utterly outmanoeuver the Romans. The legion was blocked on all sides by a wall of Carthaginians. They were doomed.

Marcus.

Elissa reached the back line of Libyans. She didn't stop. Men shouted in dismay and jumped to the side to avoid her stallion's barrelling chest. A man turned to her with his sword drawn, but by the time he started to swing, she was gone. She flew through the Carthaginians, over their white plumed helmets, past their gilded standards, and straight into the side of the tightening block of Romans.

Elissa screwed her face into a mask of determination and did the most idiotic thing she could have imagined. She lifted her legs and placed her knees on top of the saddle. Then she pushed her feet underneath her and straightened her legs.

"MARCUS!" she bellowed. "MARCUS! MARCUS! MARCUS!"

Elissa didn't bother breathing between shouts. She was standing on her horse's back and they were in the middle of a battlefield. She was probably the highest point in the battle and deadly exposed. It wouldn't take more than a poorly aimed spear to kill her.

She broke through the final line of Libyans. She was surrounded by Romans now. These men might be doomed, but they were alive for now and fighting desperately to escape. The Carthaginians would have to kill them one by one. They'd start with the outer rows of men and move inward. The bodies would pile high as they set about their grisly task. The Carthaginians would not rest until the last Roman had a sword through his heart. That was the way of war between worlds.

"MARCUS! MAR…"

A muffled shout interrupted her. Elissa shifted her head in its direction. Another cry. It was no louder than all the rest, but its sound was completely different. Amid all the death, it was the sound of renewed life.

"*ELISSA!*"

Elissa dropped back into the saddle and brought her left hand to her hip. The stallion squealed but locked his hind legs and spun toward the back of the legion. Now Elissa crouched low over his neck to make herself less of a target. She pulled her knees up to her chest to prevent someone from grabbing her leg and yanking her from the horse.

Carthaginians and Romans were locked in desperate struggles for survival all around her. Their swords rang against each other's armor and cut through one another's flesh. When their swords were gone, they attacked each other with hands and legs. Kicking, biting, scratching, all for one more moment in this terrible world. Fear vibrated in the air. Every man, no matter what side he was on, knew his next breath might be his last. Death was capricious, and it was everywhere.

"Elissa!" she heard again. It was faint this time, but it was close. She was going to make it!

The red fanned helmet of a centurion rose in front of her. The Roman was directly in her path to Marcus. His hands tightened around the hilt of his sword and he lifted it above his shoulder. His bare arms bunched as he started to swing, aiming at the stallion's neck. The edge of his sword sang as it sliced toward them through the trembling air.

The stallion slammed into the centurion chest-first before the steel could make contact. The man went down under his thundering hooves.

Marcus was in front of her, ashen and bloody, matching blows with a Libyan soldier. He still wore only the light training breastplate and he fought without a shield. The Libyan kept his own shield high and jabbed at Marcus from behind its protective cover. Marcus didn't even try to defend himself. He attacked head-on. He struck at the Libyan's side and sliced at his head ferociously. Marcus's right arm hung useless and mangled by his side. He was fighting with his left hand, and his movements were slower than normal. Elissa wanted to yell out to him but she feared distracting him. Instead, she—

Something akin to a bull slammed into her left side. Before she could tell exactly what it was, her leg crumpled into the stallion's ribs and the world started to turn. Men were no longer fighting on their feet, but on their sides. The stallion shrieked in terror as the ground rushed toward them. They were going down.

The ground felt even harder than the first impact. Elissa's shoulder drove into the dirt and her head bounced off the ground. But that pain was nothing compared to her right leg, which was now pinned under the writhing stallion. Her horse screamed and flailed as he tried to right himself, but he couldn't get his legs underneath him. Elissa twisted her left leg to take her weight off him. Her foot struck something hard. She lifted her head and saw the shaft of a javelin jutting from the stallion's side. Above that, the Roman who had thrown it was pulling out his sword to finish the job.

Elissa thrashed even harder to free her leg and allow them both to escape. But in his desperation to flee the pain in his side, the stallion was rolling toward her rather than away. The pain multiplied as his massive body crushed her hip. The Roman walked around the stallion toward Elissa. He loomed above her, his eyes tiny black points in his face. Blood dripped from his skin and saturated his beard. His chest heaved up and down as he adjusted his grip on the sword so the point was facing down. It hovered in the air above Elissa's neck. He was going to drive his sword into the soft flesh below her chin. Elissa shut her eyes. Her death would be quick. The air whistled around the edges of the sword. It was all right, she told herself; there were worse ways to die. At least Marcus would know that she'd chosen him, that she had loved him above all else, loved him to the end.

There was a dull thud above her head.

Elissa kept her eyes shut. Her body might have to die on a bloody battlefield in Italy, but she wanted her mind to be somewhere else.

Her shoulders began to shake. Something grabbed at her armpits and her body felt as if it was being stretched. Then, in her ear, "Elissa, get up, Elissa, get up now. ELISSA!"

Her eyes flew open. It was no longer the bloody-faced man above her; it was Marcus. He wrenched on her arms to get her out from under the stallion.

Elissa reached up for his face. "Marcus, Marcus, I found you," she murmured.

Tears were building inside her. They rose up through her throat, ready to spill out in a torrent of gratitude and disbelief.

Marcus ignored her. He hauled her leg loose.

"Up," he commanded.

Elissa rolled over onto her side. The bloody-faced Roman stared back at her.

Elissa jolted away from him. Tears turned to bile in her throat and she choked on her breath. A boot appeared next to the Roman's head and kicked it aside.

"Up!"

This time Marcus's hand accompanied his command. Elissa clamped her fingers around his. Marcus tugged her to her feet and straight into his arms. He slid his injured arm around her shoulders and used his other hand to hold his sword behind her back. Elissa felt the muscles in his arm go tight as he swung his sword behind her.

"Come on!"

Marcus lunged to the side with Elissa still between his arms. She could see what he was rushing toward. The stallion had managed to scramble to his feet and was lunging for an open space in front of them. There was a sharp crack as the javelin shaft lodged in his stomach broke off against the ground.

They needed to get back on that horse.

Elissa ducked under Marcus's arm and grasped for the reins. The stallion broke into a gallop and his momentum blew the reins out of her hands. Elissa jumped. The tips of her fingers brushed against his long mane streaming behind him. Elissa forced her shoulder forward and planted her fingers at the base of his neck, knotting them in the coarse hair.

"Got hi—"

The words were abruptly cut off as her other arm slammed straight into Marcus's hand. She heard his sword ring against steel a second time and then he was running with her, both of them behind the galloping stallion. Elissa needed to get onto his back and slow him down so Marcus could follow, but she couldn't release either hand.

"Go!" Marcus shouted behind her.

"No!"

"Yes!" Marcus jerked back on her arm, and suddenly her hand was free.

"No!" she screamed in shock.

But her body automatically twisted away from Marcus to keep up with the stallion. There was no time to think. She gathered her weight on one leg and swung the other in a wide arc that launched her into the air. She grabbed the stallion's mane with both hands. Her chest hit the saddle and she wrenched her leg to the far side of the stallion's back. She was up.

Elissa groped for the flapping reins and managed to catch the very end of them. She hurled her weight backward, against the reins, and pulled with everything she had. The stallion squealed and threw his head in the air. He was mad with terror and bleeding from his injury, but he slowed.

Elissa frantically whipped her head around. "Marcus! MARCUS!"

She couldn't lose him now. They were so close to breaking free! The stallion had chosen the right direction to run. A small group of Romans had punched through the wall of Libyans up ahead, and the mass of bodies had lessened enough to see the ground between the men's feet. Even the fighting was becoming sporadic.

Elissa heard a grunt behind her, and she whirled toward it.

It was Marcus. His injured arm was twisted around one of the saddle straps. He was running and stumbling as he tried to keep up with their frantic pace. Elissa looked down at the point where the strap was attached to the saddle. The leather was stretched nearly white; it could break at any moment. Elissa tore her hand from the reins and locked her fist around the strap. It wasn't going to break yet. For the second time in as many minutes, she hauled back as hard as she could.

Marcus pitched forward and Elissa lunged for his outstretched arm.

She caught him by the wrist.

Marcus wrapped his fingers around her arm and pulled himself up. Suddenly he was across from her and his hand was on the saddle. Elissa jumped forward onto the stallion's neck. Then Marcus was behind her, and they were both on the stallion. They were riding away with only a few scattered Romans in front of them. And then there was nothing but open fields, smooth plains and the hazy tinge of the ocean on the horizon.

The brave stallion carried them away from the entombed Roman army, away from the screams of dying men and the shouts of victorious ones. Away from ambitious fathers and jealous politicians. Away from it all.

As the sun beat down on the battlefield at Cannae, and the screams of life and death faded away, all that was left was Marcus. His arms were tight around her, and words that were spoken in both Carthage and Rome echoed in her ear.

Love, always.

Elissa leaned over the railing and watched the water slip under the ship's hull. The sea was brilliant turquoise. Small waves rippled across the surface and changed the light from blue to green, and back to blue again. She inhaled the smell of salt and felt the wind tickle her cheeks. It had been several days since Cannae, and sometimes she thought she could still smell blood in the air. After the battle, they'd fled all the way to the port and begged passage on the first ship that could sail. They'd traded their stallion that seemed fit to recover from his injury to a merchant who promised to care for him. They used the funds to pay the exorbitant fare.

"Not thinking of jumping, I hope."

Elissa spun around to the familiar deep voice. She laughed when she saw Marcus. He was leaning against the mast with his arms crossed, watching her. His right arm was bound in a sling.

"I wouldn't dare," she teased. "I know you'd jump in after me."

Marcus flashed her that cocky smile she loved so much and walked toward her. Elissa noticed the grimace that crossed his face when he started moving. He had suffered badly at Cannae. Aside from the broken arm, he had a dozen wounds across his chest and legs. Elissa had tended to each of them as best she could. All she could do now was change the linens and hope they healed properly.

Marcus reached over to her and cupped her cheek. "You worry too much, *cara*. A few cuts could never stop me from finding you."

Elissa arched her eyebrows. "Well, centurion. We're headed to Athens, the city of philosophers and architects, not to mention my mother's birthplace. You can't go around poking things with your sword and expect to make friends there."

Marcus chuckled and moved his good arm to the railing. He leaned forward until Elissa was lodged between him and the wooden bar at her back. His hand shifted to her hip and he spun her around to face the water. He slid his arm around her waist and squeezed tightly. He nestled his lips in her hair.

"I'd follow you anywhere, Elissa Mago."

Elissa closed her eyes and let her head rest on his chest. She breathed him in and relaxed into the closeness of his body. She'd ended up back where she'd started—fleeing on a ship to a foreign land.

Her life was just as uncertain as before. She didn't know where they'd go once they reached Athens, or whether they could truly outrun this war. Already there were rumors that Philip of Macedon was planning to join the Carthaginians after their victory at Cannae. Marcus was convinced it wouldn't matter; Rome would never surrender.

Elissa turned and looked up at Marcus. He smiled down at her. There were still so many questions to be answered. But one thing was certain.

She would be with the man she loved.

The End

KATE Q. JOHNSON is a scientist, new mom, and outdoorsy chick living in the Pacific Northwest. Originally hailing from the frigid Great White North, her creative juices only really got flowing when she moved to the warmer climate of Vancouver, BC for graduate school. Her debut novel, *Daughter of Carthage, Son of Rome* was the stuff of daydreams at bus stops, learning about epic wars and earth-shattering events through history podcasts. She figured the only thing missing was a daring heroine to save the day! Kate is passionate about bringing history to life through action-packed stories of love and adventure. Stay up to date with her latest projects at kqjohnson.com.